NO OTHER OPTION

Beverly was sure this case was winnable even if they fell short on some key evidence. The suspect had all but confessed to the killing when he threatened Judge Crawford's life and apparently never backed down from the threat. He had also been fingered by Maxine Crawford as the man who sexually assaulted her and shot her husband to death.

Trials had been won with less, Beverly told herself.

But they would still have to prove Santiago's guilt in a court of law.

And she planned to.

Or she would have to watch Rafael Santiago walk, a free man who got away with cold-blooded murder.

Other books by R. Barri Flowers:

JUSTICE SERVED
PERSUASIVE EVIDENCE

PRAISE FOR R. BARRI FLOWERS!

JUSTICE SERVED

"Vividly written. This book holds the reader's attention and speeds along."

—*RT BOOKclub*

"Flowers has given us much more than a captivating story here—he's served a wake-up call to failing judicial systems bogged down in mires of red tape and loop holes... An A+ suspense/mystery with a touch of heartfelt romance."

—Fresh Fiction

"*Justice Served* is a model of crime fiction... Flowers may be a new voice in modern mystery writing, but he is already one of its best voices."

—*Statesman Journal*

"[Flowers] weaves a magical web as well as a tangled one."

—*Huntress Book Reviews* (4-star review)

"This novel has lots of twists and turns and is a very fast read with believable characters and a tense setting."

—*The Midwest Book Review*

PERSUASIVE EVIDENCE

"Raw, primal, thrilling, incredible—that's how I would describe this book. This is one of the best books that I have read. I was completely riveted from the first page."

—*Romance Readers at Heart*

"R. Barri Flowers has written a superb legal thriller. *Persuasive Evidence* will appeal to fans of John Grisham and Linda Fairstein."

—Harriet Klausner

"R. Barri Flowers creates a story that keeps you on the edge of your seat. The suspense builds in *Persuasive Evidence* to master a page-turning story I couldn't put down."

—*Romance Junkies*

"An absorbing legal thriller, *Persuasive Evidence* is proof of Flowers's talent as an author."

—*Romance in Color*

R. BARRI FLOWERS

STATE'S EVIDENCE

LEISURE BOOKS NEW YORK CITY

*This is for H. Loraine, Marjah Aljean, Johnnie Henry,
and all the special ones to contribute to my life
and times over the years.*

A LEISURE BOOK®

April 2006

Published by

Dorchester Publishing Co., Inc.
200 Madison Avenue
New York, NY 10016

This is a work of fiction and all the characters within are entirely
the product of the author's imagination and creativity; hence
purely fictitious. Any semblance to real persons, places, or circumstances is entirely coincidental and should be regarded as such.

ISBN 0-8439-5571-6

Visit us on the web at www.dorchesterpub.com.

ACKNOWLEDGMENTS

I am thrilled to present *State's Evidence* as my third Dorchester legal novel, following the success of *Persuasive Evidence* and *Justice Served*. I hope that my fans enjoy this book every bit as much!

I would like to express thanks to all those who have been instrumental in the publication of *State's Evidence*, including my editor, Don D'Auria, as well as the wonderfully supportive staff at Dorchester and the brilliant B.J. for her excellent critique and assistance with the research for this book. I am as always ever grateful as well to my parents for encouraging me to follow my dreams, and my alma mater, Michigan State University and the School of Criminal Justice, where the seeds were planted for my most satisfying life as a literary criminologist and mystery novelist.

Yours truly,
R. Barri Flowers

STATE'S
EVIDENCE

PROLOGUE

She was a real piece of ass, he thought, feeling himself become aroused through tight jeans. He had been watching her, following her, getting to know her every move till it was time to do what had to be done.

He could have taken her any time he wanted, crushing her pretty skull between his strong, calloused hands, as easily as one might flatten a piece of dough. But it was more fun and stimulating to bide his time like a shark might before going after a helpless fish. Or even a human. He knew exactly where she was every minute of the day.

And night.

Why rush a good thing?

He considered killing a person a work of art. Like the *Mona Lisa*. It required skill, finesse, courage, determination, and a vision.

He had been born with these talents thirty-two years ago in East L.A.'s Latino community. Surviving the mean streets there had required every bit of his artistic skills, and then some. With his mama a whore and his daddy a wife-abusing heroin addict, he had literally been left to fend for himself as early as he could remember.

Joining a gang had allowed him to sharpen his skills. He imagined he had taken out or seriously injured maybe a dozen or more rival gang members by the time he was fifteen. He considered it all in a day's work. It was either them or him—which was a real no-brainer.

But he knew he was going nowhere fast in L.A.'s war zone. Between the rival Latino gangs and the black gang-bangers fighting for territory, respect, or just for the hell of it, he saw no future there. Sooner or later he figured a bullet or a blade would have his name written on it in blood—unless he quit while he was ahead.

Which was precisely why he had given up the hood and gang life and fled the city before he turned eighteen. He ended up in Northern California in a town called Eagles Landing. In comparison to the urban jungle he'd left behind, it was fairly laid back and boring as hell.

Still, he didn't miss his homeboys one bit. No damned way!

He'd hooked up with distant relatives and was cool with a few dudes in Eagles Landing.

But even that was fleeting. It didn't take long for him to realize he operated much better on his own, apart from keeping a roof over his head in living with a broad. This way he got to keep all the profits and pleasures from doing what he did best—killing people.

It was a rush like no other. Even better than getting off inside a bitch. Or the almost orgasmic feel of cocaine going into his veins. He killed for hire or just plain old desire. It made no difference to him. What counted most was that once he had targeted someone for death, it was just a matter of when, where, how, and sometimes how much.

He contemplated those very things as he studied the nice-looking broad through the window of her fancy home. She was maybe thirty, slim, with a big ass and even bigger breasts. Her yellow hair was permed in fluffy curls and she had full red lips. He imagined kissing that mouth, then sticking his tongue inside. Or better yet, having that mouth go down on him and doing its thing.

Before he gave her a taste of death.

She was sitting at the dining room table with her husband. He was a few years older than she, dark-haired, and seemingly uncomfortable in her presence, as though he didn't belong.

He looked away from the man back to his wife, watching a while longer, as he devised his strategy for her demise. A rush of adrenaline poured through him at the prospect, knowing the time was getting near to put the plan into action.

But first he wanted to allow her a bit more of a false sense of security. It was always that much more exhilarating when his victim realized that the perfect little world she or he had created was about to come crashing down around them and there wasn't a damned thing that could be done to prevent it.

Except maybe hope you got run over by a bus first. Or dropped dead of a heart attack, sparing yourself from meeting up with him.

Short of that, the person was his for the taking. And he fully intended to do just that.

Only a matter of time.

Yes, let her feel secure in her comfortable house. With that husband of hers there to protect her. Wouldn't do her one bit of good.

She would never live to see the light of day.

CHAPTER 1

The jury foreman looked tense as she responded to the judge's terse question: "Have you reached a verdict?"

The juror, an attractive Jordanian professor and mother of five, risked a furtive peek at the other jurors, as if for final confirmation. Then she raised her big brown eyes to the bench. "Yes, we have, Your Honor."

Judge Sheldon Crawford was in his mid-fifties, but looked younger with a cappuccino-toned face that was without wrinkles save for a barely perceptible crease stretching across his forehead. He had short salt-and-pepper hair, and deep gray eyes that rarely seemed to blink. Focusing them on the juror, he instructed her to hand the verdict to the bailiff.

Judge Crawford had a reputation as a tough judge, routinely doling out the stiffest penalties the law would allow. Needless to say, prosecutors and their constituents loved him and the justice he rendered. Whereas defense attorneys and their clients feared coming before the judge, often doing all they could to avoid his court, including plea bargaining at virtually every opportunity.

Beverly Mendoza, co-counsel for the state, fidgeted in her seat. It was so quiet you could hear a pin drop. Her intense green eyes studied the faces of the jurors, trying to get a hint as to what direction they had taken. Admittedly she hadn't a clue and was too smart to make any presumptions.

The case involved a woman accused of murdering her lover by pushing him off a 320-foot cliff. Her defense was that they were just fooling around—*love play,* she had called it—when he accidentally fell to his death. The fact that she didn't report him missing for two weeks seemed incidental. As did his million-dollar life insurance policy, which had only recently named her as the beneficiary.

Beverly gazed at the thirty-year-old defendant who sat there cool, calm, collected—and incredibly confident.

Does she know something that I don't?

Could this jury have possibly let her off the hook?

Meaning the prosecution would have failed to prove its case. *And I'd have a loss on my record that would be hard to swallow and harder to justify.*

Beverly snapped her head back, causing her long, straight brunette hair to bounce against the gray jacket of her Anne Klein linen suit. Her eyes landed on her co-counsel, Deputy District Attorney Grant Nunez. His Afro-Latino profile was classic with chiseled, caramel-colored features and a round head that was shaven bald. He wore a tailored dark brown suit that fit well on his muscular, tall frame. Grant was forty—eight years older than Beverly—and in line for a judgeship by all indications. Losing this case would not help his chances.

Nor would it bode especially well for my career, thought Beverly. Sensationalized cases would always be remembered for the winners and losers, no matter how many other battles were fought and won. Especially when lawyers were always looking ahead in their careers. She had aspirations of being a district attorney someday. Or maybe even a judge.

Right now, assistant district attorney for Wilameta County would have to suffice.

Sensing her stare, Grant swiveled his head, slanting cool sable eyes at her. If he was worried, he didn't show it. Instead, he gave Beverly a devilish smile that she knew was less about the proceedings than it was about them. They had been dating for four months now, though it had only become sexual in the last four weeks. Both had survived bad previous relationships and, once they had overcome their fears of failure and the unknown, had succumbed to mutual desires that left Beverly shamelessly wanting him every chance she got.

But getting her twelve-year-old son to approve of Grant had proven to be a far more formidable task. Jaime was very protective of her and did not want to see his mother get hurt—again. To him, Grant was someone who threatened the life Jaime had known for most of his young life, where it had pretty much been just the two of them.

Perhaps even more difficult for Beverly to deal with was losing her mother to breast cancer five years ago and now watching her father wasting away with Alzheimer's disease. It left him but a shell of his former proud self as a Latino who was used to being a macho man in command of his life and times. Sometimes she wished it would be over with so her father wouldn't suffer anymore; other times Beverly wanted him to hang on for as long as he possibly could. After all, having part of a father and grandfather to her son was preferable to none at all.

Wasn't it?

Beverly's mind shifted back to the attention Grant was giving her, as if they were the only ones in the courtroom. She willed herself to avert her eyes from his lascivious gaze that had managed to cause her temperature to rise, and focus on the important matter at hand. Judge Crawford read the verdict to himself. He passed the slip back to the bailiff, giving no indication by his dignified facial expression as to what it said.

Beverly felt the butterflies in her stomach as she usually did whenever a case was about to be decided. It represented weeks or months of hard work and in an instant would culminate for all parties concerned. Later there would be the penalty phase. And then, in all likelihood, appeals, and more decisions to come.

But for the moment it didn't get any more exciting and tension-filled than this.

Once the bailiff had returned the verdict to the jury foreman, the judge faced the defense table and stated levelly, "Will the defendant please rise."

She obeyed him, springing to her feet and running thin fingers through her short crimson hair before taking a breath and awaiting the judge's words that would change her life for the better or worse. Standing alongside her was her attorney, Cassandra Fielding, a fortysomething ex-prosecutor who had put up a strong, sympathetic defense. No doubt she had an eye on a hefty percentage of the insurance payments, mused Beverly. Provided they ever came.

Judge Crawford nodded at the jury foreman. "You may read the verdict."

The woman put on her glasses, almost for effect, took a deep sigh, and looked down at her trembling hands. "We, the jury, find the defendant, Suzanne Landon, to be guilty of murder in the first degree—"

The courtroom erupted in cheers from the family of the victim. Beverly let out a sigh of relief and saw victory spread across Grant's face in a big grin. The two hugged as co-counsel might be expected, formally and professionally. There would be time later for a much more private celebration.

The newly convicted murderess was led away in handcuffs, tears of disbelief or disappointment flowing down her reddened cheeks. Before leaving the courtroom, she shot Beverly a contemptuous gaze, which the prosecutor dismissed for all it was worth.

Sticks and stones may break my bones, but hateful glares will never hurt me, Beverly told herself satisfyingly.

Justice was not always blind, she thought. Not today anyway.

"We did it!" Grant Nunez declared magnanimously. He had Beverly cornered in his office, right between two file cabinets. The door was locked and might just as well have had a DO NOT DISTURB sign on it. He certainly had no intentions of being interrupted till they were done.

At six-three, he hovered over Beverly by almost seven inches. But that didn't detract from the presence she had as a woman. With her Salma Hayek looks and a hot and taut body all her own, it was all Grant could do not to want to be with Beverly 24/7.

He'd settle for twenty-four minutes and seven ways to make love to this woman who turned him on like no other with both her mind and sexuality, inside and out of the courtroom.

"Never thought for a minute we wouldn't," Beverly declared between kisses.

"You're not a very good liar." Grant put his hands on her firm breasts over her silk blouse, causing Beverly's nipples to tingle.

"So sue me," she murmured, "but only after you make me come."

"Whatever you say, Counselor." He briefly put his tongue in her mouth. "Never let it be said that I don't believe in the spirit of cooperation."

"Maybe that's why we make such a great team."

"Maybe."

Beverly tasted spearmint from his tongue, and gave him hers to play with. She put a hand to his pants, feeling the hardness of Grant's erection begging to be released. She was only too happy to oblige, unzipping him even as his hand went under her skirt and began to caress between her legs. She pulled his very sexual organ out and held it firmly as if her own, stimulating the shaft.

"Umm . . ." She heard the sound utter between their mouths, unsure who it came from.

Her back stiffened when Grant slipped fingers inside her panties and then into her. She spread her legs while leaning against a file cabinet, urging him on and giving back as much in touching his penis. Beverly bit her lip as he began to stimulate her clitoris, causing her to nearly scream with pleasure.

Instead, mindful they were someplace where noise could be easily heard, she managed barely more than a whimper. But inside her a desire to have an ache squelched had grown in leaps and bounds. While still holding his throbbing erection, Beverly looked Grant in the eye ravenously. "Condom?"

He removed one from his pocket and placed it in her palm, content to see her take the lead. She quickly removed the foil, slid the latex over him, and climbed atop Grant's sturdy hips, wrapping her arms around his neck.

Beverly inserted him inside her. "Make love to me," she demanded in a desperate voice, the sense of urgency spreading across her body like a bolt of lightning.

"It would be my pleasure, baby," he said huskily, and held on to her slender waist while plunging himself deep into her. She absorbed the thrusts while slamming herself back against him with equal zest.

Her orgasm came quickly, and a second one came shortly thereafter at about the same time that Grant climaxed with a rush of breath and a violent shudder. Both were breathing heavily, and Beverly could feel Grant's heartbeat pounding as they clung to one another till the experience had come to a mouths-smacking, bodies-perspiring, satisfying conclusion.

"We need to win as a team more often," Grant sang contentedly, giving Beverly another long kiss.

She kissed him back and climbed off him. "That may not be possible," she teased, "if you're a judge."

"True," he said, removing the condom and zipping his pants. "But look at the bright side, baby. If and when that day ever comes, just imagine what fun you and I could have in the judge's chambers."

Beverly pushed him playfully. "You're insatiable!" She put her clothes back into place, then brushed her hair.

He laughed. "And you're not?"

She blushed. "Maybe it's the effect you have on me, darling, that makes me crave your body."

He chuckled again. "I have been known to have that effect on women."

"Oh, really?" Beverly met his eyes and felt a touch of jealousy. As far as she knew they were exclusive. If they weren't on the same page there, she wanted to find out before this went any further.

Grant sensed that he'd used the wrong choice of words and quickly sought to rectify his error. The last thing he wanted was to ruin this relationship, something he'd managed to do too easily in the past. Only none of the previous women in his life could hold a candle to Beverly Mendoza and he wouldn't have it any other way.

"What's important is that this is the first time it's really meant something to me," he said in earnest. "I don't take that lightly, Bev, and I'm definitely not looking at anyone else."

She smiled, feeling a sense of relief and maybe a little leftover insecurity. "But you'll tell me if you change your mind?"

"I won't change my mind," he promised. *Not so long as there's the possibility that we can really go somewhere with this.*

"Neither will I," she thought to add, enjoying his company more than Beverly had enjoyed a man's in some time. She was in no hurry to ruin a good thing. How good remained to be seen.

Grant straightened his tie. "So what do you say I take you out to dinner for a victory celebration? Sex always leaves me famished."

"Can't," Beverly said apologetically, putting fresh lipstick on after he had taken it all off. "I promised Jaime pizza tonight." She couldn't help but think that though only twelve, her son sometimes seemed like he was twenty-five with his maturity and rapidly growing body.

Grant grinned wistfully. "Did I tell you that I love pizza?" *And would love to get to know your son better, if you'll let me.*

Beverly squirmed guiltily, knowing he wanted more than what they had. And so did she. But right now her son was still her top priority. As were his feelings on the subject.

"Jaime just needs a little time adjusting to someone else in my life," she offered contritely.

Grant looked like a wounded puppy. "How much time does he need—the rest of *your* life?"

Beverly touched her nose thoughtfully. "Not much longer, Grant." She hoped. "It's been just the two of us for so long, he's trying to come to terms with the fact that someone else is now in my life who's very important to me."

Beverly realized that along with wanting to protect Jaime, she was also trying to protect herself from being hurt and abandoned, as they had been by his father.

Grant furrowed his brow while trying to be understanding. "Seems to me it's time you let someone else take down that wall you've built around the boy."

"Please be patient, Grant," Beverly implored softly, not wanting to spoil what had just happened by applying too much pressure either way. "I just want what's best for everyone—you included." She kissed him on the mouth. "Call me."

Even as she said that, Beverly knew that it sounded like she was afraid of commitment. Was she? Not that Grant had ever suggested he wanted a commitment in so many words. Or maybe she was confused over the terms *commitment* and *exclusivity*. Didn't they mean the same thing, in effect, in a relationship? Like her, Grant had been married once before. He had no children from it and did not seem entirely comfortable at the prospect of ever marrying again. But he did care for her, she was sure, beyond the sexual compatibility.

Was that enough to constitute a real and trusting relationship at the end of the day? Beverly wondered. One that included her son as an intricate part of the team?

Would it ever be enough?

Grant showed Beverly out the door, waved good-bye, and settled back into his office thoughtfully. She was the first woman he'd been with who gave as much as she took—both sexually and as a prosecutor. He was damned glad to have her on his side in both departments.

Should he be offered a judgeship, as expected, it would be all the more reason for them to mesh, without the competition as trial lawyers that brought them together and could potentially tear them apart.

Grant's focus shifted to other issues on his mind. He picked up the phone and buzzed his secretary.

"Get the DA on the line," he ordered.

A moment later, the thick voice said, "Yeah, Grant, what's up?"

He sighed and glanced out the window musingly. "We need to talk . . ."

CHAPTER 2

He watched from the bushes as she left the office building, wearing an aqua jogging suit that looked a size too large on her streamlined frame. He watched her suck in a deep breath of the cool October air and then stretch her limbs in preparation for what was a normal jog through the park across the street. She always ran alone, almost as if she considered company an invasion of her privacy.

That played right into his hands because he liked to do his thing alone, too.

A slight rustle of the bushes off to the side of the building drew her attention. For an instant in the waning sunlight, he saw fear in her face and thought he'd been detected. But that fear disappeared when she apparently decided it was nothing but the wind.

He sighed and maintained his low position, careful not to even twitch. He watched as she glanced up at a window. The light was on and the blinds were closed. If she expected someone to open them, she was disappointed. She seemed to become deeply absorbed in thought for a moment or two before crossing the parking lot in a lazy jaunt.

He gave her a couple of minutes to enter the park, and then emerged from his hideaway. Looking around, he saw no one. Good. Now it was just him and her.

Like an addict needing a fix, he pursued her eagerly, fully expecting to be relieved of his urge.

She was in excellent shape, he admitted to himself, trailing her from a short distance as she moved at a brisk pace. But so was he. He had been lifting weights and running for years in his determination to stay fit and firm. It was the best way to survive on the streets. And in the joint, if it came down to that.

For now fitness would serve him well in tracking down someone who had become his sole obsession of late.

The park was very quiet this evening. It was almost as if others had decided to stay at home, so as not to get in her way.

Or his.

Slowly but surely he began to close the distance between them. When she realized he was behind her, she instinctively increased her speed, determined to simply outrun him. But he countered, moving even faster, his long legs giving him the advantage. His blood was pumping like crazy and he loved the feeling. It was like building up to a mind-blowing climax. The climb was always more rewarding than the result, he knew.

Not that the result would be disappointing. On the contrary, it would be very satisfying.

After all, she had been targeted for death. And now it was time to wipe the slate clean.

Collect his just rewards.

She tried to dart in a different direction amidst tall, old Douglas fir trees, as if somehow he would simply bypass her altogether. Anticipating such, he had countered her move with one of his own, taking a shortcut to beat her to the clearing on the other side of the park.

She didn't realize it, but the dumb bitch had run right into his trap like a rat.

They came face to face and he saw the stark terror in her baby-blue eyes. He even detected a hint of recognition as she tried to make out his face. His eyes. His sly grin. His taut, virile body.

He pulled out a switchblade, springing it open and moving it from hand to hand with the ease of a magician.

He might have pitied her had he not applauded himself for a job soon to be well done. They had reached the point of no return. At least she had.

The fun this night was only beginning.

Sheldon Crawford huffed and puffed while atop his wife, Maxine, feeling as if he had run out of breath. He was getting too damned old for this. But at the same time, he was determined to keep up with her. A daunting task indeed. She was twenty years his junior and in her sexual prime. Meaning she wanted to be satisfied constantly and had esoteric tastes that at times tested his limits, ability, and stamina. Not his resolve, though. The worst thing he could do was ignore his young wife's needs and allow her to leave him for a younger man as his first wife had done.

Sheldon gazed into Maxine's café au lait eyes, staring up at him from her beautiful butterscotch-complexioned face. He nibbled on one of her large breasts, as she loved for him to do. She winced and then murmured, taking his cheeks between her hands and attacking his mouth with fervor in hard kisses.

He propelled himself deeper into her splayed legs, feeling her constrict around him. She clawed at his back and he grunted from the pain, even while their kissing intensified.

"I'm coming . . ." Maxine warned him, wrapping her legs around his waist. "Don't stop, darling."

Sheldon couldn't even if he wanted to. He felt the surge of ejaculate leave him and go into her.

He heard a muffled cry as Maxine seemed to feed off his orgasm to release her own animatedly. His chest heaved against her flattened breasts and they climaxed together—

loudly—as the sounds of sexual gratification took center stage.

Afterward Sheldon collapsed onto Maxine's slender body, keeping most of his weight on his knees so as not to crush her. He was exhausted but gratified in the knowledge that he had pleased her. As a judge, he wanted only to please himself and his brand of justice. Sometimes he would bend the rules, if called for in the name of law and order—or the preservation of his career and satisfying certain obligations.

But as a man, he wanted to feel needed and loved. Maxine gave that to him. More than anyone had before. So the least he could do was provide her the financial and physical comforts she deserved.

Sheldon had barely felt her warm breath upon his cheek when a sharp pop rang through the air like a firecracker. A millisecond later he experienced a dull pain in his back. There was a piercing scream, which almost sounded as though it were coming from a distant place. Then he realized that it had come from the person beneath him.

Sheldon Crawford had been shot before, back in Vietnam. It was an experience a person never forgot. He had been caught in an ambush and took two bullets in the chest. Both had missed his heart by scant inches. He had considered it divine intervention, and promised himself that he would make something out of the second life he had been given.

That life had carried him to the judicial bench, where he had presided over the scum who threatened to one day become free to wreak havoc on the lives of other innocent victims. Not if he could help it. He didn't believe violent criminals could ever be rehabilitated. Not in his court. They needed to be kept behind bars as long as possible to ensure public safety. And be punished severely for their crimes.

But even with the best of intentions in his heart, Sheldon

knew that these desires sometimes came into conflict with powerful forces beyond his control.

In the process of passing judgment over others, Sheldon Crawford had come to believe he was somehow secure from the very dangers he devoted his life to fighting.

He was wrong.

The second scream roared into his ear like a siren gone out of control even as Sheldon felt another sharp pain explode into his body. He kept a loaded .357 Magnum in the nightstand but had never had to use it before. And though now in excruciating pain, he knew that the gun was the only chance he or Maxine had to survive this night.

But his assailant, seemingly toying with him, allowed the judge to crawl halfway out of bed and lunge for the nightstand before firing another bullet at point-blank range. This one hit Sheldon Crawford in the face, killing him instantly.

Maxine Crawford, immobilized by fear, watched incredulously as half of her husband's head separated from his body in something akin to a horror movie. Without time to even contemplate the terror she had just witnessed or the fact that she was now fully exposed for the shooter to see, Maxine could only think that she was next to die. She felt utterly powerless to do anything about her seemingly unchangeable fate as a witness to an execution. But she prayed like she never had before.

Through a shaft of diminishing sunlight filtering through the window, Maxine was afforded a surprisingly clear look at the killer, clouded somewhat by the tearful haze of her eyes.

She took an instant to study the person who stood at the foot of the bed like he was standing guard. He was a Hispanic male in his early thirties, powerfully built, and short. He had coarse black hair; dark, frightful eyes that never took themselves off her nakedness; and a scowl that almost seemed to be a wicked smile.

Wearing gloves, he held the gun at his side like in an old

Western movie and she wondered why he had not lifted it and pulled the trigger by now.

Suddenly all she could think about was wanting to live to see another day. Maybe many days and months and years. She'd worked too hard to get what she had for it all to end like this.

Commanding her mouth to speak, Maxine voiced in a desperate whisper, "Please, don't kill me . . ."

The man said nothing, but continued to enjoy his voyeuristic show at her expense, grinning. She wanted to cover up with the satin sheets but didn't want to do anything to provoke him.

He moved to the side of the bed and she saw that his mouth had become a scowl. He raised the gun and pointed it at her.

"Please," she gasped helplessly. "I don't want to die."

"Well, you're gonna die, *bitch!*" His words were hollow and menacing.

Maxine felt that she had reached the point of no return. Just as Sheldon had moments earlier. There was apparently no reasoning with a cold-blooded murderer.

She squeezed her eyes shut and tried to imagine how painful death would be.

Would she even be aware of when she was dead?

Was Sheldon aware that he had gone to the other side?

Would there be the light at the end of the tunnel? Or would they both drift off into some horrible abyss, uncertain as to where they were or why?

Then Maxine heard her husband's killer say in a chilling tone, "But not yet . . ."

He stared at the good-looking Black chick on the bed. Raven hair in box braids formed a halo around her frightened face. Pouty lips had suddenly been silenced. Her big breasts and body glistened from sex, and her long, lean legs were still spread wide as though her old man was still on top of her. He could only imagine how hard the good judge had to work to satisfy her. On the other hand, *he* was younger, hungrier, and definitely more energetic for the task.

In truth, it had been a while since he'd had a woman, at least not one who looked like her. The notion excited him to the point where he felt like a dam ready to burst. Only he intended to do so inside the bitch's mouth and vagina. He glanced at what was left of the bloody corpse on the floor, thinking, *There sure as hell ain't nobody gonna stop me from taking what I want from the lady.*

She certainly couldn't stop him. Even when he took the gun out of her face.

Who knows, she might even enjoy what they were about to do, he thought.

He knew he would. Every lingering moment of it.

CHAPTER 3

They went through an entire large pizza, loaded with cheese, sausage, and pepperoni. Beverly managed to get in a couple of pieces before Jaime took over, gobbling down bites like a garbage disposal. Normally she would have drawn the line after maybe three pieces, tops. She had been concerned about his increasing diet of junk food and a cholesterol level that was already too high. But she had promised Jaime that he could have anything he wanted if he got a B on his math test. And he had done one better, acing it with an A.

Beverly considered Jaime the best mistake she had ever made. She had never intended to get pregnant at age twenty. She was hardly more than a child bride herself. But her birth control had inexplicably failed her that night, just as Jaime's father had failed her when he found out she was pregnant.

Diego Mendoza was as charming a Latino as they came, making Beverly fall for him with barely more than his shiny red Corvette and dreams of a bright future with her. But it all turned out to be false dreams when the going got tough.

He wanted her to have an abortion. When she refused, he got scared of his responsibility and ran away. That was the last she had ever seen of Diego.

Beverly had raised her son alone, no small task with law school and mostly low-paying jobs to make ends meet along the way. But they had both survived, if not thrived, and Beverly could not imagine her life without Jaime—though she knew the day would come when he would have his own family.

Until then, she would be there for him as his father had not been. And never would be.

Jaime wiped his mouth with a greasy napkin and slurped root beer through a straw. "Want some?" he asked, as if an afterthought.

"I think not," Beverly responded, wrinkling her nose at the notion. She drank bottled water instead.

Jaime giggled. "Didn't think so." He sipped more soda.

Beverly stared at her son without making it too apparent. He had her brown hair—though a shade darker—in a short crew cut that was all the rage at school. Jaime had his father's dun-colored eyes and thick brows. At twelve, he was already nearly as tall as her and on the chubby side. Even his feet—size nine and a half—were big for a boy his age. Beverly considered that perhaps Jaime was just a normal oversized kid in today's society where most things seemed to be excessive and large. In fact, his baggy jeans and oversized jerseys actually made him look leaner than he really was.

"You didn't tell me how the case went." Jaime looked across the dining room table, as if genuinely interested, surprising Beverly.

For the most part her son had shown little interest in her law work, she thought sadly. He had been far more impressed with his best friend Paco's mother, who Jaime thought was hot, and who, as a stay-at-home mom, was always around to do things with.

Perhaps he's beginning to appreciate what I do for a liv-

ing, Beverly mused, even at the expense of being able to spend more time together. Maybe someday Jaime would even follow in her footsteps and become a lawyer.

"Well, we won," she told him, still feeling victorious, as if having won a national championship. Especially when thinking of how she and Grant had celebrated the occasion.

"I'm glad." Jaime gave her a proud smile out of the side of his mouth.

Beverly smiled back warmly. "I'm happy to hear that."

His smile seemed to evaporate. "How much did *he* help?"

She raised a brow. "You mean Grant?"

Jaime knew they had worked together on the trial and had gone out on a few dates, though Beverly was sure her son had no inkling of the extent of their relationship. She'd planned to tell him that she was seeing Grant, once she felt Jaime was ready to hear it. Maybe the time was now?

"Yeah, him."

"Actually, Grant helped quite a bit as co-counsel." She wiped her mouth with a napkin. "In fact, to be honest, I'm not sure we could have won without him."

Jaime leaned back in his chair so his head rested against the wall behind him. "Oh . . ." He stared thoughtfully. "Are you sleeping with him, Mom?"

Beverly's spine stiffened. "Jaime!" Her face colored. *Just who have you been talking to about sex? Or do I even want to know?* "That's not the type of question a boy asks his mother," she snapped.

Jaime shrugged. "I've seen the way he looks at you. Was that the same way Dad looked at you?"

Beverly bit her lip. "Grant and I are friends *and* colleagues," she told him, deciding that now wasn't the right time to say more. "And your father was too busy looking at himself to notice me for the most part."

"But he noticed you at least once, didn't he?" Jaime shot her a cold, crude look.

Beverly could barely believe he was talking to her like this. Obviously her son was being told more about intimacy between a man and woman than she was comfortable with him knowing at this stage of his life.

"Yes," she responded sharply. "And after that he didn't want to have anything to do with me—or you." She was always straight with Jaime where it concerned Diego. She saw no need to paint a pretty picture about his father for false consumption. There wasn't anything pretty about abandonment, disappointment, or betrayal.

"We're doing just fine the way we are," pouted Jaime. "We don't need *anyone* else in our lives."

Meaning *she* didn't need anyone else in *her* life but her twelve-year-old son who was growing up way too fast. There had not been anyone else in her life for a very long time. Beverly had dedicated herself almost entirely to Jaime and her career for longer than she cared to remember. Add to that responsibility of her father with his declining health the last two years.

Wasn't that enough? What more did her son want from her?

Beverly wondered if it had been a mistake to spoil Jaime for so many years with undivided affections and perhaps too little attention given to respecting one's elders. Could he ever accept another person in her life, including his ailing grandfather?

Well, he would have to, she thought, unwilling to go back to the way things had been without romance and sex in her life. Grant was someone Jaime would have to contend with sooner or later if things remained on course as they were.

The phone rang, breaking the silent standoff.

"I think that's for me," Beverly uttered, though in no way feeling that was a certainty. Lately Jaime had been on the phone enough that she was sure he'd soon be demanding his own cell phone. She reached for the cordless on the table.

She could see from the caller ID that it was Grant, making Beverly feel even more guilty of neglecting her son. After taking a breath, she said, "Hello."

"Flip the TV to channel four." Grant's voice had a tense catch to it.

"What's on?" Beverly watched Jaime curl his lip perceptively and leave the table, disappearing down the hall. A moment later she heard his bedroom door slam, giving her a shiver.

"You won't believe it," Grant said evasively. "A real shocker! Hurry up!"

"All right, just a minute."

Her curiosity piqued, Beverly went into the hall, glancing once at Jaime's closed door before moving toward the sunken living room. She'd purchased the single-level patio home nine years ago, right after passing the bar. It was in a beautiful old Eagles Landing neighborhood, separated somewhat from other homes by coast redwood and lodgepole pines.

Grabbing the remote control off the rustic log coffee table, Beverly pointed it at the flat screen plasma TV.

A female anchor, Nancy Novak, stared dramatically at the screen, stating painfully, "In a recap of our breaking story, Superior Court Judge Sheldon Crawford was shot to death at his home tonight." Beverly felt a thump in her chest in disbelief. "His wife, Maxine Crawford, was rushed to the hospital. No word yet on her condition. The assailant is apparently still on the loose and considered armed and dangerous—"

CHAPTER 4

He came in the back door of the duplex, hoping to avoid the usual confrontation with his old lady that seemed to be the story of his life these days. His clothes were wet and muddy. There was even some blood on his pants.

Damn!

He stepped into the kitchen and went over to the sink. He could hear the TV upstairs and figured it was safe to try and clean himself up a bit.

But she would never let him off that easily.

"Where were you?" The voice blared out of the shadows like a sonic boom.

He jumped, though he wished he hadn't, and faced her as she came into full view. A scowl ran the length of her olive face, which was a perfect match for her bulky body. Her dyed dark-blond hair was worn in a layered bob, and a floral purple nightgown did a poor job covering her.

"Out," he said simply.

She moved closer, eyeing him suspiciously. "What the . . . You look like hell! *Where have you been?*"

"At the lake." It was true, he thought, in part. The rest she was better off not knowing, for her own sake.

"You've got dirt all over you," she spat, giving him the once-over with narrowed chocolate eyes. "What the hell happened?"

He sniffed, the smell of death repugnant even to him. "You don't really wanna know."

Her gaze rested on the dark red spots on his jeans. "You're bleeding."

He wiped at his pants self-consciously. "It ain't no big deal."

She refused to leave it alone. Slapping a hand on her considerable hip, she demanded, "What have you done, Manuel?"

"I ain't done nothin'!" She was starting to piss him off, sticking her nose where it didn't belong. One of these days, he just might have to cut it off and shove it down her damned throat.

She glared at him. "That is *your* blood, isn't it?"

He had to think fast. He sure as hell couldn't tell her the truth and nothing *but* the truth. If something went wrong, she could testify against him. Couldn't she? He'd heard that even a married woman could squeal on her husband, if she had her mind made up to do so.

And knowing his fat old lady, her mind might already be made up if he confided in her.

He smiled at her crookedly. "It's fish blood. I told you I was at the lake. Thought I'd reel in some dinner for you, baby. Things got a little rough out there, but I stuck with it."

She darted her eyes from side to side with serious misgiving. "So where's the fish?"

"Out in the car," he told her. "I just hadn't gotten 'round to bringing it in. If you don't believe me, go see for yourself."

Her nostrils ballooned. "If you're lying . . ."

"I'm not," he insisted boldly. "Check it out. Save me a trip to the car. I'll go clean up and then fry it for you."

As he expected, she gave him the benefit of the doubt,

dragging her lazy, fat ass back upstairs without another word. He would drop by the market and pick up some fish. She'd never know the difference.

Bitch.

His secret was safe for now. Maybe forever, if he had his way, like the others.

He opened the fridge and got out a beer, opening it and taking a giant swig in one motion.

He thought about the sweet-looking woman he'd accosted at the park. She had not gone down easily. In fact, she'd put up one hell of a struggle, battling him tooth and nail to the very end. It had aroused him like never before.

He loved a broad with spunk—especially one who normally probably wouldn't have given a Latino like him the time of day. Not until he took it, and her life, as a bonus.

CHAPTER 5

Beverly had agreed to meet Grant at Eagles Landing Medical Center's emergency room, where Maxine Crawford had been taken. It was what Grant called a preemptive strike, given the attention Judge Crawford's murder was likely to generate. The Eagles Landing Police Department would be under tremendous pressure to make an arrest and the Wilameta County District Attorney's office would be equally pressured to get a swift and decisive conviction.

All else would have to take a backseat for the time being.

The fact that Judge Crawford's last trial had taken place that very afternoon, in a case Beverly had successfully prosecuted, along with Grant, meant that they would be on the hot seat on this one.

Was the trial in any way connected to the judge's death? Beverly wondered, entering the doors to the ER. Maybe it was some form of payback for upholding the guilty verdict against Suzanne Landon. But who would do such a thing after the fact?

Beverly had told Jaime she wasn't sure when she would be back, wishing the timing had been different. She was confident that in his own way he understood that her career obligations sometimes included working after hours. And with little to no warning. Fortunately, Jaime had reached the age where he could take care of himself for short lengths of time when she wasn't there, though she always tried to be there when he got home from school and most evenings. She was proud of him for his maturity and responsibility, even if he may have grown up a little too fast for her comfort.

There were still outstanding issues the two of them would have to resolve. And one of them included Grant.

Beverly spotted Grant pacing around in the lobby as though he had lost his best friend. As far as she knew, he and Judge Crawford were only casually acquainted. Which was more than her own relationship with the judge. She knew him only in the courtroom. Even then, Sheldon Crawford struck her as somewhat distant and unapproachable.

When Grant saw Beverly he met her halfway, giving her a lightning-quick hug. "Thanks for coming."

Beverly gave him a tiny nod while thinking that he looked tired and ill at ease—unlike this afternoon when he was full of life and comfortable with her . . . inside her.

"Have you found out anything?"

"Nothing." He threw his arms up in disgust. "The doctors aren't talking about her condition. Maxine Crawford could be dying in there for all we know."

"What did the police say?" Beverly could see what looked to be detectives just down the hall. She thought she recognized one as Detective Joe O'Dell of the Eagles Landing Police Department's homicide division. They had worked together on a case or two. He had proven himself to be a thorough cop and an excellent witness.

"Doesn't look like she was shot," said Grant. "Just bruised and in shock."

Beverly curled her lashes. "Who wouldn't be in shock, under the circumstances?" She tried to imagine what it would be like to see your husband murdered right in front of you.

She wondered why the assailant didn't kill the judge's wife, instead leaving an eyewitness to the crime who could testify against him. Had Mrs. Crawford gotten a look at him? Was it even a *him?* Beverly had just finished a case where the culprit was a female. Who says it wasn't a woman who offed the judge? "Do you think this could have had anything to do with the case we just tried?" she asked.

Grant scratched his cheek. "Hadn't really thought about it," he said artlessly. "Judge Crawford has undoubtedly made more than his share of enemies over the years."

"But the timing of the attack," questioned Beverly. "Maybe someone acting on behalf of Suzanne Landon decided to get their revenge on her conviction by killing the judge who presided over her trial?" Even while saying it, Beverly realized that since the penalty phase had not yet taken place, there seemed little point in killing the judge beforehand—unless the killer believed it would somehow make a difference in sentencing.

"I didn't get the feeling that Suzanne Landon had much of a fan club," Grant voiced dismissively. "Besides, if she wanted to get back at anyone, it would be the people who convicted her of first-degree murder!"

He favored Beverly with narrowed eyes, as if to point the finger at the two of them. The notion left her slightly unsettled.

"My point being that Landon is probably not behind Crawford's death." Grant's brow furrowed. "Which doesn't make it any less disturbing."

Beverly agreed. So who hated the judge enough to want to kill him? Could be anyone who ever came into his courtroom, she decided.

Danger lurked at every turn for those who worked in the criminal justice system. It came with the territory. She herself had come face-to-face with death as a result of a case she had worked on. The most recent time was last year when a serial rapist on trial and out on bail had actually cornered her in a bank parking lot. He had managed to threaten her with bodily harm and may have actually put his words into action had a bank employee not come to the rescue.

Since then Beverly had carried a loaded .40-caliber Glock in her purse, and was prepared to use it if she had to.

Surely the judge had a gun, given the routine threats he must have received. Obviously he never got the chance to use it.

Beverly cringed and gazed up at Grant. "Were you friends with the judge?" she asked curiously.

He flipped his eyelids casually. "Not really. Played some racquetball on occasion while talking shop unofficially, but never socialized much outside of that. Why?"

"No reason." She twisted her lips musingly. "Just thought that since you were here, you might have some inside information on why the judge was attacked."

Grant favored her steadily. "Yeah, I wish it were that simple. I don't know any more than you do. I came to try and stay ahead of the curve in learning just what happened at the judge's house tonight and how the DA's office might approach it."

Beverly considered Judge Crawford's wife for a moment. They had never met, but she had heard that Maxine Crawford was a good deal younger than her husband. And gorgeous. Might the attack have been directed toward her?

"It was a good idea to see what we can learn before everyone else does," she said.

"I thought you would agree."

They watched as Detective O'Dell walked toward them. He was pushing forty, tall, and had dark Rastafarian locks.

"Hello, Joe," Beverly greeted him.

He nodded politely. "Beverly. Nunez. You here to interview the judge's wife?"

Grant pursed his lips. "Not exactly. That's your department, isn't it?"

O'Dell smiled slightly. "It is. I suppose Judge Crawford has friends in high places?"

"Not friends," Beverly pointed out. And not at high as the judge was before being brought down to earth. "Just friendly observers."

"I see."

"So what have you got on this one?" Grant asked.

O'Dell scratched his brow. "It appears that Judge Crawford was shot to death at point-blank range with what looks to be a small caliber handgun. Half his face was blown away." He paused, glancing uneasily at Beverly and back again. "He and Mrs. Crawford were in bed having sex at the time. Not sure if the judge ever knew what hit him."

Beverly swallowed. She had seen enough horrific crime scenes to last her a lifetime. But the thought of death occurring under such intimate, pleasurable circumstances sent shivers up her spine.

"Did Maxine Crawford know what hit *her?*" she inquired.

O'Dell seemed to ponder the thought. "Haven't really had a chance to get a statement from her yet. At this point it looks like she's damned lucky to be alive."

Grant bristled. "Yeah, right. You call watching your husband's head explode luck?"

The detective's coal eyes shot him a nasty look. "When you consider the alternative . . ."

Beverly felt obliged to step between the two, as if they were about to come to blows. "Hopefully Mrs. Crawford will be able to identify whoever did this," she said wistfully.

"Yeah, that would be a big help," O'Dell said skeptically.

A doctor from the ER approached the gathering. He was in his fifties, perspiring, and had sad blue eyes. Beverly knew instinctively that he had just worked on Maxine Crawford.

"How is she?" O'Dell asked in confirmation.

Frowning, the doctor said, "Under the circumstances, she could be a lot worse." He sighed raggedly. "Mrs. Crawford was raped and sodomized. Also suffered some bad bruises, probably from trying to fight off her attacker. But . . . she'll live."

"Can I talk to her now?" O'Dell asked eagerly.

"Not tonight, I'm afraid. We've given Mrs. Crawford a tranquilizer to calm her down . . . help her to sleep. She's resting now. We'll keep her overnight to be on the safe side."

Grant stepped forward. "Did she say anything about who might have done this?"

"Not a thing," the doctor said unapologetically. "Sorry. Now, if you'll excuse me, I have other patients to tend to."

They watched as he walked away, stopping only long enough to confer with a nurse.

"Looks like it's going to be a long night," grumbled O'Dell, scratching his pate.

"I'm sure you're used to it, O'Dell," Grant said coldly. "Isn't that what you detectives live for?"

"Being used to long nights and enjoying them are two different things, *Counselor.*" O'Dell glared at him, then nodded to Beverly with a softer expression. "See you around."

"Bye, Joe." She forced a tight smile at him. After he left, Beverly turned to Grant with a hard look. "What's wrong with you?"

"Nothing." He cast his eyes downward.

She wasn't buying it. "Why were you so rude to Joe?"

"Didn't mean to be." Grant took a handkerchief from his pocket and blew his nose loudly. "Guess I was just reacting—or overreacting—to all the crap that goes on in this town."

"What crap is that?" She assumed it was something other than the norm.

"Crime, criminals, courtrooms—everything we have to go through to deal with all of it. Makes you wonder if we're fighting a losing battle."

"Even the small victories count," Beverly responded. Was there more to this than he was letting on? She decided not to press it. "I have to go," she told him. She wanted to get back to Jaime, reassure him that she would always love him as her child, even if she also loved a man.

It was still too soon to tell if that man was Grant.

He brushed against her, causing Beverly's body to react unbidden.

"I should be leaving, too. Nothing more for me to do here."

At Beverly's car—a white Subaru Impreza—Grant kissed her softly on the lips.

"I'm glad I have you, Bev," he said affectionately.

"I feel the same way about you," she told him.

Grant's eyes crinkled. "Say hi to Jaime for me."

"I will," Beverly promised, though not sure her son would be in any mood to receive it.

Grant was still waving when she drove off, as seen through the rearview mirror. She could still feel the tantalizing taste of his lips on hers.

Were they really meant to be together at the end of the day?

Or was it merely a temporary fulfillment of sexual and emotional needs before they went their separate ways?

Grant watched Beverly's car disappear from sight. Already he missed being with her. And being inside that hot Latina body. He hoped that they could get past any hang-ups her son might have about them being together. Maybe if he'd had children, he would have been able to better relate to them having a conniption over his ex-wife dating someone else. But since she refused to have children and he was in no position to make her, the best he could do was give his ex the freedom she so craved and move on himself.

He did, and worked his ass off to get where he was today. *I'm not about to let the judge's bad luck interfere with that,* he thought.

Grant stared thoughtfully into the night before heading back into the hospital to make sure that all the bases were covered. The last thing he wanted was more surprises. Even if he had to keep Beverly in the dark for her own good.

CHAPTER 6

The small television on the dresser served as little more than background noise to the heavier sounds of grunts and groans coming from the bed. Manuel buried his face in her massive breasts, practically suffocating as they pressed against his nose. Sweat poured from her body like running water while she cradled him, pinning his legs down with her considerable thighs.

She pulled his face from between her breasts and licked his lips, savoring the taste like fine wine. She slid up and down his hard penis, constricting around him as her excitement grew. He clutched her fleshy ass cheeks and began to lift her up and down on him, his excitement building as the time neared to get off inside her.

Only she got there first and came all over him while her big body quivered violently. She screamed into his ear while climaxing, practically shattering his eardrum.

Now it was his turn. Using all the energy he had, Manuel flipped his old lady off him and rolled on top. He clutched her breasts tightly and started ramming his erection into her like a man possessed. He muttered a couple of expletives as he ejaculated inside her tight vagina, relishing the sensation before collapsing atop her.

Kissing her mouth, he grinned sweetly. "Was it good, baby?"

She flashed dreamy eyes at him. "Always, Manuel," she sighed. "Can't get enough of you, hon."

"I know," he said confidently. He wished the same could be said of her. But the truth was that she could only satisfy him up to a point. The rest was left to others. She didn't have to know all his business, though.

They shared a cigarette while regaining their equilibrium and playing footsie. Manuel glanced at the tube. An Asian broad was reporting the news. She said a judge had been executed this night, and his wife seriously injured. The suspect was still at large.

This intrigued him.

He hated all judges. They were assholes. Judges sat on benches, looking down at the rest of them like they were the scum of the earth. He'd had his fair share of run-ins with judges and always felt they were damned lucky they didn't meet under other circumstances. On the streets he could do some serious damage to the bastards and bitches who ruled the criminal courts like they were their private property.

Which made it all the more rewarding that this judge had gotten his but good. The wife had as well, he thought gleefully, as if from personal knowledge.

The mere contemplation suddenly had his libido working again. Manuel turned to his old lady and she knew that it was time for a replay, whether she wanted it or not.

CHAPTER 7

Detective Stone Palmer hand-brushed his short graying hair and shifted his lean body in the desk chair. He had been a homicide detective for the Wilameta County Sheriff's Department for the last fifteen years, but was currently doing double-duty for the Missing Persons Division due to budget cuts and a reduced workforce. In his years on the force, Stone had seen it all: serial killers, mass murderers, sexual psychopaths, domestic violence turned deadly, runaways found murdered and buried in shallow graves, and every other morbid homicide you could think of.

No two cases were ever quite alike. He supposed that was what made the job interesting, along with the fact that he was damned good at what he did. That included investigating missing persons, where he left no rock unturned to get at the truth, no matter how painful. Other detectives avoided that detail like the plague, considering it too inactive and often lacking a real challenge.

At thirty-nine and still married to his high school sweetheart for twenty years now, Stone felt he had all the challenge he needed at home. Two of the kids were still there and two others were off in college, but never too far away to call and ask for money—which he usually gave, admittedly a sucker when it came to his children.

He trained his gray-blue eyes on the man standing at the side of his desk. Caucasian with wavy black hair, he guessed him to be in his early thirties, probably about his own height of six-four, with the type of solid upper body that made Stone believe that he lifted weights. His square-jawed face was unshaven and bags beneath sloe-colored eyes suggested a man who had gone too long without sleep. He wore a wrinkled gray suit, as if thrown on just for the occasion.

The man had identified himself as Chuck Murray and stormed into the office, worried about his wife's where-abouts.

"Why don't you have a seat," Stone urged nicely, feeling uncomfortable looking up at the clearly agitated man.

After a sigh, Chuck sat in one of two aging chairs across the desk, stretching out his long legs.

"How long has your wife been missing, Mr. Murray?" Stone asked routinely. He hoped the man didn't say one or two hours. Even three or four.

"She never came home last night," he answered tersely.

"What time does she normally come home?"

"Around seven o'clock."

Stone glanced at his watch. It was 10 A.M. He did the arithmetic. Just over fourteen hours. They usually needed at least twenty-four hours before a missing person case became official. But there was something about this one that made him suspicious. Call it instinct or a general mistrust of nervous men who maybe had reason to fear the worst for a wife missing less than a day.

"What's your wife's name, sir?" Stone looked at him coolly.

"Adrienne." Chuck's lower lip twitched.

Stone made a mental note. "Where was Adrienne supposed to be before she came home?"

"At work."

"Where does she work?"

"At a telemarketing firm."

Stone jotted this down. "Doing what?"

Chuck tilted his head. "She's an administrative assistant."

"Adrienne never phoned you to say she might be late or maybe spending the night with a girlfriend or something . . . ?"

"No!" Chuck snapped. "Adrienne would not have just gone off for the hell of it without letting me know. That's not her style."

I'll take your word for that at the moment, Stone thought. Maybe she had a reason for not wanting to come home. Or it could be that something—or someone—really had prevented her from doing so.

"Did you call her office?" he asked the husband.

Chuck nodded. "Yeah, and they said she left around six thirty."

"Alone?"

"I didn't ask. Why?"

"Because it could tell us where she might have gone, sir—and who with."

"She doesn't really socialize with the people at work," Chuck said.

"Things can change," Stone suggested thoughtfully. "Friendships form at work. Even sometimes a workplace romance—"

Chuck glared at him. "What the hell are you trying to say?"

Stone peered back. When a man got that defensive over what was a legitimate question under the circumstances, it usually meant that the prospect was not entirely without merit. At least to him. But now was not the time to jump too far into conclusions, although that was part of his job.

"I'm trying to say that there are any number of reasons why your wife may not have come home last night. In my line of work, you have to keep an open mind . . ."

"I'm open to anything that makes sense," Chuck said,

rubbing his long nose. "But if you're insinuating that my wife was having an affair, you're wrong. We're in love and not having any marital problems."

So you say, Stone thought. But what couple in America is without *any* marital problems?

"Could have been a miscommunication," he told the husband as a possibility. "Maybe you and your wife were not on the same page when she left for work . . ."

Chuck dismissed this with a twist of his head. "There was no miscommunication. Something's happened to Adrienne. I can feel it."

Stone wasn't convinced. By the same token he couldn't rule it out, either. "I can understand your concern, Mr. Murray, but the fact is, your wife hasn't even been missing for twenty-four hours. Technically, that makes her not really missing. Does your wife *always* come straight home from work?"

Chuck regarded the question like it was incomprehensible. "Adrienne likes to jog sometimes after work," he admitted, as if just remembering this. "There's a park across from her office where she runs."

"And that park would be?"

"Belle Park."

Stone wrote this down, familiar with the area. "Do you know if she was planning to jog after work last night?"

Chuck paused. "We never talked about it," he claimed.

"So then she could have gone jogging?"

He shrugged. "Yeah, I suppose. Adrienne keeps some running clothes and shoes in her car to change into at work."

"I see." Stone looked across his desk, thoughts running through his mind.

Chuck picked up on it, eyes widening. "So you think Adrienne went running and someone attacked her?"

"Not really sure what to think at this point," Stone responded candidly. He wondered if the man was being straight with him across the board on his wife's disappearance. Or was there more to the matter that he wasn't sharing? "I'll look into this and see what I can find out. I'll need a recent photograph of your wife, where she works, daily schedule, type of car she drives and license plate number. And also *your* address and phone number."

"No problem." Chuck removed the wallet from his back pocket and pulled out a photograph, sliding it across the desk. "It was taken in June at a company picnic. I have larger pictures of her at home if you want them."

"This will do for now." Stone studied the photo of the two of them. Adrienne Murray was a pretty lady: blonde, blue-eyed, slender, big-chested. She looked to be in her late twenties, early thirties. The type of lady one might never want to let go of, he mused.

And it was that very thought that troubled Stone most at this point of the investigation. He had been around long enough to know that many men could not bear the thought of losing their wife to another man—or a woman. It wasn't uncommon to see men commit murder to hang on to the wife *forever* in their own warped minds.

But it was still too soon to know if this missing woman had fallen prey to foul play. Or if she had simply left her husband, even if just for a night. Stone didn't rule out that Murray could return home to find his wife waiting for him with some kind of explanation as to her whereabouts for the past fourteen hours.

CHAPTER 8

Detective Joe O'Dell stood at the door of Judge Sheldon Crawford's house. He glanced at the unmarked sedan on the street, where a detective sat, assigned to protect the judge's wife, Maxine Crawford, 24/7. The order was expected to stay in effect for as long as her attacker, and her husband's killer, remained at large.

It had been two days since the crime occurred and O'Dell looked forward to finally being able to talk to the only living witness, having been rebuffed in his attempts to interview her during her hospital stay. He understood that Maxine Crawford was still in the grieving process and recovering from her own victimization, but some things could not wait any longer. He had a job to do and he intended to do it, even if he had been ordered to take it easy on the lady.

O'Dell rang the doorbell. He thought of the other night at the hospital when Grant Nunez was almost defending her honor, as if Maxine Crawford were his lover. Even that didn't seem totally absurd, in spite of Nunez's apparent thing with Beverly Mendoza, as reported through the grapevine. Maxine Crawford was obviously a good deal younger than her late husband and was, by most accounts—including his—a good-looking lady. Perhaps Nunez had more than a legal interest in the widow's health and welfare?

The intriguing possibilities ran through O'Dell's mind for a moment or two before the door opened. Maxine Crawford stood barefoot on the other side, wearing a full-length lavender chenille robe and a towel wrapped around her hair. Her face was free of makeup, but showed little sign of the ordeal she'd been put through, save for a slight ruddiness on the right cheek of her light brown face.

Obviously she still had a lot to deal with, the detective mused, feeling a trifle guilty that he had to intrude upon her at this time.

He took out his ID. "Mrs. Crawford, I'm Detective O'Dell, Eagles Landing PD, Homicide. I'm investigating your husband's death." *And your survival in spite of the sexual attack.* He paused for some reason while she kept her brown eyes pinned on him as if they had nowhere else to go. "I tried to talk to you at the hospital last night, but—"

"Come in, Detective . . ." She turned and walked away.

O'Dell switched the book of mug shots he held from one hand to the other and went inside, closing the pine door behind him. The Tudor-style home was as impressive on the inside as out, from what he could see, right down to the European furniture and expensive artwork hanging on the living room walls. Certainly a hell of a lot more than he could even dream of with his salary. Now he knew why judges became judges. It meant life on easy street, if this was any indication.

That was, until the master of the house ended up with his brains blown out.

"Would you like some coffee, Detective?" his host asked.

"That sounds good," he responded, the aroma drifting from the kitchen invigorating.

"Cream? Sugar?"

"Just sugar."

While she disappeared, O'Dell visually inspected the security. Or lack thereof.

According to the initial investigation, there had been no sign of a forced break-in, meaning that the attacker either had a key or was invited in. The latter seemed an unlikely possibility, considering that the Crawfords were having sex when the attack occurred. Unless, of course, the killer had been invited in beforehand. But, O'Dell noted, the Mrs. had told the police that no one was in the house when they retired to their room.

At least not that she was aware of.

O'Dell ventured across the cork flooring over to the security system on the wall off the foyer. Surprisingly it was an older, cheaper model, less reliable than some of the current high-tech systems that seemed made for a house like this. Which was odd, considering everything else he'd seen looked to be as modern and high-priced as they came. There was evidence that the system had been tampered with, causing the alarm to malfunction when it was needed most.

Whoever went after the judge obviously knew what the hell he was doing, O'Dell thought. And did it without a hitch. Except for the fact that an eyewitness was inexplicably left behind.

Was this by mistake? Had the perpetrator somehow been scared off before he could finish the job he started?

"Your coffee, Detective."

O'Dell turned and saw Maxine Crawford standing there. She held a tray with two cups of coffee. He lifted one off the tray.

"Thank you." He saw that she had removed the towel from her head, leaving long, tar-colored individual braids cascading freely across her shoulders.

"We can talk in here," she said, and led him back to the living room. She put the tray on a rectangular glass coffee table and took a seat on a white leather couch.

O'Dell sat on the adjoining loveseat. Sipping the coffee, he eyed the attractive new widow and began respectfully. "I want to say how sorry everyone at the police department is about Judge Crawford's death. He was a good man and a good judge for law and order." At least as far as anyone knew.

"Thank you. I appreciate that," Maxine said with genuine emotion, lifting her cup expertly. "Sheldon only tried to do his best as a husband and criminal court judge. Why someone would do this to him . . . and me . . . ?"

O'Dell wished he could comfort her in some way. But what could he do or say to someone who had seen what she had, and been sexually assaulted as well?

"We want to get the man who did this to Judge Crawford—and *you*," he stressed.

Maxine sipped the coffee. "I'll do whatever I can to help," she said after she had swallowed. "It all happened so fast. I'm just not sure—"

The judge's murder didn't happen fast enough, O'Dell thought, since he had enough time to get out of bed before the gunman finished him off. And from what the detective understood, the perpetrator took his own sweet time in sexually assaulting the wife in more ways than one.

"How about if we go over a description of the perpetrator first?" O'Dell took out his notepad, glancing over the information from her initial statement. "How old would you say the assailant was?"

Maxine swallowed pensively. "Maybe in his early thirties."

"Race . . . ethnicity?"

"He was Hispanic, but not black."

O'Dell looked at her. He was happy that it wasn't a brother who'd committed these violent crimes, otherwise they both would be that much more uncomfortable, all things considered.

"Height and weight, approximately?"

Maxine considered this before responding with, "Short, maybe five-ten, and not overweight but muscular."

O'Dell saw that her depiction of the person pretty much corresponded with what she'd said before, which was a good step in the right direction.

"Why don't I let you look at some pictures?" he said. "These are men who have been sent to prison by your husband and, unfortunately, recently released. Maybe you'll see someone who looks familiar."

He handed her the catalog of mug shots. Some of the pictures were in fact of ex-cons who were never in Crawford's courtroom but had a history of violent crimes, including rape and sodomy.

Maxine gazed at the mug shots nervously, though trying hard to keep her cool. She felt the hard stare of the detective and, for an instant, it was as though she were being violated again. But she knew that he was under a great deal of pressure to capture the man who murdered Sheldon.

Sheldon was in many ways the lucky one, she thought. He had lived a reasonably long and distinguished life, for the most part, and she loved him for it. Even if he didn't always live up to his lofty image by some standards. Who could in the world today with all the pressures and temptations?

Now Sheldon was gone and presumably at peace somewhere.

Whereas, for some unknown reason, Maxine had been spared death, forcing her to live with being brutally violated and humiliated at gunpoint. Facing the possibility of being infected with HIV and any number of sexually transmitted diseases. These were things she had been careful to protect herself against. Now they could become a reality.

People would look at her funny. Judge her by something that happened that was beyond her control.

Her life would never be the same again, she told herself. Her attacker had seen to that.

Maxine wiped at tears that had formed at the corners of her eyes and tried to focus on the photographs. Most looked unfamiliar. Others looked like men she may have seen before.

The face of the man who attacked her was indelible in her mind, though he was somewhat of a blur at the moment. Would she recognize him in mug shot pictures taken when his face may have been younger, thinner, or wider? His hair a different style? When she could not smell him? Feel him? Taste him?

She came to a picture that caused Maxine to freeze. The thin but well-defined facial structure and crooked grin stared back at her, surrounded by short black hair. The eyes, dark and foreboding, ogled her as if to say, *You recognize me, don't you, bitch?*

O'Dell sensed that Maxine had found someone she recognized. "Is that *him?*"

Her voice was barely audible when she said, "Yes, I think so."

O'Dell wondered if this was the break they were looking for. "Take a good look at him," he urged, recognizing the temptation to pick out someone who bore even the slightest resemblance to her attacker. "We need to be sure."

Though all the men in the mug shots were assholes of the lowest order as far as he was concerned, they didn't want to try and make a case against the wrong man. Not if it meant the real bastard would still be free to kill and rape again.

Maxine forced herself to remember the attack and all its horror. She saw his face, as if it were close enough to touch. Just as he made her do.

His eyes. His hair. His nose. His mouth. His ethnicity. His terrifying presence.

The more she thought about it, the more Maxine was certain it was *him* in the mug shot.

It had to be.

"That's the one," she uttered, trembling.

O'Dell lifted the book from her shaky hands. He recognized the dickhead. He had been convicted of murder, and was released within the last month.

"You did a good job," O'Dell said, impressed, all things

considered. For some reason, he hadn't been overly confident she would be able to pick out someone. Perhaps it was too soon. Or she had been too traumatized to clearly see the person who had done this to her. "We'll get him," he told her bluntly.

They would go through this again, O'Dell thought, only with the bastard in a lineup. That way, they could give the DA's office a bona fide suspect who wouldn't be easily dismissed. And a case that they wouldn't be afraid to prosecute.

He had seen it happen too many times. Cases thrown out or rejected because of witness uncertainty or inconsistencies about the suspect. Which then translated into a prosecutor's lack of enthusiasm and reluctance, leading to criminals walking rather than doing hard time.

O'Dell was determined to not let that happen in this case, for the wife's sake and Judge Crawford's memory. The suspect, once in custody, would not be seeing the light of day again any time soon. Not if he could help it.

What judge in his or her right mind would give this asshole bail? None, O'Dell thought, given the gravity of the offenses, including the execution-style slaying of a sitting criminal court judge.

But first they had to get the one responsible for it.

Before he hurt someone else.

CHAPTER 9

"How's your science class coming along?" Beverly asked her son during the drive to school. Or in other words, she thought, was he doing any better in the class that seemed to have given him the most trouble besides math.

"Okay," he drawled unconvincingly, his Eagles Landing baseball cap tilted onto his brow, seemingly obscuring his vision.

Beverly didn't want to baby or embarrass him. But she wanted to make sure his grades did not slip to the point of failure. "If you need my help, just tell me," she said gingerly. "That's what mothers are for." And fathers, too, were they still in the picture and responsible enough to care.

"I don't need your help," Jaime insisted. "I'm figuring it out myself."

Beverly hoped that was the case. "I'm glad to hear that, Jaime, really." She glanced in his direction. He turned to look out the window.

She didn't press the issue for now, realizing that he really was trying hard. The A on his math test demonstrated that.

Beverly recognized that her son had reached an age

where he was becoming more and more independent and, at times, distant. It scared her in some ways that someday he would not need her at all. In other ways it thrilled her that he was becoming a young, responsible man right before her very eyes.

It had been two days since they were at odds over the nature of her relationship with Grant. Since then things had remained lukewarm between them, though she had gone out of her way to assure Jaime that her friendships with men had absolutely nothing to do with *their* relationship.

Even then Beverly knew full well that her relationship with any man had *everything* to do with Jaime. He was the most important person in her life. The child she had given birth to. She would never place their relationship in jeopardy. Her fervent hope was that in the long run he would be pleased that she wanted some stable and trustworthy companionship and he would be supportive.

Until then, she would not rock the boat when it came to balancing her life as a parent and her intimacy with a man.

Beverly's thoughts turned to another touchy issue that was unavoidable between them.

She turned toward her son. "I'd like to go visit your grandfather on Saturday."

"I don't wanna see him," Jaime groaned with a frown.

"You have to," she asserted, turning her eyes to the road and then back to his profile. "He needs us, just like you and I need each other."

"He doesn't need us! Gramps doesn't even know us anymore." Jaime slouched and pouted.

"That's all the more reason why we have to try and keep whatever faint memories he has left alive." Beverly was nearly to the point of tears as she thought about her once robust father—who prided himself on having a razor-sharp memory and fit body—now being reduced to a rambling, incoherent person she hardly recognized. "He's my father, Jaime," she uttered firmly. "And *your* grandfather. No matter how hard it is, we can't ever lose sight of that fact."

Jaime lowered his head. "I still love Grandpa." He dabbed at his eyes that had begun to water.

"And he still loves you," Beverly assured him, "even if he doesn't always remember."

They drove in silence for a few minutes, each collecting their thoughts.

Jaime broke the quiet, seemingly forgetting about the previous conversation. "Can I go to Paco's house after school?" He raised his cap.

"What about your homework?" She pulled up in front of his school.

"I'll do it over there," he answered. "Or when I get home."

"What time will you be home?"

He shrugged. "Probably eleven."

"Make it ten," Beverly said, exercising what control she still had over him. Even ten seemed a bit late for a twelve-year-old to be out on a school night. But she realized that some tolerance in today's active times was almost mandatory.

"No problem," Jaime muttered, opening the door. "See ya."

"See ya." She repeated his words as he slammed the door shut and shuffled toward the building with other students.

Beverly waved good-bye, though he never saw it, and drove off. She turned her attention to her other life as an assistant district attorney. It consumed more of her attention than she sometimes cared for it to. On the other hand, it was what she had worked long and hard for, and she loved her job. With any luck, along with some skill, she could go as far as she wanted.

Beverly thought about Maxine Crawford. She had been released from the hospital yesterday. The police had spoken to her but no word on if there were any viable suspects at this point. How many people wanted the judge dead badly enough to kill him? she wondered.

Could there be others on the hit list, too?

Beverly parked in the garage of Criminal Courts Plaza. She headed to the elevator, briefcase in hand.

She had just stepped inside when she was practically bowled over by the district attorney himself, Dean Sullivan. He was sixty-three, tall, and thin in a designer gray suit. Thinning white hair slicked backward bordered a sagging face with a deep tan. He rubbed his long nose and showed Beverly his puffy china-blue eyes behind silver wire-rimmed glasses.

"Good morning, Beverly," he said in a hoarse voice, which reflected too many years of smoking before he'd miraculously kicked the habit cold turkey a year ago.

"Morning, Dean." Beverly had always been slightly intimidated by him, primarily because he was almost too friendly for her comfort. It was as if beyond his charms and easygoing demeanor there lay a vicious, manipulative man, lulling people unsuspectingly in for the kill. Of course, she was sure this was far more her fertile imagination than fact.

The elevator doors closed and Dean pushed the button.

"How's Jaime?" he asked nonchalantly.

"Growing up too fast, I'm afraid."

"Don't I know it." Dean looked up at the numbers. "My son's about to enter law school. Seems like only yesterday he was still in smelly diapers."

Beverly chuckled. Like many other men in midlife, Dean had divorced his wife and married a younger woman, with whom he had his only child. If only women could be so fortunate with their biological clocks.

Dean touched his glasses, eyeing her. "By the way, I want to congratulate you, Beverly, on a job well done in the Suzanne Landon case."

Beverly blushed. Rarely had compliments come directly from the DA. They usually came courtesy of the Deputy DA's office, where Grant just might be less than objective given their personal relationship. Or they were delivered from the DA's office via a general, indirect memo.

"Well, I had a little help," she said unevenly, in reference to Grant and a supporting staff.

"Maybe," he allowed, "but I like *your* style, Beverly. You know how to go after them the way I used to back in the day."

She was starting to like this. "Just doing my job the best way I know how," she said modestly.

The elevator opened on the sixth floor, where they both had offices. Beverly got off first.

"If you have a minute, Beverly, I'd like to discuss an upcoming case with you," Dean said, walking alongside her.

As if she could refuse him in order to go file some briefs. *I don't think so.*

"All right," Beverly said in a stilted, curious voice.

She followed him down the hall, where each greeted other staffers perfunctorily. When they passed by Grant's closed office, Beverly recalled the last time she'd been in there, causing her body to suddenly burn with desire. Though the relationship had been somewhat discreet, she was sure everyone in the DA's office knew that something was going on between her and Grant. While workplace romances were not necessarily encouraged, the unspoken policy was to date who you wanted, so long as it didn't affect the job and there was not an imbalance of power that could potentially lead to charges of sexual harassment. It seemed to Beverly that she and Grant had the perfect recipe for romance. She wondered if it would be the same should he climb the ladder and become a judge.

They entered Dean's spacious corner office. He closed the door behind them and offered Beverly a seat on an antique English chair. He sat on a matching chair at a forty-five-degree angle.

Beverly noted over his head an oak bookcase filled with law books. Though piqued, she felt more than a little ill at ease for some reason. Probably because she could count on one hand the number of times she had been allowed into his office since becoming part of the DA's team. Obviously things were starting to look up for her. Or so she hoped.

Dean wrung his hands nervously. "I'm sure you're well

aware of the tragic and senseless death of Judge Sheldon Crawford?"

"Yes." Who wasn't? Especially those involved in the local criminal justice system.

"Well, Sheldon was a personal friend of mine," he said as a preface. "Know Maxine as well." His brow furrowed. "I just received word that the police have honed in on a suspect. An arrest will happen any time now . . ."

Beverly was happy to hear this. "Who is it?"

"Name's Rafael Santiago. Judge Crawford sent him to prison for murder twelve years ago. He was released last month. The bastard vowed revenge against Sheldon when he was sentenced and apparently made good on his threat."

Beverly chewed on that. It would have to be proven in a court of law, no matter how guilty the suspect appeared to be. But she gathered that was what this was all about.

"What evidence do they have?"

Dean considered this. "Maxine Crawford picked him out of a photo lineup," he said, as if this cinched the deal.

"Anything else?" Beverly had seen more than her fair share of cases where victims picked the wrong person from mug shots in which practically every arrestee looked the same. She presumed there was corroborating evidence to back up the victim's identification of the suspect.

Dean looked at her as if he resented the question. "Detectives are putting together the necessary evidence, circumstantial and otherwise, to tie Santiago to the crime." He removed his glasses. "I want you to prosecute this one, Beverly."

"I'll be glad to," she said, knowing that the Suzanne Landon verdict had given her a leg up on this one. Though Grant could very well have said the same thing. So how did she get so lucky?

"And there will be *no* plea bargains!" insisted Dean. "We have to send a message to all the Santiagos out there that you don't go around killing judges and raping their wives and expect to get off with a slap on the wrist. This is a death penalty case all the way if there ever was one." He took a breath and peered at her. "Think you can handle it?"

She needed no time to think about it. "Yes," she said emphatically, in spite of the intense media scrutiny this trial was sure to generate.

He flashed her a satisfied half-smile. "That's what I wanted to hear. Feel free to choose anyone on staff as your co-counsel. I'll move people around if I have to."

Beverly could think of only one person she wanted as second chair during the trial. Grant Nunez. They worked well together in and out of court. There had never been a problem with egos between them, though he had been at it longer than she had. Furthermore, it was Grant who was the first one at the hospital to get the jump on investigating Judge Crawford's murder. It could come in handy.

"Thanks," she said appreciatively to her boss.

"First off," he told her, "you'll need to get down to police headquarters this afternoon. After they pick up Santiago, he'll be placed in a lineup for Maxine to positively ID."

"I'll be there," Beverly assured him.

"Good." Dean put his glasses back on and stood, seemingly indicating the meeting was over.

Beverly got to her feet. She wanted to say a few more words but decided they could wait for another time. She headed for the door.

She stopped in her tracks when Dean called out her name. She faced him.

He removed his glasses again theatrically. "I thought you might be interested in knowing that I've recommended to the governor that Grant replace Judge Crawford on the bench."

Beverly was stunned, if only because of the suddenness of the news and the circumstances that had brought it about. She had always known that Grant was headed in that direction and was very happy for him. Did he know he was being considered for the appointment? Had he known when he asked her to meet him at the hospital?

"That's wonderful news!" Beverly said with a smile.

"Yes, it is." Dean smiled too, then frowned. "Just wish it could have been under more favorable conditions. Of course, Grant has yet to be offered the judgeship. Until he is, let's keep this under wraps."

"I understand," she said, while thinking, *Do I?*

Beverly stood before her secretary's desk. Jean Arness was nearly sixty and had been with the DA's office for twenty-five years. Beverly cringed at the thought of being in any one place for that long. But then again, if it was something you loved, why not?

Jean, shaped like a Christmas tree with a gray bouffant, looked up behind avocado-colored glasses. "You've got about ten messages here," she groaned, handing them to Beverly one by one.

"And good morning to you, too." Beverly gave her an amused smile.

Jean scowled. "It's been anything but good this morning."

"I can see that." Beverly glanced at the messages. "At least there's the rest of the day to look forward to."

Jean rolled her hazel eyes. "Yeah, I can hardly wait." She looked at her calendar. "You've got an appointment at eleven with Walter McIntosh."

Beverly recalled setting up the meeting with the investigator for the DA's office. But that was before the recent developments had taken precedence. "I have a lineup to go to. Reschedule it for tomorrow."

"Not a problem, for me anyway. Maybe Mr. McIntosh might beg to differ."

"I doubt that. Usually it's Walter whose busy plate is too much for me to keep up with," Beverly said.

She went into her office. It was a good deal smaller than Dean Sullivan's, but big enough for Beverly to feel as if she belonged. Her wraparound desk was in typical disarray with open file folders, closed ones, a couple of trays filled with papers, and computer CDs piled next to her laptop. Law books lined the shelf on the back wall and a single file cabinet stood in one corner.

She sat in her ergonomic desk chair and glanced out the window. The view was largely of other buildings in downtown Eagles Landing, though if she stretched her neck, Beverly could make out the peak of Mount Tulan surrounded by some puffy clouds.

Her thoughts turned to her father. She hated the helpless feeling of watching him decline right before her very eyes. He barely recognized her now and had no memory at all of Jaime. Her son had trouble dealing with it, choosing mostly not to deal at all.

But she had to. Alberto Elizondo was still her father and Beverly owed it to him to do what she could to make him feel as comfortable as possible, and let him know that he did have family out there who cared about him.

Beverly made a few phone calls to thank those who had lent their support, expertise, or testimony in her last case. Aside from common courtesy, she was also networking, well aware that it never hurt to maintain ties with people you might have to work with again.

Afterward, Beverly focused her attention on Rafael Santiago and Maxine Crawford. The two were about to form the centerpiece of her professional life and preoccupation. She accepted the challenge. She never liked to lose a case, especially one involving such violence and a high-profile victim. But she was careful not to take anything for granted, knowing that surprises seemed to always wait in the wings, ready to potentially burst forth and jeopardize a trial at any time.

The mere notion left Beverly just slightly on edge.

CHAPTER 10

The car—a shiny, new crème Chevy Cobalt—sat unlocked in the parking lot, as if the owner had every intention of coming back to it but had never made it. At least that was what Stone told himself, surveying the vehicle, careful not to touch anything. From all indications, there was no sign that it had been broken into or vandalized.

But the fact that the car had apparently been there all night did not bode well for Adrienne Murray. Had she gone running after work? Stone stared across the lot at Belle Park, a popular park for runners and non-runners alike. He narrowed his eyes to block out the sunlight.

Someone could have been stalking her, Stone mused, waiting in the park for her expected run. Then what? Had she been abducted? Left for dead somewhere?

He had to consider the possibility that Adrienne Murray could already be a victim of foul play. If this was the case, Stone had to first look back at the husband, knowing that in spite of his apparent concern, most adult female murder victims were slain by their romantic partners.

So what type of relationship did the Murrays have? Had Chuck Murray actually done away with his wife?

Stone walked back to his car and got on the radio. "Gordon," he said calmly to the detective roaming the park, "you see anything suspicious in there?"

"Not yet, Stone," he responded. "Just the usual litter, some kids necking, people swimming, hanging out . . ."

"Well, keep at it."

It occurred to Stone that in some rare cases people had been known to disappear completely and voluntarily from one life to start another. Sometimes they were even declared officially dead, only to reveal later that they were alive and well, having staged their own disappearance.

That didn't seem to be the case here, he thought. It didn't figure that a person would walk away from a brand-new car as part of an elaborate plan to disappear into the woodwork.

Where the hell is she? Stone asked himself, growing worried that there was more than a misunderstanding or vanishing act here to account for Adrienne Murray's whereabouts.

He went inside the building that housed the telemarketing firm where Adrienne Murray was last seen, according to the husband. Looking at the business index board, Stone spied a variety of businesses sharing the space, including a realty company, a janitorial service, an investment firm, and ELNC Systems, Inc.—Adrienne Murray's place of employment.

He took the elevator up to the fifth floor and walked down a narrow corridor till coming to the ELNC Systems office. A pretty, young receptionist greeted him inside.

"May I help you?" She brushed away thick blond bangs that obscured her vision.

He flashed his ID. "Detective Stone Palmer of the sheriff's department. I'm following up on the disappearance of one of your employees . . . Adrienne Murray."

She frowned. "I'd heard that Adrienne was missing. I hope nothing bad happened to her." Color filled her pale face. "You might want to talk to our manager . . ."

Stone nodded. "I might at that."

He followed her to the manager's office where an overweight Latina met him. She was in her early thirties and wearing way too much makeup on a sallow face. A blond bob somehow did not seem to go well with the rest of her.

"Hi," she said. "I'm Claudia Sosa."

The receptionist identified him before Stone could, and also revealed the purpose of his visit, then left them alone.

"I last saw Adrienne yesterday just after six," Claudia explained calmly. "She seemed perfectly fine then."

Stone jotted this down. "Do you know if she went jogging in the park after she left?"

"Yes, I think she did, actually. Adrienne runs about three times a week, changing clothes in the bathroom."

"Does she ever go jogging with anyone?" Stone favored her intently.

Claudia rolled her brown eyes. "No one from this office. We're all females working here and, aside from Adrienne, none of us are exactly into working out, if you know what I mean."

"I think I understand," he said uneasily, using her as a prime example. "Has anyone ever come here to visit Adrienne that you know of?"

"Yes. Her husband. He probably stops by more than he should, given that this is a business we're running."

Stone took that down. "No one else?"

"No one that I can recall."

Meaning maybe someone other than the husband could have visited Adrienne, he mused, looking for even the slightest lead.

"Mind showing me where Adrienne works?"

Claudia blinked. "Sure."

Stone was taken to a partitioned cubicle, similar to

maybe two dozen others. Each had a small desk, a computer, and a phone.

There was nothing particularly suspicious about this cubicle, Stone thought. It was orderly and showed no signs of friction. He used a pencil to nudge open a desk drawer at random. Inside was a purse. He took it out.

"Is this Adrienne's?" he asked Claudia.

"Yes." She identified it. "She usually leaves it there when jogging."

Stone took a cursory look inside, not wanting to contaminate potential evidence of a crime. There were the usual things: wallet, keys, makeup case, checkbook . . . Again, no sign that anything was missing.

Just Adrienne Murray.

She had obviously gone to the park, he thought. But she had not come back.

They both looked up as Detective Gordon Chang, a ten-year veteran of the department, came barreling toward them like an out-of-control freight train. He was thirty-four, with short black hair, and a five-eight stocky frame.

"Found something out there," he said in a huff, his java-colored eyes dilated.

"Will you excuse us for a moment?" Stone asked Claudia. Reluctantly, she waddled herself a few feet away.

In a low, conspiratorial tone, Chang said, "Saw what appears to be blood, not far from the lake."

In spite of his first instinct, Stone took a low-key approach to this news. "Maybe it wasn't blood?" he suggested. "At least not human blood. Could have belonged to an animal." He knew for a fact that there were always dogs running loose in that park—and some had been hurt through owner neglect or deliberate actions by others. Even rabbits and deer managed to find their way through the park in search of food.

"I doubt *this* came from an animal," voiced Chang with a sniffle. He removed a plastic bag from his pocket. There was a piece of aqua fabric in it, about three-by-three inches. It appeared to be nylon and its ragged nature suggested it might have been ripped from a garment. Holding it up, he said, "This was found near the blood. Looks to me like part of a—"

"Running suit," Stone finished bleakly. He had one himself with the same texture. Still wasn't proof that Adrienne had run into harm's way. But things were not looking good, he thought, and called Claudia back over to them. "Do you know what color clothing Adrienne wore when she went running?"

Claudia scratched her head. "I'm not really sure. Sorry."

He showed her the material in the bag. "Does this look familiar?"

Claudia's eyes widened. "It might . . ." Her voice dropped. "Do you think it's from Adrienne's clothes?"

Stone tossed her an austere look. "That's what we were hoping *you* could tell us."

She was suddenly shaking. "The color looks right," she gasped. "But Adrienne has a couple of jogging suits she likes to wear. Maybe she was wearing the other one."

Something tells me she wasn't. Stone realized that denial seemed to be the way most people—including cops—coped with a possible tragedy. Till the facts spoke for themselves.

"Thanks for your help," Stone told the manager, though unsure just how helpful she'd been. He declared Adrienne's cubicle an unofficial crime scene, meaning nothing was to be removed or touched pending further investigation.

Outside, Stone directed Chang to get a search team out to comb the park. He also wanted to get the name of every person who worked in that building, especially those who were at work yesterday. Maybe someone saw something. Or knew something.

Or some*one*.

Could even be that Adrienne's disappearance was directly attributable to another employee in her place of employ, Stone considered, even though it was a long shot.

"I think I'll go pay the husband a little visit," he said to Chang. "Maybe Murray will be able to shed more light on a situation that's looking dimmer with each passing moment."

Stone drove to an old Victorian house on Rosewood Avenue in Wilameta County. A black extended-cab pickup truck was parked in the driveway.

Before Stone could get to the porch, the door opened and Chuck Murray came out. His face was contorted. "Is my wife dead?" he asked in a slurred voice.

"We're not certain." Stone wondered if his obvious drinking was in preparation for bad news. Or to mask what he already knew. "Mind if I come in?"

"Yeah, sure," Chuck muttered, as if forgetting his manners.

The interior of the house was stuffy, but well kept. Stone noted the simple contemporary furnishings in the living room. He spied framed pictures of Adrienne and her husband on the mantel.

"Can I get you a drink or something?" asked Chuck, looking flustered and disoriented as he picked up a glass and took a sip.

"No thanks. Can't drink on duty." Stone gazed into his bloodshot eyes. "Besides, looks as if you've already had enough for the both of us."

Chuck made no attempt to deny it. "Can you blame me, man?" His mouth hung open like it was being pulled down. "The woman I love is missing . . . probably dead and buried . . ."

Having never experienced the feeling of having his own wife missing, Stone knew he couldn't exactly relate. And yet he could, to some degree, as a detective who had been there, done that, with unfortunate results. His concern here was that Chuck Murray was acting more like a man who knew his wife was not coming back, rather than one who hoped she would. Why was that?

"I guess I can understand why you might feel the need to

get drunk," Stone pretended, hoping it might keep the man talking.

"It's helping me cope," said Chuck, licking his lips. "You know?"

Not really, but maybe you'll care to enlighten me. Stone casually walked to the mantel and lifted an eleven-by-fourteen photograph of Adrienne Murray. "You take this?"

"Yeah." Chuck was boastful. "I like to take pictures in my spare time. Call it a hobby."

Not a bad hobby, Stone had to admit. Taken fairly recently, Adrienne was all smiles and teeth and seemingly happy. He wondered just how often Chuck had photographed his wife. And under what circumstances. He put the picture back and faced the husband.

"So what did you find out?" Chuck asked nervously.

Stone approached him. "Well, for one, your wife did go jogging after work . . ." he began, "and apparently never came back to pick up her car."

Chuck buried large hands in his face, as if sensing the worst. "I knew I shouldn't have allowed her to run in that damned park! Especially at night with all the winos and gangbangers hanging out there."

Stone peered at him. "Do you know what color running suit your wife brought to work to wear afterward?"

"I think it was blue-green," he said matter-of-factly. "I bought that one for Adrienne myself. Why?"

Stone took out the plastic bag with the torn fabric in it. "Does this look like the material from her jacket?"

Chuck studied the fabric for only an instant before squeezing his eyes shut. "Yes." He groaned. "That looks exactly like a piece of her running suit."

Stone had feared he would say that, and probably with good reason. But at this point, he still wasn't sure if they were dealing with a dead wife or not. And if so, was her death a homicide? Suicide? Accident? *Maybe the husband knows more about the circumstances of her disappearance than he's letting on.*

"Why don't we wait until it's confirmed before we jump to any of the wrong conclusions," Stone voiced sensibly. In his own mind he had unfortunately already reached some probable conclusions, and they weren't very pretty.

Chuck ran a hand through his hair, as if searching for something. "Yeah, you're right," he said. "She has to be okay. I don't even want to think about life without Adrienne . . ."

You just might have to. "I could use your help, Chuck," Stone said gingerly, "trying to find your wife."

"I'll do whatever you need me to," he promised.

"Was Adrienne wearing any jewelry when she went to work yesterday—including a watch . . . rings . . . ?"

Chuck tasted more of his drink. "My wife wasn't much for jewelry. Thought it was too showy. Except for her wedding and engagement rings," he said, almost as an afterthought. "She never took them off. Wore a watch every day too. One of them two-tone Seikos." He walked to the mantel and lifted a photograph. It was a close-up of Adrienne, posing with her hands under her chin. Her rings and watch were clearly visible. He extended his arm toward Stone. "Take it."

Stone took him up on the offer, saying, "I'll bring it back." He regarded Adrienne Murray, honestly hoping she was somehow still alive. But he knew hopes often had little impact in the scheme of things. He focused in on the rings. Both sported a series of diamonds his own wife would kill to have, figuratively speaking. "These rings must have cost you a pretty penny."

"Yeah," Chuck acknowledged. "Cost me damned near all my savings and a loan. But she was worth every penny."

It was the worth of the rings themselves that concerned Stone at the moment. This wouldn't be the first time that valuable diamonds had caused a thief to become a kidnapper. Or worse.

"Does Adrienne have any identifying characteristics, such as birthmarks or tattoos?"

"No tattoos," Chuck replied. "She has a small black mole

on the inside of her left thigh and another slightly bigger one on her back."

Stone made a mental note of this. "Has your wife ever gone away for any extended period of time without telling you, Chuck?"

"Not like this." Chuck wrung his hands nervously.

What exactly did that mean? "How did she go off . . . ?"

"Sometimes Adrienne and her girlfriends would skip work and go to the coast for the day," he said. "Maybe even spend the night. I wouldn't find out until she got back, but she would usually leave a note that I didn't always see till after the fact." His eyes narrowed. "Adrienne has never taken off at night, after work, without a word to me. She wouldn't do that."

Stone found himself believing that much. But it still didn't tell him if Adrienne Murray had met with foul play or if there was something else going on here. He intended to find out one way or the other.

"I'll be in touch," Stone said assuredly.

He was already halfway back to the department when Stone got the word that a woman's body had been found in Eagles Lake.

CHAPTER 11

The pawnshop was empty when Manuel walked in. He liked it better that way. He couldn't conduct his business with too many nosy-ass people hanging around.

First he browsed around all the junk in there, wondering why people even bothered to buy or sell such garbage. Then he casually made his way to the counter.

A roly-poly man of around forty stood on the other side reading a paper—or at least pretending to. What little hair he had left was sloppily pasted to his pate.

"What can I do you for?" the man asked disinterestedly.

Manuel removed the two rings from his pocket, wondering how much they were worth. Tossing them on the dingy counter, he asked tonelessly, "How much for these?"

The man took a look. "Are the rocks real?"

"Of course," he said hopefully. "They belonged to my grandmother."

"Your grandmother, huh?" the man said mockingly. "Why are you parting with them?"

Why do you think, asshole? "I need the money," he said

honestly. "Why keep them in the drawer when she ain't around no more to wear them?"

"Whatever." The man shrugged indifferently. He took out his eyeglass and examined the diamonds on each ring. Afterward he gazed across the counter. "I'll give you three hundred for the two of 'em."

Not bad for something that just happened to fall into his hands, Manuel thought, but he decided to hold out for more. "They're worth at least three times that."

"Not in here, they aren't!" The man hit him with a hard gaze, recognizing he had the advantage. "Three hundred or try your luck elsewhere."

Manuel realized he would get no more out of this old fart. "I'll take it."

The man had him fill out some paperwork he described as standard before handing him the money.

"I'll hold the family jewels for thirty days," the man warned. "If I don't hear from you by then, they're gone forever."

Manuel smiled darkly, pocketing the money. "Yeah, whatever, man."

He left the shop three hundred dollars richer than he'd gone in. It hadn't been his intention to rob the little bitch. He was not a common thief. Not like many he knew. But since she was already dead, she would have little use for the rings. He kept the watch to give to his old lady when he needed to cover his ass.

Manuel made his way up to Broadway and Eleventh Street. There he ran into his friend, Carlos Valenzuela. They used to hang, till he went solo. Carlos was about his height and build, but darker in complexion with a thin mustache and goatee.

The two shook hands and Manuel gave Carlos a brief hug.

"What's up, man?" asked Carlos.

"Nothing much." Manuel shrugged. "Just hangin' out with my old lady."

Carlos laughed. "Right," he scoffed. "Remember, man, you talkin' to Carlos."

Manuel laughed, too. "So maybe I met this white bitch and we had ourselves a little party."

"What kind of party?"

"The kind where she gives me everything I want."

"And what does she get in return?"

Manuel laughed again and grabbed his crotch, getting turned on in the process. "Complete satisfaction."

The two had a good chuckle.

"You seen our white amigo 'round, man?" Carlos asked.

"Naw," Manuel muttered, knowing he was referring to a white drug dealer. "Ain't seen 'im. That dude is crazy." He didn't care to elaborate.

"Yeah." Carlos grinned. "If you run into the crazy bastard, tell him we can do some business."

Manuel gave an aloof nod. "You got anything on you now, man?" he asked, feeling he needed a quick high.

Carlos darted his eyes both ways, then rubbed his nose. "How much you want?"

Manuel took two of the three hundred out of his pocket and stuffed it in Carlos's hand. "Two bills' worth."

Carlos stuffed the money in his shirt pocket, then turned his back to the street and removed a tiny packet of crack. He passed it to him. "Little something extra in there, man, cause we're cool."

"Thanks, man." Manuel put the crack away. "I gotta run."

"Same here," Carlos said. "Don't use all that at once. But if you do, you know where to find me."

That he did, Manuel thought, as they shook hands again and went in opposite directions.

Once home, he got out his pipe and smoked most of the crack, making him high and horny.

He thought about the white bitch and what a good time he had with her. It made him imagine having more good times ahead with other bitches.

CHAPTER 12

Maxine Crawford stood nervously at the window as the lineup of men stared straight ahead as if they could see her. But Detective O'Dell and the attorneys from the DA's office, Grant Nunez and Beverly Mendoza, assured her that they could not see through the glass.

Still, Maxine was uncomfortable observing them, like animals in the zoo. Yet the one who had killed Sheldon and assaulted her was little more than an animal. He deserved whatever fate he had coming to him now that the bastard had shattered her life forever.

Maxine thought back to the mug shots the detective had her look at. She had chosen the man who most closely resembled the one that lived in her deepest nightmares. But how could she be sure? What if she had chosen the wrong man?

What if I choose the wrong one now?

Or what if she chose a different man from the one in the mug shot? Would that work against her in bringing him to justice?

Maxine studied the faces, as if her life depended on recognizing the one who had raped her and killed Sheldon. And, in many ways, she supposed it did.

"Take your time," Beverly said to her, aware how difficult it must be to have to identify the man you believed sexually attacked you and shot your husband to death. There would always be doubts. Wouldn't there? And there was the pressure of people like her who wanted Maxine to make their job easier by making a positive identification of the perpetrator. There could be no room for error.

She truly believed that the system ultimately worked, if given the chance.

At the same time, Beverly knew that cases were often made or broken at this stage of the process. She scrutinized the lineup, which included three Hispanic men and two Caucasian men with dark complexions. All were of reasonably similar height and build, to keep anyone from standing out too much.

Beverly took a sweeping glance at the others in the viewing room, all of whom had a vested interest in the outcome. With the possible exception of Grant, who had accompanied her there, he said, for moral support. Neither of them had spoken of his possible appointment to the bench. In her case she had been sworn to secrecy. She assumed he knew about Dean's recommendation of him, but chose not to tell her till the deal was done.

Either way, Beverly only wished Grant the best, even if his judgeship meant she would lose the best co-counsel she'd ever had. And one she had hoped would be second chair on her present case, should it go to trial.

"Could you ask number two to lift his head up?" Maxine requested. He had lowered his face, as if to hide it from her.

O'Dell yelled into the microphone, "Number two, put your head up and look directly in front of you!"

Number two complied. He was a Hispanic male in his early thirties, short and well built. Raven hair was tightly cropped around an oval, handsome face. Despite this, he wore a perpetual scowl.

Beverly felt like he was staring right at her. It gave her an eerie feeling. But at this stage it wasn't her feelings that counted most. *I'm not the one who was raped and sodomized*, she thought.

"It's him." The words were spoken almost as a whisper.

Or maybe it was a hesitation, Beverly thought.

"Are you *positive* it's number two?" she asked the victim and witness to the crime.

"Yes!" Maxine's voice raised and was more emphatic. "That man's the one who shot Sheldon and—" Her voice broke.

"Good enough," O'Dell said, sparing her any further indignity. "That will be all, Hector," he shouted into the room.

The order was meant for one of the Hispanic men, a detective named Hector Oliverez, who had volunteered to be in the lineup.

"Would you like some water or something?" Beverly asked Maxine, her own throat suddenly feeling parched.

"No," she said, looking as if she were suddenly short of breath. "Just need some fresh air."

Grant grabbed her arm to keep her from falling on the spot. "It'll be all right," he tried to assure her, hoping they were not just empty words. They needed her to remain strong at this time. But could Maxine Crawford hold up under the pressure she was about to face?

"We've got the bastard!" O'Dell declared, turning to Maxine. "He's never going to get the chance to hurt you or anyone else again!"

It was a promise Beverly had heard all too often, only to see it broken time and time again because of victims backing out of their responsibility, or because of credibility issues, mishandling of evidence, police misconduct, judicial improprieties, appeals, and even defense victories. This case was far from a done deal, she thought. But they had definitely taken an all-important first step. They had themselves a bona fide witness-identified suspect in Rafael Santiago.

* * *

"Do you want to grab a bite to eat?" Grant asked as they left the station.

"Where did you have in mind?" Beverly licked the roof of her mouth, for some reason feeling as if she hadn't eaten in weeks.

"My place," he said as casually as if it were a five-star restaurant. "I can't think of a better place to have a couple of broiled steaks, baked potatoes, and a bottle of red wine." He eyed her ravenously. "Can you?"

Beverly felt her knees buckle from his persuasive stare. "No, not really."

She missed spending quality time with him. But it had been nearly impossible of late—with the exception of their victory celebration a few days ago—given their busy schedules.

They got into a dark gray Cadillac. It matched the color of the sky, which suggested a big storm was in the making. Stormy autumn weather was just a fact of life Beverly had gotten used to in her thirty-two years of living in Eagles Landing, contrary to the belief that it never rained in California. But she wasn't complaining. She would take rain and cool temperatures any day over snow and cold.

Grant reached over and planted a wet kiss on Beverly's mouth. "I've been wanting to do that all day," he said breathlessly. And much more, he thought. But that would have to wait till later.

Beverly had to take a moment to recover. "Maybe you should have done it earlier," she gasped, "and saved us both some suffering."

He laughed. "Believe me, I would have if we both hadn't been so preoccupied with things."

Things.

Such as preparing to become a judge, she thought. Was this when he would spring it on her? Or would that be pillow talk?

"That was smart of Dean to hand you this case," Grant

said instead, starting the ignition. "I certainly can't think of anyone better equipped to put that asshole away."

"What about you?" she felt obliged to ask. "Or are you losing your touch, Mr. Nunez?"

"Not exactly." Grant regarded her. "I couldn't have taken the case even if I wanted to," he said.

"Oh . . . ?" She met his eyes expectantly.

"Conflict of interest."

"What conflict of interest?"

Grant's full brows descended over his gaze. "I happened to be the prosecuting attorney who convicted Rafael Santiago in Judge Crawford's courtroom," he said matter-of-factly. "He not only threatened Crawford, but me as well. If I took the case, I'm sure any competent defense attorney would have tried to beat that drum to get the case thrown out, or overturned on appeal. Why take the chance?"

"Then it could have been *you* Santiago went after?" Beverly's mouth was agape, horrified at the thought.

"Could have been," Grant allowed, pulling onto the street. He couldn't help but think about being shot to death while they were making love. Maybe not a bad way to die, but not exactly a good way either. "Who's to say it might not have happened sooner or later, had he not been identified?"

Beverly felt a shiver at the prospect that Grant could have been killed and *she* could have been raped. *I'd rather not even go down that road,* she mused.

"Thank goodness Maxine Crawford was able to pick Santiago out of two lineups," she uttered in complete agreement, feeling even more determined to see to it that the full weight of the law was brought down on the suspect.

Ironically, the very fact that Maxine Crawford had identified her attacker was contingent upon Santiago having allowed her to live, Beverly realized. Why didn't he kill her after sexually assaulting her? Was it that he simply didn't give a damn that she might be able to finger him? Or did he feel so cocky that he somehow believed there was only a snowball's chance in hell that Maxine would ever be able to tie *him* to the crime?

Well, he was dead wrong.

Grant lived in a Colonial house on Eagles Lake with plenty of bay windows and magnificent views of the water and surrounding land. He enjoyed living away from the city center and having his own little piece of paradise.

They barely made it past the ceramic-tiled foyer and inside the great room before their hunger pangs gave way to more urgent physical needs. Standing between an octagonal lamp table and left-arm sectional loveseat, Grant and Beverly began kissing feverishly. Their hands were all over one another.

Beverly had a sharp intake of breath when Grant nibbled on her ear while sliding a hand underneath her dress and between her legs. She cupped his face and brought his mouth back to hers, attacking it again, wanting as much of him as possible.

Grant enjoyed the sweet taste of Beverly's thin lips, his hands grabbing onto the panties that covered her buttocks and bringing their bodies closer together. "You're really turning me on, lady," he murmured, feeling hot all over.

"I think it works both ways, Grant." Beverly watched deliriously as he put his mouth on the linen of her dress, atop a breast and onto a nipple. "In fact, I'm sure of it!"

"In that case, I say we'd better do something about it—and fast!"

"Say no more," she uttered, hoping they could make it to the bedroom before things got too steamy.

They didn't, settling for a Tibetan rug next to the limestone fireplace. Each began ripping at the other's clothing till both were stark naked and admiring one another lustfully.

To Grant, Beverly was the picture of perfection, with all the right curves and bends in all the right places. Her breasts, while not exceedingly large, were high, full, and tantalizing. He noted the almond-colored triangle below her slender waist and longed to taste the delicacies within.

Beverly regarded Grant's hard body as he stood tall like a modern-day gladiator. She turned to his full erection, marveling at its size and magnificent state of readiness to pleasure and be pleasured. A twinge of excitement coursed through her at the notion.

They started kissing with open mouths and Beverly wrapped her arms around Grant's neck. Slowly they sank to the rug, their mouths managing to stay attached. Then Grant abruptly moved away and planted hot kisses down Beverly's stomach and below her belly button. He opened her legs and began to kiss her there.

Beverly winced when his tongue licked her clitoris again and again, causing her to shiver with delight.

"You taste so delicious," said Grant, enjoying making her wet and ready for him.

"Oh . . . Grant . . ." Beverly murmured as she felt herself coming. She did so on his mouth and shook like a leaf as he steadied her with strong hands.

She took a moment to come back to earth before pulling him up and wanting to give back what he gave her.

But Grant resisted, grabbing Beverly's shoulders. "Not this time, baby. I want to climax inside you."

"Please do," she said eagerly, wanting the same with a passion.

Grant slipped on a condom and planted himself squarely between Beverly's outstretched legs. When he entered her body, she was wet and ready, immediately wrapping her thighs around his upper back and riding the wave of desire with him.

They made love to each other as though there were no more tomorrows, each yielding to the demands of their bodies.

Grant yelled out when the moment of impact erupted. Beverly screamed a moment later, hurling her groin at his as a second wave of orgasm electrified her.

When it was over they clung to each other and kissed the waning sensations away. Beverly admired the seemingly tireless ability Grant had to go as long as she could. Even longer. She'd once thought such men only existed in romance novels. He had proven her wrong, for which she thanked her lucky stars.

Following the sex, they had a late lunch, talked shop, and went back to work.

Amidst their sharing of bodies and food, Beverly was surprised that Grant had remained mute on his impending appointment to the bench.

Could it be that the appointment was not going to be made after all? Or had he not considered the most important news in his career worthy of sharing with her?

CHAPTER 13

The nude body was swollen and discolored. It had been discovered by a jet skier who noticed something "funny" stuck in some vines on the south shore of the lake. Turned out to be the decomposing body of a young woman. Before even viewing the corpse, Stone had a bad feeling as to who it likely was. His feeling was confirmed by the time he arrived at the scene.

It was Adrienne Murray. Or what had once been her. This pale, bloated, bruised, and cut-up object was no longer a human being.

He recognized her from the photos provided by her husband, Chuck Murray. For further clarification Stone checked the dead woman's inner left thigh. A dime-sized mole was there, seemingly undisturbed by the trauma her body had taken. Another was found on her back, just where Chuck had indicated.

Stone noted, however, that there were no rings on her fingers and no watch on her wrist. But the white spots where they had been were clearly visible.

"You think she was dumped here?" asked a somber Detective Chang.

Stone shook his head. "I'd say it was more likely she floated south from the park. Probably would have gone all the way down to the other end of the lake had it not been for those damned vines."

"So what are we looking at here—a serial killer?"

"I don't think so." Stone looked around. "My guess is the victim either knew the killer or the killer knew her. This was personal," he decided.

Chang lifted a brow. "You think the husband did it?"

"Probably not—at least not by his own hand." This was another conclusion Stone had just reached. "The man seemed too genuinely affected by her disappearance to be her murderer, per se." On the other hand, Chuck Murray may have loved his wife irrationally and therefore dangerously. Which meant it was too early to remove him as a suspect. "Let's get this place sealed off! And I want that park combed to see if anyone saw or heard anything around the time Adrienne Murray disappeared."

"I'll get right on it," Chang said to the lead detective.

The two had barely broken up when a tall and slender thirtysomething woman with a strawberry-blond perm approached Stone. She was wearing high-heeled shoes and a trench coat that made her look like a secret agent.

"Detective Palmer?"

"Yes . . ." he said while studying her.

"My name is Lydia Wesley," she announced. "I'm a reporter for the *Eagles Landing Dispatch*. I was told I could find you here."

By whom? Stone wondered, irritated. Inquiring reporters were not supposed to be guided to crime scenes by anyone from the department. Yet he knew it happened all the time, mostly through the reporter's own determination.

He supposed she wanted to talk about the body recovered, trying to get a jump on the rest of the newshounds.

"Well, now that you've found me, Ms. Wesley," he informed her, "I'm afraid I have no comment on this investigation."

"Actually, Detective, I wanted to talk to you about another case you worked on." She batted blue eyes at him, almost in desperation. "I'm writing a book about Suzanne Landon. I understand you worked on the case that led to her arrest and conviction for killing her lover, James Wright."

Stone remembered the case well—how could he not?—even if the reporter's facts were somewhat off the mark in regards to his involvement. Or maybe that was deliberate to induce a reaction. As much as he was a sucker for a pretty face, frankly, he had neither the time nor inclination to talk with her.

But he was a gentleman about it. "Listen, Ms. Wesley, I'd love to help you," he said nicely, "but right now I'm in the middle of an investigation. I suggest you contact Beverly Mendoza of the Wilameta County DA's office. She would know a lot more about the specifics of the case than I would."

"But Detective Palmer," she persisted with a sense of desperation, "if I could just—"

"You can't!" he cut her off tersely. "Good-bye, Ms. Wesley."

Stone left her standing there, regretting that he hadn't been more helpful for some reason, but knowing he had to draw the line sometimes. This was one of those times.

Before Adrienne Murray's corpse was taken away, Stone took a closer look under the sheet that now covered her. He wanted to see the victim as she was a final time before the medical examiner worked on her and took away even more of the essence of what she once represented as a woman and wife. She appeared to be at peace. Yet he knew her permanent slumber was anything but peaceful: And would not be until Adrienne Murray could have the spiritual solace of knowing that whoever did this was apprehended and punished appropriately.

Stone honed in on her neck. Judging by its discoloration

he'd say she had been strangled. There were also enough bruises to go around. Someone not only wanted to make sure the victim was good and dead, but also defiled her as if for the hell of it. Or out of hatred of her.

After he made sure that the ball was rolling in the right direction in securing the scene and collecting evidence, Stone headed back over to Chuck Murray's house to deliver the bad news in person.

Adrienne Murray's husband said nothing at first, as if he had not heard the words that confirmed that his wife was dead. When he finally did speak it was a slate of profanities, followed by open weeping. Stone was somewhat moved, while managing some proper perspective. This type of emotion was hardly unexpected, if not overdoing it somewhat, the detective believed. It was the type of performance of either a very good actor or a man who was truly devastated that he had lost forever the one person most important to him.

Stone chose to believe the latter for now, but would reserve his overall judgment till the final facts of the case were in.

"I'll need you to come down to the morgue to identify the body," he stated straightforwardly.

Chuck wiped his eyes. "I can't, not now."

"Are there other family members who can do it?"

He sighed. "It was just the two of us. There's no one else."

Stone stepped around him. Though the ID could technically come from anyone who knew Adrienne Murray, including friends and coworkers, it was always preferable that it came from an intimate acquaintance.

"We need that identification, Chuck," he pressed, "so we can concentrate on investigating your wife's death."

Chuck narrowed his eyes, which were bloodshot from crying. "If I find the son of a bitch who did this to her, I'll kill him!"

Stone did not doubt that he could, given the man's fitness, probably with his bare hands. The same way his wife was killed, perhaps? Interesting parallel, he mused.

"Don't do anything stupid," Stone warned. "Let's leave dealing with the perpetrator to the authorities."

Chuck rubbed his nose and stewed in silence.

"We're going to need all the help we can get from you, Chuck." Stone gazed at him.

"I'll tell you whatever I know," he snorted out of the side of his mouth.

Yes, you will at that, Stone promised himself. *But what exactly do you know?*

"Good. I can drive you to the morgue if you like."

Chuck sucked in breath. "I'll drive myself, if that's all right. I need to deal with my grief *alone . . .*"

"I understand." Stone left it at that. There would be time for questions and answers later.

At home that evening, Stone sat at the formal dining room table with his wife, Joyce, and two of the kids, Carla and Paco. They were eating his favorite meal—spaghetti and meatballs with garlic bread.

Stone stared absentmindedly at his wife. A Native American, she was still as beautiful as she was when he first fell for her in high school, with a defined facial bone structure and ebony hair that went down to the middle of her back. He had been a senior and the star wide receiver for the school football team; she was a junior and the reigning student council president. Joyce had gained maybe fifteen pounds at most since then, he noted. The majority of the weight had come and stayed after having their first child, Anna. He never asked her to try and get back to where she once was, accepting that some things came with the territory. He loved her all the same.

"What is it, Stone?" Joyce asked, her big black eyes favoring him perceptively.

Stone met her gaze thoughtfully. He didn't particularly like discussing his work in front of the kids. But at the same time, he didn't want to hide from them the very real dangers in the world they lived in. Including those right there in Eagles Landing.

"A woman's body was found today by the lake," he said sadly. "Appears to have been strangled." Stone chose to spare his family the further horrors the victim had clearly been put through. "Her husband reported her missing when she didn't come home from work two days ago."

"How awful." Joyce furrowed her brow, the fork of spaghetti frozen in her hand.

"Eww," voiced Carla, flipping back her flaxen hair in the way fourteen-year-old girls liked to do.

"Yeah, eww," twelve-year-old Paco mimicked her, also flipping back his shaggy brown hair.

Stone tried to imagine losing Joyce or his kids to violence. The thought made him wonder if the city was becoming too violent for them to live in. But where would they be any safer? Perhaps Alaska, where Joyce had spent her younger years before the family relocated to Northern California?

They lived in a violent world, Stone thought. There was no getting around that. No matter where they went.

"Do you know who did it?" Joyce asked.

"No—not yet." Stone squeezed a meatball off the fork and into his mouth.

Joyce wanted more. He could read the hunger for details in her eyes. "Where did it happen?"

"Belle Park," he replied.

Joyce reacted with alarm. "We've taken the kids there!" she said, as if never having considered that such a place could be dangerous. Or that their children could have just as easily been murder victims.

"I know," Stone said, painfully aware that there were no guarantees that their kids would always stay out of harm's way—no matter his desire to protect them and Joyce at all costs.

"May I be excused?" Carla said to no one in particular.

"You've hardly eaten any of your food, honey." Joyce set her own fork down, as if for effect.

Carla sneered. "I've eaten *too* much! I have to keep my weight down to make the cheerleading squad next semester."

"You will be too weak to do any cheerleading if you don't eat more," argued Joyce.

Stone favored his slender daughter and wondered if she was becoming anorexic. He saw no such problem with his son, who was bigger than most boys his age.

"They're never gonna pick *you* to be a cheerleader!" Paco said cruelly, enjoying needling his older sister every chance he got. "Cheerleaders have to be nice to look at, even if they are super *skinny!*"

"Mom! Dad!" Carla's mouth hung open with disgust. "Will you tell that twit to keep his silly opinions to himself?"

"Apologize to your sister, Paco!" Stone ordered, if only to try to keep the peace for one meal.

Paco wrinkled his nose. "Why should I? It's true! And she knows it—"

"It is not!" Carla sprang from the table and ran toward the stairs. "And I do not!" she gave a parting shot.

"Carla—" Joyce called out angrily.

"Let her go," Stone said on a breath. He turned on his youngest son. His first thought was to verbally assault him just as he had his sister. But he knew full well that Paco really loved Carla and was merely having fun at her expense. It was up to her to get past it, like her older siblings did when they used to go at each other. "Eat the rest of your food," he told him simply. "Then it's off to bed."

Stone put one more load of spaghetti in his mouth and got to his feet, suddenly having lost his appetite, albeit for very different reasons. Joyce gave him a scathing look as if he were suddenly the bad guy.

"I'll talk to her," he promised, wondering how they had made it through the first two kids in one piece. And someday they would have to deal with a house full of grandkids.

At least their children were all still healthy and alive, Stone told himself. That was more than could be said about Adrienne Murray.

Someone had seen to that.

CHAPTER 14

The Suncrest Nursing Home was located in an upscale retirement community in Wilameta County, just seven miles from Eagles Landing. Beverly had chosen this facility after a long search for a place that could properly care for her father, without breaking the bank or being too far away to visit. It was a hard decision to put him away, but a practical one. She was ill equipped to take care of her nearly teenaged son *and* a father with Alzheimer's disease, while working full time as a prosecuting attorney.

Beverly's father, Alberto Elizondo, was in the courtyard when she and Jaime arrived. A nurse was in attendance but seemed content to allow the patients to wander around in the huge yard surrounded by geraniums and daisies, as if trying to find themselves.

"What should I say to him?" asked Jaime, uncertainty creasing his brow.

"Just talk to him as your grandfather," Beverly responded. "Even if he seems lost, he'll appreciate it."

Or so she hoped. *Family will always be family—except when they choose not to be.*

They walked up to him. Alberto was staring into space, as if waiting to be picked up by aliens. Beverly noted that where once her father had been a large man and strong as a bull, he was now quite frail and seemed to be getting thinner by the visit. At seventy-four, he still had much of his hair. It was a fine layer of wintry white, combed to the side and backward.

"Hello, Papa," she said to him, mindful that on her last visit he had responded as if he remembered she was his progeny.

Alberto stared at her with blank eyes, green-gray in color.

"It's me, Beverly." She felt like she was talking to a stranger rather than her own father.

"Beverly . . ." He narrowed his gaze at her, straining for recognition. "Have we met?"

"She's your daughter," Jaime blared out. "And I'm your grandson, Jaime. Don't you remember us, Grandpa, even a little?"

Beverly could hear the irritation yet sincere hope in his voice.

Alberto painted a smile on his weathered face. "Sure I do. You're my grandson, Jaime." He looked at Beverly thoughtfully. "And you're . . ."

"Beverly, Papa," she repeated gingerly, as if talking to a child. She tried to help him along with hand gestures, like using sign language.

"Maria?" He scratched his head vigorously. "You look like my Maria."

Maria was Beverly's mother. She had always been told she favored her. Except by her father, who had always felt her features were more reflecting of his side of the family. Beverly preferred to think she inherited the best of both parents.

It was all she could do to hold back the tears. *I have to stay strong,* she knew. Especially in front of Jaime. It was hard enough on him trying to come to grips with losing his grandfather in all but body. If she lost it, where might that leave her son?

"I'm not Maria, Papa," Beverly said gently to him. "Maria was my dear mother—and your wife . . ."

"My wife?" Alberto looked confused. "Maria . . ."

"Mama's dead now, Papa." It pained her to have to say this, still shaken by the reality herself. "She's been dead for five years now."

"Dead . . . for . . . five . . . years." Some form of understanding seemed to register. "No, not Maria," Alberto croaked. "She would never leave me. She promised me she'd never leave me—" He began bawling like a baby.

Beverly hugged her father, wanting to comfort him, just as she needed to be comforted.

"Mama didn't leave you, Papa," she promised him. "She's never left any of us. She's in heaven now, but will always be with us in spirit."

"She will?" Alberto pulled back and with watery eyes held her gaze.

"I promise, Papa."

"Yeah, Gramps, Mom's right," seconded Jaime.

Alberto smiled momentarily, as if he had forgotten the entire heart-wrenching conversation, before turning his mouth downward into a pout. He eyed Jaime, and asked, befuddled, "Why are you here? I don't know you!"

"Yes, you do!" shouted Jaime, fresh tears staining his own cheeks. "I'm your *grandson, Jaime!*"

With that he ran off, ignoring Beverly's cries for him to come back.

The nurse, alerted to the activity, came over. She was heavyset and in her early thirties. "I think it's time for Mr. Elizondo to take his medicine . . . then a nap," she told Beverly curtly. "You can come visit again."

Beverly might have objected—after all, this was *their* time with her father, no matter how much of him they had lost forever—had she not known she had to go find her son. She had to try and make him understand and learn to deal with it.

"I have to go now, Papa," she told him, forcing herself to give a cheery smile, even as tears came down. "I promise we'll come back again soon."

He gave no response, seemingly more confused than ever as the nurse led him back inside.

Beverly found Jaime sitting on the hood of the car. "You shouldn't have left like that, Jaime," she said tartly. "Can't you see that only makes matters worse?"

"No it doesn't," he muttered. "It can't get any worse! He was only pretending. He doesn't know me at all and probably not you either! I just want Gramps back, like before!"

Beverly wrapped her arms around her son, holding on to him for dear life. They were both crying.

"He's never going to be the same Grandpa you remember, Jaime," she said, anguished but honest. "I wish I could say differently. He's an old man with a memory disease that's incurable and only going to get worse. All we can do at this point is pray that Papa can somehow live out his days in relative comfort and peace."

Jaime seemed to accept this for the moment, even as Beverly tried to come to terms with what in her own mind seemed like a tall order.

That afternoon, while Jaime went skateboarding, Beverly took the opportunity to do some neglected yard work. She had once had an impressive flower garden, but had been unable to keep up with it in recent years. Now she promised herself to give it another try next spring. Maybe grow some perennials and plant some bulbs.

Beverly spent an hour doing aerobics in the den and another half hour on a stationary bike, deciding she could use a bit more firming here and there. Everyone told her she was in great shape, which she strived to be. Grant seemed especially pleased with her body. But, like most women, she always felt there was the constant need for improvement. Maintaining a steady workout regimen as a full-time mom and attorney was a challenge to say the least. Yet it was one Beverly was determined to keep up with for peace of mind and fitness.

Now if I can only get Jaime to become more physically fit and take consistent exercise seriously, she thought.

Later Beverly listened to messages retrieved from her voice mail at work. Most had to do with various aspects of her caseload, requests for interviews, and even an offer to join a prestigious law firm. She had entertained such offers in the past, but never seriously. She loved working for the DA's office, even if sometimes it could be a real pain in the ass. Mostly the work managed to tap into her skills effectively and challenge her mind in ways she could never have imagined.

One message in particular that caught Beverly's ear came from a Detective Stone Palmer of the Wilameta County Sheriff's Department.

"Ms. Mendoza, I just talked to a woman writing a true crime book on the Suzanne Landon case. Her name is Lydia Wesley. I'm sure you know the crime originated in Monroe County but ended up being prosecuted in Wilameta County. How Ms. Wesley got my name, I'll never know, since my role as a secondary investigator was only minimal in the scheme of things. Anyway, to make a long story short, I referred her to you since you prosecuted the case. So don't be surprised if she comes your way. Bye now."

Thank you very much, Detective, Beverly thought snidely. She had little time right now for someone seeking to exploit a murder for personal gain. Much like Suzanne Landon had herself. With any luck, this Lydia Wesley would forget that Detective Palmer had ever given her name as a source of information.

The last message came from Grant, who said, "Just wanted to say that I miss you and loved being with you the other day, in every way . . ." He paused, as if weighing whether to say anything else. "If I play my cards right, I should have some dynamite news to share with you on

Monday, baby. I'd better leave it at that for now, so as not to jinx myself."

Beverly smiled. *Wonder what news that might be?* She kept her fingers crossed that he got the judgeship even as she, too, thought about the last time they were together. It made her hot just replaying the intimate nature of the occasion.

As for her, she would have to settle for promotions within the DA's office for the moment. These she saw perfectly within reach, so long as she continued heading in the right direction.

Starting with the successful prosecution of Rafael Santiago.

CHAPTER 15

Manuel watched his old lady stuff her face with chili and corn bread, downing it with cheap wine. He was doing the same thing, truthfully, but he didn't enjoy it half as much.

"I need some money," he told her without prelude.

She lifted her face, chili dripping wickedly from her mouth. "There isn't any," she said, as if this pleased her. "Not till I get paid next Thursday."

She expected him to believe that? Did she think he didn't know that she hid money from him?

Bitch.

"Just give me twenty for now," he said nicely, "and I can wait for the rest."

She rolled her eyes cynically. "What *didn't* you understand, Manuel? We don't have any money. You've already spent everything the rent hasn't gobbled up. Maybe if you got a job, we'd have more money—"

Before even he knew the rage that had built within him like fire in a furnace, Manuel had backhanded her across the face. She grabbed hold of her reddened cheek like it was about to fall off. For just an instant he regretted hitting her. But he would not apologize. Hell no.

She was disrespecting him. The stupid bitch. Latino men did not take well to Latino women challenging their authority. Why the hell did he put up with her fat ass when all she did was give him a hard time other than with sex?

"See what you made me do!" He blamed her. Women were always to blame for making men do things to hurt them. They usually got what they were asking for. Even the whores.

"You bastard!" she spat defiantly.

He nearly slugged her with his fist, but thought better of it. *Control your temper, Manuel. Don't do something crazy. Not to her anyway. Not when you still need the fat bitch.*

They would kiss and make up later and he would still get his damned money. As always. Right now, he had to get out of there and clear his head.

Manuel backed his chair from the table and stood, glaring down at her blubbery frame. "Have it your way."

"Where are you going?" she asked, eyeing him suspiciously.

"I need to go out for some fresh air," he lied, knowing there sure as hell wasn't much of that in this neighborhood. "Don't wait up for me."

He knew she would. It wasn't as if anyone was waiting in the wings for her. Not that he would mind much if there were. If someone actually wanted to put up with all the crap he took from this bitch, the man could have her.

Manuel left by the side door. But not before rummaging through her purse and taking what she had.

He went down to the tavern on the corner. The neighborhood was largely Hispanic and African-American, though some Asians had recently begun to take up residence as if to escape their own hell. There were also the white whores who worked the streets and gave whatever they earned to pimps, giving the area a multicultural look. But to him, it would always be first and foremost working-class Mexican turf.

At the bar he had beer while sitting on a stool. A flat-screen TV sat on a wall like a picture. Manuel considered this his home away from home. His office, where he sometimes conducted business. He was tight with the owner, another Latino who also grew up in the hood.

Manuel put the mug to his lips and watched the ladies go by. They all knew him by name and swooned over him, wanting the chance to get into his pants—and let him get into theirs. Sometimes he was accommodating, other times disinterested. He liked it better when he took what he wanted. It gave him a sense of power no consensual sex ever could.

He looked up at the TV. The Asian broad on the news was talking about the murder of the judge again and about his wife being raped and beaten.

Now they showed the face of the man being charged. They said his name was Rafael Santiago.

Manuel gazed steadily at the man who looked enough like him to be his twin brother. Same good looks, olive skin tone, and short black hair.

Problem was he didn't have a twin brother. Or maybe he did and just didn't know it? Could be that they were separated at birth, he grinned, scoffing at the notion.

He watched with interest.

Just how sure were they that they had the right man in custody? Manuel wondered with amusement, drinking more beer.

If anyone else noticed the resemblance they weren't saying it to his face. *I just might pay Santiago a visit before they inject his ass with a lethal dose of drugs. People will think they're seeing double. That would sure as hell shake up the foundation at the place where they're keeping him.*

The Asian lady now talked about a dead woman identified as Adrienne Murray, whose body was fished out of Eagles Lake like a dead salmon. She was believed to have been murdered. Videotape was shown of the grieving husband, who promised to do everything in his power to bring the killer to justice.

Promises, promises. Manuel frowned at this. Why did everyone want to be a damned hero? Even those who had something to hide?

And just as much to lose . . .

Manuel followed the one named Penelope from the bar. She was a petite Latina, with big breasts and blond-streaked brown hair. She had on a black leather mini-dress that practically showed half of her big ass, and black stilettos.

Her apartment was two blocks away. He knocked on the door, feeling the rush of excitement just like all the other times. When the door opened he gave her his best smile.

"Manuel!" She regarded him with surprise. "What are you doing here?"

"To be honest, I followed you from the bar." He looked her over lasciviously. "I've been wanting us to get together." He hadn't really, but she had been coming on to him for months.

Penelope beamed. "Really?"

Manuel flashed his teeth convincingly. "I'm here, ain't I?"

She parted her razor-thin bangs. "Come on in . . ."

He did, locking the door behind him.

They didn't waste any time with the formalities. Both knew why he was there. At least part of the reason. The other part he was keeping to himself for now.

She took him to her bedroom. There they stripped and he was on top of her in a flash, spreading her legs wide. He played with her breasts and pinched her nipples, watching Penelope react gleefully as they turned rock-hard. He made sure she enjoyed her final moments as she ground her hips against him and whimpered at his powerful thrusts.

"Ohh, ahh, you feel so good, Manuel," she cooed.

"Yeah, so do you, baby," he returned, feeling her vagina clamping around his penis like a vise while she climaxed.

As his own orgasm released deep inside her, Manuel placed his hands around the whore's neck and began squeezing the life out of her. Penelope's eyes were agape with terror as she tried to break free of his hold, but proved no match for his strength and determination.

Manuel took out his switchblade and gave it a workout, finishing the job and putting Penelope out of her misery.

He left her limp, naked, bloodied body for someone else to find and weep over.

It was time to go back home and make peace again with his old lady.

CHAPTER 16

K. Conrad Ortega showed his ID, allowing him to enter the area at the police station where attorneys met with their clients. It was a routine he had become quite accustomed to since embarking on a career as a public defender. At thirty-eight, an even six feet, and on the husky side with closely cropped dappled-gray hair, Ortega knew he wasn't exactly Johnnie Cochran, when the man kicked ass in the courtroom back in the day. But that didn't mean he worked any less hard for the people he defended. Even someone accused of killing a popular judge in this town and sexually violating his wife still deserved the presumption of innocence and thus a fair trial.

If it went that far.

In his mind, Ortega went through the facts as he knew them pertaining to the accused. Rafael Santiago was a thirty-two-year-old Cuban. He had lived in the U.S. since 1980, coming over in the Muriel boat lift. After serving time for a petty crime, he had raised his criminality a notch by strangling his pregnant girlfriend.

It was Judge Crawford who had sentenced Santiago to

life in prison and against whom he swore vengeance, if he ever got out—which Santiago did after serving just over twelve years with time off for good behavior.

Now you're really in hot water, and I may or may not be able to pull you out, thought Ortega, setting his briefcase on the table. This was the type of case all lawyers lived for. Especially those trying to make a name for themselves and move into the salary range of the elite defense lawyers of the world, where not enough Latino attorneys had made their mark.

But Ortega wasn't ready to think about having a multimillion-dollar house built from the ground up just yet. First he had to win this case, if at all possible. Then let the chips fall where they may.

The door opened and he watched the shackled prisoner being led in by a burly officer. Rafael Santiago was dressed in orange jail overalls and looked smug, as if he didn't give a damn what happened from this point on. Or perhaps he failed to recognize the serious implications of his situation.

Ortega had the officer remove the shackles and cuffs, which he did reluctantly.

"You can leave us," he then instructed the officer. He could see that the man, white as cream, was just as uncomfortable with him as he was with Santiago.

"I'll be right outside if you need me."

I don't think I will. "Thanks." Ortega turned his Vandyke-brown eyes to his would-be client, who gave him the up and down, as if he could do better. He doubted it. Not for what they paid public defenders. "I'm K. Conrad Ortega. I've been assigned to represent you."

Santiago sneered, running a hand through his short, shiny black hair. "I'm supposed to be impressed, or what?"

"Not here to impress you, man," Ortega said, somewhat irritated but determined to keep his cool for the both of them. "Just to offer you my assistance. Now have a seat and let's talk about the case against you."

When the accused seemed hesitant to sit, as if the chair

was booby-trapped, Ortega sat first. Finally Santiago joined him.

"You're facing some very serious charges, Rafael," Ortega said up front. "If the state has its way, they may seek the death penalty if you're convicted."

Santiago seemed unperturbed by this. "That's up to them, man. Can't change what's gone down. Or what's gonna happen."

"Are you saying you're *guilty* of the charges?" Not that this would come across as a great surprise to Ortega. After all, at least half the people he represented were guilty as sin. With many not able to do much to help their own cause. Which, in effect, boiled down to the same thing.

Nevertheless, the majority of those he came across swore on their mother's grave that they were innocent, even when they weren't. But then lying was usually the least of their problems.

"What difference does it make what I say?" Santiago spat out with a flicker of contempt in his dark eyes.

"Could make a big difference," Ortega responded. "If you are innocent and I believe you, I'll go to bat for you as if you were my own brother."

"And if I'm not, what you gonna do then, *brother*—send me to the white wolves and black bears?"

Ortega smiled humorlessly. "I'm obligated to defend you either way," he admitted. "All I'm looking for is the truth . . ."

But with the truth came a price, he thought. Any lawyer would tell you that the *wrong* truth would make it difficult to generate the necessary enthusiasm to mount a credible defense.

Yet anything was possible.

Santiago shifted uncomfortably. "They've got the wrong man," he said flatly. "They're trying to railroad me, man, for something I didn't do."

Ortega looked him in the eye, usually a surefire indication of whether or not a person was being straight with him. "You're telling me you didn't shoot the judge three times at point-blank range? And then rape and sodomize his wife?"

"I just got outta the pen, man," Santiago answered, flipping his hands caustically up in air. "You think I wanna go back right away for offing a judge and raping his woman? I ain't crazy!"

Ortega was not immediately convinced. Far from it. "You were picked out of *two* lineups by Maxine Crawford, the judge's widow," he told the suspect. "One was a photo lineup, you know about the other. What do you make of that?"

"What the hell can I make of it?" Santiago hunched his shoulders brazenly. "People believe that all Latinos look and smell alike. C'mon, man, you know what I'm talkin' 'bout. I guess the judge's wife saw only what she wanted to see . . ."

Ortega mulled over his words. He did know from personal experience that some had trouble distinguishing one Hispanic from another. This was especially true when it came to Latinos in trouble with the law. But the reality was that they came in all different sizes, shapes, and shades, just like everyone else. If Maxine Crawford identified Santiago as her attacker and her husband's killer, it couldn't easily be dismissed as a simple case of mistaken identity.

Then there was any DNA evidence the police might have in their possession, the attorney thought. It rarely pointed the finger in the wrong direction.

Ortega cast a narrow eye at the suspect in this case. He wasn't buying Santiago's weak explanation for why he was in the hot seat.

But what if Maxine Crawford had bought it? What if the witness saw what the cops wanted her to see, and not the real person who attacked her and Judge Crawford.

Was it possible that there really could have been a case of mistaken identity here? Ortega asked himself. Or was it just a clever con by a man with nothing to lose? Except quite possibly his life.

Ortega thought about the evidence he was aware of so far against Rafael Santiago. It was flimsy at best, aside from the eyewitness to the crime who also happened to be the second victim. Being traumatized as Maxine Crawford had been could have affected her ability to get her facts straight.

He gave his client a steady look. "You swore vengeance against Judge Crawford for sending you up the river." He left it there to gauge Santiago's reaction.

"Man, I swore vengeance against *everyone* back then," Santiago claimed. "I was mad as hell about being sent to prison for killing that bitch!"

"You're saying you were *innocent* of that, too?" Ortega batted his eyes skeptically.

Santiago snarled. "I killed her, man, all right! But she deserved it. She was two-timing me with my cousin. Went and got herself pregnant and expected me to take care of her and the bastard. Can you believe that?" He furrowed his mouth thoughtfully. "I'd have killed my homey too, but he got away before I could put a bullet between his eyes!"

Santiago pretended he was doing just that—aiming his hands at Ortega's face. The attorney was not impressed, glaring. "So what about your threats against Crawford?"

"Just empty words, man," Santiago said tonelessly. "I said what I felt at the time, but it don't mean I spent the last twelve years of my life just waiting to get out to do in the judge and bang his woman."

Perhaps not, considered Ortega. Or, he may have done just that, putting the suspect in the unenviable position he was in at the moment. It would ultimately be up to the courts to decide.

And his skills as an attorney.

"I'll do what I can to help you, Rafael," he said honestly. "All I ask is that you be straight with me all the way. Deal?"

For the first time Santiago grinned. "Deal."

Ortega reached across the table and shook the prisoner's hand. It was cold as ice, much like his eyes. Was that an indication that this one was slated to be a frigid case all the way?

"Can you get me outta here, man?" Santiago favored him an unblinking serious look, as if he believed it was truly possible.

Ortega was all business when he stood and said, "The arraignment is Monday. It's highly unlikely there will be any bail for you."

"Why not?" Santiago's jaw dropped. "What about innocent till *proven* guilty?"

He was serious, thought Ortega with incredulity. "You've already been down this road, man," he advised. "I'm afraid all ex-cons are presumed guilty until proven innocent."

Santiago seemed to have trouble digesting his situation. Ortega found this bizarre, considering he highly doubted the man would be able to raise the money anyhow for what could only be a bail well out of his reach.

"The most we can hope for is that adequate security will be in place at the courthouse," Ortega told his client candidly. "After all, we are talking about the murder of a popular judge. And many people can be unforgiving."

He wondered if Rafael Santiago was one of those people.

CHAPTER 17

Stone read the autopsy report. The victim, Adrienne Murray, had been strangled, her windpipe crushed. She had also been beaten, stabbed repeatedly, raped, and sodomized. There was semen inside her, along with strands of hair, presumably from her attacker's pubic area. She had also been worked over pretty good. This usually indicated more than an attack by a stranger. It was almost always personal when the victim was beaten up. Almost as if to punish her for the rage of the one who wanted her dead.

"Here's a list of all the people who work in the building," Chang provided, sliding it across Stone's desk. "Can't say there's anything unusual here. Not even a criminal record among them."

"Some criminals don't have records," Stone muttered, admitting to himself that it didn't look to be an inside job. But looks could be deceiving. "Dig deeper," he ordered, just to be on the safe side in leaving no stones unturned. "Check out everyone and anyone who may have been associated or involved with employees there—boyfriends, girlfriends, husbands, wives, sons, whatever . . . Maybe we'll get lucky."

Unlike Adrienne Murray, he told himself.

Chang frowned. "Sounds like a lot of work."

"That's what we're paid for, man," Stone reminded him. Few cases were as cut and dried as they were often portrayed on TV cop shows. Usually they were just the opposite.

Chang rubbed his nose. "Whoever killed Adrienne Murray is probably someone she ran into in the park," he suggested. "That's where we should be concentrating our efforts."

Stone was not about to be told how to conduct an investigation. Especially when, as the lead detective on the case, it was primarily his neck on the line if he failed to arrest someone for Adrienne Murray's murder. Or worse, if they set their sights on the wrong perpetrator. But he also wanted to keep the peace with his partner.

"Why don't we try this my way first, Chang," he said, holding his gaze. "My gut tells me that what we're looking for is right before our eyes. We just have to find the connection and go from there."

Chang gave a pacifying nod before heading out the door. Stone stopped him with final instructions. "Oh, one other thing . . . Have someone check out the pawnshops in town. Adrienne was wearing expensive wedding and engagement rings, along with a Seiko watch. All were missing when her body was found. We have a photograph of her wearing these. Shouldn't be too hard to make a match if we find them. Maybe her killer decided to try and sell the jewelry."

It was a long shot, Stone thought. The rings and watch could have somehow found their way to the bottom of the lake. Or Adrienne could have taken them off when she went jogging, in spite of Chuck's insistence otherwise. The fact was, they weren't found among the victim's possessions at work or in her car.

* * *

That afternoon Stone was visited by an attractive young woman named Erica Flanagan, who claimed to be Adrienne Murray's best friend.

"How can I help you?" Stone feigned disinterest, but he felt just the opposite.

"I'm here to see what you're doing about bringing Adrienne's killer to justice."

Stone surveyed the tall, thin woman. She had shoulder-length black hair, pale skin, blue eyes, and a petulant pout. A hand was rested precariously on her small hip. Her leather outfit was something he could imagine his daughter Carla wearing, to his discontentment.

"The investigation is ongoing," he told her politely. "If there's something you know about Ms. Murray's death, I'd be happy to hear it."

Erica looked as if she were ready to explode. "I know her husband had something to do with Adrienne's death," she said without preamble.

Stone reacted to the passion in which she spat this out. "What makes you think Murray had anything to do with his wife's murder?" he asked bluntly.

Erica's eyes rolled. "Because Chuck was *insanely* jealous over her. He thought Adrienne was sleeping around with every man she knew. And even those she didn't know. He wanted to know everything Adrienne did, who she did it with, where she went for lunch at work, what she had to eat—everything! He even followed her around sometimes to make sure Adrienne did exactly what she told him she was doing."

"That definitely sounds obsessive," acknowledged Stone. "Maybe even sick. But that doesn't prove Chuck Murray wanted his wife dead. Or that he murdered her." *It has gotten my attention, though, and speaks of possible motive,* he mused.

"What other proof do you need?" Erica's lower lip

dropped. "The man is *crazy*. He threatened Adrienne all the time . . . told her that if she ever even thought about leaving him, he would kill her."

Stone propped his elbows on the desk. "Did she take these threats seriously?"

"Adrienne was scared to death of him," Erica insisted.

"Did she ever consider leaving him?"

"A thousand times. But each time she would back off for fear of what he might do."

Stone chewed on his lip. Very interesting, he thought. And disturbing, if true. He imagined Murray having a psychological and physical hold over his wife, fearing the possibility of losing her and deciding he couldn't allow that to happen.

"Was Murray physically abusing Adrienne?" he asked, recalling the multiple bruises found on her body. The assumption had been that most were very recent and likely caused by her assailant. But what if some had come before the attack?

"She tried to deny it," Erica said, "but many times she would show up at my house with black eyes and purple blotches on her arms and legs. She always said that she had bumped into a wall or tripped over her own two feet."

"But you didn't believe it?"

"Would you?" she sneered.

Not in a million years, Stone thought, having witnessed firsthand his own father abusing his mother. In those days it was considered strictly a family issue. Hence, no one else knew about it, and those who did weren't talking. But there was no place for domestic violence in today's world, even if it continued to happen.

So Chuck was a wife beater and a bully, Stone began to believe. Was he also a rapist? And a murderer?

"Was Adrienne having an affair?" he asked.

Erica practically jumped from her chair. "No way!" she exclaimed. "She wouldn't have dared cheat on him. Adrienne was too afraid for her life to ever consider being with another man."

"How about a woman?" Stone favored her with a straight look. He couldn't rule out that she could have been Adrienne's lesbian lover and not just a platonic best friend.

Erica's eyes widened. "If you're asking me if Adrienne was bisexual, the answer is no." She sighed. "And, for the record, I'm straight, too."

Stone smiled faintly, while making a mental note.

"Thank you, Ms. Flanagan, for coming in and providing me with this information," he told her sincerely. "I'm sure it will be quite helpful in the investigation." As far as he was concerned, it was more than enough reason to take a much stronger look at Chuck Murray in connection with his wife's death.

"Are you going to arrest Chuck?" Erica batted her lashes impatiently.

If only it were that simple. "First we need to verify the facts . . ." Stone almost hated to say.

"I have absolutely no reason to lie, Detective!" Erica snapped.

"No one is accusing you of lying about anything, Ms. Flanagan." *Not yet anyway.*

She began to cry. "I just don't want to see Adrienne put into the ground forever, while her killer gets off scot-free."

Stone handed her a Kleenex. "If Adrienne's husband killed her, I promise you he won't get off scot-free," he said earnestly. "Not if I have anything to do with it!"

Right now he had everything to do with it, Stone thought.

And the same could well be said for Chuck Murray.

CHAPTER 18

"Just say 'here comes the judge,' " Grant sang gleefully, as he embraced Beverly and did a little dance.

"When . . . ?" she asked, feigning total shock. They were in his office where he had called her in, claiming it was for some unfinished paperwork.

"The call came from the governor himself this morning. He needed a replacement for Judge Crawford and asked if I was interested. I told him I would have to think about it." Grant made a comical face. "Two seconds later I said hell yes!"

"I'm so happy for you, Grant," Beverly said, and kissed him on the mouth. "I'm sure you'll make a fine judge, even if we'll miss you around here more than anyone will admit. Except for me."

Grant laughed. "Didn't you know—they've been trying to get rid of me for years. Now I'm granting them their wish." He pulled her closer, wrapping her in his arms. "As for you, my dear, you're not going to get rid of me that easily. I intend to make sure you're never too far to miss me."

"Promise?" Beverly felt a prickling all over being in his

arms. She really didn't want his promotion to have an adverse effect on their relationship.

Why should it?

It wasn't as if he was headed to Washington. Though suddenly that no longer seemed so far-fetched. Beverly wondered if someday Grant might decide to run for the Senate. Or even try and occupy the White House.

"You have my word as a gentleman who adores you, lady," Grant said positively. He didn't even want to think about anything else that could cause a rift between them. Not today, anyway. "In fact, I'd say that this calls for a celebration. I want to take you and Jaime out to dinner tonight."

"Oh, Grant," Beverly hummed regrettably. "We can't—not tonight. I promised Jaime I'd take him to the video store to check out the latest rentals." Also, she didn't know how Jaime would feel about going anywhere with Grant. Even if he was now a judge in the making. But she knew they would have to make an effort to get along at some point, if Grant was to remain a vital part of her life. "How about Friday night?" she compromised. "If you're not doing anything."

"Nothing that can't be changed," Grant was quick to say. "Friday night it is."

"Good." Beverly smiled and kissed him again, then used her finger to wipe lipstick from his mouth. "Now, Judge Nunez, I hate to leave so abruptly, but I have to prepare for an arraignment this afternoon."

Grant frowned. "You mean the Santiago case?"

She nodded.

"Do you know who's representing him?"

"I've heard that K. Conrad Ortega from the public defender's office was assigned the case."

"Poor bastard," Grant shook his head. "Ortega is a good attorney, but not good enough to snatch victory from the jaws of certain defeat. I'm sure you won't have any problem convincing a jury of Santiago's guilt. The asshole's made-to-order for any prosecutor looking to tack one up on the scoreboard."

Beverly flashed him a look of surprise. "This isn't a basketball game, Grant," she told him. "My only interest is that justice is served as swiftly and fairly as possible."

"Of course," he said apologetically. "Fortunately, justice usually does prevail in cases like this where everything points in one direction."

Beverly agreed, though she wished the same could be said for cases that didn't involve the murder of a sitting judge. She'd been in trials where swift and decisive justice seemed blind. Or, at the very least, nearsighted.

"I hate having to try and fill the Honorable Judge Crawford's shoes this way." Grant lowered his gaze respectfully. "But if it hadn't been me, it would have been someone else."

"I'm sure he would have wanted the best person for the job," Beverly said. "And that clearly is you!" she declared, even if she was maybe just a bit biased in that assessment.

He grinned boyishly. "Thanks for the vote of confidence, Bev. I think *you* just might be the next one from the DA's office to move to the bench."

Beverly blushed, flattered that he should think so. *Do you really believe that? Or are you just trying to make me feel good?*

"Right now," she told him, "I'll settle for one victory at a time . . ."

Starting with the State's case against Rafael Santiago.

The arraignment was set to begin at two o'clock, but it was closer to three before all the parties were present. Security was extra heavy, as some threats had come in against the accused and were taken seriously. No one wanted to see Rafael Santiago gunned down before he had a chance to be convicted by a jury of his peers and sentenced appropriately.

On the bench was Judge Harriet Ireland. She was in her late forties, but looked older. Her auburn hair was stylishly coiffed and she wore tinted glasses. She nodded coolly to Beverly, who nodded back.

Representing the State, Beverly sat at the prosecution table. The second chair was empty at the moment, as no other attorney was needed at this stage of the proceedings. Given the relatively strong case against the defendant, she had more or less decided to go with one of the younger ADA's to give the person the experience and credibility she was once afforded.

Beverly looked across the room at K. Conrad Ortega. He seemed to smile at her. She did not smile back. She'd heard he was ambitious and looking to make a name for himself. Showing any signs of weakness could only encourage him.

Next to Ortega was his client. The defendant, Rafael Santiago, had only recently arrived, shackled and handcuffed. He wore the standard orange jail attire. Later, she imagined, he would be in a suit, looking like a Wall Street lawyer. And his hair, currently disheveled, as if he had been in a wrestling match, would be smoothed back or to the side. Even the smug look on his face would be toned down to one maintaining innocence. Or at the very least, remorse.

Not present was the State's key witness and crime victim, Maxine Crawford. It was unnecessary to have her in attendance at this juncture, only to be gawked at and intimidated by the monster who hurt her after he shot her husband to death.

Beverly glanced at the front row where Grant sat in attendance. He said he wanted to come in support, as well as to regard the courtroom setting from his new perspective as a judge. She was grateful to have him close either way. He smiled at her and she returned it, while thinking briefly about their dinner date and having him and Jaime emerge as friends.

"Are we ready?" Judge Ireland asked the attorneys, as if in doubt.

Both said yes in unison, standing, along with the defendant.

After going through the preliminary issues, the judge read the five current charges to the defendant. Additional charges related to possession and use of an illegal firearm were expected to be filed later, once the murder weapon was located.

With each charge Santiago was asked point-blank if he understood.

"Yes," he responded each time with little emotion.

Ireland adjusted her glasses, then asked the defendant, "How do you plead, Mr. Santiago, to count one of murder in the first degree?"

Santiago favored his attorney, who then answered without prelude, "My client pleads not guilty."

"Count two, of criminal sexual battery?"

"Not guilty," Ortega again responded.

"Count three, of sodomy?"

"Not guilty."

"Count four, of forced oral copulation?"

Ortega sighed. "Not guilty."

Ireland eyed the defendant as if to read his mind. "And count five, of breaking and entering?"

"Again, my client pleads not guilty, Your Honor." Ortega spoke without looking at Santiago.

To Beverly this did not come as a particular surprise. Few defendants facing murder charges ever pleaded guilty. At least not at the arraignment. She fully expected that later Santiago, or Ortega on his behalf, would seek a deal in which some degree of guilt would be admitted, so long as it was less than the current charges, and a softer sentence was the result.

Beverly didn't see a chance in hell that she would ever accept a plea bargain. Not in this lifetime. Not if she valued her future in the DA's office.

And her possible future as a judge.

The preliminary hearing was set for two weeks from now,

at which time the prosecution would have to present just enough of its case to show probable cause that Rafael Santiago had committed the crimes for which he had been charged. By then Beverly expected to have put together the pieces of the puzzle necessary to send this one to trial.

The issue of bail was now raised.

Beverly tugged on the ruffled cuff of her Maggy London teak jacket that was part of the silk suit she wore, along with matching mules.

"Your Honor," she began, "in light of the serious nature of the charges against the defendant and the fact that he has already served time for similar crimes, there should be no consideration of bail whatsoever." She knew that the issue itself was a mere formality to which each defendant was entitled, no matter how heinous the charges. She also realized the importance of making it clear from the start just how strongly the prosecution felt against such.

Judge Ireland seemed determined to show no favoritism as she faced defense attorney Ortega. "Counselor, what do you have to say regarding bail?"

Stepping slightly away from his client, Ortega glanced at Beverly and back to Ireland. "Your Honor, we realize that Mr. Santiago has been in hot water before," he said with lamentation. "And he paid the price for it. But that was then, and this is now! All my client wants is to have a fair bail set and then be given a chance to prove he is innocent of the charges."

Ireland glared at Santiago. "He'll get his chance to do just that," she said forcefully. "But not in this court. Bail is denied!" She slammed the gavel down and court was adjourned.

Beverly turned to Grant, who gave her a thumbs-up. A tiny smile crossed her lips.

She now regarded the defendant as he was being led from the court by bailiffs. He seemed to make a point of giving her the dirty eye all the way out. Or was she only imagining it? Might she, too, be just a little pissed off if someone stood between her and freedom?

Perhaps Santiago should have thought about that when he decided to exact his vengeance on the judge and his wife, Beverly told herself. But then that was what separated vicious criminals from law-abiding citizens. Often the former did not think about the consequences of their actions—not until it was too late.

And someone was dead and another sexually assaulted.

Well, if I have it my way, you'll never have the chance to harm another living soul, Santiago, Beverly thought, determined to see that justice prevailed in this case.

Grant watched the arraignment come to an end, pleased to see that Rafael Santiago would be headed back to jail, just where he belonged. He wished the asshole hadn't killed Judge Crawford and sexually assaulted Maxine Crawford. No one wanted to see the judge dead and his wife traumatized.

But it had happened, and now they had to deal with it, even if things could get ugly along the way.

I would have preferred to take over Judge Crawford's spot on the bench another way, thought Grant. *However, it wasn't my call. I just have to make certain I keep my eye on the ball and not mess things up any more than what's already gone down.*

He flashed a brilliant smile as Beverly approached, looking as stunning as ever. Being with her was enough to make him believe that good things really could happen, even when things went bad.

CHAPTER 19

Manuel smoked the crack, intensely savoring the high that penetrated every fiber of his body. It made him feel alive again. There was no feeling like it. Not even sex.

Murdering somebody was a high all its own. But that could only come when the time was right, the circumstances conducive to killing, the trap laid out precisely so the predator backed the prey into a corner with no chance of escape.

With crack cocaine, the thrill could come anytime, anywhere. And its potent effects always left him feeling like he was on cloud nine. Manuel emptied the pipe of its contents, allowing the stuff to filter into his system, before leaving the bathroom.

Downstairs he warmed some leftover chicken to go with red beans. By the time his old lady walked through the door from another day and half dollar on the job, he was feeling horny, hungry, and mellow.

"How was work?" he asked routinely, not much caring, so long as she kept a roof over their heads.

"Okay," she said unenthusiastically, looking worn out.

Manuel wrapped his arms around her full figure from behind. They were back on speaking terms after their last fight. At least he had forgotten about it. There were more important things on his mind.

"I missed you, baby." He poured it on a bit thick.

"Since when?" Her voice echoed with skepticism.

"Since every time you go away," he lied.

She wriggled around, still in his arms. Her gaze explored his face, as if looking for something hidden. "You're high, aren't you?"

"A little," he was willing to admit. "Ain't no big deal."

"You promised me you were gonna get off the crack, Manuel."

"I am off it," he lied again. "Just smoked a little weed. That's all." He kissed her chapped lips.

"I'm not really in the mood right now," she muttered.

He grabbed hold of her massive breasts through her dress. "I'll get you in the mood." He kissed her again while he cupped her breasts and squeezed them like pillows. "I need you now, baby."

She was beginning to warm up, he knew. Her nipples had turned rock-hard and her breathing had quickened.

"Oh . . ." she purred.

"Let's go to bed," he told her. "I'll give you what you need, and a lot more."

She did not protest.

Upstairs he orally stimulated her till she came in waves. Then she returned the favor and he squeezed his eyes shut. The dual stimulation of the crack and her active tongue had him pumped up and shaking like a leaf till he spent himself in her mouth.

Afterwards he entered her and slammed against her repeatedly until he ran out of steam.

All the while Manuel was thinking about that whore he had killed.

And the whore before her.

Even the next whore who would meet his blade made Manuel's blood boil and his imagination run wild.

CHAPTER 20

Conrad Ortega sidestepped the used hypodermic needles and other drug paraphernalia scattered across the pavement and patches of brown grass at the apartment complex like ants. It was mostly home to poor Hispanics and African-Americans. He, too, had once lived in such a drug-infested community, but through hard work and determination had left that life behind.

Too bad the same couldn't be said for Rafael Santiago, he thought, entering the dark hallway that reeked of marijuana and urine. Like most felons, Santiago had been sent back to the very environment that put him in prison in the first place.

Stopping in front of apartment 314, Ortega listened in for a moment. There was shouting, but he determined that it was from the apartment across the hall.

He knocked on the door. This was where Isabel Santiago lived. And where her son, Rafael, was placed after his release from prison. According to Santiago, at the time Sheldon Crawford was shot to death and his wife raped and sodomized, he was at home and had been all night. His mother was his witness and alibi.

Ortega's visit was routine as Santiago's attorney. The police had obviously dismissed his client's claims. He, too, had his doubts about the alibi, all things considered. But at this point, if he was to present a credible case at all, he had to give Santiago the benefit of the doubt.

And his mother.

The door opened slowly with a squeak, stopping because of the chain lock being fully extended. An elderly and frail Hispanic woman peered out cautiously.

"Ms. Santiago?" asked Ortega.

"What do you want?" she responded suspiciously.

He detected fear in her umber eyes that had heavy bags beneath them.

"My name is Conrad Ortega. I'm representing your son, Rafael Santiago."

Her gaze widened, almost in disbelief. "You mean you're his lawyer?"

"Yes." Ortega flashed a weak smile. "I need to talk to you."

She stared at him for another moment or two before closing the door and removing the chain. The door opened again and he was invited in.

Ortega found the small living room cluttered, but in an orderly way. A television was on and a cat scurried across the floor, jumping over his shoes and onto a tattered couch.

"You want somethin' to eat . . . drink?" Isabel asked hesitantly.

"No, thanks."

Ortega regarded her. He guessed she was at least seventy, with thinning hair white as snow and a face with more than a few wrinkles. She wore an ill-fitting floral print dress that looked as if it had seen better days.

Walking with a slight limp, Isabel sat down next to the cat and put it in her lap. "Is Rafael in big trouble again?" she asked, her voice quivering.

"Yes, I'm afraid he is, ma'am." Ortega sat on a foot chair, facing her.

"Ever since coming here from Cuba, the boy's been in trouble."

"Well, it's his current situation I need to discuss with you," Ortega told her. "I'm sure you're aware that Rafael's been charged with murdering a judge and sexually assaulting his wife."

"Judge Crawford," she said matter-of-factly. "I know all about the judge. He put Rafael away twelve years ago."

"For murdering his pregnant girlfriend," emphasized Ortega.

Isabel nodded reluctantly. "He did his time. Lost a good chunk of his life," she said almost bitterly. "Now all Rafael wants to do is try and make a new life for himself. Then they try to blame him for this." She rolled her eyes.

"Your son says he was here all night when the Crawfords were being attacked." Ortega favored her keenly. "Is that true?"

"Yes," she said without blinking. "Rafael never left the apartment that day."

"Did you?" he questioned curiously. If so, it would mean she couldn't account for his whereabouts every minute of the day, besides the time in his presence.

"No. I hardly ever leave this apartment," Isabel responded swiftly. "Can't get around that much these days. Also, it ain't safe when the sun goes down. Too many gang fights and drug dealing happening in the neighborhood for an old lady to venture out very often. That day me and Rafael sat in here watching TV and talking."

"You're telling me Rafael didn't go out at all?" Ortega gave her a look of doubt. Santiago didn't strike him as a man who could stay holed up in a tiny apartment for any length of time. Not after being confined in a tiny cell for a dozen years.

"The police already asked me," she replied bitterly. "I tell them the same thing. Rafael was here *all day and night*. But they don't believe me. They think I'm just trying to protect my son."

"Are you?" Ortega raised his chin skeptically.

"No!" Isabel's voice jumped. "I'll do anything for Rafael, but I won't lie for him."

Maybe not.

Or maybe you're lying right now, mused Ortega, uncertain.

"If this goes to trial," he told her, "we'll need you to testify in court, under oath. Can you do that?"

Isabel considered this. She nodded. "I'll do what you want to help my son."

"Good." Truthfully, Ortega knew she would be raked over the coals by the prosecution, probably rendering her testimony useless. But right now she could be the most important thing standing between her son and a death sentence.

He stood, noting the boarded windows that seemed to blend in, as if they came with the territory.

Isabel tossed the cat to the floor, watching it sprint out of the room, yowling like it had stepped on a piece of glass. "Thank you for taking Rafael's case," she said sincerely. "He has no one else to stand up for him."

Except for you, Ortega thought. Unfortunately, the two of them might not be enough. Not when the State had Maxine Crawford as their star witness and sympathetic victim.

And the ghost of her slain judge husband on their side.

CHAPTER 21

Beverly helped Jaime put his tie on against the backdrop of a pale pink shirt and a navy suit. It was one of the few times he had worn the suit she had bought for him last Easter. And even then he had worn it under protest.

"Why do I have to wear a suit just to go to dinner with *him?*" he whined.

"Because Grant is now a judge," Beverly told him respectfully. "And he's invited us both to a fancy restaurant that has a dress code."

"I don't wanna go," Jaime whined. "I'd rather play on my computer or watch TV."

"You have to go," she insisted. "I promised Grant you would. Besides, he's been really good to me and I want you two to get to know each other."

But at what cost? Beverly wondered. Would Jaime forever resent her involvement with a man? Any man?

This man?

Could Grant ever see Jaime as more than her son? Beverly contemplated whether the day might come when Jaime could be *their* son.

Was that what she really wanted? A substitute father for Jaime, whose real father was missing in action?

Or am I really looking for a husband in a man who may no longer be the marrying type?

Beverly feared that both would be an uphill battle. Especially since she wasn't sure if marriage was something she truly desired again in her own future after successfully separating romance and independence for so long.

"There . . ." She smiled at Jaime in the mirror. "You look very handsome this evening, Mr. Mendoza."

Jaime blushed, admiring himself in the suit. "You really think so?"

"Of course I do." Beverly beamed. "You'll have to wear your suit more often."

"You look nice, too," Jaime said approvingly.

Beverly looked at her reflection in the mirror. She had chosen a celadon charmeuse halter dress for the occasion that flattered her figure while not overdoing it. She put her long hair in a chignon and wore only enough makeup to add a bit of color to her sallow skin.

"Yes, I think I do," she laughed, and glanced at her Carlos Santana "Maiden" sandals. Inside, Beverly knew that she wanted Grant to feel the same way.

"Did you think Dad was handsome?" asked Jaime, a brow raised curiously.

Beverly favored him, knowing he considered the question important. "Yes, I did. Your father was one of the most handsome men I've ever met. It wasn't Diego's looks that were the problem—but his character and selfishness that were unattractive."

"Why did he have to be such a bastard?" Jaime snorted.

Beverly widened her mouth in surprise. Till now she had never heard him say a bad thing about his father. Or use profanity. Jaime had always managed to keep Diego alive in his head by believing him to be a better person than he ever was.

Now it was time for Jaime to take Diego off the pedestal.

Beverly gave her son a frank stare. "I asked myself the same question time and time again," she admitted. "And never came up with the answer." She doubted she ever would.

"I'll never leave you," Jaime promised.

Beverly hugged him and kissed the side of his head. "And I'll never leave you, sweetheart." It was a promise she knew only one of them would be able to keep. But that didn't mean they couldn't extend being together for as long as possible.

Even if a third party should join them for the ride.

The Creekside restaurant sat on the banks of Eagles Lake. Grant was already there when they arrived. Beverly thought it was better that they break Jaime in slowly to the idea that they were a couple. She ventured a half-wave to Grant at the table and he waved back.

He stood to greet them, wearing a tan sportcoat with a yellow shirt over dark brown gabardine trousers. Beverly couldn't help but admire what she saw. She had to admit that she was turned on, though this was hardly the time or place.

"Hello, Beverly," Grant said in an almost businesslike fashion. He gave her a friendly peck on the cheek and thought she looked gorgeous this evening. But that was always the case, which made him feel he was the luckiest man around.

"Grant," she responded, wondering if he was overdoing it a bit in his attempt to appear the perfect gentleman.

"Nice to see you, Jaime." Grant stuck out his hand. *Maybe you'll let me get to know you a little better.*

Jaime seemed surprised, maybe even suspicious, but put his hand forward. "Hi," he said meekly.

After an awkward moment or two they sat down and the waiter brought over menus.

"I'd recommend the roast duck," Grant said as an authority. "Along with a stuffed baked potato."

"Sounds good to me," seconded Beverly. "How about you, Jaime?"

He frowned over his menu. "I'd rather have the grilled steak and fries," he answered defiantly.

"That's good, too." Grant glanced at Beverly with a smile. "Then it's settled. Three grilled steaks and fries coming up."

They ordered. Beverly and Grant had coffee, while Jaime sipped lemonade through a straw.

"Your mother tells me you're doing very well in school these days." Grant looked at the boy across the table. He wondered if Jaime resembled his father, though he definitely had characteristics that reminded Grant of his mother.

Jaime gave Beverly the narrow eye, as if embarrassed or resentful that she had shared information about him with Grant. "I'm doing okay."

Beverly seized the moment, deciding this was a good subject to build on. "Jaime is getting all A's and B's right now," she said, mindful that his last science test had produced a B.

"What do want to be when you grow up?" Grant asked. "Maybe a lawyer like your mom?"

Jaime sneered. "What do you care?"

Beverly glared. "Jaime!"

"That's all right," Grant told her, prepared for such resistance. It was up to him to see if he could melt the boy's icy resolve to keep him at arm's length. "It's a good question. What do I care? Actually, Jaime, I care a lot. I've grown to care for your mother very much. That means I also care about you and what you choose to do with your life, now and in the future . . ."

Jaime weighed this, sipping more lemonade. Beverly knew that he was intimidated by Grant, as well as uncertain about his role in their lives. She hoped this might allay some of his fears.

Either that, or it could backfire and Jaime might grow even more distant from Grant. Beverly suspected it could impact her relationship with both her son and with Grant.

"I want to be a doctor," Jaime said, surprising Beverly.

Last she knew, he had talked about wanting to be a hip-hop singer. Or an entomologist.

"Good choice." Grant nodded, impressed. "Why a doctor?"

"That way maybe I can find a cure for my grandpa's Alzheimer's disease and help people like him."

Beverly and Grant exchanged sad glances. She had not realized that Jaime was so deeply affected by his grandfather's condition, enough to influence his career choice at this stage of his young life. She wondered if he somehow feared that it might be genetic, and that she and eventually he would come down with it.

"Maybe you can," Grant said with feeling. "Who says you can't make a difference someday in battling this terrible disease?"

Yes, thought Beverly. Why not? At some point someone had to develop a means to fight the ravages of Alzheimer's disease. If Jaime really wanted to be a doctor—and that was a big *if* at age twelve—then she would do everything in her power to see to it that he achieved his dream.

But she suspected that he was speaking more out of frustration and fears than real dreams. Only time would tell.

The waiter brought their food.

Grant and Beverly spoke briefly about the Rafael Santiago case before returning to other conversation as they strove to keep Jaime part of the dinner chat.

"Are you a Golden State Warriors fan?" Grant asked Jaime, knowing they were the nearest pro sports team to Eagles Landing, albeit some fifty miles away.

"Not really," he said dispassionately. "They suck."

Grant chuckled. "Can't argue with you there. Well, how about the Houston Rockets?"

"Yao Ming is awesome," Jaime said animatedly.

Looks like I may have found a soft spot in him, Grant mused. "If you're interested, I can get tickets to a Rockets game against the Warriors in a few weeks."

Jaime's eyes lit up. "Really?"

"Really." Grant smiled, aware that he had indeed made a

breakthrough. One that was sorely needed if he was to succeed in getting closer to Beverly. "I have a friend who works in the team's front office. He can get me front row seats. Maybe even arrange for an autograph or two from players." Hopefully Yao would do the honors.

"Cool." Jaime's face flushed with excitement. "Can I bring my friend Paco? He loves the Warriors, even when they suck."

Grant laughed, even as Beverly winced. "Yes, Paco is certainly more than welcome to join us," he promised, and eyed Beverly. "And your mother, too."

"I wouldn't miss it," Beverly declared, ecstatic over the prospect of some Grant and Jaime male bonding, as well as the three of them spending more quality time together.

Grant flashed his teeth. "Was hoping you'd say that. We can even drop by my judge's chambers beforehand. I can give Jaime and Paco the grand tour."

"Wow!" Jaime gave a wide smile. "That would be great! Paco will think it's cool, too."

Beverly watched with amusement, as she hadn't seen Jaime this excited in a long time. She was seeing a whole new side of Grant. Evidently he had more of a way with kids than he'd let on. She wondered what other secrets he may have been keeping bottled up inside.

"I think it's great as well," she offered enthusiastically. Especially considering that she had not seen Grant's new chambers since he had taken Judge Crawford's place. Beverly imagined that as Judge Nunez, Grant would make an immediate impact in the war against crime, leaving his own mark.

For the first time Beverly began to believe there was actually hope after all that her son and her lover could learn to like each other. Someday it could even turn to love, an emotion that Beverly could also see taking shape between her and Grant, if things continued to blossom in their relationship.

* * *

On Monday morning Beverly met with Detective Joe O'Dell and her co-counsel, Gail Kennedy. At twenty-five, Gail was one of the bright young prosecutors in the DA's office. An African-American, she had a beautiful pecan complexion and a retro blond curly Afro, which may have turned heads as much as her tall, slender physique. Her duties as second chair would primarily be note-taking, paperwork, interviewing witnesses, and sometimes getting coffee. Beverly hoped the experience would be invaluable, as it had been for her when she was coming up the ranks.

The three were going over the evidence in the Rafael Santiago case.

"There may be a problem with the DNA on the semen taken from Maxine Crawford," said Gail, razor-thin eyelashes fluttering.

"What problem might that be?" asked Beverly, though the answer was obvious, given what she knew about the case.

"She had intercourse with Judge Crawford just before being raped by Santiago." Gail colored, glancing across the table at O'Dell. He did not seem to be particularly affected one way or the other. "And it appears that Maxine also engaged in anal sex with the judge before she was sodomized. Samples of his semen were removed from her anus—along with that of Rafael Santiago."

"Damn," O'Dell hummed as if this were news to him. "So Judge Crawford liked it both ways."

"Apparently," Beverly said, wondering if this was actually turning him on. "Obviously Maxine Crawford did as well. But it was their right as a married couple to engage in any sexual acts they chose. What Santiago did to her was a different matter altogether."

Gail looked up from her notes. "Unfortunately both Santiago's and Judge Crawford's semen was found in Maxine's vagina and anus; meaning it may be tricky in distinguishing which man was responsible for any tears or other trauma she experienced as a result of the sexual assault. This could undermine both the rape and sodomy cases and make it more difficult to rely on the DNA evidence pertaining to the semen."

Beverly was thinking the same thing, but was counting on the preponderance of evidence against Santiago to work in their favor. "What about the genital hair samples taken from Maxine Crawford?"

"We should have the preliminary results in a few days," Gail answered.

Beverly said colorlessly, "Once we have the DNA match of Santiago's genital hairs inside Maxine's vagina, anus, or both, it'll bolster our case against him as a sexual assaulter."

She looked at O'Dell. He was one of the better-looking detectives on the force, she thought, and happily involved in a long-term relationship. He and his girlfriend had recently produced a beautiful little girl that O'Dell doted over like she was the most precious thing in the world.

Beverly was glad to see that he didn't seem to show any lingering effects from the cold shoulder that Grant had given O'Dell at the hospital the night Judge Crawford was killed. *Or maybe I was overreacting in the feeling that there was some genuine animosity between the two men.*

"Joe, I understand that Santiago has an alibi for the time in question," Beverly said, some anxiety in her voice. "Are we going to be able to get around that without hurting the case?" Surely Santiago could not be in two places at once.

O'Dell's face hardened. "His alibi is a bunch of bull! Any man who hides behind his mama isn't much of a man, as far as I'm concerned."

"But is it possible that the jury might actually believe Santiago's story? Or his mother's testimony?" Beverly had seen as much, even when the weight of evidence was stacked against the defendant.

"What do you think?" O'Dell tossed back with a sneer. "The woman is scared to death of her son. She would say anything he told her to—including confess to the crime herself. No damned jury in their right mind is going to give Santiago's so-called 'alibi' any credibility. Not when the facts come out."

"Where are we on *hard* evidence, Joe?" Beverly gazed at him, then Gail, and back again.

"We've got Maxine Crawford's positive ID of the suspect," O'Dell said firmly. "We also know that Santiago swore he'd get even with Judge Crawford for putting him away, and had the will and means to do it."

"What about the murder weapon?" Beverly asked dubiously.

O'Dell bowed his head lamentably. "Haven't been able to locate it—yet. Chances are the asshole tossed it into the lake, which is right across the street from the judge's house. It's being scoured, but I don't hold out much hope of finding anything. Between the currents, the depth, and the muck in the water, it will take a miracle to find the gun."

"Well, let's hope for one, as we really could use that 'smoking' gun to lock this case up," Beverly stressed, aware that many so-called open-and-shut cases had been lost without the most crucial piece of evidence. The judge had been shot with a .25-caliber automatic. Not the most powerful of weapons, she knew, but enough to fell even the strongest man at point-blank range. Especially when shot three times. It would be a persuasive piece of evidence to dangle in front of the jury.

"There's enough other evidence to get a conviction," argued O'Dell. "We've got the bullets and shell casings, which are being matched against some found at the place Santiago was staying. Fibers from clothing at the scene of the crime are also being tested with clothes owned by the suspect. It will all fit, take my word for it."

"With all due respect, Joe," groaned Beverly, "we need more than your word or my prosecuting abilities to win this case. What about fingerprints?"

"The man wore gloves, according to Mrs. Crawford." O'Dell scratched his head, clearly uncomfortable. "But we're checking for prints anyway."

"Any other witnesses?"

"One of the neighbors saw a man running down the

street around the time this happened. But she didn't get a look at his face."

"Let's get her in here, Gail," Beverly ordered. "Maybe this woman saw more than she thinks she did. At least she can give us a description of the clothing worn by the man seen fleeing."

"Will do." Gail jotted this down.

O'Dell leaned forward. "And I'll poke around and see what I can find out from Santiago's ex-cellmate."

"Good idea." Beverly closed her folder, grateful that the trial was still weeks away.

She was sure this case could be won even if they fell short on some key evidence. The suspect had all but confessed to the killing when he threatened Judge Crawford's life and apparently never backed down from the threat. He had also been fingered by Maxine Crawford as the man who sexually assaulted her and shot her husband to death.

Trials had been won with less, Beverly told herself.

But they would still have to prove Santiago's guilt in a court of law.

And she planned to.

Or she would have to watch Rafael Santiago walk, a free man who got away with cold-blooded murder.

CHAPTER 22

"I appreciate you coming in, Chuck." Stone gave a polite nod. He watched the primary suspect in Adrienne Murray's death take a seat. He'd learned that Chuck worked as a car salesman, and frequently moved from job to job.

Chuck gave a nervous cough. "Like I said, I want to co-operate any way I can to help find Adrienne's killer."

"That's good to know." Stone slid his chair closer to the desk. "Why don't you begin by telling me about your relationship with your wife."

Chuck flashed him an uneasy gaze, then shrugged. "What do you want to know?"

"Did she ever cheat on you?"

"No. Why would you ask that?"

"It's my job to ask that," Stone responded curtly, "and anything else that might help find her killer."

Chuck sniffed. "I understand."

Stone took a moment. "So you never suspected your wife of having an affair with another man?"

"Never," he insisted. "We loved each other. She never would have slept with someone else."

"And what if she had, Chuck? How would you have felt?"

Chuck's eyes half closed with indignation. "How would anyone have felt?" he asked with snap. "It would have hurt like hell!"

"Have you ever hit your wife?" Stone stared at him accusingly.

Chuck's head tilted pensively. "No. Did someone say I had?"

"Why would you think that, Chuck?" Stone could see that he was becoming flustered. Perhaps feeling guilty on maybe more levels than one.

"Because this . . . friend . . . of Adrienne's—Erica Flanagan—was always trying to stir up trouble between us," Chuck claimed. "She hates me for some reason."

"And what reason would that be?" Stone locked eyes with him.

Chuck shrugged. "Hell if I know. I think she was jealous that Adrienne had a man and she couldn't seem to hold on to one."

Stone suspected that he had to reach deep to come up with that one, doubting Murray believed it himself. He played along for now. "So you're saying you actually think Erica would make such an accusation that you beat the hell out of your wife purely out of spite?"

Chuck shifted his gaze. "I wouldn't put anything past that bitch." He paused, turning back to Stone. "So, is that what this meeting is all about?"

"No," Stone said tersely. "It's about *you*, Chuck, and the brutal murder of your wife."

Chuck twisted in the chair. "You think *I* killed Adrienne?"

"Did you?" Stone honed in on the husband's face.

"No—I did not kill my wife!"

"Did you visit her at work on the day she was killed?"

"No!" Chuck insisted.

We'll see about that, mused Stone skeptically. "Where were you between six-thirty and seven-thirty the night your wife died, Chuck?"

"At home."

"Alone?"

"Yes, alone."

"Not good enough, Chuck," Stone snapped. "You're going to have to do a hell of a lot better than that!"

Chuck put his hands to his head. "I can't believe this! Why on earth would I kill my wife, then come to you to report her missing?"

"Maybe because you wanted to cover your ass." Stone's brow furrowed. "It wouldn't be the first time a man killed his wife and tried to make it seem like someone else did it."

Chuck lunged to his feet. "I don't have to listen to this anymore. Not without my lawyer!"

Stone stood up, making it clear that he was not intimidated by this show of indignation from the suspect. But he also wanted to keep the man talking, without violating his rights. "Sit down, Chuck. This is strictly informal," he indicated.

Chuck glared at him for a long moment. "I don't think so. Sounds more like you've got your mind made up and are way off base. Unless you're arresting me here and now, I don't think I have anything else to say to you, except through my attorney!"

Stone held his disappointment in check. "If that's the way you feel." He sensed that he was looking at a guilty man in some respect. Perhaps Chuck Murray was only guilty of loving Adrienne too much when maybe it was not reciprocated equally. But Stone somehow sensed it went deeper than that. Maybe to the point of wife battering and murder. "You're free to go," he told him. "But I suggest you get together with your lawyer quickly. You may need representation soon. And do us both a favor, Chuck—don't try and leave the state."

Chuck's nostrils grew with ire and he stomped out.

Stone watched him disappear before Lieutenant Bruce Kramer came into the room. He had been observing the interrogation in another room through a one-way window.

Kramer was forty-eight and wide-bodied. Two inches shorter than Stone, he had a walnut complexion, shaved head, and thick mustache. "I'd say we probably have our man," he spoke in a deep voice. "Or had him."

"Murray definitely knows something he's not saying," Stone said positively, not willing to go beyond that for now. "But we don't have enough yet to make an arrest."

"Then get enough!" warned Kramer, his hard features crinkled. "If this man strangled and sliced up his wife before tossing her into the lake like a rag doll, I don't want him deciding he may as well add another woman or two to the list for the hell of it, so long as he's a free man. Do you understand what I'm saying, Palmer?"

Stone held his gaze respectfully. "Yeah, I think I do." All too well, he thought. He either brought in Chuck for Adrienne Murray's murder, or someone else—and soon. *Otherwise my ass is grass and I'm looking at the lawnmower.*

Stone felt the pressure and wouldn't buckle under it. After receiving several commendations over the years for excellent and professional work, he wasn't about to mess things up now. Not if he could help it.

Detective Chang walked into the room. The look on his face told Stone that he wouldn't like what the detective had to say.

"The body of a prostitute named Penelope Grijalva was found this afternoon in an apartment on Broadway." Chang glanced at a paper in his hand. "She'd been rotting there for a few days, till the stench became more than the neighbors could handle. The preliminary report is that she was strangled, raped, and cut up badly, much like Adrienne Murray."

Both Stone and Kramer gave each other looks, and then read the report.

"You think this could have been done by the same person?" Kramer asked Stone bluntly.

Stone hated to think that they had a serial killer on their hands, because it went against the grain—especially if Chuck Murray had killed his wife. It didn't figure that he would exhibit the same rage against other women with whom he didn't have the same vested interest. But the similarities could hardly be overlooked and were ominous to say the least.

"It's too early to tell," Stone responded as his way of saying he needed more time. But he had a feeling there wouldn't be any.

"Better get Murray back in here!" ordered Kramer, brows stitched. "And have him bring his lawyer along. Something tells me he's going to need good representation."

Stone had an APB put out on Chuck Murray. He had a bad feeling that if Murray was the one they were looking for, he wasn't in this alone. Only Stone wasn't sure where else to point the finger at the moment.

In bed that night, Stone tried sleeping but found himself unable to. Too many thoughts were drifting in and out of his head. Chuck Murray had been arrested without incident, still claiming innocence. He was later released when it became clear that they just didn't have enough to hold him.

There appeared to be no connection between Penelope Grijalva and Adrienne Murray, aside from the similarities of their deaths. Like Adrienne, Penelope had apparently had sex with her killer, albeit Stone suspected it may have been voluntarily in Grijalva's case. At least initially. DNA tests would show if the same man had intercourse with both women.

Joyce, sensing he was awake, wrapped her arms around him. "What is it, Stone?"

"I'm not sure." He yawned miserably. "Someone is out there killing young women and I don't know who the hell I should be looking for."

She kissed his bare shoulder. "It'll work itself out, honey," she said in a motherly tone. "It always does."

"Yeah," he muttered. The problem was that if it didn't work out soon, there would be more victims. More lives shattered.

Could Chuck have snapped after killing his wife? Stone wondered. Maybe he had set his sights on other young women who reminded him of her.

Stone contemplated the idea that Chuck Murray was in cahoots with someone else. Or was he, like his wife, an innocent victim of tragic circumstances and bizarre coincidences?

Trouble is, I don't believe in coincidences, the detective told himself. Most things that happened were not by pure chance but rather by design. Meaning these women were likely killed by the same person who knew exactly what he was doing.

There was no reason to believe he planned to stop any time soon. Unless he was caught or killed first.

Stone turned to his wife and pressed his lips against the warmth of her bosom. She was wearing Tommy Girl cologne and it was invigorating to his nostrils. He kissed her naked skin, feeling her nipples harden.

Lowering himself down her stomach with kisses, Stone went down further till arriving between Joyce's legs. He started kissing her there, then licking, aroused by the taste and her reaction to him.

"Oh, sweetheart," she gushed, grabbing onto his head and holding it firmly in place while he brought her to orgasm, her body shaking wildly and her breath quickening.

Stone felt the surge within him about to explode, but contained it till he could get inside his wife's body. Moving back up her, he planted kisses everywhere before reaching her mouth. She attacked his lips feverishly.

"Make love to me, Stone," she uttered.

Stone could barely hold back, so strong was his desire. Once his erection entered Joyce, he ejaculated almost instantly, but continued to propel himself into her for the joy of being intimate with the woman he loved.

Joyce clung to him, wrapping her legs around his buttocks, making love back to him as their damp bodies tingled with mutual satisfaction and the muted sounds of sex rang in Stone's ears.

After Joyce climaxed for a second time, Stone pulled himself out of her and lay next to her as they held each other. He felt temporary relief from the stresses of the job. And great satisfaction in knowing that someone was always there for him, no matter what.

Joyce was always only too happy to give him that reassurance.

CHAPTER 23

"Hold my calls, Jean," Beverly directed her secretary over the speakerphone, then she clicked it off.

Sitting across from her desk was Maxine Crawford. She was conservatively dressed in an expensive mint-colored skirt suit and wore very little makeup but was still stunning. Her ebony box braids were gathered into a long ponytail and hung to the side.

Beverly felt slightly in awe of the judge's widow, physically speaking, though she hardly wanted to be in her shoes otherwise. She had asked Maxine to come in to routinely go over some of the details of her assault and witness to her husband's execution.

She met Maxine's pretty brown eyes. "Can I get you some coffee?"

"Yes, thank you." Maxine smiled faintly.

Beverly headed toward the coffeepot in the corner of the office where Jean made fresh coffee every morning. "Sugar . . . cream?"

"Just cream."

Beverly made the two coffees, handing Maxine one before retreating back to her desk chair. She wondered briefly what Maxine would do with herself now that her husband was dead. There was no indication that she had an outside career and there were no children to care for at home. Not that she would be hurting for money. Beverly imagined that Judge Crawford had probably left her a great deal of it between his pension, insurance, and investments. As she was only in her mid-thirties, Beverly suspected that Maxine might well marry again someday and even have children, if she wished.

"The case will be going to trial soon," Beverly began. "I know this isn't easy, but we need to go over again what happened that night."

Maxine nodded, as if she had braced herself in advance for what was to come.

"You and Judge Crawford were in bed when Rafael Santiago broke in. Correct?"

"Yes."

Beverly glanced at her notepad, though she already knew what she wanted to say. "And what were you doing?"

Maxine swallowed. "My husband and I were making love," she replied without apology.

Beverly got a visual image, even if she wished she hadn't. "Did your husband use a condom?" Again she knew the answer, as Judge Crawford's semen was found inside her vagina and anus, but Beverly had to go through the motions. If at all competent, she fully expected the defense to try every trick in the book to paint the defendant in a brighter shade. That included going after the Crawfords, their sex life, and anything else that could cast doubt on the events of that night.

Maxine looked Beverly straight in the eye and answered succinctly. "No. Sheldon never used them; there was no need to. He'd had a vasectomy years ago."

"I see." That certainly had not come to light, Beverly thought. Had his first wife not wanted children? Or was it his choice? She couldn't imagine being without at least one child. Jaime made it all worthwhile. Beverly was sure she would have had more children, had she married again. Grant had never spoken of having children of his own. Why? Did he not want any . . . ever?

Did she really want any more at this point in her life?

Beverly refocused on the business at hand. "Was there anyone else in the house that you know of before you went to bed?"

Maxine pursed her lips. "No."

"Did anyone else have a key to your house?"

"Just the housekeeper," Maxine answered.

Beverly touched her nose. "And how often did she come over?"

"Three times a week."

"Did she come that day?"

"We gave her the day off." Maxine's eyes turned thoughtful.

Which may have saved her life, thought Beverly. Or saved her from some other type of victimization. Unless her absence was part of some larger conspiracy to commit murder.

"And her name is?" Beverly asked.

"Josephine Canseco."

"How long has she worked for you?"

"Josephine worked for Sheldon for many years before we married." Maxine regarded Beverly sharply. "If you're suggesting that she had anything to do with this—"

"Not at all," Beverly responded quickly, the implication being that because she was Hispanic, the housekeeper could have known Santiago. Did she? "Just getting all the facts straight." And trying to make sure this was not an inside job, Beverly thought. "Do you normally lock your doors when you're at home?"

"Yes . . ."

"But not always?" Beverly thought she detected hesitation in her voice.

Maxine tightened her jaw. "Who locks their doors *every* time they're home?"

I do, for one, Beverly told herself. But she knew that Jaime was guilty of leaving their doors unlocked from time to time, if not outright open, in spite of her admonitions. Did that make it any more excusable?

"What about the windows?" There had been no sign of forced entry.

Maxine shot her a fierce look. "Are you blaming us for what that man did?"

"Of course not," Beverly tried to reassure her, even if it may have come off that way. "We just need to figure out how the suspect entered your house when there's no indication that he *broke* in."

Maxine seemed to tremble as she put the coffee mug to her mouth. "I really couldn't say," she uttered. "He just seemed to come out of the woodwork."

"Could you or Judge Crawford have inadvertently left a door unlocked or a window open that night?" Beverly asked straightforwardly, dismissing the woodwork theory. It was either that, or Santiago had a key for easy entry.

"Sometimes we opened the windows a crack to let air in," Maxine admitted, pausing. "We didn't always close them before we went to bed."

Beverly wrote this down. She tasted her coffee. "When did you first become aware someone was in your bedroom?"

Maxine cringed. "When I heard the first popping sound and felt my husband react."

"You mean the shot?" Beverly asked, to be sure.

"Yes."

"While you were making love?"

"Yes." Maxine's voice quavered.

Beverly favored her. "And what did you do?"

"There was not much I could do underneath my husband's weight!" Maxine made a face. "I screamed, and was terrified."

"I'm sure you were," Beverly said, speaking as a woman, at the thought of being trapped in an unenviable situation. "Then you heard a second popping sound or shot?"

"Yes."

"What happened next?" Beverly played with her pen, hating to make the victim go through this again but not wanting to miss anything that could be important later on.

Maxine was glass-eyed as she said, "Sheldon somehow managed to crawl out of bed with two bullets in him. He tried to get his gun from the nightstand. But *he* shot him again point-blank. This time fatally—" Her voice broke.

"What then?" Beverly knew the defense would be even more demanding of the explicit details. *I hate this part of the preparatory process.*

"I thought I was going to *die!*" Maxine rolled her eyes, as if she couldn't believe she was still in one piece, alive and well, all things considered. "Why didn't that bastard just kill me, too?"

"I don't know," Beverly answered honestly. She often asked herself the same thing when one person was killed and another that could testify against the perpetrator was spared. Was it divine intervention? Or total stupidity on the part of the assailant? Had it been Rafael Santiago's wish that Maxine suffer for the perceived sins of her husband? Beverly sighed, leaning forward. "The important thing is that you were spared and Santiago will pay for his crimes."

"Will he?" Maxine gave her a doubtful look.

"Yes," Beverly tried to assure her. "We have a strong case against him, including your testimony. We'll make sure that Rafael Santiago never does to anyone else what he did to you." *Maybe he'll even get a taste of his own medicine once behind bars.*

Maxine could only hope that justice didn't turn a blind eye in this case. She wasn't sure if she could ever recover from the horrors she'd witnessed and experienced. Sheldon deserved better, no matter his faults. So did she. But there was no going back. Whatever the future held, she would have to deal with it and try not to let it break her completely.

Beverly regarded Maxine thoughtfully before saying, "I have to ask you a few questions about the attack on you."

Maxine dabbed at her eyes, though there were no tears. "I understand."

"Was there forced vaginal penetration?"

"Yes," she mumbled.

"Did he use a condom?" Again Beverly already knew the answer, given the evidence her attacker left behind.

"No." Maxine fidgeted.

"Did he sodomize you?" Beverly gazed across the desk.

"Yes," Maxine's voice cracked. She thought about the sex acts she'd had with Sheldon beforehand. They had often experimented in trying to keep their sex life exciting. It pained her to think of how such acts had turned ugly when forced upon her.

"Was there oral copulation?" Beverly asked.

Maxine struggled for words. "Yes."

Beverly took a moment before proceeding. "Was Santiago holding the gun the entire time he was assaulting you?"

"I think so . . ."

"Were you in fear of your life throughout the ordeal?"

"Yes—I fully expected him to shoot me afterward." Maxine wrung her hands.

"Did you ever try to stop him from hurting you?" Beverly had to ask.

Resentment flooded Maxine's eyes. "What the hell was I supposed to do to make that happen?" she challenged icily. "The bastard had just killed my husband. I did whatever he wanted me to do to stay alive. I had no other choice!"

"Of course you didn't," conceded Beverly, feeling like the enemy rather than the one person who could put Rafael Santiago away. Would she have done anything different had she been in her shoes? *I hope I never have to find out.* "Would you like some more coffee?"

Maxine moved her head swiftly from side to side. "I just want this to be over with as soon as possible."

"I understand," Beverly told her with empathy. "But it can't be—not until the man who did this to you and Judge Crawford is held accountable for his actions. And we need your testimony to make that happen."

Maxine gave a nod. "I know," she murmured.

Beverly composed herself. "Was he wearing anything on his hands?"

"Gloves."

"What type of gloves?"

"Leather."

"Did he remove his clothes during the attack?"

"Only his pants." Maxine gave her a sideways glance.

"What type of pants were those?"

"Jeans, I think."

Beverly noted this. "What about his underwear?"

"He wasn't wearing any," Maxine responded in an undertone.

"Were there any distinguishing marks you noticed on his body?" Beverly asked.

Maxine closed her eyes. "He had a scar on his thigh."

"Left or right thigh?"

"Right."

"Any tattoos?"

Maxine froze, envisioning this. "There was one . . ."

"And where was that?"

Maxine hesitated. "Below his waist—where his pubic hair would be."

Beverly raised an eyebrow. "Are you saying Santiago's pubic hair was shaved?"

Maxine nodded.

This certainly hadn't come out before for some reason, thought Beverly. What an odd place for a man to shave and put a tattoo. Then again, there seemed to be no place on a body that was off-limits these days. So why not the pubic area?

She looked at Maxine. "Can you describe the tattoo?"

After a moment or two, Maxine answered, "It was some sort of reptile . . . like a lizard."

Beverly wrote that down. Was there something symbolic about having a lizard on your shaved pubic area? she mused.

"What color was it?"

"Green, red, and black," Maxine responded almost mechanically.

"Do you think you'd recognize the tattoo again if you saw it?"

"Yes," sighed Maxine, knowing it was something she couldn't forget even if she wanted to.

Good, thought Beverly. That could be critical in the absence of the murder weapon in further identifying the suspect as her attacker.

"Had you ever seen Rafael Santiago before that night?" Beverly asked while tasting her now-cold coffee.

Maxine pursed her lips. "No."

"You're sure?" Beverly pressed, not wanting to find out later that her knowledge of his anatomy came earlier. Not that she had any reason to disbelieve the victim's story.

"Yes," Maxine responded curtly.

Beverly swiveled her chair. "We're just about through, Maxine," she said, sounding like her physician. "Just need to ask you a few personal questions. You don't have to answer them, but the defense is likely to ask similar questions and the judge might permit him to. I just don't want any surprises."

"I have nothing to hide," Maxine insisted testily.

"Judge Crawford was quite a bit older than you," Beverly noted. "Why did you marry him?"

"Because I loved Sheldon, plain and simple." Maxine held her gaze. "Other men only wanted me for my body or what they thought I could give them. But never my mind and soul."

And Judge Crawford was different? Beverly pondered

skeptically. He married a woman twenty years his junior for her mind . . . and soul? Couldn't he have found someone closer to his own age who fit the bill? Or did it help that she happened to be beautiful as well?

But who am I to say it wasn't true?

Beverly met Maxine's eyes and asked, "Have you ever cheated on your husband?"

Maxine stared dourly at the question. "No! I was faithful to Sheldon till the end."

"Was he faithful to you as well?"

To this Maxine was not as quick to respond. "My husband is dead, for heaven's sake," she groaned. "What possible difference does it make?"

"Maybe none," Beverly conceded. "Or it could mean that Rafael Santiago had an accomplice in killing Judge Crawford. Even a woman," she pointed out. "It could have been blackmail. Or was motivated by revenge—"

"Sheldon was *not* having an affair!" Maxine's brow creased in two places. "We had our issues like everyone else, but infidelity wasn't one of them. Sheldon and I were happy together for the most part, no matter what anyone else chooses to think. I never gave him any reason to want to be with another woman."

Men don't always need a reason, Beverly told herself. Even if a wife was willing to have oral, anal, or any other sex act her man chose to engage in. Sometimes variety, fantasy, and opportunity were more important to men than having a wife ready and waiting at home.

But was Maxine always ready and waiting for the judge's sexual desires? Beverly wondered. Or, for that matter, her own?

And was Sheldon Crawford really as faithful as Maxine claimed? Or could he have gotten hooked up with a woman who turned out to be the mistress from hell? With Rafael Santiago as her partner in crime, complete with a lizard tattoo where his pubic hair should be . . .

In any event, it was obvious to Beverly that Maxine's

mind and soul alone were insufficient for her marriage to Judge Crawford to work. The real question was whether or not the couple's sexual appetite played any role in the judge's murder and his wife's sexual victimization.

"I think that's all I need for now," Beverly told the woman she expected to be her star witness against Rafael Santiago.

After she showed Maxine out, promising to keep her informed on the progress of the case, Beverly asked Jean to get Walter McIntosh on the line.

Ten minutes later Beverly watched as the ex-cop turned DA's office investigator strolled into her office.

"Nice of you to invite me over, Beverly," he said dryly, flopping onto a leather side chair.

Walter McIntosh was forty-one, around six-two, and had no neck to speak of. His dark blond hair had receded and was pulled back into a tiny ponytail. Beneath thick brows, gray-blue eyes gazed across Beverly's desk at her.

"You're always welcome here, Walter," she said with a teasing smile.

"Yeah?" He grinned from one side of his face. "Is that why I practically have to bribe Jean to talk to you?"

Beverly laughed. They had always had a good-humored working relationship. Though he had been careful not to cross the line, she suspected that Walter was attracted to her. Unfortunately he was not her type for romance. Not to mention she'd heard that he went after everything in a skirt and heels.

"So what's up?" asked Walter, lifting a brow.

"I need you to do a background investigation."

"Okay." He rubbed his aquiline nose. "So who am I supposed to be investigating?"

Beverly's throat went dry. "I want to find out everything I can about the late Judge Sheldon Crawford *and* Maxine Crawford."

Walter scratched his pate. "Everything? That covers a lot of territory. Can you be a bit more specific?"

She had anticipated this, but it still didn't make it any easier to dig for possible dirt on a dead judge and his victimized wife, who Beverly needed as a friendly rather than a hostile witness. Better to know up front anything that could derail or otherwise call into question what seemed to be a solid case against Rafael Santiago, she thought.

"I'd like to find out about their sexual histories, financial histories, friendships, acquaintances, enemies, and any other information or innuendoes about their lives."

Walter jerked his head back. "Wow! Is that all?" He chuckled uneasily. "What *exactly* are you hoping to find in their sullied laundry? Or shouldn't I ask?"

Beverly wondered the same. "I guess I'll know when, and if, I find it."

Walter put his large hands on the desk and peered at her. "In case you don't already know, Judge Crawford was a powerful man in this town," he warned. "Asking the wrong questions about his life, professional or otherwise, could bring us *both* down."

Beverly got the picture. Judge Crawford's stature was such that Walter considered the assignment risky to his own job, along with perhaps his welfare.

And mine, should I step on the wrong toes, she told herself.

"I'm not looking to trash the judge's good name," Beverly promised assuredly. "Or his widow's. I only want to be sure that Rafael Santiago acted alone in committing the crimes against the Crawfords."

Walter's forehead wrinkled. "Are you thinking this was some kind of conspiracy to commit murder?"

"Not saying anything of the sort," she stressed, out loud anyhow. "But anything's possible. I just want to go into the trial knowing everything my opponent knows." And maybe a little extra for good measure.

There was no reason to believe that Conrad Ortega would go to any unusual lengths for a client such as Santiago, thought Beverly. On the other hand, why wouldn't Ortega try and use this golden opportunity to steal a victory any way he could? Even a hard-fought loss could do wonders for his career.

Whereas to Beverly there was no substitute for winning. She knew her own career advancement could rest on the outcome of a trial.

This trial.

As a result, she preferred to cover all the bases. Even those that may lie outside the base path.

"I'll see what I can find out," Walter told her. "I just hope you know what you could be getting yourself into."

What might I be getting myself into beyond the obvious— building a case for trial? Beverly wondered. Did Walter know more than he was letting on?

She considered whether there could actually be some sort of conspiracy against Judge Crawford, who'd had more than his share of critics in spite of his reputation as a no-nonsense, by-the-book judge. A reputation that could have resulted in murder and a brutal sexual assault.

Beverly shuddered at the thought that moving ahead could open up a Pandora's box. It was a risk she was willing to take, considering the alternative of allowing a rapist-killer to walk and justice to be denied.

CHAPTER 24

Rafael Santiago was brought into the room by an armed guard, who looked to O'Dell like he had just gotten out of high school, with a little goatee and a few freckles on a broad nose. They seemed to be getting younger each year, the detective thought, though bulkier. He wondered if the guard was taking steroids.

"Just need a few minutes with him—alone," O'Dell told the guard.

"What are you gonna do with him?" The guard wrinkled his nose suspiciously. "Or don't I wanna know?"

O'Dell gave a slight smile. "You should ask, man. If you didn't, it could cost you your job." He ran a hand across his chin, casting an eye toward Santiago. "Don't worry, I'm not going to beat the crap out of him. I don't need to have the brass all over my black ass telling me I've violated his damned civil rights."

The guard grinned with relief and went into the hall, closing the door behind him.

The suspect, who was handcuffed and shackled, flashed O'Dell a smirk, which annoyed him. He didn't like killers, plain and simple. Especially killers of judges—the men and women who took assholes like Santiago off the streets and put them where they belonged.

He also didn't like men who had their way with women by force. O'Dell considered such men to be spineless, the scum of the earth.

But he wasn't willing to test the waters with this creep by smashing his face in. It wasn't worth it.

"What you want, man?" Santiago asked fearlessly, his thin brows knitted.

"Not much, asshole," said O'Dell. "Just need to see a certain part of your anatomy."

Santiago laughed instinctively. "You a queer, man, or what?"

O'Dell got into his face, growling. "You wish, you son of a bitch! You'll get your chance soon enough to have a *daddy*. I'm way out of your league. Now get them pants down, and fast, or I'll do it for you."

Santiago smiled wryly as he pulled his orange prison pants down to his ankles. He was wearing no underwear. He grabbed himself, half erect, and pointed it toward O'Dell, as if it were a garden hose.

"You want some of this, huh, man?" he taunted the detective. "Come and get it." He began caressing himself, grinning salaciously.

O'Dell glared disgustedly. He felt like wiping that grin off Santiago's face, but thought better. He grabbed the prick's cuffed wrists tightly, lifting them over the inmate's head, and regarded the area above Santiago's penis. Just as Maxine Crawford had indicated, damned if he didn't have a colorful lizard tattoo in place of pubic hair.

"What's with the tattoo?" he questioned. "That part of the Latino brotherhood in the pen?"

"Just freedom of expression, man," Santiago responded tartly. "Nothing more. Why, you want one, *brotha* . . . ?"

"Not a chance." O'Dell squeezed his wrists till Santiago winced in pain. "The woman you assaulted will have to live with that damned reptile for the rest of her life—and so will you!"

O'Dell released him and stepped away, thinking it was another surefire indication that they had the right man. *You just sealed your fate, Santiago.*

"If it was up to me," he said out loud, "they would castrate you first *without* anesthesia—so you could see how Maxine Crawford felt when you raped, orally copulated, and sodomized her—then put the lethal drugs in your veins."

Santiago laughed crudely. "It ain't gonna happen, man. No matter what the bitch is sayin', me and my lizard friend here are innocent."

"Like hell you are." O'Dell noted the half-inch scar on his right thigh. The judge's widow had also identified the scar. Probably the result of some gangbanging, he thought. "Put your clothes back on, asshole," he ordered. "I can't stand the sickening sight of you."

"Whatever you say, man," chuckled Santiago, lifting his pants. "We through?"

"Yeah, *we through*," mimicked O'Dell. He called the guard and ordered photographs to be taken of the suspect's pubic area and right leg. They would come in handy during the trial.

O'Dell took the nearly sixty-mile drive to Folsom State Prison. He parked in the visitor parking lot and then braved a downpour before getting inside.

He used his identification to gain clearance to Cell Block D, which Rafael Santiago had called home for twelve years. O'Dell knew that the one thing that kept prisoners going during long stretches behind bars was making grandiose plans for when they were free. He was betting that a vengeful-minded Santiago couldn't resist bragging about what he planned to do to Judge Crawford and his pretty young wife when he got out.

If he had told anyone, thought O'Dell, it would likely be

the person he roomed with for more than eight years during his stint.

Nkaki Ahmad entered the room, a curious grin on his face. The thirty-eight-year-old African-American was Muslim, brawny, and shaven bald. He was serving life for beating a man to death in a bar fight.

"Do I know you?" he asked, scratching his forehead while handcuffed.

"Detective O'Dell, Homicide, Eagles Landing PD." O'Dell approached him tentatively. A guard was outside, but he wasn't worried that the prisoner would attack him unprovoked. Not when he was in cuffs and had stayed out of trouble behind bars.

As it was, his beef wasn't with Ahmad, thought O'Dell. Right now, he needed his help.

Ahmad flipped his eyelids sarcastically. "That don't mean nothin' to me, man," he said acerbically.

O'Dell bit his lip. "I just want to talk to you, that's all . . ."

Ahmad narrowed his bulging, black eyes. "About what?"

"Rafael Santiago."

Ahmad reacted. "What about him?"

"I know you were cellmates," said O'Dell. "And you could be cellmates again . . ."

Ahmad twisted his lips meditatively. "Yeah, I heard that he offed a judge and had some fun with his old lady. So what's that gotta do with me?"

"I was hoping you could tell me if Santiago ever talked about what he was going to do when he got out?"

A frown creased Ahmad's brow. "You mean snitch on my Latino brother?"

"I wasn't aware he was your brother, man," O'Dell said curtly. "But I do know that you two didn't always get along. In fact, I heard that Santiago cost you some time in the hole on more than one occasion."

"So what?" growled Ahmad. "That don't make me want to tell you nothin', man."

O'Dell felt his ire being tested. *Be cool, man. You can still reach him.* With eyes narrowed, he moved a bit closer and said, "A judge is dead and his wife was sexually assaulted. We got enough to know that Santiago is the man who committed these crimes. I could really use your help in telling me everything that he ever told you about this . . ."

Ahmad stepped back and thought about it for a moment. "If I did happen to remember an interesting conversation or two between me and Rafael about the judge," he offered, "what's in it for me, man?"

O'Dell knew he had him intrigued. Now he had to reel him in like a big fish in the water.

"I'm not going to kid you, Nkaki," he told him as the setup, "there's not going to be any reduction of your sentence. The information isn't *that* valuable." He watched the hope seem to deflate from him like hot air. "But I do know that you've been trying to get conjugal visits with your girlfriend. I believe her name is Evangeline? What if I were to help arrange that for you? Could take some of the steam out of these cold, lonely nights."

"Yeah, it could." Ahmad sat down, ready to talk.

O'Dell turned on a small recorder. "I'm listening."

"Santiago couldn't stop talking about the judge," Ahmad said, looking the detective straight in the eye. "He blamed Crawford and that prosecutor for sending him to prison, claiming he never got a fair trial."

Grant Nunez tried that case, recalled O'Dell. Obviously he was next on Santiago's hit list. Fortunately for the prosecutor, Santiago was no longer in a position to carry out his threats. Still, O'Dell imagined that Nunez had been spooked by Crawford's death. Could he have known he would inherit the judge's spot on the bench once Sheldon Crawford had been removed permanently?

O'Dell thought about that for a moment, and considered Beverly Mendoza's involvement with Nunez and the potential for a conflict of interest in the Santiago case.

"Did Santiago ever specifically threaten the judge?" O'Dell peered at the inmate.

Ahmad grinned. "Yeah. He said the judge would get what was coming to him just as soon as he was released. Said he would see to that." He rubbed his head. "Even said the Mrs. would be his for the taking . . ."

O'Dell groaned. "Would you testify to that in court?"

Ahmad hesitated. "Hey, man, telling *you* is one thing. But sayin' it in court is a whole different story."

"It's the only way the information can be useful," O'Dell said, keeping the pressure on.

In truth, an affidavit might suffice, he knew. But it wouldn't carry the same weight as direct testimony. And even that would be viewed with much skepticism, considering the source. O'Dell wasn't sure he believed one word from Ahmad himself. Yet it made sense. Guys like Santiago always ran off at the mouth, too stupid to consider that it might one day come back to bite them in the ass.

Ahmad seemed to get the picture. "Oh, what the hell," he said. "I don't owe Santiago a damned thing. He made his own bed, let 'im rot in it. I'll testify, so long as you hold up your end of the bargain."

A small concession, O'Dell thought, planning to call in a few markers.

Small indeed, if it helped convict Rafael Santiago.

CHAPTER 25

The Westside Deli was a regular hangout for attorneys and hip young judges. Beverly agreed to meet K. Conrad Ortega there as a courtesy and to see what type of strategy he might employ in his defense of Rafael Santiago. She made her way through the lunchtime crowd, finding Ortega way at the back. She wondered if he had deliberately made her walk this far as a show of intimidation. Or perhaps it was manipulation?

Ortega stood when he saw her. "Ms. Mendoza. Thanks for coming."

"Couldn't resist," Beverly admitted, regarding the chubby attorney in a tight blue suit. "And please call me Beverly." It seemed less formal that way. Which was always strategically advantageous outside of the courtroom.

He flashed her a deceptive smile. "Call me K or Conrad," he said. "Take your pick."

"I pick Conrad," she said, shaking his hand, which felt clammy.

"Heard a lot of good things about you, Beverly." He showed his whitened teeth.

"You shouldn't believe everything you hear, Conrad," she said wryly. "I don't."

He laughed uneasily. "I'll try and remember that."

They sat, studied menus, and ordered. Beverly went with the corned beef sandwich and grilled veggies, while Ortega had a ham sandwich and fries.

"You know that you've got the wrong man?" Ortega looked serious across the table.

"Right." Beverly rolled her eyes as she sipped on a mocha. "Santiago's about as innocent as John Wilkes Booth was of murdering Abraham Lincoln."

Ortega chuckled while wrinkling his nose. "Don't you think that's getting a bit carried away, comparing Santiago to Booth? Judge Crawford was hardly Abraham Lincoln, Counselor."

"Does that make his life any less worthy?" Beverly challenged the attorney. "As far as I'm concerned, your client and Booth are cut from the same cloth. Both are guilty of heinous, cold-blooded murder. In fact," she added for effect, "Santiago may be even more atrocious. He added rape, sodomy, and oral copulation to his list of bad deeds."

Ortega's gaze betrayed acrimony. "My client is not guilty of the charges!" His voice boomed. "He was at home with his mother when the crime occurred."

Beverly dropped her mouth, incredulous. "You really believe that? *Please.* Give me a break! We've got an eyewitness named Maxine Crawford who has positively identified your client as the man who sexually attacked her and shot her husband to death."

"But what *else* have you got?" he questioned. "You've got no other witnesses to place Santiago at the scene. No murder weapon, which means the *real* killer probably has it. And you have no conclusive physical evidence linking my client to the crime."

Beverly kept her cool. She understood how the game worked, aware that this was leading to something. Didn't mean she had to bite.

"The physical evidence will come," she promised, "just as soon as the DNA results are in. And we do have one important piece of evidence that is irrefutable. Your client has a lizard tattoo where his pubic hair used to be. Now I seriously doubt that Maxine Crawford could have just conjured up that interesting little detail about your client's physical makeup. Do you?"

She watched Ortega squirm. "What kind of deal are you willing to make?" he asked tensely.

Beverly pretended to think about it. "How about a plea of guilty in the first degree to murder, rape, sodomy, and oral copulation?" She let that sink in. "And, oh yes, let's not forget breaking and entering."

Ortega shook his head, smiling grimly. "Give me some slack, Beverly. I like second-degree murder and second-degree sexual battery, dropping the other charges. This will put Santiago away for a good while and give him the chance for a life afterward."

A laugh escaped Beverly before she could bring it under control. "You're really good, Ortega. Maybe Santiago should have thought about getting a life before he took away someone else's and damaged another in ways he cannot imagine. To suggest such a plea bargain with such a straight face is outrageous."

Ortega bristled. "Frankly, it's the best I would even offer the man," he said unapologetically, "considering I believe my client's being railroaded."

"By whom?" she asked peevishly. "Definitely not me! The facts speak for themselves." Beverly shot him a hard look. "My advice to you, Counselor, is that if you believe your client is *truly* innocent, then prove it in court. No deals from my office!"

Indignation spread across Ortega's puffy face like a rash. "If that's the way you want to play it . . ."

"It's not a game and definitely not play," Beverly made clear. "It's the way the system works when someone commits a shocking and despicable crime and there's an air-tight case." Now she only hoped she didn't have to eat her words.

Their sandwiches came. But by then they both seemed to have lost their appetites.

On Saturday Beverly spent some quality time with Jaime. She had resolved to make sure her career never caused her to lose sight of the most important things in life. Jaime was at the top of that list, followed by her father.

And Grant was not too far behind. It seemed that he had left quite an impression on Jaime, though her son hadn't come right out and admitted it. Now she hoped to build upon it, for all their sakes.

After going to see a movie in the afternoon, they went to a Barnes & Noble bookstore. Beverly had always been an avid reader. She had managed to instill a love for books in Jaime at an early age. He picked out the latest Harry Potter novel and several of his favorite mysteries, while she chose a few audiobook selections and some nonfiction hardcover titles.

Next they went to a music store across the street, where Jaime spent some time listening to the latest hip-hop sounds. This gave Beverly a chance to browse through jazz CDs and sip on a cafe latte.

On the way home, they stopped at Burger King. It wasn't exactly Beverly's first choice, but it was Jaime's turn to decide where they ate out, so she didn't complain.

While nibbling on a garden salad, Beverly couldn't help but notice the Hispanic man seated at the table near the window. He looked strangely familiar. When he glanced her way, she quickly shifted her eyes elsewhere.

Now where have I seen that face . . . ?

Then it came to her with alarming clarity. He bore a striking resemblance to Rafael Santiago! So much so that the man could have been his brother. He may have been a trifle shorter and a few pounds heavier, if that, but if Beverly hadn't known better she would have sworn that they were one and the same.

But how is that possible?

Santiago's background file showed that he was an only child. Could the records have been mistaken?

Beverly glanced at the man again. This time he was already looking her way, as if he knew exactly who she was and wanted her to know it. Uneasiness swept over Beverly like a bad cold.

Could he possibly be the man who murdered Judge Crawford? she wondered. The one who then viciously sexually assaulted his wife?

Had Maxine identified the *wrong* man, as Conrad Ortega had insinuated?

Was he mocking her as he chewed on a double cheeseburger?

Beverly took a deep breath and turned to Jaime. He was too preoccupied with his ketchup-coated fries and chicken sandwich to notice much of anything else.

When she turned again to look at the man, he was gone. Vanished like a thief in the night.

Now she wondered if he had really been there.

And, if so, had he really looked as much like Rafael Santiago as she had imagined? Or had she unintentionally prejudged him as a Latino male around the same age and build?

Could Maxine have done the same? Fingered an innocent man . . . ?

Stop it! Beverly ordered herself, wiping her lips with a napkin. *Have you lost your mind?*

Of course they had the right man in jail. Maxine had identified him *twice.* He also fit the part as an ex-con who had once threatened the judge's life. Even the DNA evidence they had thus far pointed squarely to Rafael Santiago as being at the scene of the crime. Not to mention the tattoo. There was simply no room now for doubts.

Was there?

She finished off the salad, washing it down with apple juice, then waited for Jaime to finish his meal.

"This is so cool," sang Jaime in the car, listening to a CD with a collection of Latin hip-hop artists he had bought with his own savings. "Wait till Paco hears them. He's gonna go wild!"

Beverly laughed. "Let's hope not too wild." It was good to see Jaime happy again. She hoped it was a sign that he was starting to accept life for what it was and make the most of it.

She checked the rearview mirror. It seemed as if the same car had been trailing them from the restaurant. Was it her imagination working overtime again? Or an assistant district attorney sensing danger like a deer?

When Beverly looked again, the car was gone, replaced by another. She breathed a sigh of relief. *Guess my mind was playing tricks on me. Get a grip, girl!*

"Do you think you'll marry Grant someday?" Jaime inquired out of the blue, snapping Beverly out of her reverie.

She elevated a brow, surprised to hear him ask since he was just coming to terms with her dating Grant. *Where did that come from?*

"We're a long ways from going down that road," she prefaced. "Grant and I really like each other, but we haven't really talked about the future. Right now, we're just taking things one day at a time."

Still, the mere subject of marriage got Beverly to thinking. She certainly wasn't opposed to marrying again, if both parties loved each other and wanted to commit to a lifetime together. Even if the idea of such a commitment as a single mom and thriving attorney scared her. Then there was the reality that Grant had not even told her he loved her, much less indicated he had any desire to tie the knot again himself. So did that mean they both had cold feet? Or simply weren't ready to go down that road yet in their relationship?

"Do you think he'd make a good father?" asked Jaime.

"Yes, I think so," answered Beverly, as though being tested before Jaime gave his blessing for such a possibility.

As it was, Grant did seem like good father material, even without direct experience. She supposed that some things came naturally. You either had what it took or your didn't.

"Not like my real father," fumed Jaime, as if he could read her mind. "Why'd he have to be such a jerk?"

Beverly eyed her son sadly. "If I knew the answer to that question, I never would have gotten involved with him in the first place."

"I wish you hadn't." Jaime stared out the window and Beverly could tell that he was crying.

She touched his face lovingly. "I'm very glad I did, Jaime. He gave me the one thing that made it all worthwhile. You."

Slowly Jaime faced her and said emotionally, "I love you, Mom."

"I love you too, honey!" Beverly blinked back tears.

That night, after Jaime had gone to bed, the phone rang. Beverly answered it in bed, where she had been looking over notes on the Santiago case.

It was Grant. "Hi, gorgeous. Didn't wake you up, did I?"

"No." Beverly felt a tingle in hearing his voice for the first time in several days. With his move to the judge's chambers, Grant had apparently been too busy to call or come by. In all fairness, she, too, had been inundated with work.

"Just wanted to hear a friendly voice," he said.

"Oh, is that all?" she joked.

"Well, also a sexy voice." His intonation was low-pitched and intimate.

"Then you probably called the *wrong* number," Beverly laughed. She had never considered her voice particularly sexy. She was too soft-spoken.

Grant chuckled warmly. "I don't think so. Fact is, I've missed you like hell, Bev."

"You have a funny way of showing it." Her body was becoming moist all over.

"My apologies. Making this transition has been a hell of a

lot more difficult than I imagined. There are procedures and initiations that have taken up every available moment."

Beverly realized she was being selfish in hoping to monopolize his time. And trying to see if he truly was the marrying and father type. After all, Judge Nunez now had a higher authority to answer to—his court.

"You're forgiven." Beverly's cadence was one of understanding and happiness in knowing Grant really did care about her.

"How's the Santiago case coming along?" Grant inquired.

She filled him in on the mundane details. "His attorney knows Santiago's in a no-win situation," she said confidently.

"Heard you grilled Maxine Crawford pretty good." Grant took a deep breath.

"Oh, really?" Beverly adjusted her position on the antique brass bed. Was it a wrong impression, or did he seem to take this personally? "And where did you get your information, Mr. Nunez?"

"I have my sources." He gave an uneasy chuckle.

Which could have been anyone from the DA himself on down the line, she realized. But what difference did it make? He was not part of the enemy camp.

So why do I suddenly feel as though he is?

"Well, if you must know, I didn't exactly grill Maxine. She's not a hostile witness and we're on the same page in our desire to win a conviction in this case. Hope that meets with your approval, Your Honor."

"Not trying to tell you how to do your job, baby," Grant said tonelessly. "But you don't want your chief witness to turn hostile because you've been digging too far into her and the judge's personal lives."

"I didn't realize I was doing that much digging." She sat up, annoyed at him. Had he been talking to Walter McIntosh? "I haven't treated Maxine Crawford any differently than I have any other witness-victims."

Have I?

Had she unwittingly been too intrusive in Maxine's life and victimization? Beverly wondered. Was the pressure of winning this case starting to get to her? Even to the point of imagining earlier today that she had actually seen a Rafael Santiago clone?

"Why your great interest, Grant?" Beverly asked boldly, sensing something here that she couldn't quite put a finger on. "I thought you gave up your job as Deputy District Attorney."

"I have," he said, sounding ill at ease. "No interest really, other than not wanting to see you blow this case."

She crossed her legs, suspicious. "Who says I will?"

"No one."

Obviously he had brought it up for some reason, Beverly thought. Maybe he'd care to share his thoughts.

"What is it you're not telling me, Grant?"

"Nothing," he claimed.

"I think it's *something*," she countered. "Whatever's going on, I'd like to know. Please . . ." She assumed he hadn't been sworn to secrecy by whomever. Or maybe she shouldn't assume anything?

Grant took a deep breath. "All right, but you never heard this from me," he instructed. "Dean Sullivan, whose friendship with Judge Crawford goes way back, does not want any pressure put on Maxine Crawford to answer questions that are better left unanswered."

"Such as . . . ?"

"Such as any that do not pertain *directly* to this case."

"I see." Beverly was not so sure she really did. She was being told indirectly to back off of the harsh questioning of her own star witness. Why? For fear that it might somehow expose Judge Crawford's soiled laundry? Maxine's? Or someone else's? Perhaps Dean Sullivan himself had something to hide, she mused.

"Now don't get all bent out of shape over this, Beverly," said Grant, seemingly intent on smoothing over the waters. "There are no dark figures conspiring against you or working to conceal evidence. If you stick to the job at hand in going after Rafael Santiago—the man we all want to see go down for the judge's murder—you'll be just fine."

And what if I do go further than the job at hand? thought Beverly, unnerved. Would she be replaced in the trial? Or fired from the DA's office?

Do I really want to test the waters by stepping on the wrong toes here?

"I think I understand," she acquiesced. Get a conviction of Santiago and forget about the Crawfords' private affairs.

Beverly decided that she gained nothing from pursuing this over and beyond what was necessary to win her case. Except maybe trouble that she did not need.

"I've missed touching your body," Grant cooed desirously, adeptly changing the subject.

Did he really? Or was this his way of diverting her attention?

Don't be silly, she thought. Why shouldn't he miss her body? She missed his hard body to the point that thinking about Grant made Beverly quake with longing.

"Just how much have you missed it?" she challenged him.

"Enough to almost taste." Grant made an erotic noise into the phone that gave Beverly shivers of delight as her imagination conjured up vivid images of him doing just that.

"I think that sounds mouthwatering." She suddenly felt in a playful, intimate mood.

"I agree." Grant hummed lasciviously. "So what are you wearing right now?"

"An oversized nightshirt," she answered, sure he'd hoped she would say a sexy silk nightie, or maybe nothing at all.

"I'd love to put my head under that nightshirt right now," he said wistfully, "and go on an exploratory journey that I guarantee would leave you breathless."

"Umm . . ." Beverly found herself already breathless at the mere prospect.

"Then when I had you all hot and bothered, I would take you in my arms, kiss you like you've never been kissed before, and make passionate love to you the whole night through . . ."

Beverly gasped. The phone sex was turning her on and now she didn't want it to end there.

"This isn't fair, Grant," she murmured. "You should be here to put your words into actions! If we're quiet, Jaime would likely sleep right through whatever happened."

Grant breathed huskily. "I wish I could come over, baby, but I've got to get up early for a meeting. If we were together right now, that would be all but impossible. So I'm afraid I'll have to take a rain check."

Beverly frowned, feeling her libido sink like the *Titanic*. "Well, let's hope it rains soon," she said, biting back her wishes when smacked against reality.

"Oh it will," Grant promised. "You can count on it, Bev. By the way," he added with a catch to his voice, "did I ever mention that I think I've fallen in love with you?"

Before Beverly could answer, she heard the dial tone, leaving her to ponder the words all on her own.

So there, you've told her, Grant thought, sitting in his study sipping scotch. Where did they go from here? Would Beverly say the same to him when he was courageous enough to listen? What then?

Admittedly, he had acted impulsively in spilling out his declaration of love without regard to how to build upon it. Even if Beverly were to love him back, it didn't mean either of them were ready to walk down the aisle. But it would signify that they were firmly committed to making this work, whatever the future held. And Jaime would be a big part of that.

Grant's thoughts shifted back to the present. The last thing he wanted to do was apply any pressure on Beverly with respect to the Santiago case. But he knew that the deeper she dug, the more trouble she could make for herself and for him. He didn't want anything to come between them or the pursuit of justice. The lines could sometimes be blurred when it came to true justice, he realized, hoping his own choices didn't cross the line any more than necessary.

He sipped more scotch and mused, *The sooner Sheldon Crawford's murder and his wife's sexual assault are put behind them, the better for all parties concerned.* Getting a conviction against Rafael Santiago was key; then they could go from there.

Grant finished off the drink and headed up to bed for what he figured to be a sleepless night.

CHAPTER 26

Manuel followed them to the house, careful to keep his distance. Though located in the same city he lived in, it might just as well have been another country. The tree-lined block spoke of folks who had money, pension plans, stocks, bonds, and something left over for entertainment. He was sure the sweet-looking Latina had no trouble paying the bills and stashing the rest away for a rainy day. Probably to send her kid to some Ivy League school someday so he could go out and make even more money.

Manuel had watched them come into Burger King. The lady had captured his attention immediately. She had the slender and shapely, long-legged body type he liked. And the small, rounded breasts that didn't take away from the rest of her. Her brown hair was in a long ponytail, hanging temptingly on one side of her chest. Even her eyes—green like grass and calculating—captured his fancy. She wore tight jeans that showed her small ass move with every step she took, arousing him.

The boy was not nearly as interesting to him. He was

overweight and wearing a burgundy jogging suit and Nikes. He seemed in his element, stuffing his face as though it were a last meal.

Manuel had watched as they took their meals to a table. He walked to a nearby table and sat, careful to appear as if he had not even noticed them.

From what he could gather from their conversation, the Latina broad was some type of attorney and without a man. At least not one who lived with them. Her father was in some old folks home, having lost his damned mind.

She and the boy seemed to be at odds about the father's likelihood of survival beyond the year. They were more in tune regarding the boy's goal to make rap music or race cars, and also shared a desire to someday move to a newer, bigger house.

He listened with little interest beyond getting a handle on their situation and learning more specifics about *her*.

For a moment she honed in on him, as if recognizing an old friend. It made Manuel uncomfortable. He didn't want the bitch to get too cozy with his face. Not yet. When the time was right, she could look into his pretty coal eyes for as long as she wanted.

When she became preoccupied with the boy, he quietly slipped away.

He was waiting for them when they came out and followed as they drove off, careful to keep his distance. Manuel even allowed another car or two to pull in front of him when it seemed that the lady lawyer was on to him.

He was always one step ahead of everyone else. That was his key to survival and getting what he wanted—who he wanted.

The thought of doing her excited Manuel. She presented more of a challenge than the others. She was a classy broad. Smart. Educated. Sexy. Sensual.

Which made it all the more exciting.

He parked down the street as the car pulled into a driveway, watching as they went inside the house. Part of Manuel wanted to go in right now, do what he wanted with her, and make sure there were no witnesses left behind.

But he hadn't survived this long by taking foolish chances. Something told him that if there was no man there, she probably kept a piece in the house and knew how to use it.

Why tempt fate?

Especially when there was plenty of time to go after the classy bitch later. He would wait until he got to know more about her and her habits. Also, he could take a look inside the house sometime when they weren't there. That way there would be no surprises sprung on him when he came calling for her.

Manuel laughed and drove off just as casually as he had followed the lawyer and kid.

He knocked on the door, deciding on the spur of the moment to pay a visit to his kinfolk.

The door opened as if she were expecting someone else. Her aging face crinkled with alarm when she saw him.

"What are you doing here?"

Manuel grinned. "Now is that any way to greet your nephew, Auntie?" He kissed her creased cheek, walking past her.

She regarded him, a mixture of fear and curiosity in her tired eyes. "I want you outta here," she spat out, heavy on the native Cuban accent.

"Just came to see how you was doin', Auntie," he said sincerely. "You ain't looking so good these days . . ."

Worse than he had imagined she would look. Manuel wondered if it was something in the water. Or maybe the rodents that littered the barrio like they owned the place had infected her.

"Don't call me Auntie!" She dragged her feet his way. "We ain't related. Not anymore."

Manuel licked his lips. "We're always gonna be related, Auntie, like it or not!"

He glanced about at surroundings as familiar as they were foreign. It was once home for him. Now it was little more than a decrepit pit stop. Not like the Latina lawyer's crib.

Favoring the old lady, he grinned. "Not here to cause trouble, Auntie. Wanted to let you know that I'll be comin' around more to check on you. Especially since it don't look like nobody else is gonna do it."

She curled a lip. "Go to hell, Manuel!"

He grinned again. "Been there, done that. All Latinos have. You taught me as much."

"I'll call the police," she threatened.

"No you won't!" he dared her. "What can they do that the gringos haven't already done? They love to split up families. Especially Latino families. But you know all about that, don't you, Auntie?"

She was speechless, as if her wrinkled lips were sealed.

He grabbed her by her frail shoulders and kissed her hard on the mouth. "See you around, Auntie."

Manuel smiled from the side of his mouth at her trembling, flushed face before leaving, satisfied he'd accomplished what he came for.

CHAPTER 27

Doctor Amie Kwan, Assistant County Medical Examiner, performed the postmortem of Penelope Grijalva. Petite and in her late thirties, Amie had short, pitch-black hair that was curled around her ears. Big brown eyes sat behind plum-colored glasses.

"Ms. Grijalva died of strangulation," she said tersely to her audience, which included Detectives Palmer and Chang. Neither of them was heading this particular investigation, but they were very interested in the results of the autopsy. "She also has several stab wounds. Most occurred before death, but some after. Before she died, the victim had intercourse. There were small tears in and around the vagina, but it doesn't appear as though it was forced sex—or at least not against her will."

"How was she strangled?" Stone asked curiously.

"My guess is that someone strangled her with his or her bare hands." Amie held her small hands out to demonstrate. "It is also possible that some sort of cloth or rope could have been used, but that is unlikely based on the imprints on the victim's neck and lack of fibers found to substantiate such."

Stone felt like he was listening to the autopsy report on Adrienne Murray all over again—minus the rape and sodomy. But in this case, it was obvious that the victim, a known prostitute, voluntarily engaged in sexual relations before being killed by her client. He wondered if the john was a stranger. Or someone she knew. Perhaps a previous customer.

Stone asked Dr. Kwan, who had also performed Adrienne Murray's postmortem, "Are we talking about the same killer here, Doctor?"

She favored him, and said wryly, "I think that's for you detectives to determine."

"How about an educated guess?" Chang pressed her.

Amie touched her glasses thoughtfully. "Well, my professional opinion is that both women were killed and assaulted by the same man. DNA tests of the semen and pubic hairs taken from the victims will be analyzed and compared. Preliminary results should be available within forty-eight hours."

At about the time that the news spread like wildfire among local law enforcement agencies that a serial killer was likely on the loose, DNA preliminary results more or less confirmed it.

For Stone this was no longer the case of a missing person turned up dead, but the murders of two young women, murders that he took personally—particularly the first one. It could have been one of his daughters. His chief suspect was still Chuck Murray, though Stone suspected that if he was involved he probably didn't act alone. And if that were true, did it mean there were *two* serial killers out there preying on vulnerable women?

"I think I may have something worth checking out," Chang said, sticking his head in the door of Stone's office.

His body followed as Stone watched with interest from his desk. "Seems like Claudia Sosa, the manager of ELNC Systems, Inc., has been shacking up with a man named Manuel Gonzalez . . ."

Stone leaned forward. He was open to any possible leads, no matter how remote, that could be tied to Adrienne Murray's place of employment, where she was last seen prior to her death.

"Tell me about this Gonzalez." He looked up at his partner.

"The man has a criminal record a mile long," Chang informed him. "Mostly drug- and alcohol-related and one arrest for forcible rape. There was also an attempted murder charge, which was later dropped due to insufficient evidence."

Chang handed Stone a copy of Gonzalez's criminal record. It said that he was thirty-two years old, Hispanic, and had been arrested an incredible thirty-one times. These included arrests for driving under the influence, possession of a controlled substance, loitering, disorderly conduct, and petty theft. The rape charge was later dismissed in court when the victim refused to testify. In spite of the arrests, the man had served less than three years behind bars since the age of eighteen.

"What do you think?" Chang asked, hovering over the desk like a bear in search of food.

He didn't exactly fit the profile of a murderer, thought Stone. Much less a serial killer.

But then not all killers fit such a profile, and were still every bit as deadly.

And since they had no better suspects at the moment, apart from Chuck Murray, it seemed a good idea that they learn more about Manuel Gonzalez and his whereabouts on the night Adrienne Murray disappeared. As well as on the night when Penelope Grijalva met her death.

Standing, Stone said, "I think we'd better pay Claudia Sosa another visit and see if she can enlighten us a bit on her boyfriend."

* * *

The detectives entered the ELNC Systems, Inc. office, identified themselves, and were about to be directed to Claudia Sosa's office when Stone told the receptionist, "I think we can find the way."

Halfway there he told Chang, "Why don't you ask around, see what the other ladies know about Manuel Gonzalez. That way we can compare notes."

"Good idea," Chang muttered and went in the opposite direction.

When Stone reached the office, Claudia was already standing over her desk to greet him.

She waddled her way across the floor. "Detective Palmer, I believe . . . ?" she said, as if there was a prize for the correct answer.

Stone nodded. "Ms. Sosa."

They shook hands. He found her grip to be as strong as any man's and wondered if those hands worked out by strangling two women.

"Have you found out anything about Adrienne's death?" Claudia's voice was calm yet inquisitive.

"We're still looking into it," Stone said colorlessly. "I was hoping you might be able to answer some more questions that might lead us in the right direction."

"Sure," she said without fear. "Would you like to sit down?"

Stone thought about it for an instant, but decided it might give the wrong impression that this was more or less a social call. "I'll stand, thanks."

"All right." She fluttered false lashes, continuing to stand as well. "What is it you'd like to know? I'll see if I can be of assistance."

He planted the weight of his eyes on her. "You can start by telling me about your boyfriend, Manuel Gonzalez."

Claudia colored. "Manuel . . . ? What about him?"

"We know he has an extensive criminal record," Stone told her forthrightly. "What we don't know is whether or not

Gonzalez might have had anything to do with Adrienne Murray's murder." Or Penelope Grijalva's, for that matter, he thought.

Stone watched her carefully. From his experience, the wife or girlfriend was usually the last to know when a man had gone bad. But in this case, he suspected that she had known up front that Gonzalez was no angel. The question was, did she know just how much of a devil he might be?

"Are you suggesting that Manuel killed Adrienne?" Claudia's fleshy knees buckled.

"I'm not suggesting anything at the moment," Stone lied. "You tell me."

"Manuel's not a murderer!" She seemed quite certain. "He didn't even know Adrienne."

"You're saying they never met?"

Claudia became pensive. "If they did, it was strictly a hello."

"So Manuel has been to this office?" Stone continued. "Or has Adrienne been over to your house?"

Claudia's lower lip quivered. "Manuel has been here a few times," she admitted. "But he's always come right to my office."

"But it is conceivable that at some point words could have been exchanged between him and Adrienne Murray?" Stone pushed. "Beyond a simple hello or good-bye."

"Yes, it's possible," Claudia granted under pressure. "But that still doesn't mean he killed her."

Stone agreed. But it did tell him that Gonzalez had access to Adrienne. And probably knew her, if only in passing. This, combined with his long and sometimes violent criminal history, meant he had to be considered a serious suspect in her murder.

"Do you know if your boyfriend was here on the day that Adrienne disappeared?" Stone fixed a stare on Claudia. When she hesitated, he added, "Another detective is here questioning your other employees about the same thing."

She became flustered. "I honestly can't remember. Maybe you should talk to him."

"Oh I will," he told her in a not-so-friendly voice. "You can be sure of that."

"Why would Manuel want to hurt Adrienne?" Claudia asked almost to herself, in a low, disbelieving voice.

"Maybe it was because of his habit," Stone suggested, mainly for her reaction. "Is he still a crack addict?"

"No!" Her voice rattled the thin walls. "Manuel's been off the stuff for the last six months."

By the look in her eyes, Stone could see that she was trying to convince herself of that perhaps as much as him.

"Does your husband solicit prostitutes?" he tossed at her impulsively.

Claudia favored him a wide-eyed stare. "No," she stated without consideration. "What does prostit—?"

Stone interrupted her by asking, "Do you know a Penelope Grijalva?"

"No," was her weary response. "Who is she? A prostitute?"

"Right now she's at the morgue," Stone said flatly. "Someone murdered her—strangled her to death, just like Adrienne . . ."

Claudia swallowed with shock. Once she recovered she said timidly, "You think Manuel had something to do with that, too?"

"That's what we want to determine, Ms. Sosa," he answered, pulling no punches. "Where can I find Gonzalez?"

"He's usually at home," she said in a throaty voice. "He hasn't been able to find a job since he lost his last one."

"And when was that?"

"About four months ago."

"Where was he employed?" Stone asked.

Claudia hesitated, then offered, "He worked for a janitorial service."

Stone seemed to recall that there was one right in this building. "That wouldn't happen to be the one located on the second floor?"

By the quiver of her lips and body language, he had his answer.

It was only when Claudia scratched her face, pulling back the sleeve of her quilted silk jacket that Stone noted the watch she was wearing. It was two-toned in white and gold. Just like the one Adrienne was wearing the day she was reported missing. Something told him that it was a Seiko.

"Nice watch," he said. "Mind if I have a look at it?"

Claudia cocked a brow awkwardly. "If you like." She lifted her arm toward his face.

"That a Seiko?" Stone asked innocently.

"Yeah, I think so," she muttered.

"Where did you get it?"

"Manuel gave it to me."

"When?" he asked, eyes narrowed.

"I don't know," she uttered hastily. "Recently. Why?"

Stone gazed at her. "Does that watch look familiar to you?"

"Should it?" Claudia touched her mouth nervously.

"Adrienne Murray wore an identical one the day she vanished," he pointed out. "But she wasn't wearing it when her body was found."

Claudia wrung her hands. "I had nothing to do with her death," she stammered.

"No one's suggesting that, Ms. Sosa. That said, if you wouldn't mind, I'd like to borrow your watch to check the DNA on it and the serial number to see if it belonged to Adrienne . . ."

Claudia removed the watch from her wrist with quivering fingers. "Am I going to need a lawyer?"

Stone met her eyes. While ignorance was no excuse, it wasn't necessarily a crime either. "Not if you cooperate and have nothing to hide," he told her, holding a plastic bag out for her to drop the watch in. "But I have to tell you, I think your boyfriend's in big trouble. Now where can we find him?"

Claudia wrinkled her nose worriedly. "When I spoke to Manuel twenty minutes ago, he was having a drink at the Sunset Tavern on Brentdale Road."

* * *

"All the girls said Manuel was a regular visitor," Chang reported in the car. "They all thought he was cute and a natural flirt. Even Adrienne was said to have a crush on him."

"But did she let it go any further than that?" Stone thought about Erica Flanagan's insistence that Adrienne was too frightened of Chuck to even think about cheating on him. Had she gained some courage along the way, only to let things go too far? "And if she didn't, did Gonzalez decide to take what Adrienne wouldn't give him? Along with her life . . . and jewelry?"

"Guess we'll find out soon enough," Chang said from behind the wheel. "My money's on Gonzalez as the person who killed Adrienne and Penelope."

"I wouldn't bet against that," Stone said. "I also wouldn't let Chuck Murray off the hook just yet, either. Since the dead do not talk, we'll have to do it for them. Meaning it's up to us to make sure that Adrienne Murray rests in peace with her killer or killers safely locked behind bars."

Taking Manuel Gonzalez into custody for questioning for at least one and probably two murders was their current order of business to that effect, Stone thought eagerly.

Stone and Chang went into the Sunset Tavern. Detective Joshua Arellano, who was investigating the murder of Penelope Grijalva, met them at the door. Stone saw no reason to muscle in on his territory without at least giving him a heads-up.

"This had better be good," Arellano grumbled. The thirty-seven-year-old detective was six-six, lanky, and had short dark hair.

"We're hoping for the same," Stone said tightly. "Have you come across a Manuel Gonzalez in your investigation into Grijalva's death?"

Arellano cast dark brown eyes at him. "Yeah, he's on a short list of men who spent some time at the tavern the night Penelope Grijalva was murdered. I hadn't gotten around to interviewing him yet."

"Maybe you'll get the chance right now," hinted Chang. "Right after we question the man about the murder of Adrienne Murray. He and the victim crossed paths and we think he may've stolen her jewelry . . . after sexually assaulting and killing her. We have it on good authority that he's inside putting liquor in his mouth even as we speak . . ."

Stone gazed at Arellano. "The way I see it, if we can nail one asshole for two murders, we can all go home and sleep lighter tonight."

"So what are we waiting for?" Arellano asked anxiously. "Let's go after the son of a bitch . . ."

The detectives fanned out inside the tavern, in search of the suspect. When they converged it was apparent that Manuel Gonzalez was nowhere to be found.

"You think we've been had?" Stone questioned the others, hoping Claudia Sosa hadn't bought Gonzalez some time by leading them on a wild goose chase.

"You tell me," muttered Arellano. "Thought you had this on 'good authority'?"

"We did," Chang said. "Or so we believed."

"Let's not jump to the wrong conclusions just yet," Stone said. He led the three to the bartender—a fiftysomething, heavyset man with a Fu Manchu mustache and a shaved head.

"How can I help you?" he asked after Stone had identified them as police detectives.

"We're looking for a man named Manuel Gonzalez." Stone peered at the man. "Know him?"

"Yeah, sure. Manuel hangs out here all the time."

"How about today?"

"How about it?" The bartender tugged at his mustache. "You just missed him by five minutes . . ."

CHAPTER 28

The photographs were blowups of Rafael Santiago's shaved pubic region. Beverly looked on with revulsion at the red, black, and green tattoo of a lizard that rested above Santiago's penis.

"He's got a lot more guts than I do," joked Gail, glancing at one of the pictures. "Though I suppose it could've been worse, like having his penis itself tattooed." She winced at the notion.

"I don't think guts has anything to do with it." Beverly studied the lizard. "My guess is that it's some sort of Latin machismo thing. Probably a gang initiation rite or badge of honor in the hood."

"So you're saying that other members of his gang or hood also could have lizard tattoos . . . strategically placed?"

Beverly laughed weakly at the absurdity of it all. "Well, I wouldn't know about that," she admitted. "But I wouldn't be at all surprised if Santiago was more of a follower here rather than a leader."

Gail wet her lips uneasily. "You do believe we have the right man in custody, don't you, all evidence aside?"

"Absolutely!" Beverly made clear. "Even if other Latino men had their pubic areas tattooed identically, Maxine Crawford identified Rafael Santiago by both his face and his lower anatomy. There cannot be two of him walking around this city."

Even if I saw with my very own eyes someone who was the spitting image of Rafael Santiago. At least from the waist up. Chances are that he didn't have a lizard tattoo on his pubic area like Santiago has as his calling card.

She thought about Maxine Crawford and the not-so-veiled warning from Grant to lay off any investigation into her and Judge Crawford's private lives. What did either of them have to hide that was so off-limits? Could it have any bearing on this case?

Or on the man they had charged with committing the crimes?

Beverly gazed across the table. "What's the latest on the DNA evidence?" she asked.

Gail met her eyes. "The DNA tests on the semen and hair samples taken from Maxine and the bed where she was sexually assaulted indicate there is a match with both blood and hair samples taken from Sheldon Crawford and Rafael Santiago."

"That's good," Beverly said. "Establishing that Santiago left his DNA calling card will make it difficult for his attorney to convince a jury he was elsewhere when the crime occurred."

"But there could still be a potential issue with the DNA evidence," Gail pointed out. "Santiago's attorney will likely try to score some points with the jury by suggesting that the Crawfords engaged in rough sex, thereby somehow mitigating what Santiago did to Maxine."

"Well, let Ortega try." Beverly felt the hairs on the back of her neck rise at the thought of what Maxine Crawford had been put through by that animal. "Juries are too sophisticated these days not to be able to separate consensual sex—whatever that may consist of—from forced sex acts. I think the evidence, along with circumstantial evidence and the victim's direct testimony, is sufficient to prove beyond a reasonable doubt that Santiago was there and did perpetrate the multiple sexual assaults, the murder, and the break-in."

"I agree." Gail picked up a coffee mug. "Unfortunately we've come up short on any fiber evidence from clothes or fingerprints that would tie Santiago directly to the crime scene. Even the shell casings found at the scene had no identifiable prints to link to the suspect and bolster our case against him."

"That's not too surprising," Beverly spoke thoughtfully. "Santiago probably dumped the clothes he wore in the incinerator or the lake anyway. As for fingerprints, considering that Maxine has stated the suspect wore gloves, it was unlikely that any would surface; and shell casings rarely turn up prints at that." She wrinkled her brow, a bit concerned about the lack of a murder weapon. "If you believe in miracles, that gun will somehow fall into our laps and eliminate even the slightest doubt in the jurors' minds about Rafael Santiago's guilt."

And in my own mind, she thought uneasily.

After she left the conference room, Beverly walked to her office. She passed Jean, who was busy on the phone and waving frantically to her, as if trying to flag down a cab. Out of the corner of her eye, Beverly spotted an attractive, well-dressed woman in her thirties. She was seated beside Jean's desk, and rose when she saw Beverly.

"Ms. Mendoza . . ." the woman said on a breath, short blond hair bouncing against her shoulders.

Before Beverly could speak, Jean got off the phone and said, "This is Lydia Wesley. She's writing a book on the Suzanne Landon murder case."

"Ah, yes," mumbled Beverly, recalling that a detective from the Wilameta County Sheriff's Department had directed the woman to her.

"Ms. Wesley has been trying to see you for a couple of weeks now," Jean said apologetically. "I told her that you might be able to spare her a few minutes this afternoon."

Beverly had a feeling she was being ganged up on. Jean, who was usually efficient in rerouting unwanted visitors, was obviously sold on this one for some reason. If nothing else, Lydia Wesley was certainly persistent, she thought.

And I've got better things to do with my time than talk to a true crime writer.

"Yes, I think I can manage a few minutes to answer some questions," Beverly told her, and gave Jean a you-owe-me-one look. "Let's go to my office."

"Thank you," Lydia said keenly.

"Have a seat, Ms. Wesley," Beverly offered, joining her in the visitors' chairs across from the desk so as to keep the meeting informal. "How can I help you?"

Lydia sat up straight, showing signs of nervousness. "I just want to get your feedback on a few things regarding the Suzanne Landon–James Wright love affair turned deadly."

"All right," Beverly nodded, noting that the clock was ticking.

Lydia removed a small tape recorder from her bag, setting it on the corner of the desk. "Do you mind if I record our conversation?"

I hate hearing my voice on tape and am not crazy about others hearing it that way, either, she thought. "Fine. Just be sure to get my approval before quoting me in your book. Deal?"

"Deal." Lydia smiled prettily, flashing small, white teeth. "Did you believe that Suzanne Landon was guilty from the very start?"

"It was hard not to when she failed to notify authorities for nearly two weeks that her lover was missing," Beverly remarked. "Only when what was left of James Wright's corpse was discovered did Ms. Landon suddenly remember that he *accidentally* fell 320 feet to his death."

"Do you think the fact that Suzanne had reported being abused several times by James Wright could have had anything to do with his death—you know, sort of a self-defense motive?"

"Oh, please!" Beverly sneered. She did not discount the legitimacy of battered woman's syndrome, and knew that some women resorted to murder to escape the abuse. But this was different. *Very much so.* "Those reports came within the two months leading up to his death, though they were living together for two years. I think it was more likely that Suzanne Landon wanted out of the relationship, but not until she knew she would be handsomely compensated to the tune of one million dollars in insurance payouts."

Lydia ran thin fingers through her hair. "Isn't it unusual for women to be convicted of murdering their lovers?"

What planet are you living on, lady? "Maybe, when compared to men who kill their significant others," Beverly stated somberly. "The truth is, women can be just as violent and deadly as men, if the motivations and means are there. As a result, those who do commit such acts are just as likely to be convicted and sent to prison as their male counterparts."

Lydia crossed her long legs and sighed. "Do you think the DA's office made you the lead prosecutor on the case to keep it from appearing to be a sexist attack on a brave woman standing up for herself?"

Beverly couldn't help but offer an amused smile while masking her indignation at the suggestion that she'd been given the case for any reason other than her ability as a trial lawyer. "First of all, I was not the lead prosecutor," she said snappishly. "Grant Nunez and I were co-counsel. Second, this trial was not about *men* versus *women.* It was about justice versus injustice. Suzanne Landon was not seen as a woman standing up for her rights, but rather as a female who murdered her lover and tried to collect on it. It's as simple as that."

Lydia's face reddened. "Is there any chance that I can get some crime-scene photos from you?" she asked hesitantly. "These days publishers practically reject your proposal from the start unless you can produce *vivid* pictures for the book."

"You'll want to talk to the police about that," Beverly passed the torch. Her own policy was never to allow photos from her cases to be handed over to the media or to writers, out of respect to the victims.

Lydia's brow creased. "I tried, but they aren't willing to release any photos without approval from the victim's family. And they won't even talk to me."

"Can you blame them?" Beverly narrowed her eyes. "Would *you* want to see the *headless* body of *your* family member in a *true crime* book for the whole world to gawk at?"

"No, but—"

"No *buts!*" argued Beverly, her point being made. She suddenly felt sorry for the author and decided to bend a little for her trouble. "I'll authorize the release of a couple of benign *crime-scene* photographs, but none of the body. Take it or leave it."

"I'll take it," Lydia said respectfully.

"Good." Beverly stood, waiting for Lydia to do the same. "Leave your number with Jean and I'll be in touch. I'll also expect a copy of the book when it's published."

Lydia smiled. "Count on it."

Beverly saw her out and made an impromptu decision to take the rest of the day off. She'd earned it, and would do something with Jaime.

Maybe she would invite Grant over for dinner afterward and they could continue where he left off when he'd said he'd fallen in love with her.

Have you really? she mused. *Since when?*

The idea excited Beverly. Perhaps as much as realizing that her growing sentiments toward Grant were exactly the same.

CHAPTER 29

Manuel watched from his car as the Latina lawyer, her chunky son, another chubby boy around the same age, and a tall black man left the house. He suspected the man wanted to get in the broad's pants. If he hadn't already. Everyone was casually dressed, suggesting they weren't on their way to somewhere fancy.

They drove away in the man's big Cadillac. Manuel wondered if he was a lawyer too. Or a stockbroker.

Or a drug dealer.

Maybe the dude was even a judge, like the one who recently got his, along with his young wife.

After they were out of sight, Manuel quietly crept from the car and made his way to the side of the house. The fact that tall, thick trees surrounded it, as if it were a fortress, made it hard for nosy neighbors to see what was going on. Which was more than he could have asked for.

He tried a couple of windows and found that they were locked. Impatient, he grabbed with gloved hands a nice-sized rock that seemed like it was waiting for him to arrive and make good use of it. He slammed it only once into a side window, causing the window to shatter, glass flying in all directions.

Undoing the lock, he raised the window and climbed in.

The first thing Manuel did was look around for a security system. Surprisingly he didn't find one. The bitch must have thought she didn't need protection in this old but well-preserved neighborhood.

Think again.

Only one light was left on in the house. He figured it was probably to scare burglars from entering.

Wrong again, he laughed.

On the kitchen counter he found the mail, half of it open. He lifted up something with her name on it.

Beverly Mendoza.

Another letter addressed her as Assistant District Attorney.

So the hot Latina wasn't just any lawyer, Manuel mused, his interest piqued. She put badass Latinos like him away in prison. Sometimes for life.

But now maybe I'll turn the tables and make you my prisoner! he thought. Give her a taste of what it was like to be in bondage, subject to another's will and desires.

He moved swiftly from room to room like a thief, surveying all there was to see. It wasn't as big as some cribs he'd been in, but still bigger than what he was used to living in. And nicer.

Manuel saw no indication that an adult male lived there. He suspected that the boy's father had probably dumped the bitch when he found out she was pregnant.

In her bedroom, Manuel pocketed some jewelry that he could hock. He wondered what that old fart at the pawnshop would give him for this stuff . . .

Then he went into the lady's lingerie drawer and pulled out a red silk thong. He put the crotch up to his nose, inhaling the faint odor of her mixed with perfume and detergent. It turned him on. He imagined her wearing them, as well as seeing her without anything covering her privates.

When it was time, he would make the bitch wear this thong just for him.

Searching the house for money, Manuel found a few bills stashed here and there and a couple of credit cards. If lucky, they would net him a few thousand before she could report them as stolen.

Manuel lay on her soft bed for a moment or two, nearly falling asleep as he dreamed of what it would be like to take Beverly Mendoza in this bed—with her doing whatever the hell he wanted. Making her enjoy it almost as much as he would.

Maybe even forcing the fat boy to watch. Learn a few things from a Latin lover.

Until it was time for the boy's mama to be put out of her misery, like a wounded animal.

Permanently.

Then he would take care of the kid. He didn't like killing kids, taking away their lives too soon. He had seen friends die before they ever got laid. Or before they knew that there was life outside the hood. Most had been victims of gang retaliation, sometimes from within the same gang.

But he wasn't going back to prison for anyone, not if he could help it. Not even for a snot-nosed chubby kid. Dead witnesses couldn't talk. Not unless there was such a thing as coming back from the dead.

Manuel took another sweep of the house, searching for weapons. If the broad had a piece, it must have been on her, he thought.

In the kitchen he grabbed a few oatmeal raisin cookies from a jar, eating them whole, one by one.

Then he waited.

Come home soon, lawyer lady. Guess who's coming for dinner and dessert?

He broke into a laugh, his libido rising like the tide as he envisioned forcing her to do his bidding. He would teach her what he wanted and demand that she give it to him.

Just like the others.

As if to psyche himself up, Manuel whipped out his switchblade and began practicing what he planned to do to Beverly Mendoza.

CHAPTER 30

The judge's chambers were large with thick new carpeting and contemporary furnishings, including a wraparound walnut desk and high-backed swivel chair. Plush, cushiony chairs surrounded a wooden octagonal pedestal table. A couple of beautiful trailing fuchsias hung from the ceiling and looked as if they belonged. Adjoining the chambers was a full-sized bathroom and a conference room.

"Nice digs, Judge Nunez," teased Beverly. They had decided on an impromptu visit to his chambers.

"Yeah," Jaime seconded, doing a 360-degree turn.

"Yeah, way cool," agreed Paco, Jaime's friend. He was about the same weight as Jaime, and a little taller. Beverly could see the Native American heritage Jaime said Paco had on his mother's side in his prominent features.

"Thanks, but they're pretty standard judge's chambers," Grant said modestly. "No big deal."

Beverly knew it was far more than that to him. Becoming a judge was the culmination of a lifelong dream. And he had made it before reaching forty-one. She wondered just how far he could go.

And how much she would have to play catch-up.

Grant smiled at her. "Well . . . let's head out to the video arcade," he said.

It was his suggestion that they go to an arcade, and the boys were quick to approve. Beverly knew that Grant was trying hard to fit in and she was grateful for that. Neither had broached the subject of love since he left her with that thought by phone the other day. But it stayed with Beverly and made her assess her own feelings and where to go with them.

"Sounds good to me," she said, face upturned to meet his eyes.

Grant held her gaze. "Glad you think so." *Damn, she looks nice. With those gorgeous eyes.*

In that moment Grant felt like kissing Beverly, but thought better of it. Now was not the time. This was his moment to be buddy-buddy with Jaime and his friend. And maybe show he could also be a good surrogate father, should it come to that.

What Grant knew for certain was that he didn't regret for one moment expressing his true feelings to Beverly. He only needed to hear the words from her to know that what they had was real and would only get better.

But that, too, could wait. For the moment he was content to be able to spend time with her, even as they worked on their careers and made the tough choices.

The video arcade was packed with young people and a few older ones. Jaime and Paco seemed to lose themselves in games and Beverly watched in admiration as Grant did his best to keep up. The boys seemed to appreciate Grant's efforts and were happy to have him around them.

In Beverly's mind, Grant was showing more and more of what she was looking for in a man to build a future with. She hoped he saw the same in her and would give them the time to continue nurturing what they had and let things develop at their own pace.

They had a meal at Pizza Hut before dropping Paco off at his home. Beverly promised that the next time she would come in to meet his mother, whom she had spoken with on the phone a couple of times.

Grant pulled up to Beverly's house. He kept the car running in the driveway, declining an invitation to come in.

"You sure you can't stay for a little while?" Beverly faced him with a look of disappointment after Jaime had already begun to head up the walkway.

"Not sure at all," Grant said in a deep voice. "But if I do, I may never want to leave. At least not this night."

"Then don't," she surprised herself by saying. "Jaime knows we're seeing each other. When he disappears into his room to go to bed, we can quietly go to mine." She wondered just how quiet they could manage to be once there.

"Tempting as hell." Grant groaned salaciously. "But I can't, Bev. I have some important work to do that will probably keep me up half the night. Can I take a rain check?"

Beverly hid her confusion. She felt like she was throwing herself at him. Only he wasn't there to break her fall.

"Of course you can," she said, making herself smile. "But honestly, your rain checks are piling up, Grant. Hope you don't end up with more than you can handle."

He laughed uncomfortably. "I can handle as many as it takes where it concerns you, baby."

She looked at him with a straight face. "You're sure about that?"

Grant honed in on her eyes. "As sure as I am about this . . ." He leaned over and kissed her hard on the mouth till Beverly felt it right down to her toes. When Grant pulled back, he said, "Does that convince you?"

Beverly touched her stinging lips, wishing more than ever that he would stay so they could explore each other further. But she would give him the time he needed to make more time for them.

"Yes, it does," she uttered.

Grant beamed. "Great. Oh, and by the way, I do love you, Bev."

She felt herself glowing and gazed at him. "I love you too, Grant."

Beverly held his cheeks and kissed him again before leaving the car. She didn't want to spoil the moment by saying the wrong thing or expecting too much, too soon.

After waving good-bye and feeling giddy inside, Beverly headed toward the house contemplatively. That was when she heard the scream.

It was Jaime. "Mom!"

Beverly bolted up the walkway and into the house. She was afraid he might have tripped in the darkness and hurt himself.

"Jaime . . . ?" Beverly saw no sign of him as she crossed the living room and dining room before passing by the kitchen.

Jaime darted from the den like his pants were on fire. "The window's broken in there!" he shrieked. "I think somebody was in the house."

Beverly raced by him and into the den. She saw the broken glass splattered across the red cedar flooring near the window. Her first thought was that it could have been a tree branch that caused the damage. Then she saw the unmistakable dirty imprint of a shoe near the window.

Panic seized her. Someone had broken in.

And might still be inside the house!

Beverly's first thought was for Jaime's safety.

"Jaime!" Her voice broke with trepidation. She ran out into the hall and nearly collided with her son. "Stay here!" she ordered.

"No!" He stood his ground. "I'm coming with you."

Beverly knew this was no time to argue. If the intruder was still in the house it was probably best that she keep Jaime within her sight.

She grabbed his hand and ran back into the kitchen

where she had dumped her handbag. Inside was her Glock. She removed the gun, released the safety, and began to search the rest of the house. She had never actually used the .40-caliber weapon, but had taken a firearms class and was prepared to shoot anyone who threatened her or Jaime.

Whoever had been in the house was gone.

But not before stealing some money, jewelry, and credit cards, Beverly realized. They had also taken away her very false sense of security.

The police came, took her report and collected evidence of the crime.

Beverly phoned Grant on his cell phone before he got home. He came right over.

"Are you sure you're all right?" he asked her for the umpteenth time.

"As well as I can be," she said, feeling almost embarrassed that this had happened in *her* house. After being given clearance by the police, Jaime had retreated to the relative safety of his room.

Beverly sat huddled on the living room couch beside Grant, his arm around her, as if staking his claim.

"It doesn't look like they made off with much," she told him, trying to keep from shaking. "At least nothing that can't be replaced."

Yet Beverly still couldn't help but feel as if she had been violated.

"Why the hell don't you have a security system?" Grant scolded her like a misbehaving child.

"Just never got around to getting one," Beverly offered as a lame response. She really had been meaning to have a system installed but procrastinated, largely because the area had an active neighborhood crime watch and strong police-community relations. Almost no burglaries had been reported since they moved there. This was a burglary, wasn't it? What else could it be?

"Well, we'll fix that!" Grant said with determination. He tried not to think about what might have happened had Beverly walked in on the home invader. Their entire future could have been derailed. Not to mention the unfinished business of the present. "First thing in the morning I'll make a call and get a good security system put in for you."

Beverly would have preferred to make her own choice in this matter, but she knew Grant was only trying to help. Besides, she found real comfort in having him take charge, as if he was the man of the house. Something that she now felt she needed in more ways than one.

"In the meantime," Grant was saying, "you and Jaime should stay at my house tonight."

Beverly appreciated this; however, she didn't want to feel too helpless or be put out of her own home.

"We'll be fine here," she insisted. "I doubt very much that the burglar will come back. At least not tonight."

Grant's brows drew together. "Don't be so naive, Beverly," he snapped at her. "Or bullheaded. You don't know that this was just a burglar. You're an assistant DA, for crying out loud! Who's to say that this creep wasn't after you—or Jaime—and just made it look like a simple burglary?"

The thought gave Beverly the jitters. What if it wasn't just a case of theft? she considered. What if the thief had a larger agenda in mind?

Had she been targeted with the intent of bodily harm? Was this more than a random act of petty crime?

Beverly mused about the man she had seen at Burger King last week. Could he have somehow followed her home and then come back at a more opportune time?

Was the man also a rapist and a murderer?

"What is it?" Grant asked perceptively.

Beverly told him about the man and his incredible likeness to Rafael Santiago.

"So what are you saying?" He favored her questioningly.

"I don't know," she admitted. "For one, he could be the

person who broke into my house. For another, maybe he broke into Judge Crawford's house, too . . ."

Beverly could not believe what she was suggesting, considering that they had Rafael Santiago's DNA and Maxine Crawford's positive identification, putting Santiago directly at the scene of the crime as its perpetrator. But what if, against all odds, this other person had committed the crime, without leaving behind DNA evidence?

Grant dismissed the notion with a flip of his head. "We have the *right* man in custody, Beverly!" he said firmly. "One thing has nothing to do with the other, assuming this man did follow you home."

"You weren't there, Grant," Beverly returned flatly. "You didn't see him. I did and it gave me the heebie-jeebies!"

"Will you listen to yourself, Bev?" He sucked in a ragged breath. "You see some guy at Burger King who resembles Santiago—a man you've admitted you may have only imagined looking like him—and all of a sudden you're questioning the entire case you have against Rafael Santiago?" Grant's gaze angled at her face. "Do you *really* believe you have the *wrong* man in custody?"

Beverly began to question her own judgment. Santiago was identified, right down to the tattoo on his pubic region. Wasn't that proof enough that he was Maxine's attacker? And the one who shot Judge Crawford to death?

Surely this other man, no matter how much he may have looked like Santiago, wasn't his identical twin with respect to his private parts . . .

But that didn't mean he hadn't followed her and broken into her house. Or that she might not still be in danger.

"We'll spend the night at your place," she told Grant.

CHAPTER 31

"Where have you been?" Claudia asked sharply, a bead of perspiration dampening her brow.

"Out," Manuel said simply, not in the mood to argue. He'd had a good buzz and now only wanted to sleep. He walked by her, getting a whiff of pungent body odor masked only slightly by cheap perfume.

"The police came to the office," she told him nervously.

"So . . ." He looked at her bloated face.

"They asked about you . . . and one gave me this . . ." She held out a business card.

Manuel took it and read: *Detective Stone Palmer, Homicide, Wilameta County Sheriff's Department.* There were two phone numbers and a fax number on the card.

Manuel felt a twinge of panic but fought hard not to show it. "What did this Stone Palmer want to know?" he asked in a nonchalant manner.

"They're investigating the murder of Adrienne Murray," Claudia said, as if *he* knew the woman.

"Who the hell is she?" He lifted his brow as though he had not a clue.

"Adrienne worked for me," Claudia said tautly. "You met her at the office."

Manuel shrugged. "If you say so." He rubbed his nose. "Why do the cops wanna see me?"

Claudia swallowed and continued hesitantly. "They think you may have had something to do with Adrienne's death."

Manuel narrowed his eyes. "What do you think?"

Claudia brazenly got up in his face. "You tell me, Manuel, that you *did not* murder Adrienne," she demanded. "Not someone I worked with, a friend . . . You couldn't have—"

"I didn't murder no one," he said coolly. "Why do you even listen to them? You know me. I'm no killer!" He stepped back involuntarily.

"I'm not sure I do know you, Manuel," she spat out angrily. "You think I'm stupid? I know you're still doing crack. I can see it in your red eyes."

He saw no use in denying it. "That don't mean I killed Adrienne whatever her name is—"

Claudia gave him a mistrustful appraisal. "No? Then where'd you get the watch?"

"What watch?"

"The one you gave me last week for my birthday! You said you bought it."

Manuel knew he'd led himself into a corner, but was not about to remain trapped in it. "Okay, so I lied. I found the watch, all right?"

"Found it where?" she asked warily.

"At the park," he offered with a straight face. "It was there on the grass. I figured someone probably had no more use for it and tossed it. I cleaned it up and wanted you to have it. That's the truth, baby."

When Manuel put a hand on Claudia's rough cheek, she winced as if he'd struck her. "You had blood on your clothes that night Adrienne disappeared," she recalled. "It was *her* blood, wasn't it? Not fish blood." When he did not respond she shouted at him, "Tell me the truth, Manuel."

His first thought was *deny, deny, deny*. But since she

didn't want to take no for an answer and it was too late for that at this point anyway, he decided what the hell.

"Yeah, it was that bitch's blood," Manuel admitted tersely. "Happy now?"

Claudia began trembling. "Why, Manuel?" Her eyes filled with tears. "What did Adrienne ever do to you?"

"She got what she deserved—okay?"

"No, it's not okay, Manuel," she huffed. "How could it be?"

"Because that's over and done with, baby," he contended. "Just forget about it."

Claudia closed her eyes, squeezing out tears, and opened them wide. "They think you killed a prostitute, too." She sighed. "It's true, isn't it . . . ?"

Again Manuel wanted to deny any such involvement. But it was obvious that she'd already had her mind made up from the beginning. Which had been a big mistake.

"Yeah, I killed the whore," he confessed. "It was just something that happened. We'll go someplace else and start over."

Even as he spoke, Manuel never believed she would go along with it. She couldn't. No more than he could now that the cat had been let out of the bag.

They had suddenly reached a turning point in their rocky relationship and Manuel knew there was no going back.

"You have to turn yourself in, Manuel." Claudia's voice shook. "It's the only way to make things right."

"Things can never be right again," he told her. "Not between us."

The empty look in her eyes confirmed it.

He faced her squarely and, without giving it another thought, took out his knife. Just as quickly, Manuel released the switchblade from its holder. Claudia stared at the shiny blade with an open mouth, as if it were an object from another planet. He thrust the knife into her stomach, feeling it slice through a wall of fat and arteries.

Then again.

Again.

And again.

"I'm sorry, baby," Manuel cried, holding her in his arms as best as possible while he continued to ram the blade into her. "There was simply no other way. I can't go back to prison. They do bad things to people like me in there."

When he finally released her, Claudia's bloodied body crashed to the floor, practically shaking the foundation. He closed her lifeless eyes and kissed her good-bye.

I've got to get the hell out of here, Manuel told himself, freaked out more about his latest kill than the others. They would come back looking for him.

But by then he would be long gone.

He took whatever money Claudia had in her purse. Then he took her car, knowing she wouldn't be needing it ever again.

CHAPTER 32

When Stone and Chang arrived at the duplex that Claudia Sosa shared with Manuel Gonzalez, the place was already crawling with cops. A call had come in from a neighbor who reported hearing a woman screaming inside the residence.

Stone feared the worst had happened before they could take Manuel Gonzalez into custody. He saw the body bag being removed from the residence. After identifying himself, he requested that it be opened.

Stone winced when he saw that the swollen and pale face staring back at him was indeed that of Claudia Sosa.

"What happened?" he asked Detective Arellano, who had gotten there minutes before.

"Looks like she was stabbed to death," Arellano informed him. "A witness has identified Manuel Gonzalez as running from the duplex. He drove off in the victim's car."

"Damn!" Stone closed his eyes in a moment of anguish. They had been so close, yet so far from nailing the culprit.

"We have a make on the car and the license plate number," Chang said. "We'll get the son of a bitch."

"Yeah," muttered Stone. "Let's just hope it's before he sets his sights on someone else. A probable crack-addicted psycho serial killer is the worst kind of criminal we can have running around as a loose cannon."

Aside from a person who betrays the ultimate in trust—a spouse killer.

Stone thought about Chuck Murray. Where the hell did he fit in all this, if anywhere? Was he really just an innocent grieving husband? Or was he a wife-abusing, paranoid, jealous bastard who would stop at nothing to keep his wife from abandoning ship?

Including conspiring to commit cold, calculated murder.

An APB was put out on Manuel Gonzalez in the search for answers and an armed and very dangerous killer.

It was past midnight when Beverly came out of the bathroom adjoining Grant's master suite. Jaime was already asleep in a spare bedroom and unlikely to come looking for her till morning. By then, she would have breakfast made and he wouldn't have to concern himself about her sleeping arrangements.

Not that he doesn't already suspect that Grant and I are having sex, she thought. *But why add fuel to the fire?*

Beverly waited till she got to Grant's hardside waterbed before removing her nightgown, exposing her naked body. She watched as his eyes feasted upon her in the low moonlight that filtered through plantation shutters. She watched him, too, lying on the bed, one sinewy arm propped on an elbow.

Without uttering a word, she climbed onto the bed and went down to his flaccid penis, taking him into her mouth. Within moments, it had become engorged and stiff, while Grant sighed and ran his hands haphazardly through her hair.

Beverly felt her own arousal match his. She pulled her mouth off him and rolled a condom over Grant's erection. Straddling his hips, she slowly slid onto him till he was deep inside her. Then she began galloping atop her lover, faster and faster as the need for satisfaction enveloped her like a warm blanket.

Grant caressed Beverly's nipples with nimble fingers, causing them to turn rock-hard. He heard her soft moan and bit back his own urge to vocalize his pleasure. Instead, he pulled her down on top of him, cupped her buttocks, and began kissing Beverly's mouth feverishly till they both exploded in orgasmic rhythm.

Beverly quavered violently as she came, feeling herself tightening around Grant inside her. Their bodies seemed to mold into one another as the final burst of ecstasy left their breathing labored before there was calm.

Afterward, Beverly continued to lie on Grant's comforting, solid body, her head against his chest. She could hear his heart beating rapidly, not yet come down from the high of sex.

Neither of them had spoken much about the break-in or Beverly's fears that someone who looked like Rafael Santiago had followed her home. Nor had they discussed the fact that Grant's rain check had come due sooner than either of them expected.

Now where do we go from here? Beverly wondered nervously. Could their declarations of love carry them further than either dreamed possible? Right now she only wanted to sleep. There would be other days to tackle the weighty issues.

Grant held Beverly in his arms, wishing they could stay that way forever. He could get used to having a woman in his life full-time again. Only this time he wouldn't let her get away. He couldn't.

He wondered if the home invasion was somehow tied into their destiny, causing them to bridge the gap sooner rather than later and become one. Or was there something more ominous afloat with the burglary and the Rafael Santiago look-alike?

Grant fell asleep on that thought, sprinkled in with his own issues concerning the Honorable Judge Sheldon Crawford.

CHAPTER 33

Rafael Santiago's preliminary hearing was held on a Friday afternoon. With the exception of the prosecution's key witness, all the parties were present for what was generally a routine obligation on the part of the prosecution to present its case against the accused. Only a minimal amount of evidence was necessary to successfully establish probable cause, Beverly knew, all but assuring that the case would be bound for trial. What this stage of the journey was really about was learning the extent and nature of the evidence both sides had discovered and what the judge would and would not allow.

Presiding over the preliminary hearing was Judge Helene Thompson. Helene was fifty years old with a cocoa skin tone and fine blond hair pulled into a bun. A diminutive frame was practically lost in her black robe.

Beverly stood her ground, along with Gail, as Ortega filed a motion to suppress DNA evidence on semen and hair samples.

"Your Honor," entreated Ortega, "this evidence is tainted *and* far too unreliable to be used against my client, Rafael

Santiago. DNA tests reveal that two blood types and hair samples were taken from the victim's vagina and anus—one belonging to Judge Crawford himself. As a result, we cannot be certain to what degree my client's semen and genital hairs prove what truly happened that night, much less that he sexually assaulted Ms. Crawford . . ."

The judge looked to Beverly for her thoughts before rendering a decision.

"DNA testing is not done with smoke and mirrors, Your Honor," Beverly said gruffly. She briefly explained DNA profiling, as though necessary, leaving the details for her expert. "Or in other words, even if there were two men who ejaculated inside the victim, their blood types remain separate and can be matched to their individual genetic codes. This is not about *consensual* sex between a husband and wife, Your Honor—it's about forced sexual relations, which we fully intend to prove, along with breaking and entering, and murder."

Judge Thompson weighed this for a moment or two before lifting her head. "I'm afraid that I must side with the prosecution on this one," she said to the defense attorney. "The State is entitled to use DNA evidence to support its case against the defendant, even if other evidence indicates that sexual activity was going on at the time of the alleged crime. Of course, Counselor, you are free to challenge its validity during the trial. Motion denied."

"Thank you, Your Honor." Beverly breathed a sigh of relief, knowing that she'd won one important round. But the battle had only just begun.

In the end, her most vital weapon against the defendant—whose smug demeanor betrayed the callousness of his nature—was the testimony of the only living victim: Maxine Crawford. She was the first witness called to the stand.

Maxine had been kept out of the courtroom until she was to testify so as not to be intimidated by Rafael Santiago or put through any unnecessary stress and strain.

After being sworn in, Maxine sat in the witness box. She was wearing a simple but expensive gray tweed jacket dress and a smidgen of makeup. She avoided looking at the defendant and appeared calm.

"Mrs. Crawford," Beverly began formally, "can you tell us what happened at your house on the night of October twenty-ninth?"

Maxine sighed. "My husband and I were in bed . . . making love," she said softly, "when I heard a shot. Sheldon reacted at about the same time and I knew he'd been hit."

"What then?"

"My husband was shot a second time." Maxine's voice broke. "He somehow managed to get out of bed. Then *he* shot Sheldon again . . ."

Beverly spared her from having to reveal further details that could be best told by the medical examiner. "Could you see the shooter?"

Maxine held her gaze, unblinking. "Yes."

"Where was he at this time?"

"Near the foot of the bed."

"What happened then?" Beverly asked tenderly.

Maxine hesitated, as if reliving the moment.

"It's all right." Beverly offered the witness a comforting look. "He can't hurt you anymore." Yet she knew the damage had already been done and was irrevocable.

"He forced me to have sex with him," uttered Maxine, making a contorted face.

Beverly happened to glance toward the back of the courtroom just in time to see Grant walk in. He gave an encouraging nod at her and took a seat in the back. She thought briefly about the hot sex they had two nights ago. She felt a prickling between her legs.

Turning to face the witness again, Beverly took a breath and asked, "By force, do you mean at gunpoint?"

"Yes."

Beverly braced herself for the next few tough but necessary questions. "Did he rape you, Maxine?"

"Yes," she answered unwaveringly.

"Did he sodomize you?"

"Yes."

"Did he force you to orally copulate him?"

"Yes," Maxine's voice dropped unsteadily. "He did."

Beverly swallowed. "Did he talk to you at all during this assault?"

Maxine considered this. "He told me if I screamed or tried to fight him, he would kill me."

Beverly winced. "Anything else?"

The strain of the moment was showing on Maxine's face. "He told me to suck his cock . . . and to turn over."

Beverly wrinkled her nose in disgust. "Can you tell us if your attacker had any distinguishing marks on any part of his body you saw?"

Maxine fluttered her lashes. "Yes. He had a scar on his right thigh."

"Were there any other identifying marks you noticed?" Beverly asked.

Maxine cleared her throat. "Yes. There was a tattoo on the area below his waist."

Beverly eyed her. "You mean where his pubic hair is?"

"Where it was," Maxine responded tonelessly. "He had shaved it."

This caused some stirring and murmurs in the court-room where the press had been allowed in along with the spectators.

Beverly allowed this to die down. "What kind of tattoo?"

"A . . . a lizard," the witness stammered.

Beverly walked to the exhibit table and introduced into evidence an enlargement of a photo of the defendant's pubic area featuring the tattoo. She showed the photo to the witness.

"Is this the lizard tattoo you saw?"

Maxine took one look then closed her eyes, full of emotion. "Yes . . ." she uttered.

Beverly had heard enough. It was time to get to the heart

of the matter. Leaning toward the witness box, she asked without preface, "Is the man who did this to you and shot your husband, Judge Sheldon Crawford, in this courtroom?"

"Yes." Maxine's voice was barely audible, but Beverly was sure the judge heard her. "Can you point him out?"

Maxine hated to have to look at the man responsible for ruining her life, but she knew it was necessary for justice to move forward and to help her try to rid herself of the nightmares. She drew in a deep breath, made her head turn, and pointed a finger directly at Rafael Santiago.

During recess Beverly thanked Maxine for a job well done and sent her home. No further testimony would be necessary on this day.

Beverly found herself wondering what deep, dark secrets lay beneath the somewhat cool veneer of Maxine Crawford. There was no doubt in her mind that Maxine had been horribly violated and witnessed her husband's brutal murder. But was there more to this woman than met the eye? Something that Beverly was being pressured to disregard?

Had the judge taken vital information with him to the grave with respect to his murder?

Was any of it germane to Maxine's credibility as a witness?

Beverly had coffee with Grant in the building's cafeteria. "Any thoughts on the proceedings, Judge Nunez?"

"Yes," he said matter-of-factly. "I think it's too bad that we have to go through this long-winded trial for scum like Santiago."

She raised a brow. "Are you suggesting we should tar and feather him without a trial?" *And the presumption of innocence?*

"Of course not." Grant reacted defensively. "It's just that we often spend taxpayer money going around in circles—only to reach the same conclusion at the end of the day that we could have reached much sooner."

"Unfortunately we both know that's the way the system works," Beverly said over the rim of her cup.

"Yeah, whether we like it like it or not," said Grant. "At least as a judge I can now exercise a little more discretion in dealing with criminals than I ever could as a prosecutor."

Beverly gave a little chuckle. "Pity on the rest of us trial lawyers who have not been quite as fortunate."

Grant smiled crookedly. "Guess I'm blowing my own horn a bit too much. Sorry."

"Don't be," she told him. "If you don't blow it, who will?"

He laughed, putting a hand on her knee. "Good point."

Beverly tasted the coffee, trying to ignore the soothing feeling of his fingers pressed against her nylons. It had been three days since what was still being described as a standard home invasion. Beverly had cancelled the missing credit cards and hoped that the thief didn't try to steal her identity as well. There had been no prints left behind or other incriminating evidence to identify the culprit. But one thing was certain: It couldn't have been Rafael Santiago. He was locked up and still clearly the man they wanted him to be.

Her home invader was someone else who had probably moved on to other victims. At least Beverly convinced herself this was the case as she bolstered her own defenses with a new security system, reinforced windows, and deadbolt locks.

But can anyone ever truly feel safe, no matter what protection devices they have?

Beverly's thoughts turned back to Grant's hand on her knee. As nice as it felt, for some reason she found herself musing about Maxine and Sheldon Crawford in bed having sex before all hell broke loose.

Grant noticed Beverly's expression change, prompting him to move his hand from her leg. "What is it?"

"Nothing." She gazed at him. "Actually, I was wondering what you thought about Maxine Crawford."

Grant reacted. "What am I supposed to think?"

No fair answering a question with a question. "Well, do you find her attractive?" *How could he not?*

Does it really matter?

Grant shifted uncomfortably in his chair. "To tell you the truth, I've hardly noticed the woman to give it much thought one way or the other," he said weakly.

Beverly thought about dropping the subject. But she could not. Something told her this was a question he was deliberately attempting to dodge. Why?

Am I suddenly getting possessive here?

"Well, now that you've thought about it," she pressed, "do you?"

Grant twisted his lips. "I suppose I've seen a lot worse," he admitted. "Why are we talking about whether or not I find Maxine Crawford attractive?"

So you do find Maxine attractive, mused Beverly. As did other men, undoubtedly. Even Santiago must have found her to be attractive, though she knew what he did to Maxine was not about physical appeal but raw, ugly power and brute force.

"Just wondering, that's all." Beverly could not believe she had just put Grant on the spot.

Grant's eyes danced with amusement. "You're jealous! That's it." He broke into laughter.

"I'm *not* jealous!" she insisted. *Am I?*

"The rosy color of your cheeks tells me otherwise." Grant cocked a brow whimsically.

"So maybe I am, just a little," Beverly once again surprised herself by saying. Why shouldn't she be? Especially when she was romantically involved with one of the city's most eligible and handsome bachelors. It was only natural to be a little insecure about the competition. Was Maxine Crawford really competition now that she was a widow and available?

"Well, don't be." Grant's full smile was replaced by a look of earnest. "Believe me, Bev, Maxine Crawford may be a fine sister, but you have absolutely nothing to worry about in the looks department—trust me. You can more than hold your own with anyone, whether it's Maxine Crawford,

Salma Hayek, Evangeline Lilly, you name it. I wouldn't give you up for any of them, baby!"

Beverly suddenly felt foolish in showing the insecurity of a schoolgirl having her first crush. There was no reason why she should feel threatened by Maxine or any other woman. At least not where it concerned Grant. He had proven to her that the rumors about his reckless abandon as a ladies' man were just that—rumors.

So why should I worry?

Beverly pondered Grant's suggestion that she stay away from digging too much into the Crawfords' personal lives. She wondered if there was something he wasn't telling her. Something that Maxine Crawford could shed light on. Or was it her imagination in overdrive once again?

"Sorry I asked," Beverly lamented to Grant, flashing him a smile. "Guess I'm really starting to get comfortable with us, Mr. Nunez. And I don't want anything—or anyone—to ruin what we have."

"Nothing and no one will," he said deeply with a flip of his bald head. "It's not about us, baby, but the pressures of this case getting to you. That's quite understandable, given the drama involving a dead judge, a young widow, and a career criminal who must be made to pay for his sins. The latest ones anyway. The sooner it's over, the sooner *we* can focus on building what it is we're working on."

Beverly agreed on that last point and was eager to stay the course, wherever it led them.

"Speaking of which," she looked at her watch. "It's about time to get back to court."

Beverly did so alone, as Grant bowed out gracefully, having his own court duties to tend to. But not before they kissed and made plans for dinner.

Following the recess, Officer Shawnnessy Dunbar took the stand. The twenty-eight-year-old divorcée and former correctional officer cast narrow blue eyes at Beverly.

"After the 911 call you were dispatched to Judge Crawford's house?" asked Beverly, gazing at the heart-shaped face before her that was bordered by short reddish-blond hair.

"That's correct," Shawnnessy said, "along with my partner, Ramsey LaPorte. We didn't know who lived there at the time."

"And what did you and Officer LaPorte find upon your arrival?"

"Mrs. Crawford was visibly shaken and had obviously been traumatized—"

"Objection!" Ortega raised his arm, as if saluting. "Neither the officer or her partner were qualified to know whether or not Maxine Crawford was *traumatized* based on appearance alone, as suggested."

"Overruled," Judge Thompson yelled. "I think Officer Dunbar and Officer LaPorte are capable of making a judgment call on a person's physical being under the circumstances."

Beverly ran her tongue lightly across her lips and resumed. "What did Mrs. Crawford say to you, Officer Dunbar?"

Shawnnessy flinched. "She said that she had been sexually assaulted and her husband had been shot to death."

"What did you do then?"

"After establishing that the house was secure, we went to Judge Crawford's bedroom and found him lying facedown in his own blood." She sighed. "A chunk of his head had been blown off."

The sheer morbidity of this struck the courtroom, filling faces with shock and anguish.

Later it was Detective Joe O'Dell who took the stand.

"Can you tell us what type of gun Judge Crawford was shot with, Detective?" Beverly asked the witness.

"A .25-caliber automatic handgun." O'Dell leaned back as though in a recliner.

"Were the shell casings from the bullets recovered?"

"Yes."

"And have these casings been linked to the defendant?" Beverly favored Santiago, who bared his uneven teeth at her like a rabid dog.

O'Dell nodded. "They matched shells found at the apartment where the defendant was arrested."

Ortega was quick to attack when his turn came to cross-examine the detective. "Do you have the murder weapon, Detective O'Dell?"

"No," O'Dell responded curtly.

"Do you have *any* fingerprints placing my client at the scene of the crime?"

O'Dell paused, risking a furtive peek at Beverly. Finally he looked the defense attorney in the eye, and said brusquely, "No."

Ortega gave a tiny smile. "Isn't it true, Detective, that the shell casings the *real* killer left behind would have matched *any* .25-caliber shells, and not only those that you found at the apartment where Rafael Santiago was staying with his mother?"

"Probably," O'Dell conceded reluctantly. "But we both know that it's much more than coincidental that your client just happened to have access to the same caliber bullets that killed Judge Crawford."

"*We* know no such thing, Detective," Ortega mocked him. "The fact that these fairly common shells were found at a residence where Mr. Santiago was merely a guest is hardly proof that my client is guilty of anything, other than being an ex-con who looks like half the other ex-cons out there."

He was good, thought Beverly with less than admiration. Obviously the attorney was insinuating that it was a case of mistaking one Hispanic male for another. But she doubted the judge, or any sensible person, would buy it—especially with Santiago's unique anatomical signature.

"Santiago's guilty as hell!" O'Dell lost his cool. "You'd better hope to hell the murder weapon never shows up. I'm betting that he didn't bury it deep enough to stay buried forever."

"I have no further questions for this witness, Your Honor!" Ortega glared at him before facing the judge.

Judge Thompson then admonished O'Dell and reminded everyone that this was still just a preliminary hearing and not an actual trial where such theatrics might be more tolerated.

Beverly, still shaken over the potential impact of the missing gun, called Nkaki Ahmad to the stand.

The ex-cellmate of Rafael Santiago was dressed in gray denim prison garb, his shaved head shining as if freshly polished. Ahmad appeared a tad nervous as he glanced once or twice at the defendant, but indicated he was ready to tell his story.

After establishing the relationship between the two men, Beverly asked, "Can you tell us what Rafael Santiago told you he planned to do to Judge Crawford once he got out?"

"Objection!" snapped Ortega. "She's clearly leading the witness."

"Sustained," Judge Thompson said. "Rephrase the question."

Beverly sighed. "Did Rafael Santiago ever tell you he planned to harm the judge upon his release?"

Ahmad grinned. "Yeah, he did. Rafael had a big mouth. He told me more times than I could count that it was payback time for the judge when he was set free."

"Payback time?" Beverly drew her brows together deliberately, waiting for further clarification.

"Yeah." Ahmad faced the defendant. "Rafael said he would put a gun up Crawford's black ass then make him eat it! And the wife was gonna get hers, too . . ."

Santiago sprang from his seat shouting profanities at Ahmad. The defendant had to be restrained by Ortega and a hefty bailiff.

Judge Thompson ruled that there was sufficient evidence to believe that Rafael Santiago had perpetrated the crimes of which he was accused.

A trial date was set for six weeks from now.

To Beverly's surprise, the presiding judge would be none other than Grant Nunez.

CHAPTER 34

The pawnshop was on East Ninety-second Street, along with several others in an area that was also lined with massage parlors, sleazy bars, and nude dance clubs. A bell clanged as Stone walked in with Chang. They had received a tip from an informant that Manuel Gonzalez had hocked Adrienne Murray's rings there.

"How can I help you?" The portly man at the counter flashed his yellow teeth.

Stone whipped out his ID. "Detective Palmer of the Sheriff's Department. And your name?"

"Stanley Zubrinski." He looked uncomfortable. "Look, if this is about the dame upstairs—"

"It isn't." Stone glanced at Chang, who suppressed a grin before peering at the man. "We need to ask you some questions about a set of wedding and engagement rings that were pawned here recently."

Zubrinski lifted a bushy brow. "What do you wanna know?"

"We'd like to see them, for starters."

"No problem, if they're still here. When were they brought in?"

Stone took an educated guess, describing the rings.

Zubrinski nodded in remembrance. "Yeah, I think I still have them. Let me check."

Stone and Chang watched him fiddle around beneath a glass cabinet before coming up with two rings and setting them on the counter.

"Are these the ones you're looking for?" Zubrinski rubbed his crooked nose. "Not much of a market for wedding bands these days. Almost cheaper to buy new."

Stone removed a picture of the rings supplied by Chuck Murray and compared them with the engagement and wedding rings before him on the counter.

"What do you think?" he asked Chang.

The detective studied the rings. "I'd say we have ourselves a match."

Stone concurred. He turned back to the pawnshop owner. "Where's the paperwork for these items?"

Zubrinski supplied a receipt that gave the name Louis Mendes and an address that did not match that of Claudia Sosa.

"What can you tell us about the person who brought these in?" Stone asked. He was betting that it was Manuel Gonzalez, but didn't rule out that Chuck Murray could have peddled them himself to get rid of them, had they been in his possession all along after he killed his wife.

"Not much." Zubrinski scratched his forehead. "I make it a habit not to focus too much on my customers. Safer that way."

Stone glared. "We're searching for a killer here. We could also yank your license should we find that you knowingly took in any hot property. Now do us both a favor and refresh your memory . . ."

Zubrinski got the message. He described Manuel Gonzalez to a tee. Looking at a mug shot of the suspect bolstered his description.

"The man told me they belonged to his grandmother." Zubrinski gave a sardonic laugh. "I knew he was full of it.

But in my business you don't ask too many questions, if you know what I mean."

Chang favored him with an unforgiving look. "Maybe in the future you should, man. Or risk seeing us in here again . . ."

"I'll remember that," he snorted.

"In the meantime, we're confiscating these as police evidence in a criminal investigation," Stone said, using a handkerchief to put the rings in a plastic bag to preserve any prints that might be evidence of a crime.

Zubrinski's jowly face sagged. "Hey, I paid three hundred bucks for those!"

"You're breaking my heart," Stone said emotionlessly. "If by chance we've got the wrong rings, you'll get them back. But don't hold your breath."

They left the shop, equipped with more evidence to point the finger at Manuel Gonzalez as Adrienne Murray's killer, a crime to go along with the murder of Claudia Sosa and, in all likelihood, Penelope Grijalva. Stone had learned that Gonzalez was fired from his last job at the janitorial business in Adrienne's building because of alleged drug use and a high rate of absenteeism.

But apparently that didn't stop him from frequent visits to his girlfriend.

Nor did it stop him from noticing Adrienne Murray. Or vice versa.

Stone thought it time to pay Chuck Murray another visit. When he arrived at the house, he found the widower in the company of his attorney, Jonathan Hutchinson. Sixtysomething and potbellied, Hutchinson sported a white goatee and had receding salt-and-pepper hair.

Stone wasted no time getting to the point. He removed the plastic bag containing the rings from his pocket and held it up while gazing at Adrienne's husband. "Are these your late wife's rings?"

Chuck peered at them, as if searching for something he never thought he would find. "Yes, it's them."

"You're sure?"

Chuck nodded glumly. "Yeah. We bought them together," he said sadly. "I placed them on her finger."

"Where did you find the rings?" Hutchinson intervened, as though to protect his client.

"A pawnshop on Ninety-second Street," Stone said. "I think they were pawned there by the person who killed Adrienne."

"So you know who this person is?" the attorney asked with interest.

Without answering, Stone took out the mug shot of the suspect. He put it in Chuck's face. "Have you ever seen this man before?"

"Don't answer that!" spat Hutchinson. He looked at the picture, as if to thoroughly scrutinize it for any possible self-incrimination for his client. "Maybe you should tell us who the hell he is—"

"I've never seen him before," Chuck spoke over his lawyer.

Stone favored him skeptically. "Take another look."

Chuck stared again at the mug shot, then met Stone's hard eyes and shook his head. "I still don't know who this man is," he insisted.

Stone put the mug shot away while keeping some thoughts to himself. "Name's Manuel Gonzalez. He used to work in the same building as your wife. Indeed, Gonzalez's girlfriend, Claudia Sosa, was Adrienne's boss."

Chuck's eyes widened. "Claudia . . . I met her there in the office . . . Are you saying this Manuel Gonzalez killed Adrienne and took the rings?"

"It's beginning to look like it." Stone watched his reaction.

Chuck furrowed his brow. "So why haven't you arrested him? Or have you?"

"Didn't I hear on the news that this Manuel Gonzalez is

being sought for the murder of his girlfriend?" Hutchinson favored Stone uneasily.

Stone saw no reason to deny it. "We're looking for him now. I was hoping maybe you could help me out there, Chuck, figuring that since you and Gonzalez had been frequent visitors to your wife's place of employment, you might have run into one another from time to time . . ."

"Even if that were true, that doesn't make them bosom buddies," Hutchinson declared. "If you're here to accuse my client of somehow conspiring in his wife's murder, then do so formally and we will formally answer to the charges. If not, then I'd say this meeting is over, Detective!"

Stone expected as much, but looked to Chuck Murray for verification. "Is it your wish that I leave now? This isn't going to go away, Chuck. Not till your wife's murder is solved. If you have nothing to hide, I suggest you convince me . . ."

Chuck met his eyes thoughtfully. "I would never have hurt Adrienne," he claimed. "She was my life. If this Gonzalez bastard killed her, he did it on his own. If you want to believe otherwise, to hell with you!"

"Keep your mouth shut!" Hutchinson glared at his client before turning to Stone. "From now on, Detective, when you have something to say to my client, it'll either be in my office or in police custody."

"Your call, Counselor," Stone stated. "And for the record, Chuck, he's right: Anything you say that doesn't hold up can and *will* be used against you. So maybe it is best not to say anything. I'll see myself out."

Stone left the house thinking that if nothing else, he had shaken up Chuck Murray, whether he was an innocent man being unjustly targeted or someone who played a role in his wife's death. Either way, Stone figured it was worth it to go out on a limb as the noose tightened around Manuel Gonzalez's neck, even though he was still on the run as a triple murderer. But had he acted alone where it concerned Adrienne Murray?

I don't believe for one minute that Chuck didn't recognize Gonzalez, the detective mused. On the contrary, something told Stone that the man knew exactly who Gonzalez was well before having looked at his picture. The question was just how well did the two know each other?

And had it cost Adrienne her life?

CHAPTER 35

"If I didn't know better, I'd think you orchestrated the whole thing," Beverly said over the phone, a hint of suspicion in her tone. She had phoned Grant the moment she got back to her office in order to discuss his judicial assignment to the Santiago trial. It was an hour later that he returned her call.

"But you do *know* better," Grant voiced lightheartedly. "As much as I'd like to take credit for positioning myself to preside over you in the courtroom, it was *strictly* Judge Thompson's call."

"I suppose," she hummed. Realistically, Beverly knew that criminal trials were assigned to judges randomly or based on the current load. But that didn't mean the rules couldn't be broken. Had they been here? If so, why?

"Besides, when you think about it," Grant said without apology, "who is more appropriate to be the judge in Sheldon Crawford's courtroom than the man who took his place?"

Beverly couldn't argue about the merits of his appointment. Or the irony. Still, the notion of Grant presiding over this trial—*her trial*—made her uneasy for some reason.

"You know, we might just have a little conflict of interest here," she pointed out for his reaction.

"Not that I can see." Beverly could picture Grant dismissing this with a quick bat of the eye. "There's nothing that says lovers can't be in the same courtroom at the same time," he said. "It's not like we haven't done it before."

"I didn't mean that." Or did she? Beverly's palms suddenly grew damp. The fact was they had always been on the same team before. On equal footing. Now he was in a position to exert authority over her.

Not to mention show favoritism one way or the other during the proceedings. After all, Grant would be standing in judgment over a man who had also once threatened his life. Might this affect Santiago's chance for a fair trial?

Although Beverly had no problem with gaining any edge she could over her opponent, she wanted to win this case fair and square. It was the only real way to savor the victory, like tasting fine wine without the bitterness.

As it was she knew that as judge, Grant was not the jury, nor were the lawyers. His power in the court had checks and balances. Meaning Rafael Santiago's guilt or innocence was not something Grant had sole authority over. Even then, Beverly knew deep down that the man she had fallen in love with was an honorable, aboveboard person.

"Relax, Bev." Grant's voice was as smooth as silk and confident. "We're both professionals. And we both want to see justice served, not make up our own brand of justice along the way. Santiago will have every opportunity to prove his innocence, without prejudice on my part."

"Well, that's a relief," Beverly joked. "For a moment there I was afraid you might show some bias *against* me during the heated proceedings."

A hearty laugh boomed into the phone. "I promise I won't treat you any different than I would any other attorney, Ms. Mendoza. But I wouldn't mind one bit if you treated me just a little kinder than you do most judges."

Beverly found herself laughing. She had always been respectful toward judges, so long as the same was returned. But she appreciated Grant's crafty way of putting the situation in its proper perspective.

It was not about her or him. It was about Rafael Santiago.

And, to a certain extent, Maxine Crawford.

Beverly watched her phone light up, indicating another caller. "There's someone on the other line," she told Grant. "Hang on a minute and I'll get rid of the person."

Before he could protest, she put him on hold.

"Beverly Mendoza. May I help you?"

"Ms. Mendoza," the voice said edgily, as if carrying a great weight, "this is Lynda Flanagan of the Suncrest Nursing Home."

"Yes . . . ?" Beverly said, her heart suddenly pounding hard. She expected the woman to say that her father had passed away. Though this was something Beverly had braced herself for, it was nothing she wanted to hear anytime soon.

"I'm afraid I have some distressing news." Lynda seemed to be trying to find the words to express it. "Your father is missing . . ."

"Missing?" said Beverly, baffled. "What do you mean *missing?*"

"He seems to have just walked away," she said tonelessly. "The nurse was watching him in the yard one moment and then he was gone."

Beverly's temples throbbed. She could not believe what she had just heard. "How does a seventy-four-year-old Alzheimer's patient simply vanish?"

"We're doing everything we can to find your father, Ms. Mendoza," Lynda said apologetically. "I'm really very sorry about this—"

"*Sorry!*" Beverly shrieked into the mouthpiece. "You let

my father just wander off to who knows where, and all you can say is you're sorry?" Her eyes burned like acid. "If anything happens to him, I'm holding you and your staff fully responsible! Do you understand me?"

"Per . . . perfectly," she stammered.

Beverly hung up with rancor and took a moment to compose herself before remembering that Grant was still on the other line.

Her voice was shaking like a leaf as she told him, "Seems as though my father has run away . . ."

Grant joined Beverly and Jaime in canvassing the neighborhood in search of her father. In spite of half the nursing home staff and the police also looking for him, so far there was no sign of Alberto Elizondo. It was as if he had simply vanished off the face of the earth.

"Do you have any idea where he might have gone?" Grant asked Beverly. They had spent the past two hours seemingly going around in circles.

Beverly crinkled her mouth. "I don't think Papa has any idea where he might go," she said sadly. "He could be anywhere."

"How far can an old man go?" Grant strained his eyes to look out into the distance in the dwindling late-afternoon sunlight.

The thought that her father could be lying in a ditch somewhere, hurt, all alone, and unable to call out for help petrified Beverly.

What if Papa has died? She tried not to even think such thoughts, praying that they would at least find him alive, if not well.

"Maybe Grandpa is trying to go home," suggested Jaime, looking miserable with concern.

Beverly wished she could reassure him that this would all turn out right. But she knew she couldn't. Alzheimer's disease had a way of destroying everything in its path like a tidal wave. Her father had been swept up in it and there was no turning back. She could only hope that they could delay the inevitable.

This required locating him before it was too late.

"Papa's old home is farther away than he could ever go," she told her son despondently. Beverly guessed that the house she grew up in was at least five miles away and out of reach for a man whose memory had been pretty much wiped out.

"But you told me that sometimes Gramps was his old self." Jaime's voice broke as if he were about to cry. But he refused to break down, trying to be strong. "So maybe he got lonely and wanted to be where he felt more comfortable and loved."

"I only wish that were true," Beverly said sorrowfully. Then at least they would know where to find him.

"I'll bet Grandpa *did* go there," Jaime persisted, the optimism in his voice mixed with angst, "looking for Grandma."

"I don't think—" Beverly started to say, not wanting him to have false hope.

"Maybe Jaime is onto something," Grant cut in. "Your father doesn't seem to be anywhere else, but we know he's out there somewhere. I'd say it's worth a try."

In this instance it was two against one and Beverly was happy to succumb to their wishes as a measure of desperation.

When they got to the house, Beverly had butterflies in her stomach. The Spanish eclectic home with its carved stonework and red tile roof reminded her of when she was young and both parents were hardworking, healthy people. Now her mother was dead and father was who knew where.

God, please let him be here, she prayed, though considering it a long shot at best.

Jaime rang the bell and Grant held Beverly's hand for support as the door opened. Beverly gasped when she saw her father standing there, looking very much like he belonged.

"Oh, Papa," she cried. "We were looking all over for you." Beverly embraced her father and felt his tears as well.

"He came here saying this was his house," explained Sonja Clemente, the current occupant. She was petite and in her early fifties. "He expected to find Maria here. I knew he was . . . lost."

She had already called the police, who were on their way.

Beverly felt a mixture of relief and sadness that it had come to this. "You had us all so worried, Papa. You shouldn't have left the nursing home."

Alberto wiped the tears from his crinkled eyes. "I just wanted to be near Maria," he sobbed. "She's here, you know."

"I know, Papa." She sought to pacify him, and agreed that her mother would always be there in spirit.

Indeed, Beverly almost felt as if she could feel her mother's presence somehow guiding her father to safety. She smiled at him through watery eyes. In spite of being inadequately dressed for the five-mile walk, he did not seem any worse for wear.

"We weren't going to let anything bad happen to you, Grandpa," said Jaime, elated that it was his suggestion that led them to find him.

Alberto looked at his grandson and flashed him an appreciative, if not confused, smile. "I'm glad to hear that."

"I gave him something to eat," Sonja said. "He had no trouble finishing it."

"I can't thank you enough," Beverly told her gratefully.

"None of us can," seconded Grant, feeling happy that the situation had not turned out worse. Beverly had enough on her plate without having to lose her father, too.

"I've been there," Sonja said sentimentally. "Both my parents were also in the same condition." She was careful with her words, so as not to have Alberto hear anything too disheartening that he might be able to comprehend.

When they took him back to the nursing home, all were ecstatic to have Alberto back safe and sound. Including the other residents, who were glad they were all one big, happy family again.

But Beverly was not happy that the staff had been negligent, nearly causing a real tragedy.

"I expected my father to be taken care of here," she spoke harshly to the director, Mildred Irwin. "How could you let him walk away, with no one trying to stop him?"

Mildred was in her late forties, tall and athletic in build, with short red hair. "I can't tell you enough how sorry I am," she expressed, sincerity visible in her freckled face. "The nurse that was on duty has been fired. Apparently your father scaled a six-foot-high fence designed to keep the residents in the yard. That's never been done before. It was as if he had a purpose and was determined to see it through . . . even in his diminished capacity."

"Papa was always pigheaded," admitted Beverly. She was amazed that of all the things her father could retain, he somehow remembered how to make his way to the house he and her mother had spent their wedding night in. "I guess some things never change," she mused, "no matter what . . ."

But that was not enough to let the nursing home off the hook. She dreaded the thought of a repeat performance.

"What assurances can you give me that this will never happen again?" Beverly asked the director straightforwardly.

"We're adding four feet of fence to the top in the yard," Mildred promised. "The ten-foot-high barrier should make it virtually impossible for anyone to scale it successfully without being noticed. Also, we're hiring some additional staff to be able to better keep track of all the patients when they are out for some exercise."

Why hadn't they done that from the start? wondered Beverly. It could have saved a lot of grief and frustration. Better late than never, she decided, choosing to give them the benefit of the doubt as a place that had otherwise been good for her father to stay in.

She, for one, resolved to pay much closer attention to the surroundings and safety of her father, as well as to the commitment of the staff to treat her father and others with dignity and respect.

When they left the nursing home, Beverly assured her father that she and Jaime would never be too far away.

In her mind Beverly added Grant to that pledge. He had come running when she called, and seemed very much like a man who wanted to be there for the long haul.

CHAPTER 36

Walter McIntosh walked into Beverly's office, seemingly looking over his shoulder, as if he were being followed. She had been anxiously awaiting the results of his investigation, if only to eliminate any potentially embarrassing disclosures by the defense during the trial. But something told Beverly that Walter, like her, was walking a tight line in what he could do.

Or would do.

He had a file folder in hand, thick with information.

"Looks like you've been busy," Beverly observed.

Walter was not smiling when he said, "You don't know the half of it."

"Enlighten me then," she said, staring up at him from her desk.

Walter sat down and wiped his brow, as if having just completed a grueling race. "I was stonewalled at just about every turn when I tried to get information on the Crawfords. Seems like the word was out and everyone's lips were sealed tight." His chin jutted out. "But that only made me more determined. Fortunately, I've got my street contacts who would sell their own mothers down the river if the price was right. And it usually doesn't take that much to qualify."

Beverly found her interest more than a little piqued. What could be so damned secretive about the judge and his widow that the powers that be wanted to suppress?

"So what did you learn?" she asked eagerly, though striving to keep her voice at an even pitch.

"Plenty." Walter met her gaze squarely. "I learned that the honorable judge was two-timing his wife every chance he got. The man was a sex addict and liked younger women, who in turn were attracted to older, wealthy, generous men. Judge Crawford may have had a reputation as being damned good on the bench, but he sure as hell made for a lousy husband."

Was his reputation that important to preserve even in death? Beverly wondered. Moreover, had Maxine been aware of her husband's infidelity? Or had she simply learned to live with it for what she got out of the marriage?

"And that's not all," said Walter, a catch to his voice. "Seems like the man was a big-time gambler. The ponies, the dogs, slot-machine poker—you name it. Word has it that Crawford was financing his habit by accepting bribes to manipulate the sentences of those who had the right connections and plenty of *money*."

Beverly was stunned. If true, it meant that any number of trials in the judge's court could have been compromised.

Did Dean know what was going on?

Did *Grant?* she mused.

Could this have had anything to do with Judge Crawford's murder?

Walter seemed to put that question to rest when he said, "So far there's no indication any of this is connected to Crawford's death. On the contrary, everyone I spoke to said that no one wanted the judge dead and buried. He was too valuable alive to too many people."

"Obviously not to everyone," Beverly said.

Walter sighed. "No one figured on Santiago taking him out before anyone could do anything about it."

"You mean like kill Santiago first so that the judge's criminal enterprise could go on uninterrupted?"

"Yeah, something like that," he said out of the side of his mouth.

Beverly tried to digest what she'd just been told. Even if it had no bearing on her case against Rafael Santiago, it did give cause for suspicion about the timing of Judge Crawford's death and the appointment of his successor.

Were the two entirely coincidental? Or had Grant's judgeship been tainted with blood?

"Turns out the wife was no angel herself," said Walter with a smirk. He leaned back. "Maxine Crawford was a dancer named Crystal Lynley when she hooked up with the judge. As in *dirty* dancing, if you know what I mean."

Beverly had an idea, but needed to be sure. "Just how dirty was her dancing?"

"The former Ms. Lynley was arrested twice for solicitation for purposes of prostitution," Walter said bluntly. "But the charges were dismissed."

"Let me guess," hummed Beverly, "by Judge Crawford?"

"You've got it, Counselor." Walter seemed to applaud her for putting two and two together.

So Judge Crawford married a woman who serviced him sexually for money, Beverly mused. Then he used his influence to keep it all quiet.

It made Beverly wonder if Maxine had ever really loved her husband, or vice versa. Or was she only serving as a paid watchdog for those who had a vested interest in keeping Judge Crawford happy and content?

Only to end up with whatever didn't go to the creditors or vultures?

Beverly recalled Maxine's words. *Other men wanted me only for my body or what they thought I could give them. But never my mind and soul.*

Either the lady was in complete denial or had been completely taken in by Judge Crawford. Or maybe it was the judge who had gotten less than he bargained for with the former prostitute, Beverly considered.

Walter leaned forward, twisting his lips. "One other thing you might find interesting." He opened the folder, removing what looked to be phone records. "On the night Judge Crawford was killed, two phone calls were made from his house to a cell phone. The times recorded suggested the calls came *after* the estimated time of death. Meaning that they had to have been made by Maxine Crawford. What's more, records show that many more calls were made to this number in the last few months," the investigator reported.

"Whose cell phone was it?" Beverly favored him expectantly.

Walter sucked in a deep breath. "It belonged to former Deputy DA, Grant Nunez," he said levelly. "Who, of course, is now the Honorable *Judge* Grant Nunez."

Beverly's pulse quickened. Grant? How could that be? He had *never* told her he knew Maxine Crawford. In fact, he'd seemingly gone out of his way to suggest otherwise. Why had she been phoning him? Could Maxine have remained in the business of prostituting herself even after marrying Sheldon Crawford?

Could Grant have been one of her clients?

Or had the man Beverly had fallen in love with also been corrupted by bribes, greed, *and* indiscretions?

And thereby handpicked as Judge Crawford's successor in more ways than one . . .

CHAPTER 37

Manuel hot-wired the car, shifted it into drive, and sped off. In the rearview mirror he could see the owner standing on the sidewalk—some dumbass old white man—shaking his fist at him.

He laughed. *Idiot!*

Manuel headed south, not exactly sure where he was going. He knew he needed to ditch his old lady's Chevy Aveo when he'd heard over the radio that they had found her and were now looking for *his* golden ass.

Problem was, he liked his freedom. He hated the sound of a cell door slamming behind him. Possibly for the rest of his life . . . or till they stuck the needle in his arm.

He definitely didn't want to be some bastard's prison boy toy.

And the food in the joint was poison. Even the rats avoided it like the plague, preferring to feast on the inmates while they slept and had bad dreams.

Manuel would sooner kill himself before he went back to prison.

But that wasn't in his immediate plans either. That's why he'd stolen the old white dude's Buick LeSabre.

Too much to live for, he thought, giggling like a teenager. Yeah, he was high as a kite and loving every damned minute of it.

The cocaine left Manuel seeing stars, but he was still in control. At least he knew that he had to hide out till things cooled down. Later he'd probably head back to L.A. He could get lost in the Latino hood and no one would ever find him.

Right now he had to lay low. Think about life without Claudia. She was a waste anyway, he thought, increasing his speed without being the wiser. The bitch could never satisfy him. Always a complainer and a lousy lay.

She had finally gotten what she had coming.

Manuel took note of the speedometer as the car neared ninety miles per hour. Though the fast speed thrilled him— made him feel like he was flying like a plane—he pushed down on the brake till he had fallen within the speed limit. It would be just his dumb luck to get stopped for speeding, only to have the cop find out that speeding was the least of his troubles.

And the cop's once Manuel pulled out his blade and cut the son of a bitch up.

Manuel laughed again, enjoying flirting with death. But he didn't feel it was his time yet.

Not when he still had some unfinished business.

He had a date with the Latina attorney, Beverly Mendoza. He'd watched the house as a security system was installed. Even seen when she and the fat boy fled the house that night with the black man they were with earlier. Manuel suspected he had probably offered to put them up for the night or however long they needed to feel safe.

But the boyfriend can't protect you forever, bitch, Manuel thought.

And neither could some two-bit alarm.

Not if he had his mind made up to go after her.

Which he had.

He always got what he wanted from a woman. Why should she be any different?

When he was done with her, she would wish she had never been born.

Or that he hadn't been.

Isn't that what the judge's wife wished after she had been forced to submit to sexual acts—or die?

Only the attorney wouldn't be so lucky, Manuel promised himself. When it was over, she wouldn't live to tell her story to anyone who would listen.

Manuel found himself at his auntie's apartment.

The truth was he had no more desire to be there than she wanted him there. But he needed a place to chill. And he doubted anyone would look for him there.

After all, he had only been in touch with her twice in the past ten years.

Both times he had only been trying to look out for her.

Now he had to look out for himself.

He heard the lock turn. When the door opened just enough to allow air in, he saw a frightened old woman. She tried to shut the door in his face. But he was quicker, forcing it open, so that the chain lock ripped from the wall.

She fell to the floor from the impact of the door crashing against her feeble body. He saw that she was dazed, but still conscious.

He closed the door, turning the dead bolt that was still functioning.

He faced the pitiful sight beneath him. "Sorry, Auntie," he said without remorse. "I need to spend some time with you for a while. And since I don't see nobody able to stop me, looks like it's just you and me."

He watched as she tried to speak, but nothing came out except for a gasp or two. As if she was asthmatic.

He wondered if she was having a heart attack or something.

It would serve her right if she was, Manuel laughed inside. Family shouldn't reject family. Especially when he was all she had left now that her dumbass son Rafael had gotten himself locked up again!

CHAPTER 38

Beverly was summoned to Dean Sullivan's office as soon as her meeting with Walter McIntosh was over. She had tried phoning Grant but was told he was out for the day.

Her mind was spinning as to what all this meant with regard to her case against Rafael Santiago.

Not to mention her relationship with Grant. Could she have been wrong about his heart, soul, and character?

His feelings for her?

Beverly could only speculate as to what had gone on between Grant and Maxine Crawford.

She wondered if it was *still* going on . . .

When Beverly stepped into Dean's inner office, she could tell by the hostile look on his face that she had incurred his wrath.

"Have a seat, Ms. Mendoza!" His brows bridged stiffly.

Beverly sat across from his wide desk, feeling intimidated and vulnerable with respect to whatever he had to say to her.

"What's going on, Dean?" Her voice was as innocent as

she could make it, though Beverly's heart was thumping hard against her chest.

Dean bent forward, and said darkly, "I understand that you were warned to lay off digging into Judge Crawford's background and personal life. Why have you ignored this and insisted on prying *outside* your jurisdiction?"

Beverly lifted a brow. She really had stepped on someone's toes. Was it Dean's? Grant's? The governor's?

Or were they all in collusion?

"I was only doing my job, Dean," she said toughly, "trying to learn *everything* I could to solidify my case against Rafael Santiago. I thought that was what you wanted . . ."

"You already have everything you need to take this to trial, Beverly!" Dean's eyes narrowed beneath his glasses. "Your job is to focus on getting a conviction against the man who murdered a sitting judge based on the evidence of the case—not turn this thing into a three-ring circus by digging for dirt in all the wrong places. Do I make myself clear?"

"You do," she protested, "but don't I have a right to know if Judge Crawford was *crooked,* thereby potentially making his murder part of a conspiracy to silence him?"

"There is no damned conspiracy!" Spittle flew from Dean's mouth. "You'll just have to trust me on that. Whatever the judge or Mrs. Crawford were into sexually or otherwise is extraneous to the case against Santiago. If you have a problem with that, Beverly, tell me right now and I'll hand the case over to someone else who's more cooperative."

He's ordering me to look the other way, Beverly pondered. Or she could lose perhaps the most important case of her career thus far.

Which meant she would likely find her career in the DA's office in serious jeopardy.

Who was pulling the strings here? she wondered. The DA? The governor?

Or could it be Sheldon Crawford's replacement on the bench, Judge Grant Nunez?

"I'm waiting for an answer, Beverly," Dean said, impatiently drumming his fingers on the desk.

Beverly bit into her lower lip. "No, sir," she said in acquiescence, "there is no problem."

"Good." He put a hand to his glasses. "Now update me on how things are going with the upcoming Santiago trial."

She told him everything he wanted to know and nothing he didn't.

By the time Beverly left Dean's office, she had been bruised but not broken. She would not step over the line officially and make it easy for him to destroy all she had worked so hard for.

But she did not intend to let Grant off the hook either. She was determined to find out what he was involved in and with whom.

If only for the sake of any future between them.

Beverly walked right past Grant when he opened the door. He had been shaving when she barged in, shaving cream still stuck to his chin like drool.

"Hello to you, too," he said with an elevated brow.

She regarded him sternly. He was bare-chested, wore tight jeans, and was looking very sexy. Though this was intriguing, Beverly's mind was elsewhere.

Was he crooked?

Or sexually involved with Maxine Crawford?

Maybe both, she mused.

"Did I do something wrong?" asked Grant, as if he hadn't a clue. "Or did you just decide you couldn't wait another moment to have my body?"

Beverly colored at the thought. But the idea abandoned her quickly, replaced by far more sinister thoughts.

"What the hell's going on, Grant?" she asked without mincing words. "Why did Maxine Crawford phone you *twice* the night Judge Crawford was killed?"

Shock crossed Grant's face like a shadow. *Damn! I'm*

dead meat! "How did you find out about that?" He had a pretty good idea, but wanted to hear it anyway.

At least he didn't insult me by denying it, Beverly thought. Not that it made her feel any better.

"It isn't important." She glared at him. "Are you sleeping with her?"

Grant stepped forward uneasily. "Hell no," he voiced unevenly. "It's not what you think, Bev . . ."

"Then you *must* be involved in the bribes Judge Crawford was accepting," she accused him. "Is that how you landed in his court? Is Dean part of this conspiracy too?"

"You're way out of line," Grant said with a snap. *Can I really blame her? I should have been up front from the start,* he thought.

"Am I?" Her hands were folded in an angry pretzel. "Is that why I've been ordered to look the other way by you? And Dean?"

"You don't understand, Beverly." Grant reached out to her, wanting to connect somehow.

She backpedaled. "Don't touch me!"

"All right," he said on a sigh. "Calm down." *I'll try to do the same and hope my explanation will smooth the waters.*

"I believed in you, Grant." Beverly's heart raced. She hadn't realized this would affect her so. But how could it not? Everything she thought Grant stood for in and out of the courtroom was suddenly in jeopardy.

Along with their romance and the possibilities thereof.

"Let me fix you a drink," Grant proffered tremulously. *I sure can use one.*

Beverly batted her lashes. "I don't want a drink!" He wouldn't worm his way out of this by getting her drunk.

"Well, I do."

He walked past Beverly to a wet bar in the corner of the living room. A moment later Grant was back in front of her, having wiped the cream from his chin, a scotch on the rocks in hand.

He regarded Beverly for a long moment and thought, *It shouldn't have come to this. But now that is has, deal with it.*

"Judge Crawford was under investigation for some time by the Justice Department," Grant said evenly. "They believed he was involved in bribery, racketeering, pimping, and other criminal acts. The DA's office was working closely in conjunction with the Feds in building a case against Sheldon Crawford and others he was involved with. Only Dean and myself knew about it, along with the governor."

"Why didn't you say anything?" Beverly asked, holding his gaze and trying to come to terms with this, though the answer was obvious to her.

"I couldn't," Grant said miserably, putting the glass to his mouth, emptying its contents in one swallow. "Aside from being sworn to secrecy, it could have compromised the investigation and put you in danger. The fewer people who knew, the better."

Beverly batted her lids thoughtfully. "What did Maxine Crawford have to do with it?" she ventured forth. "Or is that between you two . . . ?"

Grant mused. "She was working with us," he explained quietly, "gathering evidence we would be able to use."

"Against her *own* husband?" Beverly's mouth went agape. "Or were they married in name only?"

"As far as we know, their marriage was the real thing," Grant responded tonelessly. "Even if far from conventional. With regard to Maxine supplying information against the judge . . . well, it was either that or risk going down with him."

"Obviously she chose to abandon a sinking ship," deduced Beverly, thinking about how her knowledge of Maxine Crawford continued to evolve.

Beverly thought back to being summoned to the hospital by Grant after Maxine Crawford was brought in. Why had he wanted to see Maxine?

She looked up at his eyes. "You were at the hospital that night to—"

"To make sure she kept her mouth shut!" Grant answered. "Had Maxine said anything at all to the press or the police, it could have jeopardized the whole case we were building."

"Does your case have anything to do with the case against Rafael Santiago?" Beverly asked, remembering that Walter had indicated otherwise. Could Santiago have been a hired killer meant to silence Sheldon Crawford once and for all?

"The two are *completely* separate," Grant told her sincerely. "Santiago killed Judge Crawford and attacked Maxine Crawford all on his own. It hit everyone who was working on nailing the judge's ass like a sledgehammer. Believe me, giving him the easy way out was the last thing anyone wanted. But there was nothing we could do about it after the fact."

"Except treat Judge Crawford like a fallen hero," surmised Beverly. "Aboveboard as a law-abiding, honorable member of the judiciary."

"Exactly," Grant muttered sotto voce. "The investigation is still ongoing. To treat Judge Crawford as anything less than a saint might have caused others we're targeting to make a run for it. Not to mention place our informants in danger—including Maxine Crawford . . ."

"Is she still working for you?" Beverly was curious. No, she was a little more than curious. The thought of Grant having to spend more time with her beautiful key witness than she herself did bothered Beverly more than she cared to admit.

Grant shook his head imperturbably. "As soon as Judge Crawford was killed, we no longer had any use for her, other than what she'd already given us." He paused. "Except as the only one who could point the finger at the man who shot her husband and sexually assaulted her."

Beverly felt both relief and regret. She had thought the worst about Grant, when he, like she, was only doing his job. Even if it was inadvertently at odds with her own work. It was just by chance that Santiago happened to kill a man whose life was already about to be in ruins. Only in death, the judge had possibly forever escaped having his legacy ruined and reputation stained by malfeasance. She could well imagine the probe affecting other cases for years to come.

"I think I could use that drink now," Beverly told Grant, sucking in a deep breath.

"All right." He gave her an understanding look.

He poured her a brandy and had another scotch himself.

Beverly thought that Grant looked tired, as if carrying a great weight on his shoulders—one that had been weighed down further by having to divide his loyalties. She should never have confronted him like this, questioned his integrity, but she, too, had been in the hot seat. Without even a clue as to what was going on, it could have affected her ability to do her own job effectively.

"So what happens now?" she asked uneasily.

Grant gazed into her emerald eyes. "Business as usual," he said. "For both of us. What you just heard never leaves these walls."

"I understand." Beverly stared knowingly at him over the rim of her glass. "I'm sorry, Grant, for going after you."

"Don't be. You had every right to, all things considered. I'm sorry I had to hold things back from you that you deserved to know. I wasn't proud of it, especially when all I want is to share every part of my life with you."

Beverly blinked back tears. "I feel the same way."

Grant grinned broadly and brushed against her, causing an immediate reaction. "I've missed you, Bev."

They had both been too busy lately to devote much time to their relationship, causing Beverly hunger pains as well.

"So now that we've managed to be in the same room together, what do you propose we do about it?" she challenged him, suppressing her own renewed desire that threatened to tear her apart.

Grant took away their glasses, then ran the back of his

hand smoothly across Beverly's cheek, and said openly, "For starters, I want to kiss you."

The hairs on the back of Beverly's neck stood up. "Who's stopping you?" she managed before her voice gave way to raw emotions.

Without a response, Grant leaned his face into hers so that their open mouths pressed together at one angle and then another in passionate kisses. Beverly put her tongue in Grant's mouth, mingling with his own, enjoying the taste and moisture. She wrapped her hands around his head and put her all into the kiss, getting the same in return.

A gasp erupted from Beverly's throat and she felt light-headed. The long and deep kiss had become intoxicating. Suddenly her initial reason for coming there seemed like nothing more than a distant memory.

Grant felt the temperature rise in the room quickly. Kissing Beverly so succulently was causing him to lose all self-control. He wanted her now more than she could imagine.

And he aimed to have her.

He forced himself to back away just inches from her swollen lips, and murmured, "What do you say we carry this to the bedroom?"

"I say yes, and hurry. Otherwise I'll just have to continue attacking you here!" Beverly uttered boldly, encouraged by the kiss, cemented by her own unmet needs.

Grant laughed lasciviously and scooped her in his arms. "Say no more, baby. And neither will I . . ."

Beverly had Grant's full erection in her mouth, teasing and stimulating him to the base of her throat. The next thing she knew, Grant had managed to shift his body on the bed and part her thighs, so that his head was now between her legs and pleasuring her simultaneously.

The sixty-nine position left them both breathless and moaning at the same time in arousing sounds and actions.

Beverly reached her orgasm first, squeezing her thighs

around Grant's face as the moment came with a bang. Moments later he exploded in her mouth while she absorbed his throbbing climax.

Neither had any intention of settling for oral gratification, wanting much more of one another.

Beverly kissed him afterward, tasting her sex on his lips and vice versa. It turned her on even more. She grabbed Grant's shoulders, wanting to feel his weight on her, his penis inside of her.

Grant put on the condom in the blink of an eye, not wanting to waste a moment before he could make love to Beverly. He climbed atop her, reined in her splayed legs so they hung on his hips, and thrust himself into her covetously. Instantly he felt her vagina expand to greet him, then enclose to keep him.

Their mouths again interlocked and their bodies swayed back and forth rhythmically with zest and determination. Both were drenched in sweat and stuck to each other like second skins.

Beverly's contractions came in waves as Grant pounded her and she pounded back. Neither let up, not wanting this to end too soon.

Beverly opened her legs to allow Grant to move in deeper. He responded with fervor and they reached the point of no return, making them slaves to each other and their individual orgasmic needs. The sounds that came from their mouths were a language all their own of undulating lust and rip-roaring satisfaction.

It ended as it began, with hot kisses and a feeling of belonging.

Grant took a moment to catch his breath before cuddling Beverly and resting his lips against her ear. "You've really got a hold on me, baby. I can't imagine feeling as I do now about any other woman."

Beverly got a warm sensation, ashamed that she had doubted him earlier and vowing never to do so again. She raised her eyes to his chin. "You're a pretty hard act to follow too, Mr. Nunez."

Grant kissed the side of her head. "You think?"

"How could I not?" Her eyes batted flirtatiously. "It's not every man who gets me into bed. Not to mention to fall in love with him."

"Ditto, baby." He cracked a smile. "Guess that means we're stuck with each other."

"Guess it does," Beverly said. "Oh well, I suppose we'll just have to get used to that. Are you sure you're up to the task?"

A part of Beverly still feared rejection and being forced to start all over again. Even if neither of them had spoken of marriage as part of the deal. A steady, long-term relationship could be nearly every bit as rewarding for her and Jaime. Or it could be heartbreaking.

Then there were still their careers to consider. Grant was a criminal court judge whose path she would have to cross on more than one occasion in the courtroom as an assistant district attorney. Including during the Santiago trial. And even when he happened to be working in conjunction with the Department of Justice and not always in her best interests.

Could this stand in the way of their happiness as a couple?

Would it someday prove to be their undoing?

Grant imagined what Beverly might be thinking and wanted to squelch any notions she had that he would bolt at the first sign of trouble. Or that he would allow *her* to leave without fighting to keep what they had.

He lifted himself on an arm so that their eyes met, before saying with confidence, "I'm definitely up to the task, and then some, Beverly."

Grant sealed the deal with a kiss.

CHAPTER 39

As he did every Thanksgiving Day, Stone took over the kitchen. It was a tradition that he was proud of—using the cooking skills that had been passed down through the generations of his family and too often ignored by him to give his wife a break from slaving over the stove. While Joyce always griped a little about it, being comfortable with her own cuisine, overall she seemed to appreciate Stone becoming a chef once a year.

The entire family was there for the holiday feast. Anna and Chad had come home from college, and Joyce's parents drove down from Oregon, where they had moved a few years ago.

Manuel Gonzalez was still on the loose, having managed to evade the dragnet across the city for more than a week. Stone considered that he might have left Northern California, if not the state itself. But something told him that the man was still there in the Eagles Landing area, waiting to be caught like a mountain lion.

It was only a matter of time.

Just as it was only a matter of time before Stone would

be able to determine whether or not Chuck Murray had played any role in the death of his wife, Adrienne.

Stone was barely aware of the phone ringing as he poured the sweet potato batter into the two pie crusts. When Joyce stepped into the kitchen doorway, a dour look creased her face.

"It's for you."

"Can you take a message?" he asked on a sigh. "I have my hands pretty full right now."

A moment later Joyce was back. "It's Gordon," she said sullenly. "He says it's urgent."

Stone frowned. He had made Joyce a promise that there would be no police business today. Not with the kids and her parents there.

Maybe it was not so urgent, he thought. Perhaps his partner could delay whatever was on his mind till tomorrow.

"Yeah, Chang," Stone grumbled into the phone. "What's up?"

"Gonzalez has been spotted by one of our cruisers," Chang spoke loudly. "He's inside a Kelbow supermarket not far from your place. Thought you might want to be there when we make the arrest."

Stone moistened his lips. "You're sure it's Gonzalez?"

"He was seen leaving a car that matched the description of the last one he stole." Chang sneezed nastily into the phone. "The license plate checked out."

Stone thought about it for a moment. He wanted this bastard so badly he could almost taste it. Nothing would give him greater pleasure than to personally slap the cuffs on Manuel Gonzalez for the murder of Adrienne Murray and his girlfriend, Claudia Sosa. And, with any luck, he could be back home before they began to miss him too much.

"I'm on my way, man," he told Chang.

Before Joyce could say anything—and she had been watching him all the while like a hawk—Stone kissed her on the mouth.

"I'm sorry, hon. Duty calls. Looks like we've got a bead

on the man who's likely killed at least three women that we know of. I have to go."

"Where?" One hand clung to Joyce's hip like it was stuck there.

Stone told her, as he always did in a potentially dangerous situation. But they both knew it came with the territory. Didn't mean he had to like it.

"You be careful, Stone," she pleaded, fear dancing in her eyes. "If anything were to happen—especially on Thanksgiving Day . . ."

"Nothing will," he told her comfortingly. Not if he could help it. "I won't be long." Stone handed her his apron, knowing she knew what to do with it. "I love you."

Stone heard the words repeated back to him even as he was dashing out of the room and hoping they could finally get this son of a bitch before anyone else felt the cold steel of his blade.

Chapter 40

Beverly squeezed the cart past another in the too-small aisle. As had become customary for her during the holidays, she had put off getting some key essentials till the last moment. This year was no different. She was making roast beef and baked potatoes for Thanksgiving dinner, with a green salad and apple pie. But she had forgotten a few odds and ends like salad dressing and dinner rolls, along with a few snacks. Thank goodness some stores were staying open later on holidays, she thought.

Grant had been invited to have Thanksgiving dinner with them and had accepted gratefully, anxious to get closer to Jaime. Beverly wanted that too and felt that Grant had already taken some steps in the right direction, as had Jaime. She could imagine the day when they would be together as a real family and share all the holidays.

Jaime had become more open to the prospect that it might be a good idea to have someone special become part of their lives on a permanent basis.

He also wanted to bring home for Thanksgiving someone who had long been a part of their lives—his grandfather. Beverly thought it was a terrific idea, and Grant agreed. She knew Alberto Elizondo would never be the same person who raised her, but he would always be her father, no matter what. He deserved to spend a day of thanks with his family. He'd had a full life and a loving family, and for that they had reason to be thankful.

Having collected her groceries, Beverly stood at the checkout counter. In her periphery she saw a man walking out the door. She turned to look at him and saw that he was already looking at her. His dark eyes were cold and sinister.

Beverly froze. He looked very much like the man from Burger King, she thought, unnerved.

The man who was a carbon copy of Rafael Santiago.

A shiver ran up and down Beverly's spine. Had he followed her there?

Is this the man who broke into my house?

The police were of the opinion that the burglar was a professional thief who had burglarized some nearby homes recently.

But could he have also been a murderer? A rapist?

A stalker?

Chill out, Beverly ordered herself, borrowing a phrase from Jaime and his friends. Rafael Santiago was solely responsible for what he was being charged with, no matter how many other people looked like him.

And she had no proof that this other man had broken into her house. Or that he followed her to the store. Or elsewhere.

The man was probably not even looking at me, she mused. Not everyone who happened to be turned her way was actually staring at *her.*

By the time Beverly paid the elderly clerk, the man was gone. The bagger—a carrot-topped, gangly boy of around seventeen—noted the uneasiness on her face.

"Would you like me to walk out with you, ma'am?"

She gave it some thought but decided her fears were unfounded. And since she only had a single bag, he would be better off helping someone who really needed assistance.

"Thanks," she told him. "I'll be fine."

Beverly carried the bag with one arm while taking looping steps toward her car. She noted that there was a surprisingly large number of cars in the lot, though the store had seemed practically empty.

At the driver's-side door, Beverly reached into her purse for the key. She had not heard a sound, except for maybe the wind, when suddenly a figure came toward her at blinding speed. He rammed into her, causing the bag and purse to fly from her hand.

"Don't make a sound," a man ordered into her ear. The voice had a Latino accent.

He was behind her, but close enough that Beverly could feel his hard body pressed into hers. She heard the sound of a switchblade opening so close to her face that it may have nicked her cheek.

"I have a knife," he said, as if to make no mistake about that. "Scream and I'll rip your throat out!"

Beverly was trembling but knew she had to hold her composure. Was this the man she had seen in the store?

The same man from Burger King?

Why her . . . ?

Am I any more special than the next person a burglar, rapist, or murderer chooses to accost?

God, help me get through this.

The man reeked of the acrid smell of smoked crack cocaine and musty body odor. She had become familiar with these scents as a prosecutor who had visited crime scenes and jails more times than she could count.

A crackhead, she thought miserably. The most dangerous type of offender. They were very often unpredictable.

And scary.

Whatever Beverly may have thought about this bastard, it wasn't worth losing her life over.

"I'll give you whatever you want," she told him. "Just don't hurt me."

"Why not?" he laughed coarsely. "So you can go back to that fat-assed kid of yours and get cozy with the black dude?"

Beverly could barely contain her emotions.

It was him!

The man who had broken into her house. He knew about Jaime.

He had to be the same man she had seen at Burger King, Beverly decided. He must have followed her that day. And today as well.

If I could just get the gun out of my purse. Beverly noted that the contents of the purse had remained inside it when it fell to the ground. She dreaded to think what might happen were her assailant to check the purse.

"My son is my life," she pleaded, her heart racing. "You can have the car, the purse, the groceries . . . just let me go."

He kissed her cheek with wet lips. "In your dreams, bitch!" The man put the knife to her throat. " 'Cause it's *you* I want, *and* the car. Now we're both gettin' in and you'll drive where I tell you to."

The one thing Beverly knew was that she could not get in that car with him. If she did, in all likelihood she would be signing her death warrant. As long as she was out in the open, she stood a fighting chance.

She tried to look around for help but could not see much from the position she was in, her face upturned with the knife at her throat.

She needed to stall him.

"Who are you?" Her voice almost sounded friendly and made her want to gag.

"Your worst nightmare," he growled mockingly.

"You were at Burger King, weren't you?" She got bold. "And you followed us home? Then broke into my house?"

He laughed derisively. "You're smart, lady," he confirmed.

"Maybe too damned smart as an assistant district attorney! But it don't matter, 'cause you ain't gonna tell no one about Manuel."

Beverly felt the blade tickling her throat. She knew that if she so much as twitched it would slice into her skin. Suddenly the very real thought of dying at thirty-two flashed across her mind like a horror movie.

Could she actually die before her father?

Who would take care of Jaime without her?

She could envisage his getting married, having children, a successful career—all without her being able to enjoy it as a proud mother.

And how would Grant fare if she were no longer in the picture? Would some other attractive, smart, and sexy woman take her place in his life? Would she become little more than a distant memory to him?

Beverly decided that she was not ready to meet her Maker. Not this way.

"I won't tell anyone about you, Manuel," she said, managing to keep her voice at an even keel. *Manuel who?* "I'll go wherever you want me to . . . do whatever you want."

This seemed to inspire him as he pulled the knife back ever so slightly. "Let's get in your car, Beverly," he breathed obscenely into her ear. "We're going for a drive."

"All right," she agreed. "My keys are in my purse."

Beverly squatted to get her hands on the purse, but he lifted her up before she could reach it and the gun inside.

"Not so fast," he said roughly. "What the hell's in the purse that you were itching to get to? You wouldn't happen to have a gun in there, would you, Ms. Lawyer . . . ?"

"No, there is no gun," she lied. "Just my keys and normal stuff women keep in their purses."

If I can just grab the purse, I can end this the right way.

But her captor clearly thought otherwise and once again had the knife up to her throat.

"Oh yeah?" Manuel growled. "We'll see about that, bitch."

From the corner of her eye, Beverly seemed to detect movement. She couldn't be sure if it was an illusion or her mind playing tricks to somehow give her false hope.

A customer from the store, perchance?

The police? Perhaps someone had seen what was going on and called 911 . . .

But how could they have gotten there so soon?

Manuel was so self-absorbed that he didn't seem to notice the presence of anyone else.

I have to keep him preoccupied.

"Why don't you get my keys out of the purse then, Manuel. I'm not going to go anywhere. You're the one with the knife."

He breathed against her ear. "Yeah, and don't you forget it!"

Even with his macho behavior, Beverly sensed nervousness in the man, as if he suddenly felt exposed. Or perhaps it was the drugs playing with his mind. Either way, she had no intention of waiting to see how this played out. Especially since it was likely to end badly for her as things now stood.

"Get the damned keys, bitch," Manuel ordered. "And hurry."

Just as he had loosened his hold on her and Beverly saw the opening she was looking for, a voice boomed from a loudspeaker.

"Manuel Gonzalez, this is Detective Palmer of the Wilameta County Sheriff's Department. Put the knife down and step away from the lady!"

Manuel did just the opposite. With lightning-quick speed, he had once again looped a powerful arm around Beverly's neck, placing the knife threateningly under her chin.

"No way, man," Manuel shouted defiantly. "She stays with me. Try anything and I'll cut her throat. I swear it!"

Beverly watched as law enforcement suddenly descended upon them like vultures. She immediately recognized Stone Palmer. They had worked together briefly on the Suzanne Landon case. He seemed like a nice man, and one she couldn't be happier to see, albeit in a less than ideal situation for her.

"Don't be a fool," Stone blared, while hoping this thing could end without bloodshed. "There is no way out of this for you, Manuel. It's all over. Now move the knife away from the lady's throat and you won't be harmed."

His gun drawn, Stone inched closer to the murder suspect and his captive. It took a moment before he realized that the woman was none other than Wilameta County Assistant DA Beverly Mendoza. How the hell did she end up in Gonzalez's grasp? he wondered. Wrong place at the wrong time . . . ?

"Let her go, Manuel," Stone said nicely, noting the groceries littering the parking lot and the ADA's purse on the pavement. "No one else has to die. Including you . . ."

Beverly could sense that her captor was weighing his options. Did he kill her—or try to—and almost certainly be killed? Did he kill himself?

Or did he realize that it was a battle he could no longer win, even in death, and do the smart thing by surrendering?

"I'm not worth dying for," Beverly told him coaxingly. "And there's no reason for your life to end either. Please let me go . . ." The blade continued to tickle her throat, only it was hardly a laughing matter.

"Can't go back to prison," Manuel muttered audaciously.

So he had been in prison, Beverly thought. *Why am I not surprised?* What crime or crimes had he committed?

She found herself wondering if by chance he knew Rafael Santiago?

"They will kill us *both* if they have to," insisted Beverly, feeling his resolve was weakening. "You're worth more to them dead than I am alive. If you give them an excuse, they'll take you out and not give it a second thought if there is some collateral damage along the way."

She didn't believe that for a moment. But Beverly wanted him to. In her experience even the most depraved criminals still had an inherent instinct for survival. When this instinct was threatened they almost always reacted predictably.

Manuel moved the knife away from Beverly's neck, seeming to indicate his surrender. Beverly's jubilation was short-lived, however, as he seemed to have second thoughts. She saw the switchblade once again moving in her direction. But she would not give him the chance to put her at death's door once more.

Without her gun, mace, or even keys to use as weapons, Beverly counted on the element of surprise to catch her would-be kidnapper off guard. Using the heel of her mule, she jammed it as hard as she could into his leg just above the ankle.

Manuel howled like a wolf in pain, releasing his grip on her and the knife simultaneously, while hopping on his one good leg.

Beverly turned around and got her first up-close look at her attacker's contorted face. She saw Rafael Santiago staring back at her in anguish. Yet she knew that it wasn't him. Only a cruel hoax. Or was it somehow by design?

Before Manuel could begin to recover, Beverly immediately broke toward the store. She looked back as the authorities pounced on her assailant, throwing him to the ground and handcuffing him.

Her nightmare was over. Whereas his had only just begun.

Beverly was still shaking and trying to catch her breath when she felt a solid hand on her shoulder, causing her to jerk around.

It was Detective Palmer. A look of concern was on his handsome face. "Are you all right . . . ?"

"Yes," she said, running fingers through her mussed hair. "I think so."

"Assistant DA Beverly Mendoza, right?" Stone's eyes twinkled at her.

"Yes." Beverly smiled while holding back tears over what

might have been. "I don't think I ever thanked you for testifying at the Suzanne Landon trial."

He grinned. "You did by winning it and getting another killer off the streets."

Her head tilted to one side, grateful nonetheless. "You also sent the writer to me," she remembered.

Stone was stumped for a moment before it came to him. His eyes grew. "Ah, yes! Ms. Wesley, I believe. Persistent lady. Hope she didn't give you headaches."

"Not half as much as him . . ." Beverly gazed at Manuel Gonzalez, who was being placed in the back of a squad car.

Stone frowned. "Sorry you had to cross paths with that asshole. But if there's a silver lining, it could have been worse. Gonzalez was wanted in connection with three murders and at least one sexual assault . . ."

Beverly put her hands to her mouth, aghast. Her shock was not just that she had been lined up to become the next victim of this creep, but that he was suspected of committing crimes similar to those perpetrated by Rafael Santiago. Was this another coincidence? Or did bad seeds grow in the family, assuming they were in any way related?

Stone could see that this had unnerved the attorney, and rightfully so. He tried to soften the blow. "Why don't you let me help you gather those groceries."

Beverly nodded, having practically forgotten why she was there in the first place. She followed the detective back to her car and immediately lifted her purse, with all the contents apparently still inside.

She regarded Stone as he put her store items back in the bag. "So how long have you been looking for this Manuel Gonzalez?" she asked curiously, having barely kept track of anything recently aside from the case she was working on.

"More than a month now," Stone answered, "though we only identified the suspect recently."

Beverly noted that it was more than a month ago that Rafael Santiago had perpetrated his heinous deeds. There had been no indication that he committed any other crimes other than those against the Crawfords. So why did something in her imagine that he could have been in cahoots with Manuel Gonzalez?

Maybe because I see a mirror image of one in the other and am looking for a connection that simply isn't there. Other than the fact that both are brutal killers.

She favored the detective, who had bagged all her spilled groceries. "I'm glad you caught the man."

"So am I. That's one less criminal to have to deal with outside the courtroom."

"And one more for us prosecutors to try to win a conviction."

Stone smiled and looked at the bag. "If you want to pop the trunk, I'll put this right in."

Beverly took out her car keys and used the remote to unlock it. "Be my guest."

"By the way, seems like we have a little more in common than Suzanne Landon and Manuel Gonzalez." Stone met Beverly's gaze. "My son Paco seems to be good friends with your son, Jaime."

Beverly raised a brow in surprise. "Paco's your son? I knew his dad was a cop, and I've actually spoken to your wife by phone. But I never made the connection." *Maybe I should have,* she mused.

Stone's jaw squared. "To be honest, I hadn't either till very recently when Paco was gushing about going to a judge's chambers with Jaime and his lawyer mom."

Beverly blushed. "Small world."

"Yeah, I guess it is."

Maybe it wasn't quite as small as they thought, she told herself.

"Perhaps after the holidays we can all get together for dinner or something."

"I'd like that," Stone said.

"Right now I'd better get going. My son and father are expecting a big Thanksgiving Day feast. And Manuel Gonzalez aside, I'm not about to disappoint them."

Stone grinned knowingly. "Yeah, I'm in the exact same boat. Only as the chef, the meal will still have to go through me. That is, assuming my wife lets me back in the kitchen, after I was forced to make a slight detour in the name of justice . . ."

CHAPTER 41

When she got home, Beverly felt exhausted and unsettled, but thankful to be alive. In spite of her ordeal, she saw no reason why they should not be able to enjoy their Thanksgiving meal.

Grant's car was parked in the driveway. He had volunteered to pick up her father from the nursing home, while she busied herself with the meal. Beverly hoped Grant hadn't found himself overwhelmed in trying to baby-sit her father and son. Good practice, she thought.

Before Beverly could get to the front door, it was opened and Grant stepped out. "We were wondering if you'd gotten lost," he joked. "We actually considered starting Thanksgiving dinner without you—"

He stopped himself short and furrowed his brow as she stepped into the light coming from the foyer. Only then did Beverly become consciously aware of her somewhat disheveled appearance. She had tried to make herself look presentable as best as possible, but found she was too upset to care.

"What the hell happened to you?" Grant put a hand under her chin, which had been slightly nicked by the knife and some drawn blood had dried.

"Where are Papa and Jaime?" she asked first, not wanting them to hear or see her like that.

"They're in the den watching TV."

"Good," Beverly told him. After taking in a long breath, she managed, "I was nearly kidnapped."

Beverly explained every frightening detail of her encounter with Manuel Gonzalez to Grant in the privacy of her bedroom. Including being rescued by Stone Palmer and the Sheriff's Department brigade.

"Good heavens!" Grant exclaimed, incredulity creasing his face in several places. "That bastard could have—"

"But he didn't," Beverly reminded him even as her pulse boiled at the prospect. "The police were after Gonzalez. They think he killed at least three other women. Thankfully the stolen car he was driving was spotted in the store parking lot."

Grant was sure his blood pressure had risen after hearing that his girlfriend had nearly become a murder victim. He was familiar with the police investigation into Gonzalez, who was suspected of stabbing his girlfriend to death and murdering two other women. But from what he understood, the victims had all been living in his vicinity. Which didn't mean the killer couldn't have broadened his range and targets.

"Why'd the bastard choose you to go after?" questioned Grant. As though he needed a reason.

It was something Beverly had asked herself. She had no real answer, except for maybe pure chance and being in the wrong place at the wrong time, perhaps more than once.

But she suspected that the question from Grant was really more rhetorical, since he knew it could just as easily have been any female Gonzalez happened to run into by accident or design.

"He's the same man I saw at Burger King, Grant." Beverly

felt dirty in her clothes and wanted to take a shower. "Gonzalez admitted that he had followed us home that night and broke into the house."

Grant's gaze betrayed feelings of anger and regret.

Beverly broke down as her emotions came to the surface. "I never felt so helpless as when he had the knife to my throat and wanted to take me somewhere. All I could think of was never seeing Jaime again. Or you . . ."

"It's all right, babe," said Grant, doing his best to comfort her and still his own ire that was threatening to boil over. *I should have been there to protect her from that asshole.* "The son of a bitch is never going to get the chance to hurt you ever again." Not if Manuel Gonzalez wound up in his courtroom.

"He's like the spitting image of Santiago," Beverly told him. "Grant, the two could be twin brothers—if Santiago had a brother!"

Grant used the backs of his fingers to gently wipe the tears staining her cheeks. "Doesn't matter whether they're kin or not," he stated firmly. "The full weight of the law will be brought down on both of them so they get everything they deserve."

Beverly sniffed and gazed up into his eyes. He had been every bit as strong and supportive as she had imagined. She was happy that he was there for her when she needed him most.

"I have everything I deserve," she said softly, "in you."

Grant relaxed his jaw, kissing her. "We'll see about that. Right now, I suggest you take a quick shower, change clothes, and get back out there and feed your family. Otherwise they may stage a mutiny."

Beverly laughed. "You're right." It was time to get back to the true spirit of Thanksgiving.

The meal was served in the dining room and everyone seemed to be enjoying themselves. Beverly noted that even

her father seemed almost like his old self, joking and laughing. But inevitably he would become disoriented and not
know where he was or who they were.

"Why can't Maria be here?" Alberto asked, his craggy
face dreary.

"Grandma is in heaven, Grandpa," Jaime said sympathet-
ically, stuffing a buttered roll in his mouth.

"Heaven?" Alberto put his finger to his mouth, as if wondering where exactly that was.

"It's a place where all the angels gather," Beverly told
him. "A place where you will be someday, Papa."

"You think so?" he chirped questioningly.

"Count on it," declared Grant, forking a tender piece of
roast beef. "And Beverly won't be too far behind. Or Jaime,
for that matter. Isn't that right, Jaime?"

Jaime chuckled, his mouth full of lima beans. "Yeah, but
if it's all the same to you, Your Honor, I'd rather stay here
amongst the earthlings for a bit."

Grant laughed. "Oh, don't worry," he said. "Something
tells me you still have quite a few of these delicious meals
left to experience." He scooped up some candied yams.
"Frankly, I'm with you, Jaime. Let's see if we can bribe Beverly into hanging around a lot longer herself, if only for her
cooking."

"Yeah, let's do it." Jaime broke into a chortle.

Grant followed suit. Even Alberto joined in, prompting
Beverly to burst into laughter also. She couldn't help but
think that this was about as good as it got. Sharing a
Thanksgiving Day meal and joy with her family. That included Grant, who had shown that he wanted to be part of
the world she had created for herself. And she wanted him
there every bit as much.

She savored the thought of there being permanency to
what they had about as much as Beverly abhorred the
thought of what could have turned out to be a disastrous
Thanksgiving Day. She had the feeling that an angel was on

her shoulder, protecting her from evil men like Manuel Gonzalez and Rafael Santiago. It was up to prosecutors like her to do their part in putting these men away. Or live with the consequences.

CHAPTER 42

Two days later Stone walked into an interrogation room at the county jail. A handcuffed and shackled Manuel Gonzalez was sitting at the table accompanied by a burly, mean-looking guard. Gonzalez was wearing the standard orange inmate garb. Unlike the night of the arrest, the crackhead appeared calm . . . almost content, thought Stone.

He nodded at the guard, who then left, and glanced at the one-way mirror. On the other side Lieutenant Kramer and Chang watched.

"You're in a lot of trouble, Manuel," Stone told him, playing the good guy before the *bad* ones came in. He put a tape recorder on the table, turning it on.

"Think I care?" Manuel snorted.

"Not really. But *I* do." Stone narrowed his eyes. "And the family members of the women you killed care, too."

Manuel said nothing, staring straight ahead, as if in a trance. He had waived his right to an attorney during questioning, but Stone knew this could change at any time, so he had to try to get as much out of him as he could.

"Let's talk about Adrienne Murray." Stone turned a chair

backward and sat across from the suspect. "You remember her, don't you? You waited for her outside her office building—the same office where your girlfriend Claudia Sosa worked."

He detected a bit of remorse in Manuel's brown eyes for killing his girlfriend, if not Adrienne.

"Then you raped and sodomized Adrienne Murray, stabbed her repeatedly, and dumped her body in the lake!" Stone's voice grew rancorous. "Does that ring a bell . . . ?"

Manuel sneered. "Yeah, so I did it, man, okay?"

"No, it's *not* okay, *man!*" Stone said, as though speaking to a nine-year-old. But it was an important first step, as he was confessing to the crime after being read his rights. "It's *never* going to be *okay!* Not for her husband, Chuck Murray, who loved Adrienne more than life itself."

Stone watched him react to this as he hoped Gonzalez would.

"You knew Chuck Murray, didn't you?" he asked. "He visited the building where his wife worked almost as much as you did."

Manuel began to laugh snidely. "Yeah, I knew him. So what?"

"Were you friends . . . ?"

Manuel favored Stone oddly. "Yeah. Right." He paused, rolling his eyes. "All right, I did it for him."

"Did what?" Stone glanced at the tape recorder and the one-way mirror.

"I offed his old lady," Manuel declared bluntly.

Stone peered at the suspect. "Are you saying Chuck Murray hired you to kill his wife?"

"Yeah, man." Manuel swallowed. "That's what I'm sayin'."

Stone inhaled a deep breath and leaned forward. "Now why would Chuck Murray pay you to *sexually assault* and kill his wife?" he asked with some skepticism.

Manuel turned hard eyes on him. "To teach her a lesson, man. He said she was messin' around on him and playing with his head. He was afraid she was gonna leave him. He wanted her dead . . . but not before I treated her like the whore he thought she was."

Stone's palms grew sweaty. Part of him had wanted to believe Chuck was innocent of any wrongdoing. The other part had seriously doubted that was the case. He'd obviously been obsessed with his wife. But had that really led to a murder-for-hire?

They needed more than this asshole's words of complicity on Murray's part. Especially when Gonzalez would say anything if he thought it might help him down the line.

"Why would you agree to kill Adrienne Murray?" Stone's lips were a straight line.

"Why not?" Manuel shrugged without emotion.

"That won't cut it, Manuel!" Stone glowered at the suspect. "Unless you're straight with me, you're going down on this one all by your lonesome."

Manuel lifted his cuffed hands and scratched his face vigorously. "I owed him money, man," he said unevenly.

Stone reacted. "Money for what?"

"He was a dealer."

"You mean he dealt in illicit drugs?" Stone wanted to confirm.

"Yeah—crack, heroin, weed, you name it," Manuel said. "I owed him. This was a way to wipe the slate clean. I got what I wanted, he got what he wanted . . ."

Stone could almost see his colleagues in the other room with their heads spinning. Chuck Murray a drug dealer?

And a conspirator in the rape and murder of his wife?

Seemed almost too good to be true. Except for the fact that Stone had sensed all along that Chuck Murray had it in for his wife. And used a crack addict to do his dirty work for him.

But he still needed more than just words and gut instincts to go after Murray.

"Do you have any proof to back up these claims?" Stone asked.

Manuel flashed dingy teeth. "He didn't give me no receipt, if that's what you're askin', man. Why would I lie?"

"You tell me, *Manuel*..." Stone fixed his face. Since there was never any talk of a deal being offered and little likelihood that would change any time soon, there seemed to be little gained at this point by implicating Chuck Murray just for the hell of it.

"He showed up in the hood," claimed Manuel, "with some cheap crack. Ask around. They knew him as the White Amigo 'cause he like stood out from Latinos with his chalky white skin."

Stone chewed his lower lip thoughtfully. "What about Penelope Grijalva? Are you saying Chuck was involved in her murder, too?"

Manuel lowered his eyes. "I ain't gonna lie about it," he said flatly. "That bitch I did myself. She got what she wanted. It felt real good killing her. You know, like the feeling you get when gettin' yourself off."

A real psychotic asshole, mused Stone, distressed that he even had to give him the time of day.

He set his jaw. "Did it also feel good when you stabbed your girlfriend twelve times?"

Manuel gazed bleakly at him. "Hey, she left me no choice," he asserted. "I was high . . . scared. I panicked, man."

Strangely, Stone believed that something inside Gonzalez made him regret having to kill her. Claudia Sosa was probably the one person in the world who actually cared about Manuel Gonzalez and this was how she was rewarded? With three women dead, the man was facing a sure death sentence himself, as surely as the death sentence he had given his victims.

And, if Gonzalez's allegations turned out to be true, Chuck Murray would be next in line for a lethal injection.

Street snitches confirmed that Chuck—alias the White Amigo—was indeed a major cocaine dealer in and out of the Latino hood. That and Manuel Gonzalez's taped statement were enough to get an arrest warrant issued for

Chuck Murray on suspicion of conspiring to murder Adrienne Murray.

Murray's attorney was notified that the arrest was imminent, and agreed to bring his client in. When that didn't happen on schedule, Stone, Chang, and a few sheriff's deputies were dispatched to Chuck's house.

Stone arrived feeling depressed and disappointed. He had listened to this man profess his innocence. Now it turned out Chuck Murray had been guilty of far more than they had imagined. Putting crack out on the streets of Eagles Landing would undoubtedly cause more deaths, pain, and misery. And maybe spawn a new era of Manuel Gonzalezes who would be willing to kill to support a habit.

The house was surrounded and Murray was ordered to come out with his hands up. When there was no indication that he was prepared to do this, his attorney intervened, hoping to get him to surrender before force was used.

Jonathan Hutchinson emerged from the house within moments, his fleshy countenance looking weary. "He's dead," the attorney announced unceremoniously. "Looks like he killed himself."

Inside, Stone found Chuck Murray crumpled on the bedroom floor like a collapsed skyscraper. Blood oozed from a gaping gunshot wound in his temple. He had apparently committed suicide. By his side lay a .357 Magnum.

A hastily scribbled note on the dresser read:

> *I never wanted to hurt Adrienne. But I was hurting too. I was always afraid of losing her. Now we can always be together and no one can take her away.*
> *—Chuck*

The note was bagged as evidence.

Stone was satisfied that Chuck Murray had indeed solicited Manuel Gonzalez to violate and murder his wife in order to humiliate her and rid himself of his constant insecurity about their relationship. He had chosen the perfect patsy and killer in Gonzalez, who found killing to be as addictive as crack cocaine.

An unsettled feeling remained in Stone's stomach like indigestion long after the body had been carted off and the house sealed pending completion of the investigation.

It wasn't over yet, he told himself that night in bed. For his part, Manuel Gonzalez still had to be held accountable for Adrienne Murray's death.

And at least two other murders.

Then there was the attempted kidnapping of Beverly Mendoza. The Assistant DA had likely been minutes away from being driven to her grave had luck not stepped in and Gonzalez been spotted.

The thought comforted Stone. The last thing they needed was to have a dead prosecutor on their hands with a lunatic still on the loose.

Now everyone could rest a little easier—at least for tonight.

He held his wife, settling against her warm body and appreciating the fact that she was there as solace from the hard, cold realities of the world out there.

CHAPTER 43

Beverly watched through the one-way glass with interest as detectives grilled Manuel Gonzalez. He had been charged with the murders of three women, including the woman he lived with. Two had been strangled and one sexually assaulted. All had been stabbed repeatedly—apparently by the same knife he had held to her throat, Beverly thought.

It gave her a chill, the frightening reality that she had been slated to become Gonzalez's next victim. For this, he also faced charges of attempted kidnapping and assault. She had evidently been targeted strictly at random rather than for her position as an Assistant DA or for anything to do with the Santiago case.

Beverly had been given extra reason to give thanks on Thanksgiving Day. If she hadn't known it before, she did now—there was every reason in the world to be grateful for all the things in her life. For it could have all been taken away in an instant with no chance to get it back.

Her eyes latched on to Gonzalez through the window. If Beverly hadn't known better, she would have thought he was looking right at her. Laughing at her. Telling her that this wasn't over yet. That she had still better watch over her shoulder, for the Grim Reaper just might abduct her yet and do horrifying, unimaginable things to her.

And there was not a damned thing she could do about it but wait in terror until he came calling for her when she least expected it.

The truth was, Beverly knew Manuel Gonzalez, for all his smugness and seemingly cool detachment, was no longer a threat to her. Or any other woman in Eagles Landing. With Stone Palmer insisting they had a strong case against him on all counts, there was little chance he would ever taste freedom again.

But what piqued Beverly more was Manuel Gonzalez's striking resemblance to Rafael Santiago. She honestly wondered if Maxine Crawford would be able to tell the two apart. Not that she needed to.

From what Beverly knew, the similarities between Gonzalez and Santiago were strictly superficial and happenstance. Though the same age, one man was Mexican-American, the other Cuban. The hair was cut differently, albeit the same jet-black. Both were career criminals.

But the differences were even more telling, she thought. One had killed with a handgun. The other preferred his bare hands or a switchblade as his choice of murder weapons.

Manuel Gonzalez had never been in Judge Crawford's courtroom, by all accounts, virtually eliminating him as a suspect in the judge's death by way of motive. Then there was the fact that his DNA was not found at the scene of Sheldon Crawford's murder.

It was just the opposite for Rafael Santiago, who had the motive, means, and the DNA evidence, along with the victim identification to support his guilt in the slaying of Judge Crawford and the sexual assault of his wife, Maxine.

Still, Beverly remained troubled. There was something about Manuel Gonzalez that made her believe he was somehow connected to Rafael Santiago.

But did that connect him in any way to Judge Crawford's death? Or to Maxine Crawford's sexual attack?

Stone and Eagles Landing Police Department Homicide Detective Joe O'Dell sat in on Beverly's interview with Manuel Gonzalez.

"The Assistant DA needs to ask you a few questions," O'Dell told the prisoner in a gruff voice.

"So let her ask." Manuel fixed a lewd look on Beverly.

She sat at the side of the metal table directly across from the prisoner, who was flanked by O'Dell and Stone, almost as if it was Gonzalez who needed to be protected from her. Beverly recalled how her ordeal with him had ended—by ramming her foot into his leg.

Holding Manuel Gonzalez's gaze, she asked without sympathy, "How's the leg?"

He grinned halfway. "I'm still walkin'," he said toughly. "Maybe next time you try a little bit harder, huh, Beverly?"

She sneered at him. "There won't be a next time! You had your one big chance and you blew it!"

Manuel leered. "Never say never, Ms. Assistant District Attorney," he said, as if having some extra insight. "We just might be able to go at it again someday."

If they ever did, Beverly thought, the next time she would be ready for him. She imagined aiming her Glock right between his eyes and pulling the trigger.

But this was no longer about her, she realized. It was about *him*.

Keeping her voice steady, Beverly asked before she went any further, "Would you like to have an attorney present?"

"What for?" Manuel asked, as if he hadn't the faintest idea.

"To counsel you in anything you say to me that could be used against you," she told him clearly.

Manuel licked his lips. "I don't need no lawyer tellin' me what to say. I'll tell you *everything* I planned to do to you if they hadn't come to your rescue. Before I sliced you up, I would've made you suck my—"

O'Dell placed a firm elbow to Gonzalez's chest, causing him to heave. "You watch what the hell you're saying when talking to the lady, you son of a bitch! Or I'll rearrange your face so even you won't recognize it. No one will ask any questions when I say you ran into a door or two . . ."

Manuel smoldered, glaring at the detective.

"It's all right," Beverly said in a level voice, even if she was glad O'Dell had intervened on her behalf. She was used to this type of bullying from inmates who saw this as possibly their last chance to exert some fear and intimidation. Unlike before, this time she was strictly in the driver's seat. "Do you know a man by the name of Rafael Santiago?"

Manuel showed no sign of such in his blank stare at her. "Rafael who . . . ?"

"*Santiago,*" she repeated.

"No, I don't know no Rafael Santia—whatever the hell . . ." He grinned wickedly. "Why? He some Latino gangsta or somethin'? Or just another Latin lover like me?"

Beverly had the feeling he was mocking her. And giving all Latinos a bad name in the process. But there was no reason to believe he wasn't telling the truth.

"Have you ever heard of Judge Sheldon Crawford?"

Manuel rubbed his chin. "Who hasn't? Ain't he the judge who was shot to death a few weeks ago? Heard his old lady got somethin' for her trouble, too."

"What else did you hear?"

He looked confused. "What the hell does any of this have to do with me?"

"Maybe nothing," Beverly was willing to admit. Or perhaps everything.

Stone was less accommodating, narrowing his eyes at him. "Just answer the damned question, Gonzalez!"

Manuel regained his cool. "I read the papers. I know they arrested some dude for blowing away the judge. So what?"

"But you've *never* heard of Rafael Santiago?" she inquired again.

"I already answered that one!" he retorted curtly.

"You'll answer it as many times as she asks, asshole!" blared O'Dell.

Manuel widened his eyes. "Never met the man," he said simply.

Either he had never read about Santiago's arrest or he was lying, Beverly mused. But why would he lie? What would he gain by lying about not knowing Santiago?

She gazed across the table. "Have you ever met a woman named Crystal Lynley?" It was Maxine Crawford's real name. Admittedly Beverly was grasping at straws here. There was certainly no reason to feel that even in her former life in the sex-for-sale business, Maxine had ever come across Manuel Gonzalez. But it was worth a try, just to be sure.

"Don't know. Is she as pretty as you?" Manuel showed his teeth, running a tongue across them lasciviously.

O'Dell snarled at him, making Gonzalez lose the flippancy and salaciousness in a hurry.

"I know lots of women," he bragged. "But I don't know no Crystal Lynley. Should I . . . ?"

"What about Maxine Crawford?" she pressed.

Manuel considered the name before responding, "Ain't that the judge's wife?"

"You tell me." Beverly's jaw tightened. "Do you know her?"

Manuel flashed her another vulgar look. "I'd sure like to. Maybe you can have her drop by for a visit. I hear that black bitches are the best in bed."

Beverly glanced at the detectives, wondering what they were thinking. That she had wasted her time? And *theirs?*

She was beginning to feel they might be right.

"Do you own a handgun?" she asked Gonzalez, mindful that the gun that killed Judge Crawford had yet to be recovered. Who was to say that Santiago didn't pass it to Gonzalez when finished, or vice versa?

"Don't you do your homework, *Beverly?*" he taunted her. "Guns are dangerous. Some innocent kid might get caught in the crossfire. Knives are more my speed. That way you have more control. You get to pick out a whore and carve her up like a turkey. You know what I'm sayin', *Miss* Assistant DA?"

"I think I do," Beverly said under her breath.

She was reasonably convinced that Manuel Gonzalez, sick and pathetic individual that he was, was not connected with the murder of Sheldon Crawford and the sexual attack on Maxine Crawford.

CHAPTER 44

The People versus Rafael Santiago trial began the first week of January. Seven women and five men sat on the jury. Both sides had carefully screened them, each seeking every edge they could get. Beverly was confident that she had the people she needed to produce a guilty verdict.

And she had a defendant who, by his very nature, fit the composite of a killer you might find in a college course called Violent Homicide 101.

Beverly sat at the prosecution's table alongside Gail Kennedy, stealing a moment or two to go over the case while waiting for the judge to make his entrance.

An innocent glance at the defense table and Beverly saw K. Conrad Ortega conferring intently with his client. Rafael Santiago looked almost like a different man from the one she had first seen in a lineup. His hair was cut shorter with a part in the side, making him look almost preppy. He wore a sharp blue suit that under other circumstances could easily have given the impression that he was a successful businessman.

Would the jury buy into this?

Or would they see through the facade to his *true* character?

"It'll be strange seeing Grant on the bench as a judge," remarked Gail, wrinkling her nose.

"Not half as strange as it will be for him seeing *us* in action as prosecuting attorneys," laughed Beverly. In fact, she had butterflies fluttering in her stomach, though she wasn't sure if they were the normal ones that came at the start of every trial, or if they were a direct reflection of this particular trial.

This defendant.

This case.

This courtroom.

This *judge*.

She and Grant had spoken little about the trial, almost as if to do so invited trouble at a time when they were trying to get past the recent tests to their relationship outside the courtroom. For her part, Beverly expected Grant to be a fair judge, if not extra tough on her and himself.

She accepted the challenge, wanting only to have the chance to present her case and let the jury decide guilt or innocence.

When the court clerk announced Judge Grant Nunez, everyone rose respectfully. Grant was in his element, it seemed to Beverly, with his black robe worn over a Hugo Boss gray wool suit that she had helped him pick out last week. His head was freshly shaved and seemed to actually give him a more judicial look, she believed.

They exchanged warm glances that only they could read into before he allowed everyone to be seated.

Beverly's first witness was Maxine Crawford. The two had remained cordial even after Beverly learned of her shady past and her willingness to spy on her husband to try and save her own neck. And collect what was left of his estate after the government took what was theirs.

What would I have done had I been in her shoes?

Beverly felt the question was impossible to answer, since

she could not imagine having ever taken the route that led to Maxine now being in the witness box.

Maxine sported a new hairstyle, wearing her blond-tinted hair in a flat twist. Beverly thought it gave her an air of sophistication and went well with a khaki suit and white blouse with ruffles in an almost school-teacher look that always played well with juries.

"What happened on the night of October twenty-ninth?" she asked the witness without preface.

Maxine sat poised and demure. "My husband and I were attacked," she said pointedly.

"Your husband was Judge Sheldon Crawford?" asked Beverly, an eye on the jury.

"Yes."

"And where did this attack take place?"

"In our bedroom."

"Can you explain to the court the nature of the attack on your husband?"

Maxine gave a long swallow. "My husband was shot to death," she said painfully.

"While you were in bed?"

"Yes."

Beverly gazed down at her. "And how many times was Judge Crawford shot?"

"Three." Maxine closed her eyes for a moment, as if saying a prayer.

"Did you see the man who shot your husband?"

"Yes, I did."

"Is that man in this courtroom?"

"Yes, he is."

"Can you point him out to me and the members of the jury, please?" Beverly requested.

Maxine lifted her finger and pointed it squarely at Rafael Santiago.

"Thank you," Beverly told the witness, satisfied that she had held up well thus far. "No further questions." She would recall her to the stand later.

Ortega stood, buttoning the jacket of his brown suit. "Mrs. Crawford," he began, "you testified that you were in bed during the time your husband was shot. Can you tell the court what you were doing?"

Beverly flew up like a rocket. "Objection! This is totally irrelevant!" she snapped, even if she didn't entirely agree that it was.

"Sustained!" Grant peered at Ortega. "I don't think we need to go there. Keep your questions where they should be, Counselor."

Ortega pursed his lips. "How far were you from the person who shot your husband?" he asked the witness.

Maxine considered this. "About five feet, more or less."

"Well, is it more? Or less?"

She looked at Beverly. "Five feet."

"Was the light on?"

"No."

"So you were able to see this person who fired the shots with the light off from five feet away?" the attorney questioned.

"It was still light outside," Maxine responded nervously. "I could see his face . . . his body."

"It was around seven o'clock when your husband was shot," said Ortega. "Correct?"

"Yes," came a tentative reply.

"Well, as far as I know," Ortega attacked her, "it's pretty dark in Eagles Landing after six o'clock in late October. Too dark for most of us to be able to make out anyone clearly in a room with no lights on—"

"Objection!" Beverly was steaming. "Your Honor, he is *not* qualified to know what she saw in the room that night. Nor can his speculation on what constitutes *pretty dark* be presumed to be the gospel insofar as lighting conditions in a house. Besides, our eyes can adjust to even 'pretty dark' conditions, enabling us to see what's before us."

"Sustained," blurted out Grant. "Mr. Ortega, there has been no indication that inadequate lighting was a factor in this crime. I think the witness had sufficient illumination to be able to see the man she identified as having shot her husband!"

"He cut the light on . . ." Maxine blurted out.

"What?" Ortega fixed her face in a moment of confusion. "But you just told this court there were no lights on. Are you changing your story now?"

Maxine gulped while holding his gaze. "You asked me if the light was on when he shot my husband. It wasn't. But then *he* cut it on before he raped me . . ."

Ortega rolled his eyes skeptically. "Now why would he do that, Mrs. Crawford? Especially when you consider that he let you live. Not the type of thing you'd expect from a man who just murdered your husband and wouldn't want you to identify him."

Maxine sighed, turning her eyes to the defendant and back to his attorney. She explained tearfully what only now had come to her, "He said he wanted me to see him and remember what was about to happen for the rest of my life. Then when he made me suck on his penis while he held the gun to my head . . ."

Ortega grimaced and for a moment was speechless before saying tonelessly, "No further questions, Your Honor."

Grant nodded and eyed Maxine sorrowfully. "The witness may step down."

Beverly watched Maxine walk away. The two exchanged glances and Beverly silently applauded her for standing up to Ortega. And helping their case at the same time with an important piece of information they had not previously discussed, but that was powerful for the prosecution in going after Rafael Santiago.

Beverly next called the medical examiner for Wilameta County to the stand.

Doctor Julia Duval was an attractive woman in her early fifties. Her platinum blond hair was swept in a chignon. Silver glasses hung low over blue eyes.

"Dr. Duval, can you tell us the results of the postmortem examination on Judge Crawford?"

"Certainly," she said evenly. "Sheldon Crawford died from a gunshot wound to his face, just above the right cheek. It caused a massive rupture in his brain."

"And what other injuries did he sustain?" Beverly asked.

"Aside from his face being shattered, Judge Crawford was shot once in the lower back, fracturing his spine," explained the witness, "and another time in the upper back. This one caused extensive internal damage, including a punctured lung and several cracked ribs."

Beverly winced, though she managed a smile at the doctor and thanked her.

"Just a couple of quick questions, Dr. Duval," said Ortega, approaching her. "What was the approximate time of death?"

"I'd say between seven and seven-thirty."

"That's P.M.?"

"Yes," she responded with a straight face.

Ortega paused, giving the jury the benefit of a sweeping glance. "Were you able to learn anything else about Judge Crawford's condition that could have contributed to his death?"

Beverly voiced an objection. "The witness has already testified as to the cause of death, Your Honor!"

"Overruled," Judge Nunez said weakly. "You may answer the question."

Julia Duval looked uneasy as she wrinkled her forehead. "Judge Crawford had advanced liver disease," she informed the attorney. "This would likely have killed him in six months to a year. But there's no reason to believe that—"

"No further questions," Ortega cut her off expertly.

"Maybe it would have been better if *you* had gotten Dr. Duval to talk about the liver disease," Grant told Beverly in his chambers during recess. "It was a heads-up counterstrike by Ortega."

Beverly fumed. "It was *dirty* ball," she insisted, dismissing Crawford's prior medical condition, in spite of the irony. "What killed the judge, plain and simple, were the three bullets fired into him by Ortega's client at point-blank range."

"And I'm sure the jury will see that," Grant said coolly. "Give them some credit for having brains, Beverly." He put his hand on her breast.

"Don't," Beverly said harshly, pushing his hand away from the front of her quilted blouse, despite feeling a tingling in her nipple. "Now is not the time."

"Will you lighten up, baby?" Grant looked annoyed. "This isn't the end of the world, either way. And short of a smoking gun, there certainly isn't any reason I can see that you won't get a conviction here. Not unless you find a means to self-destruct and allow Ortega to jump all over it."

"I have no intentions of self-destructing," she pouted.

"Good to hear." He grinned unevenly.

Why am I acting like a first-year prosecutor? Beverly chided herself. Ortega was only fighting tooth and nail for his client, as any good attorney—or even a bad one— should do. But that hardly meant she had a major fight on her hands in winning this case.

Not when virtually everything pointed to Rafael Santiago as the perpetrator of the crimes in which he was charged.

Any competent jury would weigh the facts above the innuendoes in rendering a just verdict.

Beverly sucked in a breath and offered Grant a genuine smile. "I'm sorry."

"Don't be," he said. "Just continue to kick ass out there. You're doing fine."

She kissed him softly on the mouth, and then used a finger to wipe the carnation-colored lip gloss from his lips. "Can you come to dinner tonight?" she asked anxiously.

Grant licked his lips appetizingly. "Try and stop me."

Beverly smiled wickedly. She wouldn't even if she could. If he played his cards right, she thought, there might even be dessert afterward.

In fact, she was certain of it.

CHAPTER 45

The following morning criminalist Harold Bledsoe took the stand. Fiftysomething, he wore gold-rimmed glasses and had a dark blond toupee.

"Dr. Bledsoe," Beverly began deliberately, "you did a DNA analysis on semen and genital hairs extracted from Maxine Crawford. Is that correct?"

"Yes."

"And these were found where?"

"In and around Mrs. Crawford's vagina and anus," he said tightly.

Beverly favored him. "I understand that your tests revealed that the semen and hairs found belonged to two different individuals, one being the victim's husband, Sheldon Crawford. Correct?"

Bledsoe nodded. "Yes."

"Which could be expected, given that it has already been established that the Crawfords were engaged in sexual relations when the crime occurred." Beverly faced the jury, looking self-assured in a Tahari fringed bouclé cream blazer and pants. "Can you tell us who the other semen and genital hair samples belonged to?"

She looked back at the criminalist in time to see him respond evenly, "They matched the DNA of the defendant, Rafael Santiago."

Beverly nodded, satisfied that she had given herself the setup for the next set of questions.

"Were there also strands of human hair found on the Crawfords' bedspread that did not belong to either Judge Crawford or Maxine Crawford?"

"Objection, Your Honor," Ortega shouted. "Sounds to me like she's leading the witness."

Grant dismissed this without even giving the attorney the benefit of a glance. "I don't get that impression, Counselor. Overruled. The witness may answer the question."

Bledsoe eyed Beverly. "Yes, there were a few hairs found on the spread that did not match those belonging to Sheldon or Maxine Crawford."

"And who did they come from?" she asked pointedly.

Bledsoe regarded the defense table. "They matched the DNA of the defendant."

Beverly paused purposefully. "Dr. Bledsoe, perhaps you could be so kind as to explain to the jury what it means to have a DNA match, whether semen, hairs, or blood . . ."

"No problem." He touched his glasses. "Without getting too technical, DNA profiling allows us to differentiate one person from the next by analyzing small segments of DNA called polymorphisms that make us who we are as individuals. In DNA criminal profiling, samples of one's DNA can be obtained from blood, semen, hair follicles, saliva, or urine. With the exception of identical twins, the likelihood of two individuals having the same DNA is by some estimates 1 in 100 billion."

Beverly let that sink in with the jury for a moment. "So what you're telling us, Doctor, is that there is no doubt in your mind whatsoever that the DNA testing of the semen and hair samples collected in relation to this crime belonged to the defendant, Rafael Santiago?"

"That is correct," Bledsoe answered without prelude. "And for the record, the polymerase chain reaction—or PCR testing method—used to analyze the DNA fragments in this case is widely respected as a reliable forensic tool in DNA fingerprinting."

Beverly couldn't resist a tiny smile that the witness managed to get that in as a further blow to the defense, who were likely to attack the DNA evidence as presented. In her mind, even the possibility that Rafael Santiago had an identical twin in say, Manuel Gonzalez, wouldn't hold up in this case, DNA aside. Especially when considering that Santiago had motive and the witness identified his signature lizard tattoo in a rather conspicuous place.

"No further questions," she told the judge and walked away as the defense attorney rose for cross-examination.

Ortega wasted little time getting to his feet. He glanced once at his client, then glared at Beverly as she walked away, before taking looping strides toward the witness box.

"Dr. Bledsoe, you testified that the odds that two people could have the same DNA were 1 in 100 billion, *with the exception of identical twins.*"

"That's right." The witness eyed him thoughtfully.

"So you're telling us that if two people are identical twins, their DNA would be identical as well?"

Bledsoe pushed his glasses up, hesitating.

Beverly sucked in a deep breath, having anticipated such a line of questioning.

"Do I need to repeat the question, Doctor?" Ortega pressed.

"No," he responded tersely. "Yes, identical twins do have the same DNA, or genotype, in fundamental nature. However, recent studies have been able to identify minute differences in identical twins' DNA."

Ortega cut him off. "I'm not aware of any such research

being admitted as evidence in a criminal proceeding. If I'm wrong . . ."

Bledsoe averted his stare. "As I said, the research in this area is fairly new."

"And therefore not relevant to this case," argued the attorney. "What is relevant is that the possibility exists that there may be an identical twin of Mr. Santiago with the same DNA in this city who could have committed this crime. Isn't that right, Doctor?"

Bledsoe sighed. "Well, yes, I suppose so, in theory, but there are other means to differentiate identical twins, such as fingerprints—"

Ortega interjected brusquely, "But from what I understand there were no fingerprints found at the scene of the crime that matched my client's. Therefore, much of the case rests with DNA evidence that could very well belong to another individual!"

"That's highly unlikely," Bledsoe protested. "The chance that Mr. Santiago has an identical twin in Eagles Landing that no one knows about is—"

"Is *possible*," Ortega blasted, not allowing him to finish. With a steady gaze at the jury, he told them, "They say we *all* have an identical twin somewhere in this world, whether we're aware of the person or not. Who's to say that Rafael Santiago's *identical* twin brother isn't somewhere in *this* city, hoping to get away with rape and murder while his innocent twin takes the rap . . . ?"

Beverly had heard enough, objecting with a hard edge to her voice while rising. "Your Honor, this is ridiculous! The witness has already testified that the odds of two people having the same DNA number is in the billions. That should speak for itself in spite of Mr. Ortega's pathetic attempt to have us believe the unlikelihood that his client has an evil twin walking around Eagles Landing with identical genetic codes. Besides, I'm prepared to introduce evidence that will further show that Rafael Santiago did in fact commit these heinous crimes for which he is charged."

She gave Ortega the benefit of her frosty green eyes while fearing that he might have scored some points with the jury in spite of the weakness of his argument.

Grant narrowed his gaze sharply at the defense attorney. "I'm warning you, Counselor—you're skating on thin ice here. Unless you have something more than sci-fi speculation, I suggest you move on."

Ortega cracked a wry smile and did just that, clearly pleased with his performance.

Beverly next called to the stand Raymond Kaiser, a firearms and ballistics expert. He was in his late thirties and thickly built, with wavy black hair and misty gray eyes.

"You examined the bullets that were removed from Judge Crawford's body, as well as shell casings found in the room. Is that correct?"

Kaiser blinked. "Yes, I did."

"Can you tell us what kind of gun was used in the attack?"

"It was a .25-caliber automatic handgun."

"What were the results of your analysis of the bullets and shell casings?" she asked.

Kaiser cleared his throat. "The bullets taken from the judge's body were fired from a gun barrel that had five lands and grooves with a left-hand twist." He used his hand to illustrate. "The ejection and firing pin marks found on the shell casings near the bed were identical and indicative of coming from the same weapon."

Beverly met his gaze. "You also examined shells found in the apartment where the defendant was living when the crime occurred?"

"Yes," he confirmed. "These were also .25-caliber shells."

"So they could have come from the same batch as the ones used to kill Judge Crawford?"

"Yes, I'd say that's very possible."

"Thank you, Mr. Kaiser." She smiled at him for what she believed was an effective testimony.

Ortega favored Beverly with a look of contempt as they

crossed paths. He walked up to the witness box. "Mr. Kaiser, were there any fingerprints found on the bullets or shell casings that you analyzed from the crime scene evidence?"

"No, there weren't."

"Did you find Mr. Santiago's prints on the shells you took from his mother's apartment?"

Kaiser sighed. "No."

Ortega leaned forward. "Well, were you able to make a positive match between those shells and the bullets and shell casings taken from Sheldon Crawford's body and his bedroom?"

Kaiser dropped his shoulders. "Actually, no. But—"

"No buts, *sir!*" Ortega interjected triumphantly, then faced Judge Nunez. "I have no further questions for this witness."

"Detective O'Dell, what happened after you saw the body of Judge Crawford on the night of October twenty-ninth?" asked Beverly.

O'Dell brushed his nose with the back of his hand. "I tried to see if there was any sign of a pulse," he said. "When there wasn't, the medical examiner's office was notified and the crime scene secured."

Beverly took a couple of well-practiced steps toward the jury box and back again. "When was Maxine Crawford first able to identify the defendant as the man who shot the judge?"

"Two days later, at her home. It was from a photo lineup."

"Can you explain this *photo lineup* to the jury?"

"Sure." He faced them. "They are front and side color mug shots of people who have been arrested."

"Was there any reason for showing these mug shots in particular?"

"They were of people who either fit the profile for the types of crimes committed that night," explained O'Dell, "or men who had been sent to prison by Judge Crawford and released."

"Did you coerce Mrs. Crawford into picking out the photo that she did?" Beverly had to ask.

"Absolutely not!" O'Dell shook his head adamantly as though he needed to.

"Was there anything about the photograph lineup that may have unfairly made the defendant stand out?"

"Nothing unfair about seeing and identifying a rapist-killer among other lowlifes," O'Dell stated brashly. "Rafael Santiago murdered the judge and defiled his wife—"

Not surprisingly, Ortega objected vehemently. "*Highly* prejudicial," he barked. "It has yet to be proven that my client did anything, Your Honor!"

Grant had no choice but to sustain and have the comment stricken from the record.

"Did Maxine Crawford have another opportunity to identify the defendant?" Beverly favored Santiago. He looked back at her with a nasty glower.

"Yeah," said O'Dell. "She picked him out of a lineup."

In Beverly's mind it had been another important step toward building a case against the defendant whose appearance—similar as it may be to another murder suspect—would betray him at the end of the day.

Her eyes met O'Dell's. "Thank you, Detective."

Beverly locked glacial stares with Ortega as they passed each other, coming and going.

"Isn't it unusual to bring photo lineups to a witness's house, Detective?" Ortega asked O'Dell casually.

"Not really," he hissed. "Depends on the situation."

"You mean like if the murder victim happens to be a judge's wife?"

Grant jumped in. "I want that stricken from the record," he ordered. "We both know, Ortega, that such a remark is highly prejudicial and uncalled for. Photo lineups are commonly used under a variety of circumstances. And may I remind you that Mrs. Crawford was a victim here, too . . ."

Ortega offered a lame apology.

O'Dell sneered. "And she had to *live* through what your client did to her. In my book, that's much worse!"

Grant admonished O'Dell and moved things along.

"How many other Latino men were in the photo lineup, Detective?" Ortega asked.

"I couldn't tell you," O'Dell said. "We don't distinguish photo lineups by ethnicity."

"But didn't Maxine Crawford claim that the man who broke into the house and committed these other crimes was Hispanic?"

O'Dell twisted his body unwaveringly. "Yes. But we still decided to show her all the photos that were available and fit the criteria already established."

"Or, in other words," Ortega challenged, "just in case the perpetrator was *not* Hispanic after all. Isn't that right, Detective?"

"No!" bellowed O'Dell. "Just standard procedure."

Ortega seized the momentum. "And I suppose it was also standard procedure that there were only *two* Hispanic men in the *human* lineup—and one was ten years older than my client?"

O'Dell took offense to this. Baring his teeth, he growled, "The lineup was fair and the men in it similar in their characteristics. The witness and victim positively identified your client. Nothing you twist around can change that!"

The detective was excused, having stood up fairly well to cross-examination, in spite of the defense lawyer's attempts to the contrary.

Court was recessed for the day.

"What are you doing?" Beverly gingerly opened the door. Jaime had been holed up in his room ever since getting home from school.

"Just playing around on the computer," he told her without looking up.

She stepped inside his kingdom, which was usually off-limits to her. It had all the things you might expect in a twelve-year-old boy's room, much of which was haphazard. The walls were decorated with posters of athletes and rap and hip-hop artists.

On Jaime's desk was the Hewlett-Packard personal computer Beverly had bought him last summer for his birthday; soon after he had started logging on to the Internet. Since then he'd spent at least two hours a day online, often much longer.

Admittedly Beverly knew far too little about computers, other than the basic operation. Looking at the screen over his shoulder, she could see that Jaime was apparently conversing with someone named The Wizard.

"Who's that?" she asked, dumbfounded.

"Just a kid I met online," Jaime said casually.

The so-called Wizard was asking Jaime about some mystical land called Myztantropolis. Beverly had heard of pedophiles trying to lure young boys away from home. Could this be one of them? Though she had educated Jaime on the dangers of cyberspace and child molesters, she was always concerned about some slick, charming man pretending to be someone he wasn't, manipulating her son into doing something wrong. Or going somewhere.

The dangerous online predators found ways around parental controls.

"How old is The Wizard?" Beverly asked, concerned.

"Thirteen."

"How do you know?"

"He sent me a JPG," Jaime said matter-of-factly.

"What's a JPG?"

Jaime guffawed. "Geez, Mom! Get with the program," he teased. "It's a computer photograph." He calmly clicked his mouse and a picture filled the screen of a Latino boy with dark hair and bold, brown eyes. "He's a friend of Paco's, too."

Beverly blushed, feeling foolish and maybe a little like she was still living in the Stone Age.

Get with the program, girl.

If Stone Palmer's son is part of this circle of online pals, it must be safe. Surely the detective would not allow Paco to get in with the wrong crowd.

"Will you teach me how all of this works?" she asked interestedly.

"Sure," Jaime chuckled. "Obviously *someone* needs to."

Beverly pulled up a chair and got an elementary initiation on the Internet and instant messaging. She had no idea just how much information was available out there for children. And adults.

She wondered if it was a good thing. Or bad.

She imagined some steamy instant messages between her and Grant, mixed in with some real, long chats.

"You want to go out for a bite to eat?" Beverly asked when her eyes grew strained from staring at the screen too long.

Jaime, who seemed to have no problem sitting practically on top of the computer, said, "Why not? As long as I get to pick the place this time."

"You're on," she said. At this point Beverly was willing to eat just about anywhere.

They ended up at McDonald's.

A chill enveloped Beverly as she remembered first seeing Manuel Gonzalez at Burger King. She thought further of how he had followed them home, broken in, and stole from them, as well as sized her up as a kidnapping victim and sexual slave.

She still could not get over Gonzalez's likeness to Rafael Santiago. How on earth could there be two such evil, unrepentant and unrelated people who looked like they could be twins?

Oh well, stranger things have happened, she mused. *At least both Santiago and Gonzalez are in custody where they can't harm anyone in the outside world.*

"I've been thinking about it . . ." Jaime said mysteriously, between chomps on a Big Mac.

"Thinking about what?" Beverly was almost afraid to ask.

"Grant's not so bad after all."

"Oh no?" She smiled at Jaime, happy to hear him say

that. More than he knew. "You mean you're only now realizing that?"

He giggled. "Nah. But it's taken me this long to make up my mind about him. Just don't want you to end up hurt by Grant and left all alone—again."

Neither do I, thought Beverly. There was no reason to believe either would be the case. On the contrary, things seemed to be going very well between her and Grant, ever since they had admitted they loved each other and gotten over a few bumps in the road.

Knock on wood.

Only time would tell if what they had would result in true lifelong bliss and contentment. Or be another bitter disappointment that could be the hardest yet to stomach.

Beverly took Jaime's Houston Rockets cap off his head and playfully put it on hers before wrapping her arms around his neck from behind. "How did I ever get to be so lucky to have such a terrific son?"

"Probably because you're such a terrific mom."

"Yeah, probably." She chuckled, again counting her blessings.

CHAPTER 46

Natalie Pena walked steadily into the interview room. The defense attorney had been appointed by the court to represent Manuel Gonzalez, who faced multiple murder counts and related charges. She was there to tell him that the situation looked bleak at best, in spite of her efforts to do what she could to try to at least spare his life.

Under other circumstances the thirty-one-year-old Latina beauty might have been easily mistaken for a model. Five-ten and streamlined, her flaxen hair was smartly cut above the shoulders, and contacts made her eyes seem even bluer. Though she had put on a fresh coat of plum gloss, her lips still felt dry. She wondered if it had anything to do with taking the case of a man whom she had little doubt was as guilty as he seemed.

Her client was already seated at the table. He was still handcuffed and fidgeting, as if he had to use the bathroom. She often wondered why people like Manuel resorted to such violence in their lives.

And why others like her managed to escape lower-class

beginnings, a dysfunctional family, and ethnic discrimination to make a life other Hispanics could be proud of.

Maybe she would never know.

"Hello, Manuel." Natalie gave him a much-practiced smile that she gave all her clients, most of whom couldn't afford a private attorney. Often it was to keep from crying, for usually it was a depressing situation she found herself in as a public defender.

This time was no different.

"What's up?" he said, as if they were just hanging out as old friends.

At first he had sought to ridicule her as his attorney, insisting that only a man could help him. But gradually she had gained his trust, and maybe even admiration.

Natalie sat across from her client. "I just talked to the DA," she said levelly. "I'm afraid the news is not very good, Manuel. I tried to get the charges reduced to first-degree sexual assault and second-degree murder, which could have allowed you to avoid the death penalty. But he insisted that the charges stand."

"Meanin' what?" Manuel kept his eyes planted on her like they had nowhere else to go.

Natalie avoided his stare, focusing instead on the dreary wall behind him. "Meaning that unless there is something else you can give me that might influence their position, we're looking at an almost certain death sentence . . . if you're convicted." She knew that given his confession and the solid evidence, this was a more or less inevitable conclusion. But she owed it to him and her profession to do whatever she could, which wasn't much at this point.

Manuel continued to gaze at her thoughtfully before saying, "Maybe I do have somethin' else to say."

"I'm listening." Natalie tried to read his mind, but couldn't see anything that might give her a clue as to where this was headed.

Manuel moved restlessly in the seat, as if it were vibrating. "You heard about that judge that was killed last October . . . ?" He paused, adding, "His old lady was raped."

Natalie mused. Of course she had heard of the case. Who hadn't? She had actually been considered to represent the accused, since Hispanic public defenders were in short supply in the state of California. But the case went to another lawyer named Conrad Ortega.

Personally, she believed they had a problem with a Latina representing a Latino male accused of killing a criminal court judge. The same judge the suspect had threatened years earlier.

She locked eyes with her client. "Yes. I'm familiar with it. The trial is underway right now."

Did he know something about that crime?

Manuel favored her with a deadpan look, and said as though it had been weighing heavily on him, "I was responsible for it."

"What do you mean *responsible?*" Natalie separated her lips. "Were you *involved* in the attack?"

A half grin sat on his mouth. "I killed the judge and raped his whore of a wife!"

Natalie sat back, stunned. Was he trying to manipulate his way out of a really tight jam? Or was he being straight with her?

"Manuel, there's a man on trial for his life right now," she said, her voice on edge. "Are you saying he's *innocent?* Or did you commit the crime together?"

Manuel did not flinch when he met her gaze. "He didn't do it," he responded succinctly. "I did—period!"

Natalie swallowed, her mouth gone dry. "Assuming you're telling the truth, what do you want me to do?"

"Use it to cut me a deal," he said bluntly.

"What kind of deal?" She elevated a brow warily. Multiple murderers were not in much of a position to bargain. Adding more murders to his resume was hardly worthy of a commuted sentence.

Manuel reached across the table and took her wrists,

holding them tightly between his cuffed hands. Natalie's first thought was to scream. But something made her feel that it was not his intent to hurt her. Maybe he just wanted her to listen.

"I decided I don't wanna die," he muttered with trepidation. "Not till I reach the ripe old age of ninety-nine. Even a hundred. Maybe I can sell my life story and be a millionaire in prison." He loosened his hold on her. "You can save me. And *him*."

Natalie sank back as he removed his hands from her wrists. "Can you prove this?"

Manuel leapt up so fast, shackles and all, that for an instant Natalie thought he was attempting to escape. Or assault her before anyone could stop him.

Instead, he yanked down his pants like they were ablaze. Staring across the table at Natalie was Manuel Gonzalez's erect penis.

She actually flushed at its enormity.

"What are you doing, Manuel?" she asked for lack of more appropriate words.

"Just showin' you somethin'." He crossed to her side of the table in two steps before the guard could come rushing in. He forced down his penis so she could focus instead on the area above it. "Have you ever seen anything so pretty in your life?"

Natalie's eyes widened with surprise. His pubic hair had been shaved. In its place was a tattoo of a beautiful multicolored lizard.

CHAPTER 47

Beverly recalled Maxine Crawford to the stand.

She wasted little time in getting to the hardest part of her testimony, but it was the part that would most likely resonate with the jury.

"On October twenty-ninth, your husband, Judge Sheldon Crawford, wasn't the only crime victim. Can you tell the court what happened to you that night?"

Maxine sighed unevenly. "I was raped and sodomized—" her voice broke.

"*He* raped and sodomized you?" Beverly turned her head and glowered in the direction of the defendant.

"Objection!" Ortega shouted. "She's leading the witness."

"Overruled," Grant said equably. Nevertheless he looked to Beverly, and said firmly, "I think you've made your point, Counselor. Maybe a little too much since we know exactly who's on trial here. Move on."

Beverly nodded without protest. "Did this person do anything else to you?"

Maxine lowered her eyes shamefully. "He forced me to . . . go down on him."

"You mean he forced you to give him an orgasm by putting his penis in your mouth?" Beverly clarified for the jury, though she had little doubt the implication was loud and clear.

"Yes."

Beverly entered into evidence photographs that showed bruises the victim had sustained during the assault. They were passed around to the jury.

"Were you able to see the person who did this to you?" asked Beverly.

"Yes," Maxine testified laconically.

Beverly paused dramatically as she faced the jury. "Is the man who shot Judge Crawford and brutally sexually assaulted you in this courtroom?"

Maxine riveted her eyes on the defense table. "He's over there!" She pointed a long finger.

"You mean *this man*?" Beverly asked loudly, stepping toward the defendant. "Rafael Santiago?"

Maxine gulped. "Yes, he's the one."

The jurors reacted, some appearing visibly shaken.

Beverly produced eleven-by-fourteen-inch photographs of the defendant's pubic area for the witness to view. "Do you recognize any of these?"

Maxine cringed. "Yes." She honed in on the enlargements of a lizard tattoo.

"Where have you seen this?" Beverly asked.

Maxine raised her eyes at Santiago. "The tattoo is on *his* body, where pubic hair normally is. Only he shaved it . . ."

Beverly identified the photographs as in fact pictures taken of the defendant's anatomy, entering them into evidence.

She handed the explicit pictures to members of the jury, all of whom appeared mesmerized and disgusted at once.

"When you were being assaulted," Beverly asked the witness while the photographs were still being circulated, "was the defendant holding a gun on you at the same time?"

"Yes," slurred Maxine, her composure breaking.

"And did you fear for your life?" Beverly favored her with a knowing look.

"Yes," the witness uttered emotionally. "I did. Every second he was in me . . . on me . . . in my house . . . It was horrible."

Maxine wiped at her eyes in what Beverly considered a prize-winning performance, but real nonetheless. She knew the courage it had taken to testify against Santiago and to relive the brutalities he had inflicted upon Maxine and her husband.

For an instant Beverly wondered if Maxine had ever been afraid of turning state's evidence against Judge Crawford. Would she have actually testified against her husband had it come down to it? The man who, in effect, had rescued her from a life she would no doubt have just as soon forgotten?

Fortunately Maxine had been spared such a gutwrenching decision, she thought.

Beverly thanked her star witness, whom she truly felt sorry for in more ways than one.

K. Conrad Ortega lifted a yellow envelope from the defense table and strode directly toward the witness box. Beverly watched as alarm bells rang in her head.

Ortega kept the envelope at his side as he faced the witness. "Mrs. Crawford, you have testified that the man who raped you had a tattoo of a lizard in the area of his shaved pubic hair. Am I right?"

Maxine nodded tentatively.

"Is that a *yes?*"

"Yes," she said, her voice going up an octave.

Without another word, Ortega whipped an eleven-by-fourteen-inch photograph from the envelope and stuck it in her face. "Is this the lizard tattoo in the pubic hair region that you saw, Mrs. Crawford?"

There was a buzz in the courtroom as Beverly jumped to her feet. "Objection, Your Honor!" she shrieked. "I have no idea what he's trying to pull here. Under discovery, that picture was *never* made available to the DA's office!"

Grant furrowed his brow. "Mr. Ortega, you'd better have a good reason for this."

"Oh, I do, Your Honor," he responded confidently.

Judge Nunez ordered both attorneys to approach the bench.

"Explain, Counselor . . ." Grant angled his eyes at Ortega.

Beverly was as curious as she was angry at the defense attorney's attempt to put something past her.

"Your Honor," said Ortega, "the witness has testified about this lizard tattoo being on the lower body of the man who assaulted her. I have very recently come into contact with some photographs that were taken by another attorney of her client and *his* private parts. Since Mrs. Crawford is accusing my client of having done these terrible things to her and her husband, I am entitled to dispute that with evidence to the contrary."

"May I?" Grant held out a hand for the photograph, which Ortega passed to him, along with another similar close-up photograph of a man's genitalia.

While the judge studied the pictures, Beverly assaulted its highly prejudicial presence. "Grant—Your Honor," she corrected, "you cannot allow these photographs into this trial. I have not had a chance to study them. For all we know, they could have been faked."

Ortega's nostrils grew and his brown eyes were hard as rocks. "I can assure you, Your Honor," he stated tautly, "these photos are *very* real!"

Grant creased his brow disturbingly and favored the defense attorney. "Who the hell is the man in these photos?"

Ortega removed a glossy picture from the envelope. Handing it to Grant, he said, "His name is Manuel Gonzalez." Ortega met Beverly's eyes squarely. "I believe you two have already met."

Beverly's knees buckled and she might have actually fallen had she not found support in the railing beneath the

bench. She looked up at Grant, who flashed her a disbelieving gaze.

"He's being held in a Wilameta County jail on multiple
murder and rape charges," said Ortega. "As you can see,
Your Honor, the man's a *dead* ringer for Mr. Santiago. No
pun intended."

"It doesn't matter," sputtered Beverly, dismissing what
she knew to be true about Santiago and Gonzalez
appearance-wise. "Any resemblance between the two men,
including their shaved pubic regions and tattoos, is totally
coincidental."

Did she really believe that?

It seemed unlikely that Gonzalez and Santiago would
put the same lizard tattoo in the same place on their bodies and look like twins purely by happenstance.

But it was too much to believe that both men were active
participants in the crimes committed against the Crawfords.

"Maybe you should take a look at these," Grant advised
Beverly.

She viewed the photographs and quivered while studying the enlargements of the lizard tattoo. It was distinctive
because of the color patterns, which were embedded in her
mind based on Maxine Crawford's chilling description and
photos Beverly had observed of Rafael Santiago's tattoo.

*These photographs could very well have been taken of
Santiago's private parts,* she thought remarkably. Even the
picture of Gonzalez himself was a virtual clone of Santiago.
Had she not known better, Beverly might have thought the
two men were one and the same.

Except that she knew for a fact that Santiago was in the
courtroom at that moment; whereas Gonzalez was
presently locked up. Making it impossible that there was
only one man responsible for at least four murders and two
sexual assaults.

Aside from that, facts were facts. Rafael Santiago had
been positively identified by Maxine Crawford as the man

who attacked her and Judge Crawford, and the DNA evidence had backed that up.

Or had it?

Beverly mused on the expert testimony on DNA and identical twins. But there was no indication that Santiago had an identical twin. And no reason to believe it was Gonzalez, appearance aside.

"I admit," she finally told Grant, "that these photos do show a *strong* likeness to the defendant on trial today—in more than one respect. But they are *not* pictures of Rafael Santiago!" Beverly gave Ortega a stern look. "To allow the jury to see or even hear about these would seriously jeopardize the case against the man who was identified by the witness in *two* separate lineups . . ."

"I tend to agree," Grant said waveringly.

Ortega drew his brows together. "Your Honor, from what I understand, Manuel Gonzalez has *confessed* to killing Judge Crawford and sexually assaulting the witness!"

Beverly's mouth hung open with shock. "That can't be!" she protested. "I questioned Gonzalez myself about this case and he denied any involvement in the crimes."

"That was then," Ortega voiced curtly. "And this is now! Obviously the man had a change of heart, developed a conscience, or whatever. My client is entitled to be given every chance to prove his innocence, Your Honor. Why not let Mrs. Crawford decide for herself if she identified the wrong man?"

"We cannot allow this trial to be turned into a circus, Your Honor." Beverly tried to appeal to him, desperation in her tone.

But it had apparently fallen on deaf ears.

"I'm sorry, Beverly," Grant lamented, wishing there were some other way. "But he's right. This evidence is potentially too strong . . . too damaging to simply ignore. If the witness rejects it altogether, then we'll move on. If not, I'd say we have ourselves a *real* problem here."

Beverly could hear her heart thumping madly as she sneered at both the judge and the defense attorney before storming back to her table.

Deep down inside Beverly knew she had no solid ground to stand on. And could not expect Grant to bail her out, lover or not. This was the only way to be certain the right man was on trial. Or at least it was the first step in getting at the truth, assuming they weren't already there. A victory was not nearly as important as justice being served.

She could not really live with herself if her prosecution caused the wrong man to be convicted, and quite possibly executed down the line. Even if Rafael Santiago was clearly a despicable human being who deserved little mercy for his past sins.

But did that make him guilty of the crimes for which he was on trial?

"The witness will answer the questions to the best of her ability." Grant regarded Maxine judicially. "And take as much time as you need."

Ortega stood before the witness. He handed her a photograph. "Mrs. Crawford, do you recognize this? It's a lizard tattoo—just as you've described as being on your attacker's body, just above his penis . . ."

Maxine studied the picture. It took her back to that awful night. She remembered how he had made her put his penis in her mouth. She found herself focusing on the tattoo as a means to not think about what he was forcing her to do.

This was the same lizard, Maxine believed. *Wasn't it?*

Or was it a legal trick? she considered. She hadn't been able to make out what the attorneys were saying to the judge. Did this tattoo belong to the same man who sexually assaulted her after murdering Sheldon?

How could it not?

"Mrs. Crawford?" Ortega hissed impatiently.

"Yes, I recognize it," Maxine uttered tentatively.

His eyes pinned on her. "And what is it you recognize about the picture?"

She gazed at Beverly, but Maxine knew instinctively that she would get no help from the attorney. After a sigh, she responded, "It looks like the tattoo *he* had."

"You mean the tattoo your attacker had on his pubic hair area the night he attacked you?"

Again Maxine paused, not wanting to say the wrong thing, but under oath to be truthful. "Yes."

"You're sure about that?" Ortega pushed her.

"Objection!" Beverly stood, trying to mitigate the damage before it got any worse. "The witness is obviously *not* sure she's looking at—"

"Overruled," Grant said lowly, refraining from looking at Beverly. "The witness will answer the question."

"Perhaps this will help you," Ortega said, and he handed her a second photograph. This one showed the tattoo from a slightly different angle and included the man's penis.

Maxine looked from one picture to the other. The penis she saw was flaccid and she could not remember her attacker's penis when it was not hard. But the lizard tattoo was indelibly etched in her mind like a nightmare that wouldn't go away.

The photographs had to be of Rafael Santiago's private parts, she thought. *I wish I could see the face of the person in these photos, to be sure.*

Could she have possibly identified the wrong man as her attacker?

But when Maxine went back to her identification of Rafael Santiago—first in a mug shot catalog and then a police lineup—she felt certain she had picked the right person out. She would never forget that face and those eyes for as long as she lived.

Or the tattoo of a lizard that kept her sane in the darkest hour, even while reminding her of what that man had put her through.

"Yes," Maxine said with renewed faith, "that's the tattoo I saw on him." Her eyes shifted toward the defendant, as if to leave no doubt.

Beverly's mouth dropped. She knew that this bombshell threatened to blow their entire case out of the water. And who knew what effect that might have on her career as a trial lawyer?

A headache was beginning to develop and she feared it would only get worse.

Ortega quickly took the photographs from the witness and handed her another. "Is this the man who raped you and killed Judge Crawford?" he asked straightforwardly.

Maxine scrutinized the face, as if it were actual human flesh and not a picture. She saw the face she'd seen in her head over and over again.

It was *his* face, she told herself, stealing a glance at the defendant.

Wasn't it . . . ?

Unless he had a brother. An identical twin.

But Beverly had never suggested such during their preparation for the trial. Wouldn't she have said something if there was doubt about the man Maxine positively identified? Hadn't the DNA evidence backed up her testimony?

On the other hand, Maxine questioned whether or not the defense attorney would show her these pictures if they were of his client.

Maybe he was simply trying to confuse her. Make her doubt what she saw?

And *who* she saw attack her?

She looked again to the Assistant DA whose face betrayed concern but was otherwise emotionless.

"The witness will answer the question," directed the judge.

Maxine closed her eyes. When she opened them, she was hoping the image would somehow be different. More or less like the defendant.

But it was the same.

"I cannot say for certain," Maxine finally responded, deciding it might be best not to give the answer she believed to be true in her heart.

Ortega's eyes narrowed. "You've already identified the tattoo worn by your assailant, Mrs. Crawford," he snapped. "Now I suggest you take another look at this face and tell the court if it's the man you identified in a police lineup as your rapist and your husband's murderer."

Maxine studied the picture again and looked up twice to see Rafael Santiago leering at her. The two had to be one, she thought. She couldn't let him get away with this.

Looking up at the defense lawyer, she said in a barely audible voice, "Yes . . ."

"I couldn't hear you," Ortega pretended. Then he demanded, "Can you repeat your answer for the jury?"

Maxine felt tears smearing her mascara as she favored the jury box and lifted her voice an octave, uttering, "Yes, it's him . . ."

Ortega took the photograph from her and faced the jury, announcing gleefully what even he had trouble believing was true. "Ladies and gentlemen, this is a picture of a man named Manuel Gonzalez. He's currently being held in a Wilameta County jail on multiple murder and sexual assault charges."

The courtroom was abuzz on that note and Judge Nunez called for an immediate recess.

Beverly sank back into her chair, this unexpected turn of events leaving her nauseous and uncertain where to go from there.

CHAPTER 48

The hastily arranged lineup was ordered by the DA, pending the results of a DNA test performed on Manuel Gonzalez. This, after Judge Nunez had granted a continuance to Beverly in order to further investigate the State's case against Rafael Santiago.

In her heart of hearts, Beverly believed they had the right man in custody, even if her key witness to the crime was second-guessing her positive ID of Santiago. Photographs, no matter how clear, could be misleading. Misinterpreted. Unsettling. Especially under the pressure of an intimidating, grueling cross-examination.

But I saw Manuel Gonzalez with my own eyes and could barely tell him and Rafael Santiago apart, thought Beverly. So why couldn't Maxine be just as uncertain, given the obvious similarities between the two men, right down to their lizard tattoos?

Beverly felt from experience that a victim's first instincts were usually the correct ones. That along with enough direct and circumstantial evidence against Rafael Santiago would have been enough to get a conviction in most instances.

And still would be in this case, she believed, should Gonzalez's DNA fail to match that of Santiago's, as expected.

But what if that weren't the case? What if the two men were identical twins? Though both men had vehemently denied this, as had the woman believed to be Santiago's birth mother, Isabel Santiago.

Then we've got a real problem, Beverly told herself. With the same DNA and no fingerprint evidence to link either man to the scene of the crime against the Crawfords, and Manuel Gonzalez confessing to the murder and sexual assault, the case against Rafael Santiago would crumble.

Especially with the eyewitness no longer sure which man she saw the lizard tattoo on.

Beverly hoped that by seeing both suspects in a lineup together, Maxine Crawford would bolster their case against Santiago by picking him again as her attacker.

Santiago and Gonzalez were separated in the lineup by two other Hispanic men and one tanned, white detective who could have passed for Hispanic. All were of similar build and height, while wearing the same orange jail-issued attire.

Present in the viewing room were Beverly, Maxine Crawford, and Detectives O'Dell and Palmer. Both men had been cooperative in sharing information from their respective investigations and in their determination to get to the bottom of this unfolding drama involving two men charged with murder and sex offenses.

"Take a good look at every man," Beverly ordered Maxine. "If you need to look a second and third time, do it. And don't pick out the man you think *we* want you to," she added, glancing at the lineup herself. "We have to know that you can *positively* identify the *actual* man who broke into your house and committed the crimes against you and Judge Crawford. Even if that man is someone other than Rafael Santiago."

Maxine sucked in a long breath as she peered through the one-way window. She was easily able to separate the two men who most fit the image from those who did not. She looked from one man to the next.

Unlike the photographs, she was better able to discern the differences between the men. One was slightly taller, the other a shade heavier. One had a curlier hairstyle, the other had straighter trimmed hair.

But she had not paid as much attention to these characteristics at the time the crime occurred.

Only the face of the man.

His penis.

And the lizard tattoo in his shaven pubic area.

The faces were very similar, Maxine told herself, trying not to shake but doing so anyway. So were the eyes—dark and sinister. Each seemed to be glaring at her as if they could see her, daring her to pick him. Or not.

She wanted so badly to put this dreadful nightmare behind her. Yet Maxine knew this would be impossible so long as the man who did this to her and Sheldon was not held accountable.

But what if she identified the *wrong* man?

Would the other go free . . . come after her . . . rape her again, and then kill her?

Maxine strained her eyes as she tried her best to see the man she had seen that night. She rested her gaze on Number Two. He seemed to be mocking her, much like the rapist-murderer.

"Can you ask Number Two to smile?"

O'Dell shouted into the microphone, ordering the man to put a smile on his face.

Yes, thought Maxine. She could see him smiling when he was raping her and when she had orally copulated with him.

It was the same self-satisfying grin he wore when he shot Sheldon three times.

Turning to Beverly, she asked diffidently, "Can you have him pull down his pants?"

Beverly could see the detectives inside the room rolling their eyes and probably allowing their imaginations to run wild.

She had O'Dell bring the suspect up to the window and expose himself.

Maxine looked above his circumcised penis, in spite of the erection, honing in on the area above it. There was a little more hair there now, but she could still make out the lizard tattoo with its multiple colors against his sallow skin. It almost seemed to glow back at her.

She gulped and raised her eyes to the cold face of the man. He had a wicked half grin and seemed entirely amused by the whole ordeal.

As if the devil in disguise.

Then, without warning, he slapped his foot on the floor, causing her to jump back involuntarily as if the man were about to break through the window and assault her. He then began to laugh loudly.

Maxine remembered that laugh, its particular nuance. It rang in her ears like the night he viciously had his way sexually with her.

"That's him!" Maxine heard the roar of her voice echoing in her head.

"You're sure about that?" Beverly stared at Number Two, unnerved by his ruthless, calculating demeanor.

"Yes." Maxine did not back down. She was sure this was no mistake. "That's the man who hurt me . . . who murdered Sheldon!"

Beverly winced and regarded the detectives.

It was Manuel Gonzalez.

Beverly met Grant that afternoon at a coffeehouse in downtown Eagles Landing.

Both sipped on cappuccino as she broke the depressing news to him.

Grant, who had steadfastly thought Santiago was the perpetrator, almost from the start, could not hide his shock and disappointment. "Can't believe she *really* picked Manuel Gonzalez out of the lineup this time."

"I know," muttered Beverly, sharing his sentiments. She also knew that as a judge he was obliged to be objective in going with the ebb and flow of this case. But as a human being he was entitled to his own feelings on the matter.

She was also bound by the rules of evidence, testimony, and, yes, positive identification of the suspect. Yet these had to be supported by each other to make or break a case.

"On the other hand, you could see this coming after she failed under cross-examination to keep the focus on Santiago," muttered Grant. "I don't think Maxine Crawford really knows who she saw, given the resemblance between the two men. You could hardly tell them apart yourself."

"Don't remind me." Beverly rolled her eyes, remembering that Gonzalez tried to kidnap her and worse. He was also sure to be convicted on three counts of murder and related charges. But that still didn't mean he killed Judge Crawford and sexually assaulted his wife.

"When will the DNA test results come in?" Grant fixed her gaze over his cup.

"Should be any time now."

"Good. I'm betting that the results will not support Gonzalez's confession which, from what I understand, seems to be a half-baked effort to avoid the death penalty. It won't work."

"That's what I'm thinking," agreed Beverly. The entire thing still made her nervous, though. And left her case hanging for the moment as if in midair. "How do you think the jury will react to this, even if the DNA still points squarely at Santiago?"

Grant put an arm on the table. "I think they will act responsibly and let the evidence speak for itself—especially DNA evidence that would put the perpetrator right at the scene of the crime. The fact that two men look so much alike that their own mothers would have trouble telling them apart, assuming they have different mothers, I doubt the jury would fault Maxine for her confusion. They certainly won't let Santiago walk once it becomes clear that Gonzalez's desperate attempt to save his own neck failed to hold up under scientific scrutiny."

Beverly licked cappuccino from her lips thoughtfully. "Looks as though you left the DA's office just in time. I think I've got an open-and-shut case and disaster strikes."

Grant chuckled. "Don't put the cart ahead of the horse, Bev. The case is still yours to be won or lost. But you can't expect Ortega to roll over and play dead. He has every right to challenge your case against his client, even if he's grasping at straws in my unbiased opinion."

"Well, we'll see about that," she said, her confidence returning. "I just want this to be over already, so . . ."

"So what?" Grant asked after Beverly hesitated.

She gazed at his eyes. "So I can turn my attention more to my boyfriend and son."

He frowned. "Hope that doesn't mean you plan on an early retirement?"

She smiled. "It doesn't. I think I still can do some good in bringing down the bad guys for years to come. But I also have a life and want to devote more time to it. Is that so bad?"

Beverly wondered if she sounded like a clinger to him, wanting more than he did out of the relationship.

Grant smiled at her, reaching out to touch her hand. "Doesn't sound bad at all. In fact, I was thinking the same thing."

"You're not just saying that?" A doubtful look danced in her eyes.

"Not at all, baby. I think we both could use more time together, away from all the headaches of the legal profession. In fact, I was thinking that after this case is over, maybe we could head to Cancun or Maui for some R&R."

Beverly smiled dreamily. "That sounds really nice; I'd love it."

"Glad to hear it." Grant lifted his cup and sipped coffee happily. "Oh, and by the way, who says I won't find the courtroom from the bench's perspective just a bit stiff and want to go back to being a trial lawyer?"

"Yeah, right," she laughed. "That'll be the day." *But I'll take you, whatever you choose to do with your life.*

Grant laughed back. Truthfully he had no intentions of returning to the legal profession any time soon. But he would never say never, especially if he really got the ache to get back out there and fight like hell for justice.

Or if it meant losing Beverly, something he had no intention of ever doing. Right now he just wanted to be there to support her in this difficult and suddenly complex case she was embroiled in. No matter which way the pendulum swung.

CHAPTER 49

Stone was still mulling over Manuel Gonzalez's confession to yet another killing and sexual assault. In this one he claimed to have murdered criminal court judge Sheldon Crawford and to have sexually assaulted his wife. Maxine Crawford had validated his confession by picking Gonzalez out of a lineup. This in spite of having previously identified another man as her rapist and the killer of Judge Crawford. Rafael Santiago's trial was now underway.

At least it had been up until this latest wrinkle in the State's case against Santiago, Stone pondered. He was en route to the Wilameta County crime lab where the results had come in on Manuel Gonzalez's DNA. Everyone involved was holding their collective breath on this one. No one wanted to believe that the DA's office had screwed up and put the wrong man on trial. But then letting the guilty man off the hook would have been an even greater injustice.

Personally Stone had his doubts about Gonzalez's involvement in this other crime. Yes, he'd seen the uncanny resemblance between him and Santiago. And both men had the lizard tattoos and penchant for sexual violence.

Not to mention the crimes occurred on the same night.

But the MO was all wrong here.

From his experience, killers did not like to vary their way of killing people. It had something to do with a comfort zone.

Gonzalez favored knifing and strangling his victims over shooting them. There were no guns found at the apartment he and Claudia Sosa shared.

That was not to say it was inconceivable that he had shot Judge Crawford and tossed the murder weapon, Stone thought. Sometimes killers proved to be highly unpredictable.

But were that the case, why would Gonzalez go after the judge and his wife? What possible connection could there be between the two crimes that night?

Furthermore, Stone had a problem with the timeline. Based on the estimated time of death in both murders, he had driven the distance from Belle Park to Judge Crawford's house. If Manuel Gonzalez had committed the crimes against the judge and his wife, he would have had to clock it there on mostly county roads and city streets at about seventy miles per hour after killing Adrienne Murray.

Though possible, Stone was not about to bet the house on it. Nor, he had to admit to himself, could he afford to bet against it, either, considering the gray area between what they knew and didn't know about the actual events that took place during the course of a crime spree— including sometimes under- or overestimating the time frame.

All the speculation could be eliminated if the DNA tests showed that the semen and hair found at the scene of the crime could not have belonged to Manuel Gonzalez.

Stone hesitated to think beyond that. He finished off his coffee, tossed the cup into a plastic trash bag in the back of the car, and headed outside.

It was a cold, dreary day, and Stone could see his breath as he walked up the steps of the building.

He fully expected things to heat up inside, one way or the other.

"The DNA tested positive," Harold Bledsoe said dispiritedly to his audience, which included Assistant DAs Beverly Mendoza and Gail Kennedy and Detectives Stone Palmer and Joe O'Dell.

"So what are you saying?" O'Dell asked. "That Manuel Gonzalez did kill the judge and rape his wife?"

The criminalist touched his glasses and frowned. "I wish it were that simple, but it's not in this case. What the tests show is that there is a match between the DNA sample taken from Manuel Gonzalez and DNA evidence collected from the crime scene—including semen found on Maxine Crawford's body."

Beverly gazed at him contemplatively. "Then you're telling us that Manuel Gonzalez and Rafael Santiago are in fact *identical* twins . . . ?"

Bledsoe met her gaze, reading the shock and irritation in the prosecutor's eyes. "Yes, it looks that way."

"Either they are or they aren't!" Stone added his two cents. "We need to know that we aren't going around in circles here. If you have any doubts that Gonzalez's DNA—"

"I don't, Detective," Bledsoe assured him. "The tests have been thrice repeated and the results are the same. Gonzalez and Santiago have the same DNA, as only identical twins could. As such, with more definitive DNA studies only in the preliminary stages, you have two men who could legitimately be your perpetrator in the crimes against the Crawfords. Particularly the sexual attack on Maxine Crawford."

Beverly tried to keep from falling apart at the revelations that threatened to turn her case against Rafael Santiago upside down. "We need to find out which man was *really* at the crime scene," she stressed to the criminalist. "At this point, both seem to be guilty as sin, but clearly only one of them was present. If there is any other scientific way to differentiate between the two . . ."

Bledsoe rubbed his nose. "There is, in effect," he suggested. "Even identical twins have different *phenotypes*—or physical traits such as appearance and fingerprints. Aside from a confession, it's up to you to establish a criminal identification based on such characteristics." He knew that this would be an uphill battle, given that the only witness could not be certain which man assaulted her with the naked eye alone. He favored the attorney and offered meekly, "Good luck. I think you're going to need it . . ."

"In this case, I think we've pretty much run out of luck," Gail remarked bleakly. "What we need now is something more akin to a miracle to get our man before he worms his way out of this mess."

No one was prepared to argue the point.

Beverly sat grim-faced in the conference room on one side of the table. She had reluctantly agreed not to seek the death penalty against Manuel Gonzalez should his confession be accepted. This was a big if in her mind, as she still believed that Rafael Santiago was the guilty party in invading the home of Judge Sheldon Crawford and in what followed. But she went along with this for now under pressure from all sides to bring this case to a head.

Sitting across from Beverly were Gonzalez, who seemed to be enjoying this attention, and his attorney, Natalie Pena. At opposite ends of the table were Stone Palmer and Joe O'Dell, each with more than a vested interest in the proceedings.

Two tape recorders sat on the table in record mode, while a camcorder stood in the corner recording the interview.

"Will you please state your full name?" Beverly asked the suspect, as if she hadn't a clue who he was.

He favored his attorney with a sly grin and watched her nod to him before facing Beverly. "Manuel Roberto Gonzalez," he said as calmly as she could have expected from an admitted serial killer.

The memory of having a knife placed at her throat by this man bothered Beverly more than she cared to admit.

"You recently confessed to the murder of Judge Sheldon Crawford." She looked him in the eye. "Is that correct?"

"Yeah." He smirked at her.

"You also confessed to sexually assaulting Maxine Crawford, the judge's wife?"

"That's right," he said smugly.

Beverly glanced at her notes. "I interviewed you on December twenty-first of last year," she said. "At that time, I asked you point-blank if you had any knowledge or involvement in those crimes. You denied it. Why are you now saying you did it?"

Manuel tilted his head and grinned again at her. "I lied then."

"How do we know you aren't lying now?"

"Hey, you got the DNA results. What more do you want?"

"All the results told us was that you and Rafael Santiago have more in common than appearance." Beverly paused pensively. "He is your identical twin?"

"You tell me." Manuel made a face as if daring her to come across the table and hit it.

She refused to swallow the bait. "How long have you known you had a twin brother?" Longer than they knew, no doubt.

"All my life, I guess," he hissed.

"But you have different names . . . nationalities. What's up with that?"

Manuel shrugged. "Who knows or cares. Guess you'll have to ask my auntie about that."

They planned to do just that, Beverly thought. But Isabel Santiago could only answer questions about their birth. Not the misdeeds the identical twins had made a career out of perpetrating.

Beverly peered at the suspect. "I want to believe that you are telling the truth in your claims, Manuel, and not simply playing us all for your own amusement. Oh, and to have your life spared."

Manuel grunted. "Guess you'll just have to trust me on this one, *Ms*. Assistant District Attorney," he told her curtly, "won't you?"

Beverly kept her cool as she looked around the table. She knew that the detectives were dubious at best that this was anything but a waste of time and money, though the real perpetrator was still in dispute among all concerned.

For her part, Beverly was skeptical but not close-minded, in spite of the still strong circumstantial case against Rafael Santiago. After all, she was the only one present who had experienced firsthand the terror of this maniac.

"This is not about trust," she told the suspect, a hard edge to her voice. "Your credibility was shot to hell a long time ago as far as I'm concerned. It'll be up to you to convince everyone in this room, with the possible exception of Ms. Pena, that what you have to say is worth hearing. Otherwise you can go straight to hell."

Beverly had not meant to be so forceful, though the nodding heads of O'Dell and Stone told her she had their full support.

Natalie Pena was not nearly as accommodating. "Counselor, badgering my client is not helpful to anyone, least of all you. I suggest you keep your temper in check if we're to get this done."

Beverly gave her a tight smile. "Whatever you say."

Manuel conferred with his attorney for a moment or two, as if no one else was in the room. Then he fixed Beverly with a leer, and said as though there had not been a break in their direct communication, "Not ready to go to hell yet, Beverly. Least not till I'm old and senile . . ."

If she had not known better, Beverly would have thought his comment was in direct reference to her father. Had Gonzalez somehow found out about his weakened state of mind? And perhaps where her father was living?

Was he making a threat against her in his own warped way?

"Truth is," said Manuel, licking his lips, "I killed Adrienne Murray 'cause her old man thought she was having an affair. He wanted the bitch dead . . . and her lover . . ." He gazed levelly at Beverly. "Judge Crawford."

Everyone present reacted to this stunning accusation.

Beverly flipped her lashes at him disdainfully. Her first thought was that it was absurd. Judge Crawford and Adrienne Murray? Lovers?

But she knew of Judge Crawford's sordid history and reputation as an adulterer.

Was the idea that he could have become involved with this Adrienne Murray any more inconceivable than his clandestine relationship with and eventual marriage to Maxine Crawford?

"You don't really expect us to believe that the judge and Ms. Murray were having an affair?" Beverly sneered at Manuel. To her knowledge there was no connection between the two, other than that they were both murder victims in Eagles Landing on the same day.

O'Dell drew his brows together menacingly. "This whole thing sounds like a load of crap."

"I agree," Stone said dismissively. He was sure that this asshole was embellishing his story to try and get the deal he was after. "But let's hear what the man has to say. This should really be interesting."

Stone scoffed at the notion that Adrienne Murray was seeing the judge. Though Chuck Murray was obsessed with the belief that his wife was cheating on him, there had been no credible evidence of such.

At least not yet.

Manuel grinned. "Hey, I got no reason to make this up. The judge liked his women young and younger. Like that bitch he married. He met Adrienne Murray in cheap motels. They both liked the really kinky stuff."

"Are you saying you followed them to these cheap motels?" asked Beverly, her voice betraying disbelief.

"Yeah," Manuel answered matter-of-factly. "A couple of times. I was curious . . ."

Assuming it was plausible that Judge Crawford was sleeping with Adrienne Murray, Beverly still had trouble believing Gonzalez had killed the judge. Sounded more like he was trying to protect his brother. Or had they been in cahoots all along in committing serial sexual homicides?

"Why don't you tell us how you killed Judge Crawford?" she asked.

Manuel whispered to his attorney, then faced Beverly. "I shot him."

"Is that you talking or your lawyer?" Beverly eyed him suspiciously.

Natalie shot her a nasty look. "My client can speak for himself. He just wants to make sure he doesn't say anything that will only get him into more hot water."

Stone couldn't resist saying, "The man's confessed to four murders and about as many sexual assaults. No reason to be too concerned about trying to cover his ass now." He knew Gonzalez was trying to avoid the death penalty. Maybe they could find a way around that, no matter what happened here, so he would pay the ultimate price for his sins.

Beverly watched as the detective and defense attorney exchanged glares. She turned back to Gonzalez. "How many times did you shoot the judge?"

"Three."

She was not especially surprised that he answered these questions correctly, since they had been reported often enough in the paper. *I can't rule out either that Ms. Pena could have easily spoon-fed the responses to him.*

Beverly wanted to see how the man did with less commonly known details.

"What type of firearm did you use?" she asked pointedly.

Manuel again spoke to his attorney, who mostly listened and nodded or shook her head.

"A .25-caliber pistol," he said evenly.

"Where did you get it?"

He hunched a shoulder. "Can't remember."

"Well, try to remember," Beverly pressed. "It might help us to believe your story."

Natalie intervened. "Ms. Mendoza, we're not here to get my client to divulge information on an illegal weapon that might get someone else in trouble. He wants only to confess to crimes he *himself* committed."

Beverly sneered. They had clearly come well prepared for this interrogation and knew where the line had to be drawn.

"Fine," she told the attorney curtly. "Maybe your client can tell us where this gun is right now?"

Natalie whispered to him. A moment later Manuel turned to Beverly. "I threw it in the lake," he practically bragged. "I ain't crazy. No way I'm gonna keep the piece after shootin' the judge."

"Why shoot him, Manuel?" Stone stepped in, more than a little unmoved by his explanation. "Especially after stabbing Adrienne Murray to death? And why didn't you get rid of the knife—instead of using it to *kill* Penelope Grijalva and slicing up your girlfriend, Claudia Sosa?"

Again Manuel conferred with his attorney. Afterward he eyed the detective and said flatly, "A gun is the *only* way to kill men. Too much flab on their bodies for a knife to penetrate cleanly." He sniffed, as if snorting cocaine. "I always kept my switchblade, man. Knives can't be traced. Besides, it was more fun to cut women different ways. I like to see 'em bleed and squirm."

"You bastard!" O'Dell blasted at him. "If it were up to me, you wouldn't get off with anything less than a death sentence. Just like the people you butchered."

"Fortunately, it ain't up to you, *Detective!*" Manuel snapped brazenly.

"But it is up to me!" Beverly glowered at Gonzalez and his attorney. "If I were you, Manuel, I wouldn't press my luck."

She watched the smirk disappear from his face. "I'll try to remember that."

"How did you get into Judge Crawford's house?"

"I picked the lock," he said without preface. "It wasn't hard to do."

"And what time was this?" Beverly asked.

Manuel rolled his eyes. "Around seven, I guess. Can't really say I was spendin' much time watching the clock."

"Did you break into the Crawfords' house before or after you killed Adrienne Murray?"

"After," he said decisively. "Had to get the main business taken care of first. You know what I'm sayin'?"

"How did you get from point A to point B, Gonzalez?" Stone asked. "In other words, how did you get from Belle Park to the judge's house?"

Manuel put a finger up his nose and dug in. "I drove," he responded coolly.

"Drove what?"

"My old lady's car."

"How fast were you driving?"

Natalie seemed to take exception to this. "Exactly what is it you're getting at, Detective?"

Stone played dumb. "Absolutely nothing, Counselor," he uttered. "Just a simple question, requiring a simple answer."

Beverly could see that Stone had managed to strike a note of uncertainty in Gonzalez. Did this mean something? Or could he actually account for narrowing the distance between the two locations in a manner consistent with the timeline of the separate crimes?

"No problem," said Manuel, dismissing his attorney's stern gaze. "I was probably doin' around eighty, man. Except when some dumb assholes got in my way. You got a problem with that? You gonna give me a ticket for speedin' now?" He laughed at his own poor attempt at humor.

Stone regarded the confessed multiple murderer carefully.

Admittedly he wasn't quite certain what to make of Gonzalez's story. At least he was willing to entertain that there may have been some element of truth to it. But how much?

"Assuming you're being straight with me, Gonzalez, are you also saying that Chuck Murray knew his wife was having an affair with Judge Crawford?"

Manuel stared the length of the table at the detective. Raising a brow, he answered sarcastically, " 'Course he knew, man! How do you think I found out the judge was doin' double duty in bed?"

"Are you saying that Murray ordered the hit on Judge Crawford?" Stone wanted to be sure this was the implication, giving Gonzalez the benefit of the doubt. Not that it would exonerate him as the hit man, were that the case.

Manuel grinned wickedly. "Yeah, he ordered it. The White Amigo told me that once I'd gotten rid of his wife and the judge, I'd be debt free. So I did it." His tone was unapologetic, almost euphoric.

Stone could almost believe him, knowing what he did about Chuck Murray and his obsessive, maniacal jealousy involving his wife. But the fact remained that Murray was no longer able to defend himself against the charge. Stone also still had trouble buying that Adrienne would have gotten involved with Sheldon Crawford. But then, stranger things had happened, he was willing to concede.

Manuel Gonzalez really is a coldhearted bastard, thought Beverly, regardless of whether or not he was telling the truth regarding Judge Crawford, Adrienne Murray, and Chuck Murray. Since all three were now dead and unable to verify or refute his tale, it was still pure conjecture at this point.

Even so, Beverly knew his allegations were beginning to build up steam in the room, for better or worse.

She glanced at her notes that contained details of the killing of Judge Sheldon and the sexual assault on Maxine. Meeting the eyes of Gonzalez, Beverly asked directly, "Why don't you tell us what you did to Maxine Crawford?"

Manuel licked his lips lasciviously. "You want *all* the gory details?"

Beverly sneered. She could have said to keep it short and sanitized. But she knew that only the killer would know the explicit account of what really happened.

"I want to know *everything* that happened between you and Maxine Crawford," she told him bluntly. Would he be able to respond adequately to details that were not as generalized as those regarding Judge Crawford's death?

Manuel chuckled sinfully. "Is this how you get your kicks, *Beverly*?"

O'Dell nearly lifted from his chair in indignation. Glaring at Natalie, he roared, "Counselor, I suggest you ask your client to show more respect to Ms. Mendoza. Or I will—"

"Do what?" Natalie challenged him, knitting her thin, arched brows together. "Beat him up before *all* these witnesses, Detective? Maybe that's how you get *your* kicks!"

O'Dell sank back down, aware that he was almost helpless in this situation.

Beverly appreciated him coming to her aid, but she told him firmly, "I can take care of myself, Joe."

"Yeah," he muttered. "I'm sure you can."

Her gaze shot to Gonzalez. "Either you tell me what I want to know, or this interview is over."

Natalie, sensing the urgency of the moment, began to scold her client in his ear, though loud enough so everyone could hear. He seemed to get the picture.

"All right," he told Beverly, "I'll tell you what I did to his wife."

And, gloatingly, he described in explicit detail the rape, sodomy, oral copulation, and degradation of Maxine Crawford.

Beverly winced at the chilling account, which she believed sounded like it was coming from the person who sexually assaulted Maxine. But lingering doubts still remained.

Not to mention Rafael Santiago's threats against Judge Crawford and his wife.

"Were there any distinguishing marks on Mrs. Crawford?" Beverly asked the suspect, her own face flushed.

Manuel conferred with his attorney, as if anticipating this question and shaping the perfect answer. Showing his teeth, he responded, "Yeah, I remember she had a birthmark right below her belly button. And guess what? She even had a strawberry tattoo on her ass—right cheek. Not as pretty as mine, but it left an impression. You know what I mean?"

Beverly did not even dignify that with an answer, though she jotted down the details. Maxine Crawford would be able to verify them easily enough.

"I suppose you wiped the place clean?" Beverly suggested in an attempt to trip him up. "We were only able to get a partial fingerprint from the bed." She glanced at O'Dell, whom she knew understood exactly what she was doing.

Natalie spoke quietly in her client's ear and he returned the favor. When this was done, Manuel looked at Beverly and said confidently, "That partial wasn't mine, baby. I wore gloves while I took care of business. I wasn't really lookin' to send the cops on a beeline right to my front door." He paused. "Not that night anyway . . ."

Beverly leaned forward, her eyes narrowed at the suspect, thoughtful. "I'm curious, since you seem to enjoy strangling and slashing helpless women, Manuel. Why didn't you do the same to Maxine Crawford?"

Natalie tried to defend her client. "The point is he *didn't* kill her," she stressed. "*Why* is not really the issue here."

"I think it is," Beverly held her ground. "We all do. I find it hard to believe that, given your client's track record, he would leave a female victim alive to be able to identify him." She sighed theatrically. "Unless, of course, he wasn't the one who sexually assaulted her and shot the judge to death?"

Natalie said something incomprehensible to Gonzalez, who nodded a couple of times and never appeared to be rattled.

Regarding Beverly with a disparaging look, Manuel said cynically, "I do what I do on impulse. With the judge, I was payin' off a debt, okay. No reason to give the white amigo more than what I owed. I took care of the wife, Adrienne, and her lover. With Maxine, I just wanted to have some fun with the bitch. She gave me what I wanted, and then I left her alone. It's as simple as that."

"Is it now?" questioned Beverly.

"Yeah," he grinned callously. "Guess it just wasn't her time to go." Manuel gave Beverly an amused smile. "Like it wasn't yours, Ms. Attorney."

Beverly had a momentary flashback of her brush with death at his callous hands. She fought the urge to say a choice word or two to the rapist-killer, realizing she would only be doing just what he wanted. Obviously he got a vicarious thrill out of taunting women whether or not he was in police custody.

She almost marveled at the fact that Gonzalez seemingly knew all the right answers. It was as if he had been coached.

Or did it come directly from memory, having truly been there?

Could he possibly have been in consultation with Santiago? Rehearsing their stories till they knew them word for word by heart?

"Would you be willing to take a lie detector test?" Beverly challenged Gonzalez. These were not admissible in a court of law but would certainly lend credence to his story if he passed it. Especially considering that Rafael Santiago had refused to take one, though insisting on his innocence.

"Why should I?" Manuel retorted uneasily. "I told you how it went down."

"Because it would further bolster your claim," she replied flatly. "Unless you have been lying about this whole thing?"

Beverly knew that he had given them enough to take to court and get a conviction—were it not for the fact that they already had his twin brother in custody for committing the same crime. She still needed more to feel certain that Manuel's confession was not false or somehow coerced.

And that a guilty man would not be set free irresponsibly.

Manuel again talked this over with his lawyer. She, in fact, did most of the talking. At first they seemed very much at odds over this, then appeared to form a joint front.

Natalie sighed and brushed her nose lightly with the tip of a finger. "Mr. Gonzalez has nothing to hide, as volunteering to give a sample of his DNA would attest to. He would be happy to take the lie detector test, Counselor."

Beverly met the chilling, calculating eyes of Manuel Gonzalez. It was as if he was toying with her, reminding her that she had once been under his power. No matter how this turned out, she thought, knowing that he would never be allowed to walk the streets again gave her some solace. She would feel even better once the bond between identical twins was broken and one of them was held fully accountable for the brutal crimes perpetrated against Sheldon and Maxine Crawford.

CHAPTER 50

Beverly accompanied Stone Palmer to visit Isabel Santiago, the woman who was apparently the mother of both Rafael Santiago and Manuel Gonzalez.

The lady has some explaining to do, Beverly thought. She assumed that Manuel had been given up at some point for adoption. Or had it been Rafael who was adopted? The birth records hadn't been very clear either way.

While they waited for the lie detector test to be administered to Manuel Gonzalez, Beverly hoped to gain some insight into both him and Santiago from the one person who might be best able to fill in the blanks on the two violent men.

"Do you think Gonzalez did it?" Beverly asked the detective.

Stone glanced at her from behind the wheel. He hated to be wrong on this one with so much at stake, but owed her an opinion. "Well, there's no question in my mind that the man's a cold-blooded killer with at least three victims. As to whether or not Gonzalez was responsible for Judge Crawford's death and for attacking his wife, it doesn't exactly fit.

But then again, Gonzalez is making a strong case for himself. What do you think?"

"I think that Gonzalez and Santiago are guilty of trying to manipulate us to serve their own best interests," Beverly answered bluntly. "As to which one committed the crimes against the Crawfords, my gut instincts tell me we've got the right man in Rafael Santiago. But the lie detector test may make me rethink my position. And maybe whatever Isabel Santiago has to say . . ."

"Fair enough." Stone knew her neck was on the line here as much as his. Any missteps for either of them could hurt their individual cases and adversely affect their careers.

When Stone identified himself and Beverly to Isabel Santiago, she unlocked the door and let them in.

"You're here to talk about my son, Rafael?" Isabel asked warily.

Beverly gazed at her. "We're here to talk about your *other* son, Manuel Gonzalez." She detected fear in the old woman's craggy face at the mention of the name. "He is Rafael's identical twin?"

Isabel nodded, slumping onto a chair. "How did you find out?"

"DNA testing confirmed that they were identical twins," Stone said.

"Both of your sons are in serious trouble," Beverly told her. "We need to know why. Our records had shown that they weren't related. We'd like you to help us out here—for them . . ."

With some effort, Isabel leaned over and picked up the cat that scurried over to her. She sat it on her lap and became thoughtful. "I was still living in Cuba when I got pregnant. My lover didn't want anything to do with me when he found out, so he went back to his wife and I was left all alone. When I found out I was carrying twins, I knew I couldn't raise them both by myself. I had to choose between them . . ."

"And you chose Rafael?" guessed Beverly.

Isabel nodded sadly. "If I could do it over again, I would've kept them both. But I gave one to my American friend, Rosa, who'd always wanted a child but couldn't have any of her own. She knew the right people and was able to pass him off as her own. She brought Manuel to live with her in this country. Later I came here myself with Rafael."

She paused, petting her cat almost mechanically. "When Manuel got into too much trouble in Los Angeles where my friend lived, she sent him to live with me here. We agreed that Manuel would be my nephew. But he was more like a stranger. He and Rafael didn't get along very well. Both were in and out of trouble with the law. I finally had to ask Manuel to leave my house, to try and save Rafael."

"But you couldn't save him?" Beverly regarded the woman, knowing that Rafael had killed his pregnant girlfriend at the very least.

Isabel wiped at tears in her eyes. "No. I lost them both to the streets and drugs."

"When did they find out they were identical twins?" Stone asked.

Isabel stared at the question. "Manuel made me tell him three weeks ago," she confessed. "He suspected it for a long time. I thought if I told him it might help get his life back on track." Her eyes lowered, defeated.

"Do you know if Manuel has been in contact with Rafael?" Beverly asked. Prison and jail records had shown no interaction between the two, but she knew there were ways around that for experienced inmates. Or determined criminal brothers.

Isabel's mouth furrowed. "Neither of them have talked about it—but yes, I think my sons have been communicating since Rafael was arrested. Now Manuel is in the same boat. Maybe it's best. I don't have to be scared no more."

Beverly felt sorry for what this woman had already been

put through. She wished they could leave it at that, but as a prosecutor she had a job to perform in the interest of justice.

"Manuel has confessed to crimes that Rafael has been charged with," she pointed out. "Since their DNA matches, we're not sure who the real culprit is. Maybe you can help keep one of them from taking the rap for crimes he didn't commit."

Beverly recalled that Isabel had been Santiago's alibi at the time the crimes against the Crawfords took place and was to be his attorney's key witness. Was she lying then? Would Isabel lie now to protect the son she most called her own?

Isabel tossed her cat to the floor and it scrambled away. She wiped her eyes and looked at Beverly and Stone.

"Manuel is a very good liar, but also a very bad person," she said. "I wouldn't put anything past him. Don't know why he'd want to help Rafael. Maybe he just wants to do the right thing . . ."

Yeah, sure, like prolonging his own life, Stone mused. The sadistic killer would probably kill his own mother if it meant saving his ass from a similar fate.

But Stone conceded that despicable as he may be, Gonzalez could still be right on the money in taking responsibility for another murder and sexual assault.

Or more interested in letting his twin brother off the hook in some sort of symbiotic pact.

CHAPTER 51

Beverly played the videotape back for Maxine to watch. She stopped after Manuel Gonzalez had described the birthmark below her belly button and the strawberry tattoo on her bottom. All the while Beverly studied her star witness's reaction.

Maxine appeared almost expressionless.

The way Beverly saw it, Gonzalez was either lying outright or had somehow been supplied with this intimate information from the real rapist.

Or he had the opportunity to see the birthmark and tattoo firsthand under other circumstances.

Which was it?

Beverly arched a brow as she asked straightforwardly, "Do you have a birthmark below your belly button?"

Maxine looked confused, as if spoken to in a foreign language. "Yes," she finally stated like she was on the witness stand.

It occurred to Beverly that it was theoretically possible that Gonzalez—or even Santiago for that matter—could have seen the birthmark when Maxine exposed that part of her body as a fashion or personal statement. Or even while dancing and selling her body during her previous life.

"It's about the size of a dime," Maxine uttered reflectively. "I always wondered why there of all places."

"What about the strawberry tattoo?" asked Beverly for verification.

"Oh that," Maxine said coyly. "I got it before I met Sheldon. It seemed like a good idea at the time. Most women I knew were getting tattoos on their asses—as a kind of freedom of expression thing." Her voice waned. "I suppose I would have been much better off without it."

Not necessarily, thought Beverly. The tattoo itself had nothing to do with her attack. Though it was certainly another reminder of it.

"May I see the tattoo?" she asked sanguinely.

Maxine wrinkled her nose. "Sure. Why not? Apparently everyone else has."

"I only want to see for myself what Manuel Gonzalez claimed to have seen," Beverly defended herself. "We have to know that this is truly the man who assaulted you."

Maxine stood and turned her back to Beverly. Then in a single motion she pulled down her black, cropped slacks. She wore a honey-colored thong, revealing a firm, shapely bottom. On her right buttock was a small strawberry tattoo.

Beverly couldn't help but think in that moment that this case could ultimately be decided on the strength of two tattoos in unusual and intimate places.

She had seen enough.

After Maxine had taken a seat again, Beverly asked evenly, "Is it possible that you could have met Manuel Gonzalez before you were attacked?"

Maxine flung her a sharp gaze. "I'm not sure I like the implications of the question . . ."

"This isn't an inquisition into your past," Beverly tried to assure her. She saw no reason to bring up any specifics unless Maxine chose to. "However, if there is any chance that Gonzalez could have seen that tattoo or birthmark *before* the night in question, I need to know."

A vein bulged in Maxine's temple. "I have never seen that man before he shot my husband in cold blood and forced me to perform sex acts with him!" she answered vehemently. "If I had, I would tell you. I never forget a face . . ."

Except when identical to *another* face? Beverly mused.

Which face was it she remembered seeing?

Which body?

Which lizard tattoo?

Beverly wondered if Manuel Gonzalez was indeed the right assailant, as he'd insisted and as Maxine had identified the second time around. Or could Maxine's *first* positive identification have been the correct one?

Beverly stood at the window observing as Manuel Gonzalez was being readied to take the polygraph exam. He appeared fairly calm and confident—whereas her stomach was in knots and her confidence faltering.

In spite of the general reliability of polygraph exams, they were hardly foolproof, she thought. She had known of instances where the suspect had passed the test, only to fail the weight of evidence. Or vice versa.

How would Gonzalez fare? Could he outsmart the polygraph?

Was he even capable of showing the range of emotions usually present in establishing whether or not the subject was telling the truth?

Beverly looked askance at Natalie Pena, standing several feet from her as though a wall stood between them. Gonzalez's attorney had just as much riding on the outcome as she did. Probably more, considering the lady was putting her trust in a man who had already proven himself to be unpredictable, dishonest, and dangerous. Not to mention who would almost surely be convicted of three other murders in which the evidence against him was overwhelming.

It scared Beverly, as she realized that the very same characteristics she attributed to Manuel Gonzalez also applied to Rafael Santiago.

Others present with a vested interest in the exam results included Detectives Palmer, Chang, and Arellano, whose investigation of Gonzalez led to his arrest in the first place, and Detective Joe O'Dell and Gail Kennedy.

Inside the room, Jackie Hampton sat at an angle from Manuel Gonzalez. The polygraph examiner was in her thirties, small-boned, with brunette hair severely pulled into a bun. She had been briefed on the circumstances involving the subject and was certain that the test would either confirm or refute his confession. For an instant, she tried to imagine herself as the victim of the vicious sexual assaults he was being charged with. The thought was revolting to Jackie as she tried to concentrate on the matter at hand.

"Are you ready, Mr. Gonzalez?" she asked politely after glancing at the brawny guard standing impassively in the corner.

"Yeah, go ahead," he responded tartly, bracing himself as if about to run into a stone wall.

"Try to relax," she urged him, knowing the results depended on it. "Just answer the questions as truthfully and precisely as you can and I'm sure you will do fine."

Jackie chided herself for making it seem like a simple school exam where one was rewarded for one's efforts. Whatever the outcome, she realized he was in a no-win situation as life imprisonment was hardly a picnic for anyone.

"What is your name?" she asked.

"Manuel Roberto Gonzalez." He grinned at her, as if an introduction for a date.

She viewed the instruments. "How old are you?"

"Thirty-two."

"Have you ever killed anyone?"

He flashed his teeth. "Yeah."

"Please answer with a yes or no, Mr. Gonzalez. Have you ever killed anyone?"

"Yes."

The instruments showed no great variation. "Did you kill Adrienne Murray?"

"Yes, I did."

Jackie drew in a ragged breath. "Did you kill Claudia Sosa?"

Manuel lowered his lids ruefully. "Do I have to answer that?"

"Yes," she stated. "Please."

"Yes," he muttered tonelessly, looking Jackie straight in the eye.

She averted her eyes from his stare, instead studying the polygraph, trained to interpret the meaning of the lines crossing over, zigzagging this way and that.

"Did you break into Judge Sheldon Crawford's house on the twenty-ninth of October of last year?" Jackie asked.

"Yes."

She made herself look at him. "And did you kill Judge Crawford?"

Manuel said flatly, while barely opening his mouth, "Yes."

Jackie moved her eyes from him to the instruments. "Did you shoot him?"

"Yes." He held her gaze.

"How many times?"

"Three," he answered tersely.

"What did you do with the gun?" she inquired, fixing on his face.

"Threw it in the lake."

"What lake?"

"Eagles Lake," Manuel said without hesitation.

The instruments zigzagged.

Jackie read them then shifted slightly, preparing for

questions that were more uncomfortable to ask as a woman.

"Did you rape Maxine Crawford?"

"Yes," he smiled.

Jackie favored the monitor for a moment or two. "Did you sodomize Mrs. Crawford?"

Grinning, Manuel answered, "Yeah or yes, I did. And loved every moment of it!"

What a jerk! Jackie felt hot under the collar. "Please just stick to answering the question." Her voice was elevated slightly.

"Anything you say." He peered at her lustfully.

"Did you force Maxine Crawford to orally copulate with you?"

"Yeah." He licked his lips invitingly.

Jackie studied his response. "Would you please answer that question again?"

"Why not?" he laughed. "*Yes,* I made her go down on me."

She felt the color go to her cheeks. "Did you wear gloves?"

"Sure did."

"Leather?"

Manuel chuckled. "What other kind are there?

"Leather?" she repeated sharply.

"Yes, they were leather," he snapped. "All right?"

Jackie sucked in air through her nostrils. "What happened to the gloves?"

"Got rid of 'em," he said quickly.

She took note of the polygraph instruments at work. "Where did you get rid of them?"

Manuel thought about this. "Tossed them in the lake. No reason to keep 'em after I took care of business." He put a hand to his mouth sardonically. "Oh, I forgot, I ain't supposed to drag it out."

Jackie peered at him. "Do you love your identical twin, Rafael Santiago?"

The question appeared to catch the subject off guard. After a moment or two, he replied with a sneer, "What kind of question is that?"

"The kind that needs a yes or no answer!" she snapped.

"No, I detest him. The bastard got to be with my auntie, or my mother, while I was stuck for years living with someone else."

Jackie saw the strain in his face in giving a longer answer than she wanted. But she let him keep talking to help the assistant district attorney and detectives in assessing his state of mind.

"Why are you confessing to crimes attributed to a man you say you detest?" she asked, again stepping outside her bounds.

Manuel ran a hand across his face, then grinned. "Because I don't want someone else to take credit for what I did. I'm man enough to admit to killing the judge and raping his woman. Why let Rafael go down for it?"

Jackie considered his response before getting back to her work. "Did you and Rafael Santiago plan to murder Judge Sheldon Crawford together—yes or no?"

"No," Manuel responded stiffly.

She read the chart. "Did your brother ask you to take the rap for something he did?"

"No!"

"Have you and your brother communicated since he was arrested?"

"No," muttered Manuel. "Not at all."

"Do you hate your mother?"

He grinned slyly. "Yeah . . . yes, I think I do. Wouldn't you if she gave you away and made life hell?"

Jackie supposed she might have had a problem with that. But then she wasn't the one being questioned here. She ignored the question.

"Had you ever met Maxine Crawford before the night of October twenty-ninth of last year?"

Manuel gazed at her musingly. "No, never. But I wish I had."

I'll bet, Jackie sneered. "One last question: Do you believe there are extraterrestrial beings living on this planet?"

Manuel cocked a brow and chuckled. "Good one. No, I don't. But I believe there are some hot broads living in this city—like you . . ."

Jackie got the chills. She was glad there was a guard standing by. The sooner she got away from this maniac, the better.

The wait was agonizing for Beverly, as she imagined it was for the others present. She tried to determine from the facial expression and body language of Gonzalez and Jackie which way the test was going. But she was unable to ascertain what the gestures and body movements meant one way or the other.

After Gonzalez was escorted out of the room by deputies and back to his cell without any indication of how it went, Beverly went inside. Natalie Pena was close on her heels.

"Well?" Beverly hovered over the examiner. "What's the scoop?"

"I'd also be interested in knowing how my client fared," said Natalie, her timid tone belying her concern.

Jackie took another look at the graphs, as if to be sure. "It wasn't exactly a grand slam as far as polygraph tests go," she said. "But in my professional opinion, on the questions pertaining to Manuel Gonzalez's claims to having shot Judge Crawford and the sexual assault of Maxine Crawford, I'd have to say that Gonzalez is telling the truth . . . as far as he believes it."

CHAPTER 52

At home that evening Beverly mulled over the analysis of the polygraph examination and the other aspects of the case against Manuel Gonzalez.

As far as he believes it . . .

The thought raced through her mind like a locomotive. Did that mean Gonzalez could have somehow convinced himself that he killed Judge Crawford and brutally sexually assaulted Maxine Crawford, when in fact he really was *not* guilty of these crimes? Sort of like self-hypnosis?

Beverly was sitting on a club chair in the living room, a glass of Chenin Blanc in hand. The TV was on but she was barely aware of it. Jaime had gone to see a movie with Paco, leaving her all by her lonesome.

No matter what I want to believe, the bottom line is that as an expert in polygraph exams, Jackie felt Manuel Gonzalez was truthful in his assertion of committing the crimes Rafael Santiago was accused of.

Who am I to question it?

She couldn't prove Santiago was the guilty party if the tide had swung in Gonzalez's direction.

Instead Beverly was left to wonder if her instincts in this case had been all wrong. All she wanted was for justice to be served correctly. Even if it meant having to drop the charges against Rafael Santiago, who may have been innocent in spite of his criminal history, which included committing murder.

One thing that troubled Beverly was that Gonzalez had apparently failed the polygraph on the question of whether there had been any communication between him and Santiago, according to the polygraph examiner. Though Jackie conceded that the reading was more or less inconclusive, Beverly believed that there could be a darker explanation. The identical twin brothers could have conspired in concocting their stories. Or even in perpetrating their crimes.

Unfortunately I can't rely on supposition, she mused. Bottom line, at this point it would be nearly impossible to get a conviction against Santiago.

Unless some earth-shattering revelation should suddenly fall into her lap.

The phone rang, giving Beverly a start. She lifted it off the coffee table and saw that the caller was Grant.

"Hey, baby." His voice was cheerful and it warmed her to hear it.

"Hey back to you." She tasted the wine, wishing he were there to share it with her. Instead they had made a pact to temporarily pause their personal relationship so there would be no conflict of interest while dealing with the legal crisis that had just come up.

As soon as the Santiago case was settled one way or the other, Beverly and Grant agreed that nothing else would stand in the way of their happiness together.

Not even the continuing investigation into Judge Crawford's illicit activities, wherever it may lead.

"So how did the lie detector test go?" Though the question was casual, Beverly knew that the results would carry a lot of weight for Grant's inclination on the guilt or innocence of Santiago and Gonzalez.

"He passed it," she said almost sadly, though only wanting to see to it that the right man was convicted in this case when all was said and done.

Beverly discussed it with Grant, as well as the DNA results. As Conrad Ortega and Natalie Pena had access to all the same information she didn't feel it was stepping out of bounds in talking to the judge about the case.

"I blame Maxine Crawford for this screwup," Grant said, conceding that Gonzalez's confession was probably valid when coupled with the DNA match. "She positively identified Santiago as her attacker. You just took the ball and ran with it. Now some will argue that there may have been a rush to judgment . . ."

Beverly curled her lip. She saw Santiago as possibly wronged. Maybe even singled out based on past history. But there was no rush to judgment. The pieces fit. Or at least they had, till Manuel Gonzalez thrust himself into the picture.

"No one could have imagined that Santiago would have an identical twin," she found herself defending Maxine. *Or am I defending myself?* "Much less that the two would have identical lizard tattoos above their genitals."

"I suppose," Grant said begrudgingly. "Luckily Gonzalez decided to come clean and back it up before an innocent man was put away and most likely sentenced to death."

"Not sure it had much to do with luck," Beverly hissed. "It's not like Gonzalez confessed out of the goodness of his heart. The man was already in hot water for killing three people. He had every incentive to tell his story as part of a plea bargain to spare his life."

Which was, she considered, still motive enough for a false but convincing confession.

Yet there was no denying that the facts—including Gonzalez's intimate knowledge of the crimes against the Crawfords—pointed squarely at the confessed multiple murderer and rapist.

It still hardly meant that Rafael Santiago was a reformed man. Or innocent in the true sense of the word.

"You're right, Bev." Grant breathed into the phone. "Why don't we just let this play itself out in the court and see what happens."

Beverly agreed, while hoping for the best and not the worst, though unsure if she could tell one from the other.

"I love you, Beverly," Grant said. "Nothing will ever change that."

Such as my career being irreparably damaged by the blunder in suspects? she wondered.

Or was he bracing himself for future crises in the courtroom?

"I love you too, Grant," Beverly told him, leaving it and the speculation at that.

CHAPTER 53

Stone entered the brand-new massive bookstore in the re-vitalized downtown Eagles Landing. The next time he would bring the entire family and let everyone go his or her own separate way to find something worth reading.

Stone cruised past several aisles until coming to one where he found Erica Flanagan on her knees, placing books on a low shelf. He had tracked her down, hoping she might be able to help fill in some blanks left open by Manuel Gonzalez's confession.

"Detective Palmer . . ." She smiled faintly at him, still on her knees as she put a final book into place.

"Hi, Ms. Flanagan." Stone helped the young woman to her feet. "Hope I didn't catch you at a bad time?"

"You didn't, not really," she said as she brushed her hands on the back of jeans. "That doesn't mean I'm not surprised to see you."

He spoke out of the side of his mouth, "I'm surprised to be here, to tell you the truth. Something's come up."

She eyed him curiously. "All right. It's just about time for my break anyway. Would you like to buy me a cup of coffee? They've got every type you could imagine at the Starbucks next door."

Stone smiled. "You're on."

They sat at a table near the window. There Stone updated her on the Adrienne Murray murder investigation.

"I can't say I'm surprised that Chuck was involved in Adrienne's death," Erica said pensively. "He was determined that she would *never* leave him alive."

"Looks like he got his wish," Stone muttered sadly.

"Figures he would kill himself. Coward!" She wrinkled her nose. "That's just like Chuck to take the easy way out, rather than own up to what he did."

"Maybe by committing suicide Murray thought he was doing the world a favor."

Stone didn't really believe a word of that. Chuck Murray was a gutless, sick bastard. The man was personally responsible for at least one death and sexual assault; and if Manuel Gonzalez was to be believed, had also orchestrated the murder of Judge Sheldon Crawford and was responsible for the brutal sexual attack on his wife. Stone would have liked to see Murray go to trial to explain his actions, and then let the justice system decide when and where he died.

"Right!" Erica rolled her eyes dubiously. "At least the man he hired is in custody. Maybe some justice can still come out of it."

"Maybe," said Stone, while thinking that there wasn't enough justice to be dispensed on the Chuck Murrays and Manuel Gonzalezes out there. He put the coffee cup to his mouth. "You said before that Adrienne would never have had an affair. Was that more to protect her reputation or to convince me that Chuck was out to get her?"

Erica considered this. "I suppose a little of both," she admitted.

Stone peered at her. "So are you saying she *did* have an affair?"

"Not that I knew of." Erica slurped coffee. "Adrienne was

forever looking around. She was the flirtatious type. But there was always Chuck to bring her back down to earth with his threats and intimidation."

"Did Adrienne ever mention anything to you about flirting with a judge?"

"A judge?" asked Erica, as if a foreign word.

"Yeah."

She hesitated.

"This is important," Stone stressed, sensing she was holding back on him. "Her case hasn't been closed yet . . ."

"Never a judge," Erica insisted. "One time Adrienne talked about being attracted to a traffic cop who gave her a ticket along with his phone number. As far as I knew, she never called him. That's about the closest she came to knowing a judge that I'm aware of. Sorry."

"Don't be," Stone uttered over his coffee. "I'm not." For some reason he preferred to believe that Adrienne had not gotten mixed up with a married judge. Even if her jealous husband had chosen to believe it.

But he still didn't rule out that Adrienne could have had a clandestine affair with Judge Crawford without her best friend's knowledge. It happened all the time, Stone knew. Hadn't he once read that three-quarters of all married people had at least one affair during the course of their marriage? Maybe this was one of them . . .

Why would Gonzalez have concocted this wild tale if it weren't true?

What did he gain other than leniency from the courts?

"So who is the judge Adrienne's alleged to have been involved with?" Erica asked, her lashes flickering as if not a clue.

Probably better that way, Stone thought. "Maybe no one at all," he said, though keeping the book open on this one for now.

The Curbside Motel was located in Northwest Eagles Landing, along a stretch of other cheap accommodations. It was one of the motels Manuel Gonzalez claimed he had seen Sheldon Crawford and Adrienne Murray rendezvous at, mused Stone as he drove into the almost empty parking lot.

His shift was over and he should have been on his way home to Joyce and the kids. Yet here he was working on his own time, trying to allow the spirit of Adrienne Murray to be put to rest. If that was even possible, considering the ordeal her husband and Gonzalez had put her through in life.

Not to mention in death.

Maybe I should quit while I'm ahead, Stone thought, standing outside the door. *Oh, what the hell. Might as well see if there's anything to learn that's useful.*

He went inside. The tiny lobby reeked of mildew. A pudgy woman in her forties stood at the counter, as if she had nothing better to do. A nametag identified her as Barbara.

"How many nights?" she asked routinely, scratching through a blond bob.

"Just this one." Stone flashed her his badge. Producing a photograph of Sheldon Crawford, courtesy of Beverly Mendoza, he set it on the counter before the woman. "Can you tell me if you've seen this man in here recently?"

Barbara regarded the picture. "Hmm . . . How recently?"

Stone realized it wasn't that recent, in fact. "Let's say between August and the end of October of last year," he guessed.

Her false lashes curled upwards. "Maybe. Can't say really. They all start to look alike after a while." She took a deep breath. "What's his name?"

"Sheldon Crawford." The man wouldn't possibly use his own name. Would he?

Barbara lifted a brow. "That wouldn't happen to be Judge Sheldon Crawford, would it?"

Stone saw no reason to keep it a secret. "Yeah, it would be. Has he been here . . . ?"

"Not to my knowledge," she quickly said. "I just recognize the name from the news. Too bad about his death and what happened to his wife."

"Yeah, it is." And that may not be the half of it. "Why don't you see if the name shows up in your records?"

Barbara nodded obediently. "Let's check and see . . ." she mumbled to herself, typing the name into a computer. "What makes you think a high and mighty judge would spend time in this dump?"

"Oh, I have my reasons." Stone left it at that. He had been hearing rumors that even without this alleged adultery, Judge Crawford's hands were soiled. And maybe more than just his hands.

Barbara frowned. "Don't show a Sheldon Crawford in that span of time or even the month before. Of course it's always possible that he could've used a fake name. Most people do who come in here."

That was quite possible, Stone thought. Or maybe the judge had never set foot in this dive and Gonzalez was lying about it as part of his twisted con job.

Stone handed her a photograph of Adrienne Murray. It was part of his official collection of the murdered woman.

"Try the last six months of last year," he ordered. If Adrienne was having an affair with Crawford, it made sense to use her name over his, if they were going to use a real name at all.

Barbara came back empty-handed again. "Sorry." She grabbed the photograph and studied it once more. "Pretty lady," she offered admiringly.

"Yeah," Stone said solemnly. "She was. Once upon a time."

He drove home thinking that he might have been on a wild and foolish goose chase. There was nothing but the word of a rapist-murderer that Adrienne Murray and Judge Crawford were having an affair. It hadn't made sense then and it didn't now.

As far as Stone was concerned, Manuel Gonzalez had fabricated this affair. So what else was he making up along the way?

Could the man have manipulated the polygraph to give the wrong results?

Stone was unnerved at the thought that Gonzalez and Santiago were both guilty as charged. And the possibility that one of them could get away with it for the wrong reasons.

CHAPTER 54

The courtroom was filled to capacity as jurors, media, and other spectators sensed that something significant was about to happen.

Beverly sat beside Gail, both trying hard not to tip their hand. On the defense side, Ortega conferred with Santiago, seemingly advising him of the likely outcome of today's proceedings. Judge Grant Nunez sat on the bench, having just slammed down his gavel and pronounced the court in session.

A sharp intake of breath caused Beverly to tremble inadvertently. Every trial had its defining moment. She knew this one would be defined by its abrupt and surprising outcome. She was as prepared as she could be to deal with any fallout that might result from her decision.

On the plus side, she had the full backing of Dean Sullivan. He'd told her this morning, "It's your call, Beverly. I'll stand by you one hundred percent. Just be sure you don't make a mistake and let the wrong man off the hook. Judge Crawford's real killer has to be held accountable, if only for public consumption."

Now I'll have to make that call, Beverly told herself firmly. And live with the consequences either way. *I can only hope that history will prove that I made the right move.*

"Are you prepared to call your next witness?" Grant asked her routinely.

Rising to her feet, heart pounding, Beverly swallowed, and said in a heavy voice, "Your Honor, recently new evidence has come to light that gives the State reason to strongly believe that another man is in fact responsible for the crimes for which Mr. Santiago has been accused."

"Is that so?" asked Grant, as if he had been caught completely off guard. In truth, he knew exactly what the evidence was and where this was headed. He didn't try and influence Beverly one way or the other, trusting her judgment based on the facts of the case. "I'm listening, Ms. Mendoza. . . ."

Beverly made herself look in the direction of Rafael Santiago. His eyes were already glued on hers spitefully. So too was the gloating gaze of his attorney. Facing the front of the court again, she said unevenly, "Due to this convincing evidence, including a confession to the crimes by another man already in custody for committing three murders, a sexual assault, and attempted kidnapping, among other charges, the People motion that all charges against the defendant be dismissed."

The courtroom reacted to this stunning development. Jurors glanced at each other in disbelief. A low hum spread across the room like a slow fog. The judge tried to maintain order, but was mostly ignored.

Grant met Beverly's eyes in a moment of understanding and loving compassion before he turned to the defendant. After a long pause in which the courtroom became totally silent, he dropped the charges unapologetically, finishing with a sober, "Mr. Santiago, you're free to leave."

Rafael Santiago nodded respectfully before he and Conrad Ortega embraced in a bear hug of jubilation and victory.

Beverly watched them motionlessly. She felt numb and

unsatisfied. Yet she knew she had done the right thing under the circumstances.

Even if doubts lingered.

Santiago stopped his celebrating just long enough to favor Beverly with a callous look. She tried to ignore it but realized that she could feel its wicked intensity right down to her spine.

It was as if he was telling her, *You've been conned, lady. Better keep your doors locked. You never know just who might be paying you a little visit . . .*

"Grant's invited us to his house for dinner, honey," Beverly told Jaime that night.

"Sounds okay," he said. "Hope he's a good cook."

"Oh, I think he does all right in the kitchen. And if that fails, there's always carryout."

Jaime chuckled. "Yeah, I guess."

They were playing Monopoly on the living room floor. Beverly felt relief that the trial was over and she could move on for better or worse. She honestly had no idea what dropping the charges against Santiago midway through a trial that had once seemed like a slam dunk might do to her career aspirations. Perhaps it would make no difference once the press coverage died down. After all, how many prosecutors had to deal with identical twin killers with the same DNA? She hoped to never again be faced with such circumstances.

"Your turn, Mom," Jaime whined.

Beverly flipped the dice and moved four spaces to Park Place, which Jaime owned.

He grinned victoriously. "Pay up!" he demanded.

She complied. "Thought we'd go to see your grandfather this weekend. He gets really lonely about now. It's the time of year that Mama died."

Beverly wasn't sure just how much longer her father would be cognizant enough to feel loneliness. Or if it was already a thing of the past. But she wanted to hang on to what was left of him for as long as possible.

"Cool," Jaime said without protest, making Beverly happy. "Maybe they'll even let us take him out to dinner. Bet he hasn't had anything good to eat since Thanksgiving Day!"

"You're probably right about that," she conceded soberly. "But when you get to be Papa's age, you're not so particular anymore."

"I'll *always* be particular," her son said, frowning.

"I have a feeling you will," Beverly agreed with a smile, noting that his love for foods rich in calories was showing more and more. She would have to find a way to get him to eat fewer fatty foods and more foods rich in nutrients and vitamins.

"What's going to happen to that man who was set free?" Jaime lifted one brow whimsically.

"I don't know," Beverly told him truthfully, wishing she could shield him from her work. She knew it was all but impossible, given the news coverage of the trial that had ended so abruptly. "I guess he'll just get on with his life."

Not much of a life at that, she mused, and imagined that trouble would likely follow Rafael Santiago wherever he went.

"What about the guy who confessed to killing the judge?" Jaime played with the dice while gazing at her.

"He'll be formally charged, and when it's over, he'll likely spend the rest of his life in prison." This thought was a comfort to Beverly, all things considered, even if Santiago's release made her more than a little nervous for some reason. Hadn't he already paid his dues? Didn't he deserve a second chance to get his affairs in order? And to be left alone?

Yes, I believe he does, so long as Santiago is really innocent.

Beverly decided that it did no good to second guess at this point. What was done was done and there was no turning back.

"You don't think he'll come after us now that he's out, do you?" Jaime favored her with apprehension in his eyes.

"Of course not," Beverly insisted with a steady voice. "Now that he's free, the man wouldn't want to risk doing anything that might put him back where he was."

Would he?

The very notion left her feeling a trifle queasy.

CHAPTER 55

Rafael Santiago breathed in the taste of freedom, relishing its feel like a second skin. He could barely believe this moment, never imagining it happening while he was still on his feet and not in a pine box. But then a miracle of sorts happened. The miracle of kinship, blood is thicker than water and all that stupid crap.

Now that he was out, Rafael planned to make good use of his time. And that included settling old scores.

Along with some new ones.

He knocked on the door of the apartment. A moment later it opened and Rafael regarded the woman who had brought him into this world. She looked as though she had aged ten years in the three months since he'd last seen her face to face.

"Rafael!" she cried, and hugged his hard body.

He pushed her away, glaring. "Why didn't you tell me about him, Mama?"

Isabel ran a hand across her wrinkled mouth pensively. "I didn't know how. It all happened so long ago . . ."

"I deserved to know there was another me—and not a damned cousin!"

"I'm sorry," she sobbed. "I did what I thought was right at the time. Afterward, there seemed no point in causing you both—and me—pain . . ."

Rafael held his anger in check. After all, he'd gotten the better of the deal at the end of the day. So why complain openly that she'd screwed up his life, and his identical twin brother's?

He gathered her in his powerful arms, which Rafael had maintained with a vigorous exercise routine while in jail.

"It's cool, Mama," he lied to her.

"Yeah . . . ?" There was doubt in her voice.

"Yeah, Mama. I just want to chill for a while and get on with my life."

"Happy to hear that, Rafael. I've lost Manuel again. Didn't want to lose you, too."

"You won't." He noted the cat on the floor observing it all with those damned eerie yellow eyes. "Think I'll go take a bath, get some of the stink from being behind bars off me."

Rafael grabbed a beer from the refrigerator en route to the bathroom, his thoughts buzzing.

He left the door open a crack and took his bath while drinking the beer and waiting for the dumb cat to come in.

It did and moseyed over to the tub, eyeing him warily as though Rafael were his worst enemy.

Maybe the cat wasn't so dumb after all.

"Come to Papa," Rafael whispered. "Time for you to get wet . . ."

Twenty minutes later, Rafael came out of the bathroom dressed in a fresh shirt and jeans. His black hair was gleaming wet and combed backward. Isabel thought that he looked nice, like when he was a boy.

She wondered if he could ever change and become good. Or had the bad seed implanted in her sons by their father doomed them both to a life filled with hate and deviancy?

It was only when Isabel saw the scratch on one side of Rafael's face that she became alarmed. In fact, there were three long scratches, close together, and they were bleeding a little bit.

"What happened?" she uttered.

Rafael shrugged. "Cut myself shaving, that's all."

Isabel gazed at him with concern. "I have a first- aid kit."

"Don't need it," he stated tersely. "It ain't that bad."

Isabel wanted to object but thought better. She could see that he was about to leave. She hoped it wasn't for good.

"Where are you going?" she asked hesitantly.

"Out," Rafael responded.

"When are you coming back?"

"Whenever. Don't wait up."

Isabel dared to touch his arm, having a sinking feeling. She could smell the alcohol on his breath. "You're not gonna get yourself in more trouble are you, Rafael?"

Her son peered at her with unblinking eyes. "What do you think? It ain't me who causes trouble. It's the ones who get in my business." His voice softened. "Don't worry about me. I just need to take care of a few things and then we can talk . . ."

Impulsively Isabel hugged Rafael and kissed him on the cheek. "Yes, I'd like to talk."

He met her gaze with a halfhearted grin and left.

Isabel felt herself trembling even before she went to find her cat, Loda, fearful that it could have been the last time she ever saw her son.

She found it odd that Loda wasn't running around, as she loved to do. Maybe the cat had been intimidated by Rafael's presence and was hiding. Isabel looked here and there and still no sign of Loda. The last place she tried was the bathroom. The door was shut and she might have thought it was still occupied had Rafael not just left.

Isabel walked up to the tub. It was filled with dirty, soapy water. She was just about to pull the stopper out when she noticed something in the water.

Isabel jumped back and put a hand to her mouth in horror. Loda was in the soapy water, a victim of drowning.

CHAPTER 56

Stone was just getting out of the shower when he was greeted by his wife with a fluffy pink towel.

"Better dry off in a hurry," Joyce said. "You have a phone call from an Isabel Santiago. Isn't she the mother of—"

"Yeah—of both of them," Stone said succinctly.

"I thought so. Well, I told her I'd have you call back, but she insisted on talking to you now. So . . ." Joyce handed him the towel, a worried look on her face. "What does she want with you?"

Stone considered the question while drying off. He had given Isabel Santiago his work and cell phone numbers, promising to help should Rafael prove to be more than she could handle. Now Stone wondered about the wisdom of sticking his nose where it probably shouldn't have been. This case was more or less over and it was time for him to move on. Or be left behind.

His brows touched in gazing at Joyce. "Guess we'll find out in a moment."

Stone took the call in their bedroom. "Mrs. Santiago," he spoke politely.

"You said I was free to call you. Did you mean it?" Her voice shook.

"I meant it," he said. "How can I help you?"

"It's Rafael . . ."

"What about him?"

"I just wanted to keep my son from going back to prison. That's why I told the police what I did."

Stone recalled hearing that Isabel was Santiago's alibi the night Sheldon and Maxine Crawford were victimized. "Are you saying you were lying to cover for your son?" Not that it made a hell of a lot of difference at this point. The deal had already been made to send her other son to prison for the rest of his life while freeing Santiago.

Without making a liar out of herself, Isabel deflected the question and said instead, "Rafael killed my cat . . ."

Stone reacted in disbelief. "Are you sure?"

Again Isabel moved on to something else on her mind. "I saw the look in his eyes . . . I don't want nobody else to get hurt."

"Like who?"

"Whoever he's carrying a grudge against . . ."

Stone watched as Manuel Gonzalez entered the interrogation room in handcuffs and shackles, along with a jail guard who looked like he could have been a starter on the Oakland Raiders front line.

Why the hell am I here on a wild goose chase instead of home with my wife and kids? the detective asked himself. Could be because the department would never have authorized it and Stone's instincts told him this case wasn't over, even if everyone wanted it to be.

"You can remove the shackles," Stone told the guard. "Manuel isn't much to fear when he doesn't have a knife or gun to use."

"Suit yourself, man," the guard muttered and detached the shackles before leaving them alone.

Manuel flopped onto a chair. "Why am I here, man?" he asked curiously.

Stone sat across from him, sharpening his gaze. "Had a question for you."

"Yeah, what?"

"How'd you do it?"

"Do what?" Manuel chewed on his lower lip.

"Fool the hell out of the polygraph machine."

Manuel laughed. "What makes you so sure of that?"

I'm not sure, but I want you to think I am. "For one, your story about the alleged affair between Adrienne Murray and Judge Sheldon Crawford doesn't check out."

Manuel rolled fingers through his hair. "Yeah. So sue me. Just don't expect to collect. They don't pay much in prison."

Stone pinned his gaze on the prisoner. "Must pinch a little knowing that your twin brother is a free man—free to do the things you used to do."

Manuel shrugged. "That's the way it goes. He served his time."

"So what, now it's your turn to do a stretch in the pen—to make amends for the time he spent there? You think that's what identical twins are supposed to do, cover for each other?

"You don't know what you're talkin' about, man."

"Don't I?" Stone sensed otherwise. "Look, Manuel, your deal is already in place and nothing can change it. The DA's office is not about to make more of a laughingstock out of itself than it already has by retrying Rafael."

"Yeah, so what do you want from me?" Manuel set his jaw.

"The truth, just for my own peace of mind," Stone said.

"And why would I care about your peace of mind, man? What the hell's in it for me?"

Not much, asshole. But maybe just a little compassion for the one person on this planet who may still give a damn about you.

"You're right, Manuel. Wouldn't expect you to lose any

sleep on account of my peace of mind." Stone paused and waited till their eyes connected. "I was hoping that you might make it easier for your mother. Yeah, I know all about how she dumped you off on another woman, causing you to have one problem after another. I also know she regrets it and never stopped loving you."

Manuel licked his lips. "I don't wanna hear this."

"I know you don't," Stone said. "I'm not asking you to forgive her. What I am saying is that if you have a decent bone in that body of yours somewhere, you'll give her a break. Right now she's scared to death that Rafael is out to do more harm. Especially after he drowned her cat in the bathtub . . ."

"What?" Manuel favored him with an expression of anger. "Rafael wouldn't do that."

"You're preaching to the choir, man. We both know what he's capable of doing. We just don't know who's next on his hit list. If we can stop him before he starts then no one else has to suffer—including Isabel."

Manuel leaned forward. "You wearin' a wire or something?"

"I'm not wearing anything." Stone stood and patted himself for the prisoner's benefit. In fact he was wearing a wire, just in case anything useful came out of the conversation. "What you have to say is just between you and me."

Manuel seemed to mull this over. "All right. I'll just say that Rafael ain't through yet. He still blames that black judge Grant Nunez for sending him to prison back when the dude was still a prosecutor. And he also wants some payback from the good-lookin' Latina lawyer bitch for trying to bring him down again."

Beverly Mendoza, Stone mused. He had considered that Santiago had a beef with Beverly and Grant Nunez, but didn't figure him to be stupid enough to actually go after them.

Well, think again.

Stone looked across the table at Santiago's twin killer.

"Just one more question . . . How did you manage to nail your story about the crimes against the Crawfords so accurately? Or were you really there?"

Manuel eyed him askance, grinning. "Already said what I'm gonna about that." He paused and seemed to have second thoughts. "Rafael gave me the scoop word for word, man, blow by blow—passing the information through other inmates. It was easy. I just memorized what I needed to and made up the rest. Guess it was close enough."

"Yeah, guess it was."

Stone doubted that the conversation would be enough to put Rafael Santiago back on trial for the crimes he committed. But it was enough to convince him that the lives of Beverly Mendoza and Grant Nunez were in danger.

They needed to be warned, and Santiago needed to be located before it was too late.

CHAPTER 57

The gun was buried in a shallow grave not far from the apartment building. It was one of many such burial grounds scattered across the vacant lots and dilapidated, abandoned buildings in that part of town. Rafael dug it out with his bare hands. He had somehow felt that he would be reunited with the piece again some day.

Looks like today's my lucky day! But not so lucky for others.

Kissing the .25-caliber handgun, he stuck it inside his pants. He had some unfinished business to take care of.

It was time to collect from those who owed him.

That bastard, Judge Crawford, already got his.

His whore wife was a freebie, and worth the effort. Rafael had recognized her the moment he saw her pretty face. Before she hooked up with the judge, he had watched her dance in the strip clubs, knowing then that she would do whatever men with enough cash paid her to do.

Only he took his for free. And made the bitch beg for her life for his trouble.

Maybe when this is over I'll pay her another visit, Rafael thought. This time it would be for keeps.

Right now it was time for the lawyer who had sent him to prison to get what was coming to him. The asshole was now a judge. One who had tried to put him away again.

Just like his lady lover bitch had tried to do.

Both would pay dearly with their lives.

But with the prosecutor broad, Rafael would have some fun first. Just as Manuel had tried to do before they stopped him in his tracks. He would make Beverly Mendoza feel everything the judge's whore felt—only twice as much—before he killed her.

Maybe he'd torture and kill the bitch's son right in front of her. Then she would know what it really meant to hurt in ways she could not even imagine.

Already Rafael was starting to feel good again and glad to get another chance to make things right before disappearing for good.

He had Judge Grant Nunez to thank for that. He intended to thank him personally.

Along with the Assistant DA, Beverly Mendoza.

CHAPTER 58

Grant greeted Beverly with a kiss on the cheek and gave Jaime a low-five. He was glad to be able to get together with them again socially, without a cloud hanging over their relationship. The Santiago–Gonzalez situation was unfortunate for everyone, but ended as it should have: with someone in custody for the murder of Grant's predecessor and the sexual assault of Maxine Crawford. Maybe a quiet, or not so quiet, dinner was just what they needed to get back on the right track toward what Grant hoped would become a real family.

"I'll bet you're hungry, champ," he said to Jaime.

"Yeah, kinda," he said from the corner of his mouth.

Grant smiled. "Well, we'll see what we can do about that. I don't claim to be the world's greatest chef, but I know enough to have cooked up something appetizing. Of course, you'll have to be the judge in this case—along with your mother."

Beverly laughed. "At least someone else gets to be the judge this time around."

Grant laughed at her weak attempt at humor and Beverly

marveled at the sight of him in an oatmeal-colored blazer over a white boatneck sweater and black slacks. For an instant she imagined him with no clothes on at all. It warmed her up and Beverly quickly shut off such thoughts until later.

"This is way cool," exclaimed Jaime, studying a model of the *Titanic* that Grant purchased last year at an estate sale.

"Yes, cool," agreed Grant. "Although I'm afraid it was downright frigid for those 1,500 plus poor souls who failed to escape the real *Titanic*."

Jaime cringed at the sad news, then perked up when Grant smartly switched subjects and began talking about sports and going to see the San Francisco Giants or Oakland A's in the spring.

Beverly thought that the two were getting along better than she could have expected these days. She'd long wanted Jaime to have a father figure in his life. Especially when her own father had developed Alzheimer's disease. Grant seemed to have voluntarily stepped in to fill the role and for that she was grateful but not greedy. When and if the time came to make that official, she would be ready and more than willing.

"Can I go outside?" Jaime looked to his mother, then Grant. "I just want to stretch my legs."

"I'm sure dinner will be ready soon," said Beverly, seeking to discourage him from going out. Not that Grant didn't live in one of the better parts of Eagles Landing, with crime rarely an issue. She recalled feeling the same way recently about where they lived. Before Manuel Gonzalez had shattered that myth into a thousand pieces.

"Actually dinner is still about a half hour away," Grant said. "Why don't you go play in the backyard for a bit? There's a hoop back there and plenty of room to stretch those legs."

"All right." Jaime grinned at his mother as she was outnumbered. "See ya in a bit."

He scurried away before Beverly could utter a word of

objection, bouncing out the door. She could hear his footsteps stomping across the concrete toward the backyard.

Grant smiled sheepishly. "Sorry, baby, if I said the wrong thing. He'll be okay. I know it's hard to let him grow up, but it has to happen sooner or later. Besides, I think I like being a parent. Or at least someone that Jaime can look up to for guidance and authority."

"I like that too." Beverly certainly did not want to discourage the bonding between her son and Grant. Even if part of her was still a little scared to have Jaime out of her sight.

"Did anyone tell you today that you look terrific?" Grant gave her the once-over and Beverly felt warm beneath her navy crewneck shell and long raven print skirt.

"As a matter of fact, no one has—till now."

"Then I'm glad to be the first. You look terrific!" He showed his teeth and got the same in return. It ended with a long kiss that practically lifted Beverly off her feet.

Grant finally pulled away. "Think we'd better get into the kitchen, before I lose my appetite for anything but you. I could use some help on the salad."

"My specialty," murmured Beverly, enjoying the taste of his lips on hers, which were still throbbing.

The kitchen was gourmet with new cupboards, vinyl flooring, and a state-of-the-art stove and microwave combined. Grant had marinated pork chops in the oven and rice pilaf was simmering on the burner.

"I hope you're not beating yourself up with the way it all ended with the Santiago trial," said Grant, chopping carrots.

Beverly shook her head while rinsing off the lettuce. "I'll leave that up to the media to do. I was handed a case and followed through to the best of my ability. If anyone has a problem with that, to hell with them. I can't change what happened."

"No, you can't. Neither of us can." He put the carrots in a bowl, along with chopped cucumbers. "And I like your attitude about it, baby. Getting one scumbag for another is hardly a losing effort. Bottom line is that we nailed the person responsible for Sheldon Crawford's murder and Maxine's ordeal. All in all, I'd say that's a pretty damned good day's work."

Beverly was inclined to agree, even if a part of her still wished that it had been Rafael Santiago who went down in this case as the man she had put on trial. But justice had prevailed in the final analysis. Manuel Gonzalez was where he belonged and people like her no longer had to fear being victimized by him in the future.

"How about your investigation into Judge Crawford's illicit activities?" Beverly looked up at his successor on the bench, though the subject was officially supposed to be off-limits.

Grant favored her with an unreadable expression. "We expect a grand jury to hand down indictments any day now against a number of people involved in this scheme."

"Oh . . ." She batted her eyes with curiosity. "Anyone I happen to know?"

He smiled at her. "Well, let me put it this way—the good guys aren't always good and the bad ones aren't necessarily as bad as they seem."

Beverly laughed. "Uh, okay . . ." *Looks like I won't get any more from him than that.*

Grant came up behind her, wrapping his long arms around Beverly's slender waist like an octopus. "What I can tell you is that it'll all be over soon," he promised. "And I fully expect that you'll have some new and interesting cases to sink your teeth into."

"I see." Beverly was piqued at the thought and happy to move on as a prosecuting attorney.

Grant nibbled at her neck. "Then we can begin seriously thinking more about ourselves and Jaime. Maybe becoming a *real* family . . ."

A real family.

The words hit Beverly like a bolt of lightning. The word *marriage* popped into her head. It was something that was beginning to agree with her more and more. Maybe even having another child. Or two?

The mere prospect filled her with glee.

"I'd like that," she murmured dreamily.

The phone rang, disrupting the mood.

"Hold that thought," muttered Grant. He grabbed the cell phone off the granite countertop, clicking it on. "Yeah . . ."

Beverly watched as he said with mild surprise to the caller, "Detective Palmer. Nice to hear—"

Grant was apparently cut off by what Stone had to say. Beverly wondered if Paco's dad was calling for some follow-up work on his case against Manuel Gonzalez, which had suddenly grown in leaps and bounds as if it weren't already a workload for the detective.

She saw Grant frown, mutter an expletive, then tell Stone, "Thanks. I'll be in touch."

He hung up and Beverly asked, "What is it?"

Grant pursed his lips. "A warning. Detective Palmer seems to think that we're in danger."

Her lashes batted. "From whom?"

"Rafael Santiago. Palmer believes that Santiago may come after us now that he's free."

"But why?"

"Revenge. Looks like Manuel Gonzalez practically bragged about switching places with his brother just so Santiago could finish what he started."

As Beverly tried to digest this, with the clear implication being that Rafael Santiago had been guilty as charged in attacking the Crawfords, there was a shattering sound that came from the great room.

Immediately Beverly thought that Jaime had hurt himself somehow. She raced from the kitchen with Grant hot on her heels.

The first thing Beverly noted was the replica of the *Titanic* on the floor, smashed to smithereens. Then she saw Jamie, a frightened look on his face.

Only he wasn't alone.

Behind him was Rafael Santiago. He had a gun pointed at Jaime's head.

Trepidation gripped Beverly like in a bad dream. But she knew this was real life and her son was in trouble.

"Has he hurt you, Jaime?" were the first words to come from Beverly's mouth.

The boy shook his head, as if unsure. "He came out of nowhere, Mom," Jaime stammered apologetically. "I'm sorry—"

"Shut the hell up!" ordered Santiago, a streak of pure evil in his tone.

"Let the boy go," urged Grant, keeping his voice firm but not hostile. *Any false move on my part could get Jaime killed. Have to deflect the attention to myself.* "If you want me, Santiago, you can have me. Just leave them alone."

Santiago let out a hoarse laugh. "In your dreams, man," he taunted. "We're gonna have ourselves a little payback party, *Yo Honor.* And this fat-ass boy is gonna be a part of it, whether you or your girlfriend like it or not."

Beverly felt almost glued to where she stood. The mere notion that Jaime could die . . . that they all could . . . was almost more than she could bear.

God, please don't let this happen. Don't let this man win.

"You killed Judge Crawford, didn't you?" she had to ask him.

"Figure it out, Ms. Assistant DA!" Santiago bared his teeth at her like a vampire out for blood. "He got what he deserved; so did his cunt of a wife! You had me right where you wanted me, bitch, but you couldn't hold me. Thanks to my twin bro, Manuel."

Beverly exchanged sorrowful glances with Grant. Both knew they had been conned by two homicidal maniacs. Now it just might cost them their lives.

"It doesn't have to be this way, Rafael," Beverly tried to reason with him somehow. "You won. You have your freedom and there's nothing anyone can do to take it away from you. Unless you harm us."

"She's right," seconded Grant, reluctant to try anything foolish under the circumstances. Not till he could get Jaime and Beverly out of harm's way. "If you let the boy go and turn around and walk right out of here, I swear we'll forget this ever happened. We'll call it even, the past friction between us . . ."

Santiago grinned amusingly. "Man, you must really take me for a dumb-ass Cuban," he cursed, pushing the barrel of the gun against Jaime's tender scalp. "You ain't never gonna forget this, any more than I can forget what you did to me, asshole."

"I didn't do it to you," spat Grant, inching closer to them. "You did it to yourself, Santiago. You murdered your girlfriend and were held accountable. If it hadn't been me who prosecuted the case, it would have been someone else."

"But it was *you*," boomed Santiago, ignoring all reason, "*both* of you. And now it's time to pay the piper."

He shoved Jaime to the floor and pointed the gun at Grant.

"Say good night, Judge Nunez," he said gleefully.

Like hell I will. Grant lunged at Santiago as a last desperate measure to save Beverly, Jaime, and maybe even himself.

But Santiago, anticipating the wild move of a desperate man, easily evaded Grant's long, outstretched arms. He then fired off a shot, hitting his target in the shoulder. Grant winced from the searing pain but continued to move toward the rapist-killer.

Santiago grinned and aimed the gun straight at Grant's head. "Once you're dead, I'm gonna have some real fun with your lady, before she begs me to kill her."

Grant took another swipe at Santiago, missing badly. Santiago slammed the gun into Grant's injured shoulder, causing him to cry out in pain; then rammed a fist into Grant's jaw, dropping him to the floor.

Beverly watched in horror what was happening so fast; she had trouble breathing. He was going to kill Grant. Then her and Jaime. She had to do something, or else watch her whole world collapse.

Santiago stood over Grant, the gun aimed at point-blank range over Grant's right ear.

"Noooo!" A bloodcurdling scream erupted from Beverly's mouth as she flew toward them. The sound of a gunshot exploded in her ears like cannon fire.

She expected to see Grant's head splattered onto the parquet floor. Instead it was Santiago who tilted backward, glass-eyed as if in shock, before dropping the gun and falling forward, flat on his face.

Looking to the entryway, Beverly saw a tall, familiar figure standing there. His long arms were sticking straight out, a revolver held tightly in his hands.

It was Detective Stone Palmer.

"Are you all right?" he asked her, moving forward while keeping the gun pointed at the motionless Rafael Santiago.

"I'm not sure," she uttered honestly, her pulse racing. "He shot Grant."

Stone favored her for a moment, along with her son, as both scrambled to their feet, frightened, but apparently unharmed. So this was Paco's buddy, he thought, gazing at Jaime. Glad to know that their friendship had been spared. Had he been seconds later, the situation could have been far worse.

Ignoring Grant Nunez for the moment, Stone ambled over to Santiago, ready to shoot him again if he moved so much as an eyelash. Kneeling, he felt his neck. Nothing there. The bastard would not kill, rape or sodomize again, Stone knew. Not in this world.

"Santiago's dead," Stone announced without an ounce of remorse.

He stood and checked the condition of the judge. Beverly and her son were huddled around him like guardian angels. Grant was only semiconscious, a bullet having ripped through his shoulder.

"He'll live," Stone assured them, recognizing the special bond between the three. "I got here as fast as I could. Others are on the way, including medical assistance."

Beverly thanked God that they had somehow survived this ordeal. Then she thanked the detective who had saved their lives. As she expected, he shrugged it off as only doing his job. But she suspected that the job had become personal with him, as it had with her, and it had led Stone right to Grant's front door.

And had given them all the opportunity for a future.

Grant stirred, his eyes watery, focus distorted. He could barely make out the concerned faces of Beverly and Jaime.

"You got shot in the shoulder!" Jaime informed him, seeking to be strong in the face of terror.

"An ambulance is on the way," Beverly said.

"Looks like we got more excitement than we bargained for," Grant joked, doing his best to tolerate the pain and dizziness.

Beverly wiped away tears while smiling. "Story of our lives lately."

Grant made himself smile at his beautiful lady. There was something he needed to say and now seemed as good a time as any to do so. "Bev, this isn't exactly the way I planned it, but will you marry me? I'd hate to die without ever having popped the question . . ."

Beverly was stunned at the proposition, coming as it had. But she wouldn't trade it for any other time in the world. "Yes, I'll marry you, Grant Nunez. And don't you even think about dying. Not till we're both ancient and living the good life in Hawaii or the Cayman Islands."

She kissed him on the mouth. Grant returned the kiss, whispered he loved her, and lost consciousness.

"I love you too, baby," she whispered back.

Beverly cried as she cradled Grant in her arms. The thought that she could have lost him and Jaime in one fell swoop left her slightly disoriented.

But they would live to see another day. And take on whatever new battles and victories that life had in store for them.

CHAPTER 59

Stone sat in the bar, having a drink with Chang and mulling over another day of detective work. Three months had passed since Rafael Santiago's plan had been foiled, costing him his own life in the process. While the killer's remains had been cremated, his identical twin was set to do some hard time. Although the plea bargain between Manuel Gonzalez and the DA's office sparing his life stood firm, new evidence had shifted the murder of Judge Sheldon Crawford and Maxine Crawford's sexual assault back to the original suspect in the case.

This evidence included Gonzalez's taped admission about the scheme he plotted with his brother; the recanting by Isabel Santiago that Santiago had been with her at the time of the crime and, most importantly, the murder weapon. As such, the case was now considered closed and the DA's office vindicated in its dogged pursuit of Rafael Santiago.

Or at least the lead prosecutor in the case.

Stone sipped the mug of beer and smiled in thinking

of his good friend. Make that good friends. Grant Nunez and Beverly Mendoza had not only survived the assassination attempt, the lovebirds had gotten married and, from what Stone understood, were honeymooning on a cruise ship somewhere in the Pacific. He wished them well, while counting his own blessings in having a wife who he wouldn't trade in for anyone. Or his kids, for that matter, growing up faster than he could keep up with their shifting needs on a homicide detective's salary.

"Stone, are you with me, man . . . ?" Chang lowered his eyebrows with annoyance.

Stone focused in on his partner and realized he hadn't been entirely. "Drifted off there for a moment," he admitted. "What were you saying?"

"I wanted to get your take on the Butterfly Killer. Just who the hell is he? And what makes him tick?"

Stone tasted more beer and ruminated. Their latest case involved a serial killer who had strangled three women over the last six weeks. The press had dubbed him the "Butterfly Killer," because the killer had left a butterfly in the mouth of each nude victim, all of whom were pretty, red-headed, and had been sexually assaulted.

It never ends, Stone thought forlornly. Not for them anyway. All they could do was keep going after the bad guys and hope that maybe some victims could be spared along the way.

Much like Beverly and Grant had been.

Abruptly Stone got to his feet.

Chang looked up. "You going to take a leak?"

"I'm going home," he answered unceremoniously. "Think I'll take my wife out to dinner."

Chang, who was divorced, frowned. "What about the Butterfly Killer?"

"Something tells me he'll still be out there tomorrow," Stone chirped. "And we'll be hot on his ass. Tonight I need

to take a breather and remember what's really important—
or rather who. See you later."

Outside Stone breathed in the spring air and got on his
cell phone. He hoped Joyce hadn't made any special plans
for dinner, as he had.

CHAPTER 60

The private balcony in the suite gave them breathtaking views of the Hawaiian Islands and the endless sea. Beverly had come to treasure all the beautiful things in life that she may have once taken for granted. That included a lifetime commitment to the man who stole her heart and soul and made them his own.

They had cemented their love through marriage and taken a cruise as the perfect way to explore one another in an idyllic, romantic setting.

After making love for the umpteenth time in every position imaginable, Beverly felt exhausted and incredibly happy to be in the arms of her virile man. She was finally Mrs. Grant Nunez and intended to soak it up for all it was worth, which in her mind meant everything.

She thanked God again and again that they had escaped Rafael Santiago's wrath. Not in small part due to the heroic efforts of Stone Palmer. Grant had made a full recovery after being shot in the shoulder, with only a half-moon scar left to remind them.

Jaime's nightmares, lasting several weeks, had stopped.

When they had invited him to go on the cruise, he had declined, opting instead to stay with his friend Paco and his family. Stone and Joyce had graciously agreed.

Beverly no longer allowed the stress and strain of a case that went awry, before ending on a more positive note, make her question if she were in the right profession.

Indeed, over the last three months, she had found herself reenergized as a trial lawyer, using the unusual nature of the Santiago case and its eerie connection to and alliance with Manuel Gonzalez as a motivator to press forward with her career. Along the way, Beverly had been given more responsibility and now believed that some day she might even be able to join her husband on the bench.

She lifted her mouth so that it brushed against his and turned into a passionate kiss.

"Love you," she murmured, their naked bodies pressed together, the perspiration from the earlier heat they generated beginning to dry.

"Love you too, baby," Grant assured her. More than he could ever say, but not more than he could show Beverly. He fully intended to do all the little things that spelled love in a big way.

Both his and Beverly's careers were in full swing, making it all the better in their personal lives.

Just last month indictments were handed down against thirteen people, including a sitting judge, in connection with the investigation into bribery, fraud, and racketeering charges first initiated with Judge Sheldon Crawford. Grant fully expected some convictions and serious prison time to come out of this, with Beverly prosecuting several of the defendants at the state level.

He kissed the top of her head. "So are we going to spend all our time in bed or what?"

Beverly felt his erection beneath her, causing her temperature to rise once again. "You tell me, Mr. Nunez. I'm game to see what's happening on the ship, if you are . . ."

Grant thought about it for a moment or two, then, recognizing his overpowering desire for this woman and his need to be inside her, declared, "Well, maybe later. Right now, I think I'd like to enjoy the view inside this cabin a while longer."

Beverly laughed amorously. "Sounds like a plan. A very good one at that."

She waited till his mouth descended to kiss hers. It happened like clockwork and the ticking began once again.

R. BARRI FLOWERS
JUSTICE
SERVED

There is a killer on the prowl, terrorizing the streets of Portland, brutally beating men to death. Each victim was recently on trial for domestic abuse, but each was released. The press is having a field day with the new vigilante killer, but it's up to Detective Sergeant Ray Barkley and his partner, Detective Nina Preston, to stop the killer.

Among the suspects is Criminal Court Judge Carole Cranston, who presided over the trials of each victim. As the case heats up and the body count rises, Ray sees signs pointing toward Carole as the killer—but he also begins to realize he might no longer be objective where she is concerned. But neither is Nina. She's determined to prove Carole is the killer for hidden reasons of her own....

Margaret Murphy
Darkness Falls

This morning Clara Pascal had everything. A high-power lawyer with a loving family, she is envied and admired by her friends and colleagues. Now she lies chained to a stone wall in a dark cellar—without food, warmth, sleep, or simple communication. Her kidnapper won't even tell her what he wants.

While Clara fights against fear and despair in her captivity, Detective Inspector Steve Lawson leads the police in a frantic search for her. Was she abducted by a criminal she previously sent to jail, now out for revenge? The ruthless drug lord she's currently prosecuting? As the police desperately follow every lead, Clara begins to realize at last why her captor has kept her alive…so far.

COLD BLOODED

ROBERT J. RANDISI

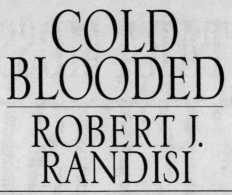

NYPD Detective Sergeant Dennis McQueen has his hands full with a very bizarre case. A series of dead bodies have been found, all frozen—killed by various methods, but disposed of in the same manner. Just a coincidence, or is there a serial killer at work?

Things heat up when McQueen is sent to investigate a body found in the rubble of a fire and meets FDNY Fire Marshal Mason Willis. Willis is investigating it as an arson, but the medical examiner's report makes it obvious that this is a case for McQueen. McQueen and Willis have no choice but to work together. Will even the combined efforts of the NYPD and the FDNY be able to stop the killer…or killers?

TARA MOSS

FETISH

Mak is young, beautiful—and in grave danger. An international fashion model, she arrived in Australia on assignment, only to find her best friend brutally murdered, the latest victim of a serial killer with a very deadly fetish. Before she knows it, Mak herself is caught up in the hunt for the killer…and trapped in a twisted game of cat-and-mouse. Who can you trust and where can you turn when you are the dark obsession of a sadistic psychopath?